"This book is a work of fiction, but some works of fiction contain perhaps more truth than first intended, and therein lies the magic."
– Anonymous

TRWPB2
ISBN: 978-0-9567700-0-4
Published by BenGalley.com
The ReWritten Edition 2017
First Published by BenGalley.com 2010
Cover Design by Mikael Westman
Original Illustration by Ben Galley

about the author

Ben Galley is an author of dark and epic fantasy books who currently hails from Victoria, Canada. Since publishing his debut Emaneska Series, Ben has released a range of epic and dark fantasy novels, including the award-winning weird western Bloodrush and standalone novel The Heart of Stone. He is also the author of the critically-acclaimed Chasing Graves Trilogy.

Ben can be found on Twitter or vlogging on YouTube @BenGalley, or loitering on Facebook and Instagram @BenGalleyAuthor. You can also get a free ebook by signing up to The Guild at www.bengalley.com.

OTHER BOOKS BY BEN GALLEY

THE EMANESKA SERIES

Pale Kings
Dead Stars - Part One
Dead Stars - Part Two
The Written Graphic Novel

THE SCARLET STAR TRILOGY

Bloodrush
Bloodmoon
Bloodfeud

THE CHASING GRAVES TRILOGY

Chasing Graves
Grim Solace
Breaking Chaos

STANDALONES/SHORTS

The Heart of Stone
Shards
No Fairytale

My eternal thanks to Charlie, Sarah, and the Clarks, without whose help I would have surely succumbed to a mind-numbing banality.

This book was written for my parents, because without them I wouldn't be where I am right now, nor would any of us.

Prime Map of Emaneska, created by Arka scholars of Arfell in the year 819

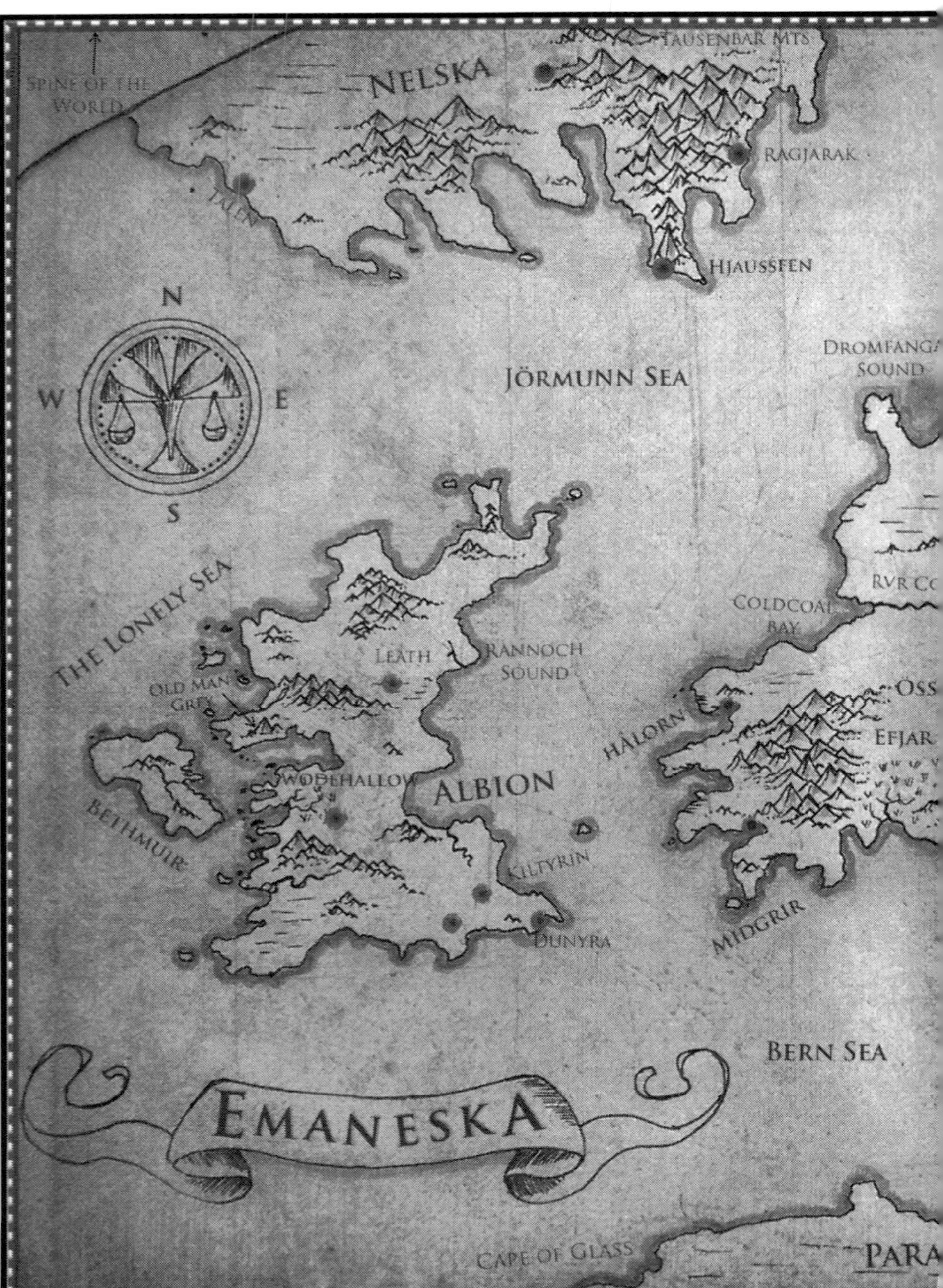

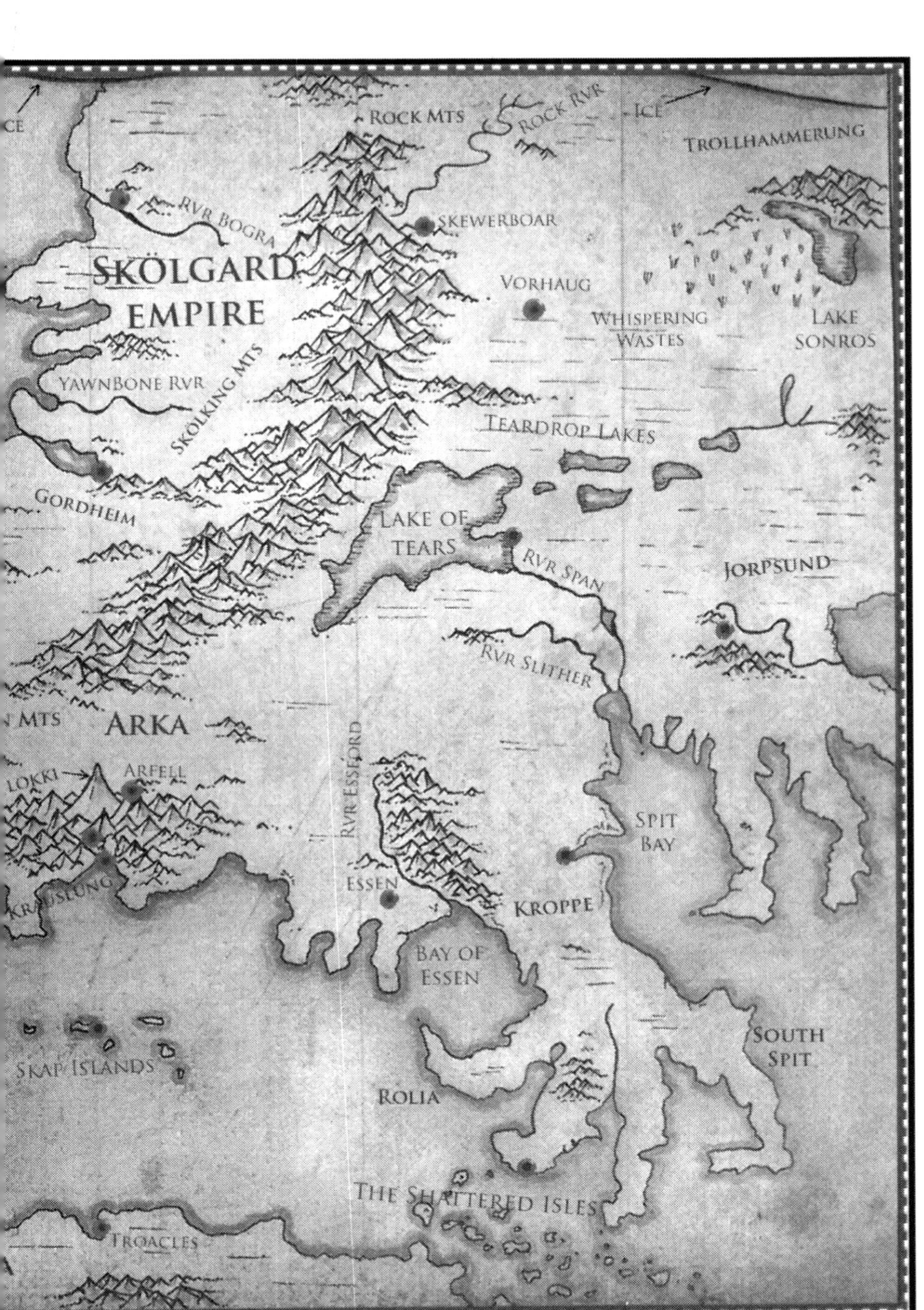

ROCK MTS
ROCK RVR
ICE
TROLLHAMMERUNG
RVR BOGRA
SKEWERBOAR
SKÖLGARD EMPIRE
VORHAUG
WHISPERING WASTES
LAKE SONROS
YAWNBONE RVR
SKÖLKING MTS
TEARDROP LAKES
GORDHEIM
LAKE OF TEARS
RVR SPAN
JORPSUND
RVR SLITHER
ARKA
ARFELL
RVR ESSFORD
SPIT BAY
ESSEN
KROPPE
BAY OF ESSEN
SOUTH SPIT
SKAP ISLANDS
ROLIA
THE SHATTERED ISLES
TROACLES

By Ben Galley

part one
IT BEGINS WITH SNOW

When the sons of gods went to the daughters of man and had children by their wombs, they became the giants of old, the nefalim, "men" of renown and infamy, dangerous like wolves amongst sheep.
From the *Gathered Prophetics*

It was snowing outside. The white flakes drifted lazily in the chill night breeze, dusting the rocky mountainside with an ivory blanket. Ice crystals flurried and spun, dancing through the cold air, skittering along the windowsill. By all rights, it was a foul night for Arfell.

The tall spire rose like a forgotten nail from an outcrop of quiet buildings huddled together between the snowy crags. A lonely window glowed brightly through the white-out. Framed in the yellow light was a silhouette of a wizened man, standing at the windowsill with his arms crossed. He fought back yet another yawn, staring at the snowflake lingering on his fingertip. He shivered, but stayed put, and pressed his warm palms to the frigid stone. After a long day of hard study, the weather was calming, cooling. And it had been a hard day indeed.

Behind him, gathered around a desk awash with papers and maps, sat a group of four aged men, each of them still poring over the small black book. It sat in its own circle of polished wood, isolated from the papery chaos surrounding it. Alone and aloof.

The room around them was cavernous, packed floor to ceiling with bursting bookshelves, each one filled with an impossible amount of paper and knowledge. Loose pages poked out from every crevice. Scrolls lay under chairs and side-tables. Old maps and notes littered the floors and shelves like dried autumn leaves. One single candle, almost at the end of its wick, clung to life on the corner of the wooden desk, throwing yellow light and distorted shadows against the walls whenever the breeze toyed with it.

'What makes us so sure it is Siren?' asked the man at the window. He absently twisted a strand of his long white hair around a wrinkled finger as he reached for a nearby cup of warm wine. The papery wattle of skin around his neck made his chin non-existent.

'Of course it is, Gernn, just look at the scales of the front cover!' replied one of the others, avidly. He waved his hand in a somewhat dismissive gesture. He coughed hoarsely, as if the cough had caught him by surprise, and then dabbed a handkerchief to his lips. Spectacles made from thin slices of rare crystal balanced precariously on his nose and a long beard, streaked with grey, cascaded down his neck and chest. 'Dragon. No doubt about it. And one doesn't simply go around borrowing their scales for book covers.'

The group of scholars mused for a few moments. 'Where was it found again?' asked another, peering at his colleagues from under wiry grey eyebrows.

The bespectacled man spoke up again. 'No one knows exactly. Some village in southern Nelska,' he said, and there was a silence.

'Fifteen years later and only now do we get to study this manuscript. Who knows the incalculable value of the magick held inside this book,' said Innel, tugging his long blue robe about him. It was now too cold. He shivered as he pulled the stained glass windows shut with a bang. He turned and sighed, leaning back against the stone sill and looking to the man with the tiny glasses. 'The only real question is this: how do we get the confounded thing open? Have we had a reply from Krauslung yet, Innel?'

The scholar with the wiry eyebrows answered. ‘No, no not as yet. They’re always late…’ He trailed off, distracted. He leaned forwards to take a closer look at the book lying on the desk. It was small; no wider or taller than the span of a man’s hand. Black dragon scales adorned the cover, overlapped and pressed flat, then trimmed to fit its square shape. *Probably from an infant wyrm*, thought Gernn, as he let his fingers trace the ridges and dips of its cover. A thick gold lock, simple but sturdy, wrapped around the book’s waist, sealing it tight. There wasn’t a keyhole or opening mechanism in sight.

The ancient pages poking out from the edges were scored and dirty. Gernn tried once again to split a few pages apart with a long yellow fingernail, but the book was locked fast, and not even the tip of a knife blade could squeeze between them. After a rather dramatic sigh, he entwined his fingers and reclined in his chair. The ornate wood creaked as he did so.

‘Well, nothing’s changed since this afternoon. The bloody thing’s still locked. And, as none of us here possesses the skill to unlock it, or could even guess what spell might force it open, I suggest we just wait for—’ Gernn was interrupted by the sounds of heavy boots on stone.

A loud voice made them all turn. ‘Having trouble, wise men of Arfell?’ A tall figure stood in the doorway, hooded, with hands clasped behind his back. The newcomer walked from the door to the desk in just a few long strides and stomped the last bits of snow from his black leather boots. The scholars were startled to say the least, but as the man moved from the shadows and into the candlelight they recognised a familiar face. The man threw back his hood and a chorus of respectful smiles followed, even a few groaning, creaking attempts at bowing.

Innel jumped up to greet the man with a warm handshake, the wattle of skin beneath his neck wobbling like a turkey’s. ‘Your Mage, what an unexpected honour! With the weather and all, we didn't expect you or Åddren to arrive for another two days,' he rattled.

The tall mage kept his smile as he removed his hooded green-gold robe and folded it neatly over an armchair. There was a long sword at his waist, sheathed in an ornate scabbard, and his expensive tunic was made of a fine emerald cloth, trimmed with white and gold.

'Do not be ridiculous, scholar. The weather has never stopped me,' he chuckled. 'When we heard that you had uncovered a long-lost book of secrets, I decided that no time should be wasted in coming to examine it!' The man crossed his muscular arms and looked at each of them with hard, hazel eyes. 'Please, show me what you have found.'

Innel retreated slowly to a chair. Gernn rose, obviously eager to impress, while the others remained silent and seated, fingers entwined in their long flowing beards.

'It is most definitely Siren, your Mage, as we thought, but this book is not from the time of the war. It seems to be very different from the other texts we recovered from the dragon-riders. Much older, perhaps.'

'Continue,' said the man.

Gernn pointed to the gold on the black cover. 'It has a lock on the cover, and no key or keyhole with which to unlock it. Magickal, clearly. We've come across this type of thing before, but this is too powerful and too ancient for our minds, or for the library mages. And so, as of yet we have been unable to read it.' Gernn shrugged, gazing wistfully at the little book. 'Hence our humble request.'

There was a moment of silence while a smile crept over the visitor's wind-burnt face. Unusual, for him.

'Perhaps I should take a look.' His hazel eyes flicked around the circle. 'If I can get it open, can you translate it?'

One of the other scholars answered. 'If it is legible, your Mage, then we can read it. The scholars of Arfell have tackled almost all of the languages that Emaneska has ever spoken or written down.

There's hardly a book we have come across that we couldn't translate.' He spoke his words with a slow and constant nodding of his head. He was the oldest by many a mile, greyer than a winter's day and waiting patiently at death's doorstep.

The others murmured their assent with a symphony of throat-clearing and the scratching of chins and facial hair.

'Good.' The mage strode forwards and flexed his hands. He loomed over the oak desk, humming and musing and making a sucking noise with his teeth. The scholars watched him think, looking between themselves with a mixture of intrigue and uncertainty.

The mage muttered incoherently as he reached towards the book, his fingers rigid and outspread. A ripple of air pulsated from his hand, like a wave of heat over a fire. A purple spark danced over the cover.

'This book is strong,' he muttered between pursed lips. He seemed to be straining to keep his fingers spread now. His hand pulsed again and he took a firmer stance, spreading his feet and gripping the edge of the table. More sparks fizzed over the cover and then, quite abruptly, something inside the gold band clicked, and smoothly rolled open.

The scholars leaned forwards with open mouths, rheumy eyes wide in their eagerness to see what the dark book held between its dusty yellow pages.

The mage wiped a drop of sweat from his brow and smiled. He clenched his fist several times, as if the magick had stung him.

'Read your book, gentlemen,' he said.

The oldest scholar wiped something from his nose and carefully lifted the scaly cover. With agonising slowness, he bared its paper to the light, and tested the crinkles with his fingers. He peered at the script. 'It's Elvish. Dark elf, if I'm not mistaken. A very strange dialect. I—I haven't seen a text like this for years,' he said, shakily.

'Elvish. An old language indeed,' said the mage. It may have been the flickering candlelight, but it seemed to Gernn that his eyes widened at the news.

'One of the oldest, your Mage,' he answered.

The old scholar shuddered as he read onwards. He coughed as he turned page. 'It reads *The Testament of... Bringing*? But that word could also mean, erm creating, or—'

'*Summoning.*' Gernn adjusted his crystal spectacles and peered at the writing.

The mage turned to him, looking down his nose at the scholar. 'Summoning?'

Gernn nodded eagerly, almost losing his glasses. 'Yes, the dark elves were capable of raising all manner of creatures from their wells of magick, as I'm sure you're aware.'

The scholar tapped the page. 'It is a manual of some kind, your Mage. Here, warnings to acolytes.'

Innel took up the lecture. The subject of elves was a passion of his. 'They could summon huge beasts from the darkest places of the world at the cast of a single spell.' Innel went to a bookshelf and brought back a rare slice of tapestry covered with crude pictures. They depicted battles with strange goblin-type animals and giant winged creatures with many horns, wearing what looked to be golden crowns.

'I remember,' muttered the mage, as he turned the tapestry to face him. The others looked up questioningly. 'I said I remember seeing something like this before, in other books and old paintings in Krauslung.'

'Of course, your Mage,' Gernn nodded, wondering if he had seen any such paintings in the Arkathedral. There was an itch in his mind.

'If it's a spell manual, where are its keys?' he asked, leaning over the book once more, casting it in shadow.

Gernn and the others all peered at the faded, flowing script. Keys could be found in every spell book and any book without them was useless. They were the start of any incantation, the unlocking words to begin a spell.

The oldest scholar turned a few pages carefully, where more runes were scribbled. 'For this spell? Well, this is a very old spell indeed. Very powerful.' He pointed to a few symbols hiding at the corners of one page. 'Erm, there, and the other, there. These are the main words, *me* and *hear*. Saying them in the other order, of course, would open the spell. I don't dare to read aloud in its language.' His voice cracked and his words trailed off into silence. The scholar's hand was shaking more than usual. 'It seems we have uncovered a very special book indeed. It must be over a thousand years old, maybe more.'

Innel pointed. 'This needs careful translation. Look, it seems to reference something called *thy darkness swallowed,* or *mouths of darkness*. Yes, that's it, over and over again on these two pages.'

'And you are sure this book is not another fake?' The man had a hungry look in his eye, looking at the scholars like a wolf standing over a huddle of grey-haired rabbits. His arms were crossed, but his voice was now low and dangerous.

Innel nodded eagerly. 'Oh, it's very real, your Mage. A Dark Elven summoning manual, if you ask me.'

'It's dangerous, whatever it is,' said Gernn. That itch had become bothersome, as if he'd left a candle burning somewhere.

The man flashed teeth. 'How interesting this all is.' He drummed his fingers on the desk absently. 'Well, it seems you have been most useful to me this evening. I am sure Åddren will be as pleased as I am to hear of this discovery.'

The oldest scholar rose shakily from his chair and bowed his head. 'Thank you, your Mage. We will continue to study this manual with diligence. There is much more knowledge to be gained from it, and without you, sir, we would probably still have a locked book.' He smiled, and the other scholars managed a polite laugh. The air had become stale and thick.

The mage laughed heartily, startling them as the noise broke the hushed atmosphere. 'And without *you*, old fools, I would have nothing!'

The smile was replaced by thin lips. In a silver blur, the mage drew his sword and slammed the blade into Gernn's chest. He fell from the blade with a gurgling scream.

The mage swung right, cutting the throat of the old scholar. Dark blood painted the books and pages scattered across the desk. Sparks of electricity danced around the man's free hand. With a snarl and a flick of his wrist, a bolt of lightning surged into the others, burning the clothes from their backs and their skin to charcoal. An acrid smoke filled the room.

His business concluded, the man calmly sheathed his sword and lifted the black book from the desk. Wiping the blood from its cover, he turned on his heel, picked up his robe from the chair, and left without another sound.

Gernn choked, spitting blood on the floor. He attempted to crawl, but found his strength ebbing away with every withering beat of his heart. He died with his arm stretched out to the door.

Hundreds of miles away, in the west, a yellow dawn was breaking over an empty, snow-covered countryside. The cold morning light shone through skeletal trees, scattered patterns across winter snowdrifts. The wilderness was undulating, with rolling hills and patches of scrawny woods springing up between boulders, frozen streams, and endless snow. Apart from the drip of melting ice and the rattle of wind in the bone-like branches, not a sound could be heard.

A broken castle rose from a tall mound, crowned by concentric rings of ruined walls and dilapidated stone ramparts. A round tower squatted in disrepair at the centre of the castle, still sporting an empty flagpole. The massive stones of the walls were covered in brown moss and hanging icicles; the crenellations adorned with cuts and gashes forged by the war engines of old.

The pale morning was disturbed by the faint noise of a heavy-breathing newcomer. The hooded figure came from the south, trudging through the deep snow towards the castle, his long brown cloak billowing behind him in the icy breeze. Hot breath escaped in smoky plumes from his mouth, and the sound of his labouring was loud against the silence.

The man paused to pull his cloak about him and catch his breath. In the half-light of the early morning his keen eyes picked out an arched doorway set deep into the thick outer wall.

'Carn Breagh,' he muttered, lowering his red scarf from his face. After spitting in the snow, he checked the woods to his left and right with a wary glance, and then trudged on through the deep snow.

Beneath a black cloak, the man wore light, steel-plate armour over his shoulders, chest, and thighs, which clanked noisily as he moved. Around his waist was a thick leather belt holding his supplies, and an old sword encased in a dark red scabbard. Something gold and scarlet and metal peeked out from beneath the sleeves of his thick cloak. The man's sturdy black boots wearily plunged into the pure white snow, making creaking noises with every step.

The stranger reached the small stone archway and spread his hands over the thick oak door, feeling the splintered wood and the thick spikes that held the gate together. The man gave it a light push, but nothing budged. It was locked tight from the inside. He shoved a shoulder against it in a futile attempt to move the ancient wood, but still nothing. He looked at the door quizzically. The planks were weathered from hundreds of years of wind and snow, yet for some reason they had not rotted away like the other wooden features of the ancient castle.

The hooded man stretched his back and neck before rolling up his sleeves. Adorning his wrists and lower forearms were thick vambraces made of interwoven red and gold metal scales. They glittered faintly in the dawn light and clanked as he held them together. He closed his eyes as he placed his palms flat on the door. A pulse rippled across the wood and there came a dull clang from the other side. He gave it another push and the door swung open with a creak.

He allowed himself a faint smile as he peered into the gloom. He wrinkled his nose. It smelled like a thousand years of damp, blood, and little glory. The faint sound of dripping on stonework echoed from somewhere in the darkness. Mould hid between the cracks in the walls.

Without a sound, the man ducked under the thick stone archway and stood in the dim corridor, listening. He made a fist. White light shivered around his fingers, bathing the corridor in a pale moon-like glow.

Surrounded by his light, the stranger began to investigate the old castle, poking around in holes and long-lost underground chambers.

Cavernous halls and old rooms spread out like a warren as he went deeper and deeper into the castle. Everything was rotting and damp. Old curtains had decayed where they had been ripped down. Chests and furniture had been smashed against walls and lay in dark heaps and broken postures. In old, abandoned barracks, benches and tables were pushed up against splintered doors. Rusty swords hid under the rubble. There were no bones. No clothes. The rats had taken everything long ago.

For hours, the man searched the dank castle and found nothing except darkness and ruin. In a tiny room deep underground, he carefully took a seat on one of the less broken chairs and rested his feet for a moment. He was beginning to tire from keeping up his light spell, but he was sure there had to be something inside the old castle. His orders had stipulated he be thorough, and Carn Breagh was not a small castle by any means.

Absently, the man picked up a small piece of rubble and toyed with it for a few moments before tossing it across the room in boredom. To his surprise, the stone sailed straight through a frayed tapestry, landing with a clang somewhere far behind it.

He clenched his fist again and a fresh wave of light penetrated the gloom. He ripped the tapestry from its rusted hangings and threw it on the dusty floor. Hidden behind it was a staircase that spiralled down into the dark shadows. Curiosity sparked, he jogged down the steps, his footsteps echoing against the narrow walls.

After barely two turns around the pillar, the stairs came to a halt and a long hallway snaked out around a corner. Sconces holding long torches poked out from recesses in the walls. The man moved to the nearest one and felt the oil-soaked wick between his finger and thumb. It was dry enough. The man clicked his fingers over the torch and sparks flew, sending flame curling up the wall.

Dousing his light spell, he continued down the corridor, lighting each torch as he went. It was not long before he came across a huge door set deep into the stonework, held by thick hinges and a massive bolt that was fused to the metal bracing it. Eyes closed, the man ran his hand over the wood, searching for the right spell to use, but when he threw a wave of magick at the door it didn't even move an inch.

Irritated, he tried again. The air hummed as he hit the wood with another spell. Nothing happened. He thumbed his stubbled chin and thought for a moment. It was then that a deep boom rang out somewhere below his feet. It made the torches shiver in their sconces.

The man drew his sword from its scabbard as a few specks of dust fell from the ceiling. He squinted at the torches. The flames were shifting, leaning far out from the wall as if blown by a stiff breeze. He listened, watched, ready for anything. Nothing came, and all was silent again in the old castle.

Bored, the stranger sheathed his sword with a metallic ring. He climbed the stairs, turning left, then right, then left again, up more stairs, retracing his steps. Soon he was out in the snow once more, with the bright morning sun stinging his dusty eyes. He slammed the door behind him and stepped out into the white glare.

'What a pointless trip that was,' he spat, bending to pick up a handful of snow to rub between his fingers and wipe off the castle's muck. As he reached for another handful a shadow passed over him without a sound: a large, fast-moving shape that his eyes had to chase.

The man sighed as he straightened, throwing off his cloak and drawing his sword with a flourish. Spinning the blade in his hand, he calmly surveyed the peaceful countryside. His steel glinted in the sunlight.

'It's not even noon yet and a man has to deal with wyrms,' he muttered to himself as his eyes roved.

A screeching roar came from the skies above. The man leapt sideways, narrowly escaping the massive claws that plummeted into the snow behind him with a huge crash and a shower of snow. The man got to his feet and disdainfully brushed the white powder from his armour. He looked up as a snarl came from the white haze.

The wyrm reared its ugly blue head, shaking its horns with a rattle and spreading its stunted turquoise wings. A ridge of sharp brown spikes ran from its head to the tip of its serpentine tail. The monster's claws pawed at the snow, razor sharp and curved like a cat's. Its eyes were like black pools of jet. It was old for a wild dragon, and the ones that survive the longest are nothing if not notoriously hungry.

The wyrm let out a deafening hornlike scream and took a step. It had been a while since the man had seen such a large wyrm. It towered above him. He felt the wafting of its stink: old meat and something musky and reptilian.

The man began to circle the creature, holding his sword out straight towards it.

'Leave now, or this will end badly for you,' he ordered, in a measured tone, still treading sideways through the deep snow. The wyrm snarled, obviously lacking the capacity to understand him, and stamped its enormous feet like an impatient bull. It screeched again and foul spit flew into the man's face.

He grimaced and wiped the phlegm from his cheek and forehead, careful to keep his eyes on the snarling beast.

'I will take that as a no.'

The beast charged with frightening speed, but the man was more than ready. Dropping swiftly to one knee, he dug his blade into the snow with a thud. A solid wall of magick tore through the snow like a rippling earthquake, knocking the reptile to the snow with a disappointed whine. The man was on it in a flash, dragging his sword across the beast's belly. The blade cut a bloody path across its scales, splashing the snow blue.

The beast's whip-like tail lashed out and struck the man hard in the chest. He somersaulted into a nearby snowdrift with a crunch of armour. A star or two swam before his eyes. Before he had time to take a breath, the hungry wyrm charged at him again.

It scratched and it spat, and the man waved his sword wildly to keep the claws at bay. A stray talon scraped across his armour and found soft pale skin underneath. With a cry, he rolled sideways through the snow and managed to escape. Red blood stained the dirty snow beneath him, mixing with the blue.

Getting swiftly to his feet, the man smacked his vambraces together and a blast of flame shook the cold air. The fireball hit the wyrm in the chest and sent the creature reeling backwards. It roared with pain, frantically thrashing its tail in an effort to fend off the man, but it was futile.

He sprinted forwards, a light pulsed down his forearm and his blue-stained sword wreathed in flame. With a grunt, he hurled the glowing blade with both hands, and like a fiery arrow, it buried itself hilt-deep in the dragon's ribcage. The beast uttered a last mournful whistle and toppled over against a nearby tree in a shower of broken branches.

Breathing heavily, and wiping snow from his face, the man strode forwards to wrench his blade from the wyrm's smoking ribs. He felt a pain as he pulled it free. He put a hand to his side and winced, feeling the wet blood seeping from the long cut.

Retrieving his bloody cloak from beneath the wyrm's leg, he sighed, and began to follow his footprints back south.

Chapter 2

The Long Winter started gradually during the years of our long war with the Sirens. The heat was slowly taken from our days, one by one, and the sun from our sky, until our seventy-sixth year, the year of our last summer. The snowstorms gathered, and the ice fields grew, creeping inexorably south until they almost threatened to cover Nelska, and ever since the end of the war our weather has remained cold and bitter, and the proud mountains of Össfen stay covered by the eternal snow.

From writings found in the libraries of Arfell

The hooded stranger travelled without rest for two days, heading south through field and forest and river and hill. On the morning of the third day, he crested a muddy knoll and took a moment to catch his breath.

Before him in the valley lay a small village called Leath, built on a rocky crag that overlooked a metallic river and muddy fields. He narrowed his eyes at the tiny town. Its inhabitants had always been wary of strangers and feared his kind especially. They were a superstitious lot, concerned only with their farming and their drinking. Mages weren't to their liking. He decided to give the village his usual wide berth and take the winding route back to the Arkabbey. He hopped over a few rocks and slid over some shale, then headed west around the town, sticking to the wilder roads and the copses.

A few hours later, the man was treading through the thick loam of the Forest of Durn, a shady wood south of Leath that was seldom entered or explored by the townspeople. Rumour had it that a fierce vampyre lived somewhere amongst the dark trees, feeding off the blood of any Albion soul that would trespass in his woods. The stranger clearly didn't believe in any such rumour, and paid attention only to the surrounding forest, still deep in the clutches of the Long Winter. The snow-laden trees were alive with the breath of a light wind. Bark creaked over the low moan. A few brave animals scuttled around in the frozen loam. Somewhere a bird cried out. The man kept walking, following the almost indistinguishable trail through the undergrowth.

At last, he made it to his destination, taking a small winding trail between a wall of bushes and pine trees. Brown needles crunched underfoot as he picked his way under branches and around rocks. Soon, he spotted the light of a hidden clearing ahead and he walked towards it.

The trees gave way, revealing a small glade and a tall brick building that had been completely concealed by the forest. This was an Arkabbey, one of many that had been quietly built across the lands of Albion and Emaneska.

Smoke rose from the windows of the kitchen and the noise of axes biting wood and other work echoed over the grounds. The tall bell tower rose high above the trees, with glass windows and balconies punctuating its thick granite walls. The bell had been silent for decades, and the man couldn't remember the last time he had heard its doleful pealing.

Workers and soldiers were milling around the gardens and taking in the brisk air. The man nodded to a few familiar faces as he walked across the lawn. The cold grass underneath his boots was slippery and well-tended: clipped short and tidy, if not a little brown from the cold. To his left, a few beehives hid amongst the trees. They seemed lifeless and quiet.

An armoured soldier standing by the door saluted him with his spear. The man strode inside the arch and felt the warmth of the busy building on his cold skin. He rubbed his hands and shook the mud and ice from his boots, listening to the sounds of cooking and cleaning echoing against the stone walls. With a yawn, the man tackled a dozen flights of stairs and as many corridors until he came to a simple oak door. He pushed it open with a bang.

A woman jumped and dropped the bundle of tunics she was carrying and put her hand to her chest in fright. 'Oh! Farden, it's you.' She flapped her hand like a fan.

'Same old.' The man threw his hood back and smiled at the girl. Elessi was his maid and somewhat of a friend to him, having done a bit more than just picking up after him over the years.

Her face knew only two expressions, either wearing a cherubic smile or a concerned frown. Her deep brown eyes were always gleaming, as if she had just been handed the juiciest tidbit of gossip. Farden would never have admitted it to her, but Elessi's notorious stubbornness had kept him on track more than once in the last few years. Like any good Albion woman, she liked to put a man in his place.

Blowing her curly brown hair from her blushing cheeks, the maid started to pick up the dropped clothes. 'You could have knocked,' she said, flustered.

'To my own room? You shouldn't be sneaking around in here.' Farden threw her a smile to melt her frown. He threw his cloak on the small bed and sat on the windowsill, watching the trees shiver outside.

'Gods know someone needs to look after you mages. Where've you been to this time? Oh! Is that blood on your side?' Her face creased up with worry as she rushed to the window to see.

Farden glanced down at the roughly-bandaged gash that the dragon had gifted him, running along the right side of his ribs. He waved Elessi away as she tried to see the damage. 'Don't worry about it, you know it will heal. Elessi, calm down! It's fine.' He shooed her away gently and covered it up with a shred of tunic.

'What was it this time? Another minotaur? It was a bandit wasn't it? I knew it.' Elessi stood there with her hands on her hips like a scolding mother. Farden looked at her.

'Elessi, we've known each other a long while, and you've seen me heal from worse wounds before,' he said. She just raised her eyebrows at him. He grimaced as he stretched. 'I'll be fine in a day,' he said, then closed his eyes and rested against the cold stone to end the matter. 'It was a wild wyrm. They hunt magick.'

'Well, no matter what it was, it looks bad to me. At least let me put a poultice on it to bring out any poison,' Elessi tutted. 'You're not indestructible, Farden, and gods know I've told you before, jus' like 'is lordship in the tower!'

'A thousand times,' muttered Farden, listening to her earnest rustling. She moved to a nearby jug of water and brought back a wet cloth. The chambermaid dabbed the crusted blood from his ribs as Farden clenched his teeth.

'Sometimes I think you like throwin' yourself into danger all the time,' she chided him.

Farden didn't answer. Instead, he stared at the leafless trees waving at him outside. Her hands were cold and so was the water, but it felt good on the burning skin, hot and sweaty from the long trudge south. He felt her hands stray to his back and the silence became awkward. The mage spun around and deftly caught her wrist.

'How many times do I have to tell you?' Farden's voice was low, sharp in severity. He stared into her chestnut eyes, and slowly let go of her arms.

Elessi looked upset. 'I'm sorry, I just wanted to s—' But Farden held up a hand. He rested his head against the wall and closed his eyes again.

'Enough,' he said, and the maid backed away. She picked up his cloak and some other clothes and turned to leave.

'Durnus is waiting for you upstairs,' she said.

Farden nodded and heard the wooden door click shut. With a sigh he held the wet cloth to his side. Elessi was a kind soul, but her curiosity was dangerous. It felt harsh keeping her at arm's length, but it had to be done. Her feelings had to be sacrificed for her own safety. There were rules, and even though she was his friend, those rules came first.

It was refreshing though, to be treated with respect, as opposed to the usual uncertainty and fear he received from most of the population of Albion. Farden was usually treated with mild neglect, as more of a dark omen than a blessing, stared at with wary, melancholy eyes, like a lone soldier passing through. Farden didn't really like people. People were rude, and people were ignorant, oblivious to how the real world worked and moved. They were like ants on a chessboard, and Farden had no time for them.

He grunted and scratched at his back and bloodied side. His vambraces felt heavy and he could feel weariness slowly creeping over him, but with resolve he made for the door. It was time to see Durnus.

A thin old man sat with his back to the door, watching the flames crackle and pop in the fireplace. Drapes hung thick and heavy over the windows, making the huge room dim and full of flickering shadows. Candles dotted the floors and walls, stars in a stone sky, ensconced in holders and perching on tall piles of books. A massive map of Albion hung on the far wall, showing the distant shores of Nelska, and the cliff cities of Halôrn to the southeast.

Farden closed the door behind him, completely silent. His bare feet slowly crept across the cold stone floor towards the old man in his comfy armchair.

'You're late,' said the old man, in a rasping voice. His words made Farden flinch. The travel-weary mage laughed and moved to an empty chair by the fire.

'Gods' sake, Durnus. How do you do that?'

Durnus laughed a whispering cackle, grinning widely and baring a pair of sharp fangs. Farden slumped into a comfy armchair and sighed, wincing as his wound scraped against his tunic.

'You always forget that I have hearing to rival that of a bat, Farden, whereas you have the footfall of a work-cow.' Durnus chuckled again and poked at the fire with a long metal rod. 'The sun is still up then, I take it?'

Farden nodded and stared into the fire in silence. The old figure in the chair next to him was his closest friend, and one of Emaneska's sharpest historical minds. Farden often found himself wondering how old the vampyre truly was.

Durnus' eyes were a blue so pale they almost bordered on white, and his skin was like white paper stretched over an angular frame. His features were sharp and bony, his grey hair swept back and slicked down behind his tall ears, stopping just short of his shoulders. His fangs peeked from behind pale lips when he spoke.

'Good,' he said. The vampyre settled back in his chair and closed his eyes. 'Report,' he whispered.

Farden went to it with a will, recalling every detail of his journey to Carn Breagh, telling Durnus of the strange corridor inside the bowels of the castle and his fight with the wild wyrm. The vampyre merely nodded along, humming at the appropriate points, occasionally clearing his throat and stroking his sharp chin with a frail hand. When Farden ran out of words, Durnus opened his eyes.

'I shall send a full account to the Arkathedral in the morning,' he said, 'but Carn Breagh can wait for now. Something terrible has happened in Arfell.' Durnus' face took on a grave quality.

Farden looked confused. 'The library?'

Durnus nodded. 'Indeed. I received a hawk from Krauslung this morning, relaying some of the darkest news I have heard in a long time.' He paused for some sort of dramatic effect. Farden knew the old vampyre loved mystery and intrigue, so he waited, playing along.

'Two nights ago, somebody broke into the library and murdered five of the scholars in cold blood. It was late at night, and nobody saw or heard a thing. Several of the scholars were found burnt to a crisp. It seems that a valuable object, an ancient book of some kind, is the only thing that's missing.' Durnus drummed his nails on the arm of his chair.

Farden let the information sink in. 'What was it?' he asked.

'No one knows. A message had arrived at the Arkathedral only that day, saying that the scholars in question had found a book in their collection, a Siren book. Something we stole during the war, when we were busy plundering Nelska's coasts. The scholars had only just begun to examine it. They requested that the Arkmages travel to Arfell to help with the opening of it.' Durnus recounted, leaning forwards to warm his hands against the fire.

'This book must have been quite something to request the presence of the Arkmages,' mused Farden.

'Precisely. And before Åddren or Helyard had a chance to leave, the scholars were murdered, and the book was stolen. And let me tell you, from what I gathered from the message, the Arkathedral is in uproar. Helyard is blaming everyone under the sky, especially the Sirens, and the good Lord Vice has ordered a regiment of his guards up to the mountains to see if the assassin returns for more books,' replied Durnus, his eyes wide with excitement.

'Well, what is this book? Why is it so powerful?'

'Again, nobody has a clue. The hawk sent from Arfell wasn't exactly full of information. You know what the old men at Arfell are like, full of secrecy and intrigue. All the message stated was that the book was in good condition, locked tight, and of the utmost importance. Apparently, it was small, covered in black dragon scales and protected by a powerful golden seal, with a spell that would require one of the Arkmages to crack. They assumed it was Siren or perhaps even older, and that it might contain an immense amount of formidable magick. That was it.'

'Sounds dangerous,' Farden said. He got up and revived the dying fire with a few logs and a spark of flame from his hands. Durnus flicked a tongue around one of his sharp fangs in thought.

'Indeed,' he muttered.

Farden knew his friend had a theory, but that he was waiting to be asked, so he relented, and smiled. 'What are you thinking?'

Durnus crept further out of his chair, making the frame squeak. 'One explanation I can muster is that the Sirens have a spy in the council. They are the ones we stole it from in the first place. It seems sensible to assume they would want it back.'

Farden shrugged as he leaned on the fireplace. 'A fair idea, but we can't dismiss that it was someone other than the dragon-riders. It's been fifteen years since the war and the ceasefire has yet to be broken, so why would they risk breaking it to retrieve one little book?' Farden asked.

'That depends on the value hidden within its pages, my good mage. Who else? Skölgard has no interest in magick, nor could their sorcerers know of such a book's existence. We Arka did not know of it until a couple of days ago. If this book is as powerful as we think it might be, then the Siren wizards would most definitely risk a ceasefire to get it back into their scaly hands.'

Durnus' words made sense, but Farden didn't like the sound of them.

'In any case, the Arkmages have sent word that you are to find a man named Jergan in the south of Albion. My research indicates that he might know what this book is, and therefore, who might have stolen it.'

Farden cocked his head. 'Jergan. Who is he?'

'He was once a scholar in his own right, who lived at Arfell before the war. He might have come across this book before when he lived with the dragon-riders.'

'Jergan worked with the Sirens?'

Durnus made a face. 'He *is* Siren. He studied in Hjaussfen before the war broke out. A historian, like me. Led all sorts of expeditions. But, ten years ago he was attacked by a lycan somewhere on the ice fields. He fled to Albion, hiding in the mountains to the north, where he lived for many years, fighting the wolf-curse. However, I've had word that a year ago he took up residence in the Dornoch hills to the south and is now living alone somewhere on the moors. It would seem the locals have lost many a sheep,' he said, before pausing to shudder. 'The very thought of a lycan makes me sick.'

Farden smiled, distracted. A lycan in Albion was peculiar. They stuck to the far eastern wilds, on the steppes and pine forests of eastern Skölgard. 'When do I leave?' he asked, reaching up to stretch his back. His wound sang out, and he winced.

Farden could feel the numbing fingers of tiredness creeping over him. The fatigue spell he had cast the day before to keep him moving was finally starting to wear off.

Durnus wagged a finger at him. 'Tonight Farden, you rest, and no arguments. You have plenty of time for slumber. It's not as though the Arka will fall apart overnight.'

'As long as nothing happens to their gold, then I think we're safe,' said Farden, and the vampyre laughed.

'Politics, Farden. Politics, rules, and using them against others. That's what they care about. People like us belong out here on the fringes, where it matters. Somehow I can't see us cooped up in a hall debating the finer points of civilisation.' He chuckled.

The mage nodded. He wandered around the room, flicking through interesting-looking parchments and book covers. 'So you don't miss it then?' he asked. Durnus threw him a quizzical look.

'The city?'

'Being in the thick of it.'

Durnus shook his head. 'No. I thought one of the reasons you came here, Farden, like I did, was to get away from all the pressure of the gossip and the politics. I was never at home in the Arkathedral.'

Farden picked up another book, fighting a yawn.

'What's wrong?' asked Durnus.

Farden shook his head and managed a weary smile. 'I'm fine, don't worry.'

The vampyre nodded, showing a sliver of fang between his chalk lips. 'Fancy some wine?' he said, pointing to table in the corner of the room. An ornate green bottle filled with a dark liquid sat upon it, with two glasses for company. Farden picked up the bottle and wiggled the wooden stopper free, then gave the liquid a careful sniff.

'As long as it's not the blood of some poor local, then yes, I would,' he replied, narrowing his eyes at his friend. Durnus laughed, gesturing to the chair. Farden sat.

Despite his tiredness, the mage remained holed up in Durnus' room for the rest of the evening, their tongues wagging over war, peace, murder, and magick, washing their words down with plenty of fruit wine.

When the night stretched into early morning, Farden finally left the vampyre's room. His head was spinning with tiredness, alcohol, and snatches of regurgitated conversation. He could feel himself starting down a trail of thought that he disliked very much.

The mage wandered through the dark corridors of the Arkabbey and tried to calm himself.

As Farden lay down on his cold bed, thoughts began to dance around his head like insects around a candle, second-guessing and doubts rife in his shallow dozing.

Smothered by the darkness of his room, he tossed and turned until, finally, he buried his fist in the pillow in frustration. Farden got up and stumbled across the stone floor until his foot kicked at his travelling bag, full of supplies. He rummaged around for a while before finding what he was looking for. He had hidden it deep.

Farden moved to the door and locked it quietly. He started unwrapping a small, scrunched-up bit of bark-cloth. He stopped for a moment to listen to the noises of the night, then quietly put a small pinch of something on his tongue.

Farden went to the windowsill and looked out at the dark forest, listening to a lonely owl hoot. He closed his eyes and chewed, waiting. After a while, the mage felt the numbness gradually climb from his mouth into his spine, and the stuff began to sour in his mouth. Farden spat, and heard the thoughts quieten, felt himself slowly forgetting.

Before he got lost in the dizziness, he grabbed a nearby candlestick and wedged the bundle of bark-cloth into its hollow base. With a thud, he put the candlestick back on the bedside table and let his world begin to melt. His head felt like water spilling over a never-ending wheel.

Farden gradually let sleep take him hostage, allowing it to cut away his problems, one by one. Forgotten for now.

The mage was in a desert.

Farden lifted his hands to feel the hot rays of the strange red sun dance across his skin. He wore only his trousers and the red-gold vambraces. His feet were bare. The cracked, dusty earth quivered and shook in the sweltering heat. Pebbles floated from side to side across the sand, hiding in the spaces between his blinks.

In the haze of the distance, the horizon was darkened by huge black mountains scraping at the heavens. Farden looked up and around him, in all directions. He had never seen a sky so big, so massive, or so empty.

He felt something scratching at his leg and looked down to find a skinny black cat impatiently clawing at him. The thing mewed at him, yawning cavernously, a yawn too big for a cat that small.

Farden watched the thing scratch about. It fixed him with an obsidian gaze, eyes like two black scrying mirrors, and cocked its head on one side.

'What?' Farden asked, not sure if he really expected an answer. *This was a dream, wasn't it*?

He became aware of his skin starting to tingle and shiver. Bolts of pain began to shoot up his arms, as if he had slept on them for too long and now sought to move them.

Farden looked down to see flakes of burning skin peel from his hands and wrists. His arms and chest started to brown and blacken. The veins and arteries under the skin melted into rivers of fire. His vambraces cracked and splintered into pieces before his eyes, then fell to the dust with a dull clang that reverberated and roared, becoming an unbearable cacophony in his ears, like the mountains were dragging themselves across the desert towards him, inch by inch but closing in.

Farden lifted his hands to his face and felt the charred bone underneath, watching shreds of flaming skin fill the air like a swarm of locusts in the hot wind. Farden opened his mouth to scream but his tongue was too dry, refusing to move, sitting smouldering between his black teeth.

Before his eyes were burnt to dust, Farden looked down at the cat. It stared at him with a placid, bored look, then its tiny mouth seemed to curl into a smile. The mage heard a voice in his head speak clearly over the fire and the roaring wind.

Follow the dragons, it said. Then the wind swallowed him.

❦

Sunlight streamed in through the open window, piercing the sleeping mage's eyelids like a yellow spear and sending pain jolting through his skull. Farden swore darkly and hoisted himself out of bed. Remnants of a dream swirled around him, but they quickly dissolved to nothing in the morning light. The early sun had a habit of stealing the memories of dreams from the mind, as if they were too dangerous to cling onto.

There came a knock at his door and Elessi shuffled into the cold room, holding a small wooden cup of something and a bowl of homemade porridge.

'Good mornin',' she said with a bright smile, her face the opposite of Farden's mood.

'Is it?' Farden coughed and tried to look awake, fighting off the haze of the night before. He grabbed a nearby shirt and threw it on to cover his wound and his back.

Elessi put the breakfast on a table in the corner of the room and began to sort out clothes for his journey. Farden stalked over to the table and sniffed the juice. Apple. He downed it in one gulp and grabbed a spoonful of porridge. He managed one mouthful before feeling ill.

'How'd you sleep?' asked Elessi, as she set to cleaning some of his armour. His battered sword was on the bed.

The tired mage swept the blade from his scabbard and looked at the notched edge, scarred from many a battle. *Many a wyrm-claw, too.* 'I need a new sword,' he said, absently, before turning his attention to the maid bustling around his room. 'I slept well, thank you for asking. Durnus and I talked long into the night. Is he up yet or should I go wake him?'

'Rumour has it he went out huntin' last night, but he should be back in his room by now. It makes my skin crawl when I think of what he's been up to.' Elessi shivered involuntarily.

'He can't help his nature. And it does wonders for keeping the townspeople out of the forest.' Farden smiled wanly at his own joke. His head pounded like a drum.

'There, your armour is all clean, and there's a fresh cloak and tunic 'ere for you. Fresh supplies are in your 'aversack as usual. I know how you don't like searchin' the kitchens for food, what with the other maids there,' she said, and made to leave. She lingered at the door for a moment.

'Thank you, Elessi,' said Farden as he tried another spoon of breakfast. She looked as if she were about to say something but thought better of it and closed the door.

Farden milled around in his room for a bit, struggling to shake the numbness he still felt from the drug, the nevermar, and the strange remnants of vivid dreams he could have sworn were real. The mage rubbed his cold skin and shook his head from side to side to see if it would rattle some sense into him.

He could feel the hangover dimming his magick, like alcohol diminishes the ability to walk in a straight line. Farden took a warm cloth from a bowl of warm water and dabbed the wound at his side. It was healing up nicely, but was still angry, red and sore. It would be healed by the next day. His fingers traced something on his back for just a moment, before he turned to face a bronze mirror in the corner of his modest room and stare at his reflection.

Farden looked exhausted. His dark, almost black, hair was in a wilder state than usual, and from behind the tangled strands that lay across his face he could see dark rings surrounding his grey-green eyes. The mage ran an exploratory hand across his face, examining the rest of him, rubbing stubble and dust between his fingertips, blinking at his bronze alter-ego to try to make it more acceptable.

Farden was a tall man, just over six foot, and well built, perhaps a few years over thirty. Nobody but Farden was sure. His arms and body bore countless scars from blade and magick: random streaks of pinky white criss-crossing his already pale skin like the paths of a snail. There was a small tattoo on each of his wrists, a black outline of a skeleton key, edged in tiny lines of script. He rubbed at them briefly before sliding his red and gold vambraces over them.

Next came a brown tunic made of rough cloth, and over that went his thick and simple steel plate armour. It hugged his body closely, but still allowed him to move if needed, unlike the thicker, more elaborate suits of armour from Skölgard or Nelska. Farden strapped on a thick rust-coloured belt, some more plate armour for his thighs, then stuffed his feet into a pair of heavy black ranger's boots. Lastly, he donned a long black cloak with a hood and strapped his sword into its scabbard on his back, arranging a red scarf to wrap around his neck. Despite the pounding headache and dizzy stomach, Farden smiled a rare smile at his bronze reflection. He was ready to go once again.

Farden slammed the door to his room and bounded downstairs, barging past a few kitchen boys carrying pitchers of milk. They stood dumbstruck as the dark character swept past them and down the hallway, muttering only the briefest of apologies.

The mage went straight to the main hall of the Arkabbey, where a small shrine sat against the north wall. His footsteps echoed loudly on the stone.

Farden knelt before the shrine, where a statue of a powerful looking woman sat. She held out a pair of marble scales, as if demanding something. Her stern stone gaze looked out over the myriad of candles that had been lit on her plinth. This was Evernia, goddess of magick to the Arka, and keeper of balance.

After he whispered a standard prayer to the goddess, Farden tossed a small coin onto a stone dish. The old gods didn't hold as much sway over the lands of Emaneska as they did in the ancient days, but it was still wise to stay on good terms with the fickle creatures.

Durnus dropped to one knee next to Farden and whispered something to the stone statue. There was a moment of silence as he finished his prayer. 'I don't often see you paying homage to the old ones,' he commented in a hoarse voice.

Farden shrugged. 'It seems like a good idea to keep on their good sides,' he said. The vampyre nodded.

'That it does. How did you sleep?' he asked. Durnus himself looked tired. His eyes were even paler than usual, and the large hooded cloak he wore did nothing to conceal the fatigue hiding in bags under his skin.

'Everyone always asks me that as if I were a stranger to a bed.' Farden smiled wryly. 'Well, thank you. I hear you had a good night?'

'Gods damn those maids; they have tongues like town criers. I would cast a mute spell on every last one of them if I had the chance to do so. I take it Elessi told you?' Durnus cursed, bowing his head to the statue as he stood up. He turned to leave and Farden followed him towards a thin door. The thick cloth curtains on the archway shifted in a chill draught.

'That one does like to talk,' grinned Farden, as they walked down a dark corridor. The Arkabbey was still in the process of waking up: the servants were preparing breakfast for the slumbering soldiers, and a few scribes wandered the halls, rubbing sleepy eyes and yawning.

'So I have noticed. You haven't said anything to her about what happened at Arfell, have you?' Durnus' pale eyes grew narrow, and he furrowed his brow at his friend.

Farden shook his head 'No. I went straight to bed after I left your room last night. I barely talked to her at all this morning when she woke me with breakfast. I know the rules, and with a dangerous matter like this, I wouldn't exactly go shouting it about.'

'Good,' said Durnus. The vampyre seemed satisfied and sniffed imperiously. He ducked under a random shaft of sunlight coming from a high window and folded his gloved hands behind his back. The two walked slowly and silently for a moment before Durnus spoke up again. 'You look tired, Farden. Anything the matter?'

The headache of an anvil and stomach-gruelling dizziness, thought the mage.

'Absolutely nothing. Deep sleep and I'm still waking up,' lied Farden. *Far too easy.*

Durnus waved a hand. 'Now remember, get as much information out of Jergan as you can. I'm not sure how he's fared since his exile, and the wolf-curse does strange things to a man, so be wary of his answers. After all, he may have a mind like that of soft cheese and be completely useless, but above all, make sure that you get the truth! If the Arkmages are going to base their actions on your words, then they had better be the right ones,' the vampyre lectured.

Farden's head ached. His old friend pulled a roll of parchment from the folds in his cloak.

'Jergan was last seen somewhere near Beinnh, south of the Dornoch hills. You can rest up in the town and then face him the day after. Unfortunately for you, the pull of the moon is strong this month, so he'll be able to change at will.'

Farden nodded. 'Trust me, I can handle him.'

Durnus flashed him a toothy smile. 'It's not you I'm worried about, my dear mage. He's the only lead we've got to putting an end to this book debacle. What I mean to say is don't kill him, Farden,' he ordered with a chuckle, but both of them knew there was a serious undertone to the command.

'I won't.' Farden paused in an arched doorway. Durnus stayed in the shadows of the corridor and away from the morning light. Farden held out a hand and the vampyre gripped it an iron handshake. Durnus smiled.

'Don't wait up for me.' Farden pulled his red scarf around his neck and chin.

'I never do,' Durnus replied.

Farden turned around and jogged over the wet lawn and into the thick forest. The mage disappeared behind the trees, and Durnus returned to his room, saying more than a few charms for good luck.

Chapter 3

A dragon's claws are curved and deadly, much like the strange daggers from the east. Beware the teeth, too. A large dragon can have up to three rows of teeth and gnash them in a fearsome manner before eating. A dragon may have a long or short tail, but either invariably has a forked or barbed tip that swishes around angrily should a traveller choose to approach! Their scales have the power to mystify, with rippling colours that can hypnotise the unwary, and some may even change colour to match their backgrounds.

From *Dragons and their Features: Lessons in Identifying the Siren Beast* by Master Wird

It was raining hard when Farden walked through the industrious streets of Beinnh. Townsfolk and strangers trotted through the muddy streets. Carts pulled by cows and donkeys splashed through puddles, soaking the passers-by and dirtying the colours of the market stalls lining the road. People crowded in the shadows of the tall houses. The wooden buildings leaned out over the thoroughfares as though they would topple at any moment, heavy with tall, arched slate roofs, brick chimneys, and gurgling gutters.

Farden shrugged rainwater from his cloak for the hundredth time and drove his hands deeper into the pockets, hoping to find a dry spot somewhere. His grey eyes roved over the various wares that were on offer in the little tents, their tables adorned with food, clothing, weapons, and cheap trinkets. The shopkeepers brayed tenaciously through the downpour with offers of bargains and special prices. A wet, miserable customer is still a customer.

Ahead, a building jutted into the road. A striped tent had been hoisted up to cover some benches and a well, where gloomy figures hunched over pots of ale, plates of bread and *farska*, a cheap beef stew sold in taverns all over dreary Albion and Emaneska. Farden trudged through the muddy puddles and cart ruts, dodging the brown rivers of rubbish. After three long days of urgent travel, he was starting to run out of food.

As he neared the tent, the mage spied a small blacksmith's shop nestled in the back of the building. A table of shining weapons glinted in the bright firelight from the forge and a thin, soot-smeared man stood holding a file to an axe. Patrons milled around the tables holding various blades and sharp objects, stocky grim men, the sort that oozed dark aspirations and malicious intent. A group of them hunched over the end of the table, clad in long dark cloaks and smoking cheap tobacco from even cheaper pipes.

Farden made his way to the front of a table and ran his hands over the shining swords and knives. His eyes picked out a longsword, sheathed in a thick black leather scabbard, with thick crossbars and a long, steel, leather-bound handle with a pommel-stone shaped like a huge black diamond. Farden unsheathed the weapon and ran a careful thumb over the blade's sharp edges. It was a fine sword, that was for sure.

'See something you like, boy?' A bald skeleton of a man croaked in a thick Albion drawl. The dirty blacksmith tugged at the grey-white gloves covering his bony hands. They were made from salamander wool, impervious to fire and perfect for working a forge.

'How much for this, old man?' Farden asked, waving the sword at him.

The smith looked at the blade and chewed something in the back of his mouth. 'Hmm, one 'undred silver.'

'One hundred? You've got to be joking. I'll give you sixty, fair price for this blade.' Farden shook his head and crossed his arms. The nearby men had gone silent, intrigued by the sale and the foreign-looking mage.

'Eighty, or no sale.' The old man stuck out a greasy palm.

The mage unbuckled his notched sword from his back and tossed it to the blacksmith with a grunt. 'Sixty, and you can have that, old man. It's still got a few swings in it.' Farden strapped the new longsword in its place and fastened the thick buckle around his armoured chest. The old smith cleared his throat grumpily, shrugged, and finally nodded.

Farden took a coin-purse from the travel pack at his side and counted out sixty silver pieces. The smith swiftly spirited them away, sliding each coin into his pocket with relish. Farden noticed the silence at the table and turned to meet the stare of a bald thug on his left, a man with a scar across his forehead. He managed to hold the mage's piercing gaze for a moment before turning away to grin at his companions. With a nod, he walked away and his minions followed him like loyal dogs in their master's wake.

Their business concluded, Farden turned to go, but something polished and bright on the next table caught his attention, something shining with reflection of the hot forge. It was a hand mirror, ringed with black iron and cheap coloured stones. It lay propped up against a wooden post at the far edge of the stall, surrounded by cheap cutlery and barely polished ornaments. 'Smith! Is that mirror silver?' asked Farden.

The smith turned and looked at the glimmering object, rubbing his filthy chin with equally filthy fingers. 'Yeah, 'tis. Made it last week, for the posh ladies of the town y'see, give 'em somethin' to look at their pretty faces with.' He leered, exposing empty gums where teeth should have been. He paused to spit into a clay pot near the crackling forge. 'Ye want that, too?'

'This is important, old man.' Farden levelled a finger at the blacksmith. The mage knew his magick lore, and of the rules that bound each creature. If Jergan was a lycan, then he would fear silver. The rumours about using silver blades or arrows to kill the creatures were absolute rubbish: any blade would do as long as it was sharp enough and thrust into the right place. However, if a lycan saw their reflection in something silver, like a silver mirror for example, then the curse would break momentarily, and they would return to their naked, shivering, human forms, dizzy and exhausted after the sudden transformation. It would give him an hour with the man, without the wolf to bother him. Maybe two, if he were lucky, and if the moon stayed out of sight.

Farden had faced a lycan only once before, on the ice fields in the far north. He had been let off easily that time; the skinny creature had merely stalked him for a day or two at the most, only once getting close enough for a spell, but otherwise keeping its distance. Farden remembered the fear as if it were yesterday. Lycans were incredibly dangerous. Their vicious claws and teeth were matched only by their strength and lightning speed. And, of course, it only took a single bite or scratch to curse a man.

'This mirror has to be *pure* silver, you understand? If I find out it's a fake there's going to be trouble between you and me, and more than just the mirror will be returned to you.' Farden tapped his new sword's hilt menacingly with one hand, and with the other he summoned a little flame to burn on his palm.

The old smith took a step back and held up anxious, shaking hands. 'Easy, easy. Ain't no reason to get violent 'ere. It's silver, have no fear, mage.' The smith flashed an uneasy smile. 'How 'bout a special price of twenny-five silver? Between you and me?' he offered. Farden didn't trust him at all, but he needed something shiny and silver. He had forgotten to find one before he left. The mage nodded, and the smith rushed to fetch the mirror from amongst the other trinkets at the back of the oak table.

Farden looked about him once again. The nevermar was still numbing his magick ability, and now a fresh throbbing had taken up residence in his head. Assured that nobody had seen his little demonstration, Farden counted out the overpriced sum of twenty-five silver coins to the fidgety little smith. He put the mirror in his travel bag and let the man scurry back to the safety of his smouldering forge.

Farden stepped back into the pouring rain and went to look for a few food supplies for the last part of his journey. After purchasing some dried meat, tough biscuits and apples, he headed down the hill towards the south gate of the muddy town. He found his pace getting a little quicker with every step closer he got to Jergan. It was nothing but his nature.

A short while later, Farden found himself striding along a quiet road near the south wall of Beinnh. Night was slowly approaching, and lamps of the town were busy being lit. A hundred twinkling lights hiding behind curtains, sitting on tables and in iron sconces. It almost made the town look pretty, but only in a futile way. It was like painting a corpse gold. It still rotted underneath.

The persistent rain fell hard, and the downpour was now driven by the approaching wind. In the distance, white lightning ripped through the cloudy darkness. The flashes tore at the night, etching the hills and bringing rumbling cracks and deep, faraway booms to the mage's ears.

Farden watched his own boots slosh through the mud, as if his eyes kept them moving, not his muscles. It was foul weather even by Albion standards, but his cloak was warm and kept him protected from the elements. This new sword was a touch heavier, but it felt good to have a decent blade for a change, he thought.

Through his musings he heard a muffled cough from behind him. He turned to see a burly figure following in his wake, about twenty yards behind him. Turning back, Farden cast sideways glances at the silent, dripping houses and tiny alleyways.

Another man, skinny and bedraggled, was leaning against a wall, smoking a pipe. In the rain ahead of him, yet another thug was coming up the road. Even though the rain hammered noisily at the puddles and mud, the sounds of splashing strides were ominously loud.

Farden clicked his neck from side to side and tensed his wiry muscles, summoning the magick from the base of his skull. A wave of hangover washed over him, dimming his power and sending throbbing waves of pain ricocheting behind his eyes. Farden grunted. *We'll have to do this the old-fashioned way then*, he thought.

The thug in front of him brandished a knife in his right hand, the thin blade glinting in the far-off glow of the town. It was the bald man from earlier at the forge, and in the half-light of dusk, Farden could see the rain bouncing off his shiny head and running down the scar on his brow. He grinned and waved his dagger at the smoker and the man behind Farden. They moved in, striding confidently through the mud. Farden suppressed a smirk.

'Jus' give us yer coin and we'll be on our way,' warned the thug, in a low voice. 'You don't want any trouble 'ere, do you mate?'

Farden spoke calmly yet sternly as the men surrounded him, keeping their distance. The other two took out their weapons: a hammer and a club. Farden took a wider stance and stood firm.

'If you and your men know what's best for you, then you'd be on your way now, without my coin, and with your limbs still attached. I don't want to have to hurt you.'

'Don't know if you noticed, mate, but there's three o' us, an' just one o' you, so it ain't lookin' too good for yer, is it? Like I said, give us yer fuckin' coin an' we won't 'ave to leave yer body for the guards to find in an alleyway, alright?'

The bald man made little cutting motions in the air with his kitchen knife. He was a brute. Thick-set and swarthy, with a face that had been introduced to more than its fair share of fists. A threadbare cloak hung from his wide hunched shoulders. No mail. Just a tunic. *Good.*

Farden sighed. He should have known better than to flash his coins around in the view of men like this. He gave them another chance.

'You idiots don't get it, do you? Walk away, or you won't live to see another day.' Farden's eyes drilled into the hungry, frog-like glare of the bald thug. The man spat.

'Get the little shit, lads! Get 'is coin!' he yelled. He charged wildly at the mage, feet pounding through the muddy street, dagger flailing.

The two men collided with a raucous crash. Farden turned deftly to the side and let his elbow greet the man's face. He was stopped dead in his tracks, blood mixing with the rain as his legs slid out from him. Farden knocked the knife from his hand in one swift strike, letting him crash to the ground in a shower of mud.

The mage dropped to his knees and drew his sword with a metallic ring, waiting for his prey to come to him. The next thug was already running at him, barely three yards away. Farden swung the longsword in a wide arc, catching the thief square in the ribs. There was a sickening crunch as it smashed through bone and flesh to bite into spine. The man let out an unearthly scream and crumpled to a bloody heap next to his bald comrade, writhing and spilling vital organs into the incarnadined mud.

The last thug ran in with a shout, waving a long club high above his head. 'I'll kill yer!' he was yelling. He really should have known better.

Pushing through the pain, Farden smacked his wrists together with a clang. Fire unfurled into the night, exploding from his hands. The bolt burst against the man's chest with a flash of flame that seared the clothes from his skin. He hit the mud flat on his back with a hiss, choking on pain and rainwater.

Farden dashed towards him as he struggled to lift his head up from the cloying mud. Without missing a stride, he sent his boot flying into the grimy thug's nose. The man's face exploded in a spatter of blood and bone as his head slammed back into the muck with a nauseating thwack. He did not move again. Farden skidded to a halt and crouched, listening to nothing but the dripping rain.

The bald man stirred under the grotesque carcass of his friend. His face looked like a crimson landslide. He lifted shaking fingers to feel the damage, breathing through cracked teeth.

Watching the thug struggle, Farden retrieved his grimy sword and wiped it on the leg of the charred man. Durnus would not have been happy with such a vicious display, he thought. *But Durnus wasn't here.*

'Told you to walk away.'

The man had only malformed curses for him. ' 'Uck ou!'

Farden shrugged and turned his back to him, walking away into the night. He let the rain drip down his face, cooling his hot, angry skin. Farden let the fight replay in his head, a guilty smirk curling at the corner of his mouth. *Might as well start the night as I mean to go on.*

He reached into his pocket and pulled out the soaking piece of parchment. He looked at the lines and contours of the map, at the word *Jergan*, then shoved it back into his pocket. Farden began to jog.

Six hours later, a lone figure crouched on the summit of a low hill, his long cloak billowing in the stormy wind, rain lashing his unblinking features. The man was staring avidly at a small hovel that cowered in a shallow valley between two hills. Gods only knew how it was surviving the weather; its rough wood and stacked-stone walls were shaking violently in the howling gale and vicious rain. A single struggling candle peeked from a tiny window.

The man's eyes flicked up to the cloudy sky as a fleeting gap in the clouds revealed the white saucer of a full moon, radiating blue light down on the hills for just a moment. His gaze returned to the hovel.

Farden had been watching this poor excuse for a house since discovering it three hours earlier. His headache had finally gone, thank the gods, and now he could feel the power swelling in his wrists and skull. The magick ran through his veins like a strong river surging through a canyon. A faint glow came from under his cloak, but he tried to keep it under control; creatures like Jergan could sense magick, smell it, like the wyrm had at Carn Breagh. They hunted it, given the chance.

The wind slammed into him with hurricane force. Rain pelted his face, yet Farden didn't blink, so focused was he on his task.

Something moved in the corner of his eye. The mage snapped his head in its direction and slowly rose to stand. He inched his sword from its sheath and gripped it with both hands. An unusual nervousness crept over him and his breathing quickened.

For what felt like an age, Farden waited, frozen, watching the stormy hillside getting lashed with curtains of rain. *Nothing*. He slowly crouched down again and looked back at the hovel.

The candle had gone out.

A huge shape barrelled out of the rain and into the mage, driving the air from his lungs and sending him flying down the hill. The hairy creature fell with him, snarling savagely as its jaws snapped in his ear. Farden felt his sword fall from his hand and dig into the grass, and he clawed at the ground.

The beast slid off of him as he latched onto a boulder, grinding to a halt. He scrabbled upright and thumped the ground hard with his fist. A searing light cut through the darkness of the stormy night, revealing a hulking creature standing a dozen yards down the hillside, matted hair drenched with rain, hot breath escaping in great plumes from a mouthful of fangs. It growled and snarled, words slipping through the yellowed daggers it called teeth.

'Leave this place,' the lycan barked. Its long arms hung low, dangling beside thick, muscular legs. Its curving claws were dripping with water.

'I've come to find Jergan! I must speak with him!' Farden shouted above the gale. He slowly moved back towards his sword and the lycan took a menacing step forwards in return. The thing's eyes were red pools of pure madness. Farden slid a hand into his pack and searched for something shiny.

'Jergan is dead! He doesn't live here and never has, so LEAVE!' The lycan crouched low. His thick wolf's mane stood upright, flapping in the wind. Farden took another step back and a sword hilt knocked against his leg. The mage held out a hand, warding the animal off, trying to get through to the man inside him.

'I don't want to hurt you, Jergan, I just want to talk!' Farden's heart was beating double time against his breastplate.

'Rarrrgh!' The lycan snarled and leapt towards his prey. Farden smacked his wrists together again and stamped his foot. A wall of fire burst out of the ground and ripped through the rain, but the agile creature jumped over the flames. He bared his teeth in the red glow.

Farden whirled his sword and dodged as Jergan flew past him. The lycan skidded on the wet grass and with a terrible clicking he unhinged his jaw even wider.

The mage summoned a huge globe of fire and aimed it at the growling animal. The fireball smacked into the lycan's shoulder-blade, sending him sprawling. Farden bravely strode forwards and held his longsword high. Jergan roared deafeningly. He sprinted towards the mage, swinging his claws in mad arcs. Farden blocked and cut straight across Jergan's left arm. It sent the lycan reeling backwards, yelping, but he managed to reach out with one wild punch. The knock caught Farden on the breastplate, winding him and cracking a rib.

The mage might have stumbled, but did not falter, and jabbed back at Jergan, finding the skin at his neck beneath the matted hair. With a yell, Farden yanked the mirror from his bag and showed it to the cowering lycan, lifting his light spell to blinding levels.

'Look at this!' the mage yelled. Jergan blinked and squinted at the silver trinket, covering his eyes with bleeding hands.

'Look!' Farden marched forwards, mirror outstretched before him. The beast barked a guttural laugh and shouted above the rain.

'You should tell your maid to buy you better mirrors, mage!'

Jergan kicked out at Farden with his long hind leg, catching him right below his throat. Farden tumbled backwards with a cry, but as he fell, he flung a small bolt of fire at Jergan. The lycan leapt back, swiping fire from his face.

Farden regained his stance, the wind blowing the smell of charred hair and flesh to his keen nose. Gritting his teeth, Farden threw a massive bolt of fire at the creature and followed it up with a quick spell to drain the lycan's strength. Jergan barked as he threw a rock. The mage side-stepped the missile and continued to throw spell after spell into the night.

A blast of lightning threw the lycan to the ground. Farden seized his chance, throwing his arms out wide and grunting. A ripple of magick spread through the ground, like a carpet being shaken. Rocks flew in all directions.

The quake spell hit the lycan in the back and the crack of several bones was audible. Farden reeled from the effort, a cramp striking his arms like a hammer bouncing off an anvil. Farden staggered forwards, watching the beast scrabble upright. Jergan's fur and skin were raw in patches, and blood gushed from his arm wound.

'Leave!' the lycan hissed.

Farden held his arms wide, twin balls of fire spinning in each hand. 'Let me talk to Jergan! I know he's in there somewhere,' he roared. He felt the drain tugging at his legs, making them shake, pulling his eyes upwards into his skull. He was struggling to maintain this level of spellcasting, but it was the only way he could make the lycan retreat.

'NO!' Jergan pounced and Farden clapped his hands together with a blast of flame. But the lycan was too quick. The spell broke, sending the two of them flailing to the ground. Farden struggled for his life as razor teeth snapped an inch from his face. Claws dug deep furrows in the grass next to his head. Farden used all his strength to hold back the beast with his sword, shoring up his efforts with an iron spell of force.

'Get off!' Farden shouted, rolling to the side. His blade sliced across Jergan's chest and raked down his ribs. The lycan leapt back, but not before scraping a claw across Farden's breastplate.

Farden could not chance even the smallest of scratches. He whirled his sword around like a madman in an effort attempt to keep the beast back. Relentless magick was the only weapon fit for Jergan. If he had to fight until the sun came up, then so be it.

Lightning forked the sky above them and a roar of thunder followed it. Jergan howled a haunting cry, arching his head towards the heavy clouds.

The two of them circled again, both breathing hard and shaking with effort. The creature was bleeding from multiple places, but the wounds already seemed to be healing and scabbing over. Farden cursed.

The mage ran the flat of his sword over his left gauntlet and the blade burst into flame, spitting and crackling. He threw two more spears of fire at the lycan. Jergan ducked and rolled, the flames licking his flanks. Lightning washed over him as Farden hit him with another spell. Jergan was getting tired. The wolf-curse was starting to break under the pressure of such relentless magick.

Farden was starting to crack as well, but he was far from giving up. He slammed the sword into the ground and began to concentrate on the wind around him, forcing a vortex of rain to spin around the snarling lycan. The wind howled like a banshee, battering Jergan mercilessly. Farden kept straining, driving the vortex faster. The wind tore back his hood and rain lashed his face, but his jaw was set. His face drained of colour.

Jergan fell to his knees. 'Leave me alone!' he shrieked, scrambling to be free. He turned tail and scampered away into the night, howling as he disappeared.

As the wind died down, Farden swayed on his feet. He lowered his hands and collapsed into the soaking grass with exhaustion, still trying to keep his eyes open and fixed on the hills around him. It was useless. The night swallowed him.

Morning brought him iron skies and a light drizzling rain. The rolling green hills lay quiet and sodden, the outcrops of rock black with dirt and flame from the night before. Farden lay in a trance, hunched up with his knees at his chin, cloak gathered around him in a tight bundle. He had forced down some meat and water at some point in the morning, in an attempt to stay awake.

Exhausted, he wiped rain from his face for the thousandth time. In the scales of his vambraces, he saw his reflection. His eyes were surrounded by dark rings and his lips were white with the cold. Black sodden hair covered his face and stubble was starting to decorate his chin. *A mess*, he thought.

In the valley below him lay the wooden and stone hovel, which Jergan had retreated to earlier that morning. After the battle, the lycan had disappeared into the storm, howling occasionally and spying on Farden from a nearby hill. When dawn finally broke over the moors, Jergan had begun to transform. He had slunk back into his hovel, and locked the door.

With a sigh, Farden forced himself to his feet and drew his sword. He gripped the cold steel and bound leather with his frozen fingers and cleared his dry throat with a crumbly, hoarse cough. After taking a final swig of rainwater from his flask and relieving himself gratefully behind a boulder, the mage strode determinedly down the sloping hill.

'Jergan! Come out here and talk! Don't make me cut your head off, you cur!' Farden barked. He marched up to the poor excuse for a door and banged loudly on the rough wooden planks. No answer.

'Jergan! Get up!' Farden kicked the door in and cast a light spell to burn the darkness out of the hovel's interior. It was a stinking mess. The rancid smell of wet dog and rotten meat caused the mage to gag. A clatter of pans came from the corner behind the door and Farden stormed inwards, sword raised.

'Don't! Don't kill me!' pleaded Jergan. He held up his muddy hands in defence and covered his eyes with his arms. Pale skinny legs flailed in the air as the gaunt man writhed in the dirt. The mage's magick burnt his eyes, and he spluttered and coughed. 'Please, I'll do whatever you want!' he managed, and Farden let his spell die. He looked down at him, wrinkling his lip.

The years and his curse had not treated him well. They had eaten at his soul as well as his muscle. It was obvious in his faintly purple eyes. Wild as they were, at their core, something had died, replaced with a coldness that made Farden shiver if he looked too long. It can eat away at a man, knowing that he is truly a monster underneath, and that there is nothing to be done about it. It turns him into a shadow of himself.

Jergan's arms were stick-thin, more bone than skin. His brown fingernails were long and wiry, and starting to curl with age. A scrap of cloth was all he wore: half a tunic, soiled with mud and blood, with holes where his ribs poked out through papery skin. His straggly white hair hung thick over a weary face, eyes poking from deep holes above sharp cheekbones and cracked lips. Scales adorned his chin amidst grey stubble. Little flecks of blue striped his cheeks and ears, memories of a life spent elsewhere, as something else.

This wretched creature was the complete opposite of the foul beast he had faced in the night. Jergan was now the antithesis of threatening, just a broken old man lying in the muck, and the mage felt a tinge of pity for him.

Scaly feet and ankles kicked pans as the exhausted Siren lycan hauled himself to a sitting position.

Farden leaned against the doorpost and waggled the fierce tip of his sword at the cowering man. 'You'd better have whatever I came for, or you'll wish I had killed you last night,' he spat.

Jergan was still breathing heavily, his bony chest heaving up and down with his panting. 'I thought you were here for sport, like the others.'

'What others?' Farden snapped.

Jergan flinched. 'The others that come here to hunt me. Every year or so, somebody tries. How was I supposed to know who you were and what you wanted? I haven't spoken to anyone in months, or years.' He looked down into the mud, cocking his head on one side like a dog. 'What do you want from me, Arka?'

Farden sheathed his sword. 'Information that you have, old man, or *had*.'

Jergan shook his head, as if his fate had already been decided for him. 'And what could I possibly know that's of any value to you?'

Farden scowled. 'Well, let's find out, shall we? Three days ago something was stolen from my people—'

'And you think I had something to do with it?' Jergan interrupted, his voice suddenly coarser. He glared up at Farden, baring the edges of his teeth, and the mage saw a little of the wolf come closer to the surface. Farden felt his own anger boiling in his chest. This cursed old skeleton was being petulant.

Farden crouched down, bringing his face close to Jergan's. 'Listen here, old man, and listen well. After last night, you're lucky I didn't just set fire to your hut and be done with you. But I've been sent here for information, and I don't intend on leaving without it. I suggest that you give me what I want. And if you interrupt me again, it will be the last thing you do. Tell me what I want to know, and I'll leave you in peace or end your miserable existence, if that is your wish.'

The mage's eyes burnt with fire. Jergan nodded, simmered down, and they both rose warily. The old Siren found a seat by the small stove and Farden remaining standing, arms crossed and stern. Jergan took a few deep breaths, licked his dry cracked lips, and gestured with a wave of his papery hand.

'Please, go on.'

Farden flashed a humourless smile. 'The stolen item was a book that was taken from the Sirens during the war. It was a book of great magick, small with a black dragonscale cover. My masters think you studied this book years ago when you lived in Nelska.'

The lycan looked away. 'That was a long time ago, mage.'

'Well, I need you to remember.'

Jergan thought for a minute. It seemed to hurt him. His eyes were full of pain and hunger.

'I have tried to forget these parts of my life, and for years I've pushed them from me, burying them in the damned beast. If I can't remember having a life, then I have nothing to miss, do I?' He paused again, narrowing his eyes.

'A long time ago, years before the war, my expedition discovered a cave near the Tausenbar Mountains, and in the depths of this cave lay a hidden fort, dug out of the cliffs. Inside we found a library filled with books we scholars had only dreamed of. It had been a dark elf stronghold in the old times, now long abandoned but left full of old relics and forgotten treasures. The elves had left all their belongings in a manic retreat, even leaving all their food and clothing behind in their rush. One of the treasures we found buried beneath the dust was a little black book like the one you've lost.'

'Was it this book or not?'

'That was such a long time ago, and my mind isn't what it used to be, but it sounds the same. A small book covered with black dragon scales, and a small gold latch on the front, with a very strong spell sealing the lock.'

Farden nodded. 'That sounds like the one.'

Jergan shrugged. 'Well, there you have it.'

The mage shook his head. 'I need more than that. What was inside the book?'

An irritated sigh. 'We took all the books we found back to the halls of Nelska to study them. It took years to accomplish. When we uncovered the black-scale book, I happened to be one of the few Sirens working on a translation, trying to uncover the secrets of elf magick.' Jergan paused for a swig of nearby water.

'You Sirens should know better than to mess around with elven magick,' said Farden.

'We knew that, but at the time it seemed the best thing to do for our people. The Skölgard were expanding. You Arka were encroaching further north with your ships. With power like that of the dark elves, we would have been unstoppable,' said Jergan, even managing to grin, if not a little wistfully.

'Then I'm glad we started the war before you did.' Farden returned the yellow smile.

'Perhaps, but in any case, that book was the most fantastic example of elf magick we had ever seen. Once our most powerful spells had opened it, we were able to learn the summoning incantations that brought forth monsters and ghosts from the other side, calling them to fight and follow our orders. We tested some of them against several Skölgard prisoners. The results were brutal. The creatures would do anything we asked them. That is, if you were strong enough to summon one; several of our wizards died from the strain of summoning such terrible beasts.' Jergan let his eyes haze over, remembering an age long forgotten, like a torn-out chapter of a book he had once read.

'Shame,' Farden spat, breaking the spell.

Jergan seemed hurt but thought better of complaining. He went on. 'There was one spell in the manual for summoning an ancient and terrifying monster, something even the elves feared to breed for war. None of us dared to read it. The incantation alone scared us witless. However, the Old Dragon called a stop to such free use of dark magick before we could learn any more and called off our whole investigation. Farfallen had the book banished to southern Nelska, where apparently your soldiers stole it and whisked it away to Arfell.' Jergan crossed his arms.

'What was this spell for then?' Farden asked as he took a seat on a small wooden box.

'We never found out. It referred to something named, *rivistokjunn*.' Jergan made a guttural sound of some foreign language in his throat.

Farden shook his head. 'Something I can understand, please?'

Jergan made a face as though he were teaching a child. '*Thine mouths of darkness* or *terrible dark*, something like that. All that we managed to learn was that this monster was different from the other dark creations, a crossbreed of daemon and dragon. Something that old Farfallen feared greatly. That's why he put a stop to our research and had dark magick outlawed in Nelska. None of us spoke of that book again.'

'*Research* is hardly the word I would use, but at least your Old Dragon was wise enough to end the madness,' Farden admonished him.

With a grunt, he reached into his travel bag for food. He tossed Jergan a red apple and munched on another. The old man caught it awkwardly.

'Thank you,' he whispered, before attacking the apple.

Farden shrugged. He mused as he chewed, turning over Jergan's words in his head. For a while, the two sat in silence, until Jergan piped up, mouth full of squashed apple.

'I take it you're one of the Written, then?'

Farden set his jaw. It was an invasive question, but he humoured him. He saw a little of Durnus in the bedraggled Siren, and it was more than he could ignore. 'Yes, I am.'

Jergan nodded slowly, a hint of something flashing in his hollow eyes. Hunger maybe. 'Then I applaud you,' he said. His hungry eyes roved over the mage. 'Carrying a Book is not an easy task. I've heard the stories about the unlucky ones, those that have the magick eat away at the mind? Terrible stuff.'

Farden shuffled on his box. 'I suggest you keep your observations to yourself, Siren. Now, why would someone want to steal this dark manual? How much would it be worth on the magick market?'

'As I said, it has been years since I talked to anyone, mage. As you can imagine I usually just end up eating my guests.' Jergan's face went icy cold and his eyes glazed over again. Farden tried to find patience somewhere inside him.

'I saw as much last night. Come on, who would want to steal this book?'

'Why would anybody want it? For power. But to cast the greatest spell in that book you would have to be one of the most powerful mages in Emaneska. I only know of a few, and two of them are the ones who sent you. The Arkmages are probably the only Arka that could open the book and cast the spells within. You're probably asking the wrong person,' Jergan shrugged, but Farden didn't buy it.

'There are other powerful mages in the land besides the Arkmages. A few of the wizards from your own lands could do it, I bet. Maybe a few Skölgard master-sorcerers could give it a good try. Besides, why would my masters steal their own book?'

'You tell me, mage,' muttered the Siren. He narrowed his eyes. 'I wonder, do you think you could do it? Summon the beast?'

'Don't be so ridiculous,' Farden snapped, and the lycan shrugged.

'If someone wanted to steal the book then they would have to know of its existence. Excluding the dark elves, who are obviously not an option, that leaves the Sirens or your own people. That's the truth of it.' Jergan shuffled on his rickety chair.

Even with the stiff breeze sneaking through the open door, the air inside the hovel was still thick and stale. The more Farden looked at the old Siren, the more he pitied him. He obviously hadn't eaten anything for days; Jergan had scoffed the whole apple already. He had even eaten the wooden stem. The mage shook his head and focused on his task.

'And if it wasn't the Arka, that means the war is far from over,' concluded the mage. An ominous silence hung between them.

Farden's mind ran through fields of possibilities and jumped over hedges of doubt. Could, gods forbid, one of his own Arka have committed this crime? Murdered the scholars and stolen this book? Farden's mind clouded stormily with fears, but he shook them off. There was still the matter of the Sirens. And the distinct possibility that the murderers were working completely or ir own, independent of either race, Arka or Siren.

Despite the dread, he felt the heat of resolve prick Farden clenched his fists. Somebody had to put a stop skin. before it got out of hand. Farden had to get back to Durnus. ess

Jergan filled the silence. 'If the book was stolen b powerful enough, strong enough to summon that terrible crea all of Emaneska would be in danger, not just our peoples. If the things I saw, the things we brought over…' Jergan drifted

Whatever colour had returned to his old skin quickly away. His tone more urgent. 'But it's not just about being powe being able to cast the spell that is the challenge, but this par beast needs a well of magick to help it cross over. The elves built caverns to house their magick power, reservoirs of strength for the weapons, much like the Book you carry. There used to be hundreds of these wells all over the lands, but when the elves left, they were hunted down and destroyed. I'm sure you know of them: "Lost by dark ones all forgotten," ' he recited.

' "Lakes of magick below paths untrodden." Yes, I've heard the Dust Song. Everybody has. But the last elven wells and troves are all gone, lost to time. So where else would someone take the book to release its power?' Farden crouched, elbows on knees. Against his better judgement he was beginning to trust the Siren's words.

'That's assuming you're right and that all the wells have vanished?' The corner of Jergan's mouth rose ever so slightly, as if he had a won a small hand in a verbal card game. But Farden wasn't in the mood for playing games.

'Then tell me where I can find one.'

Jergan cackled as heartily as his starved frame and rasping throat would allow. 'Hah! No one has uncovered one for decades. I wouldn't have the first clue where to look.'

tures of your kind are drawn to magick. You might have
your time with the Sirens, or maybe as a lycan you know
founis,' he said. Farden wore a dangerous look in his eye.

wAll I know is that there are still a few left, maybe two, maybe
ion't know.' Jergan held up his scarred palms in honesty.

'But you don't know where?'

'We never found one. That was one of the reasons we never
aged to summon the beast from the manual.' Jergan flopped his
s on his lap.

Farden clenched his jaw. 'So if whoever has stolen this book
tends to release this creature, they'll need to find one of these wells. Or they already know of one.'

'And the only way of doing that would be through the dragons of Nelska. Arfell's books don't stretch back far enough, but in the memories of the older dragons there may be a clue to where an elf well might lie,' offered Jergan. 'We never got the permission to examine their tearbooks. Farfallen was outraged when we asked, gods rest him.' Jergan briefly bowed his head.

'Then I suppose I'll be hunting dragons next, instead of lycans.' Farden made for the door, but Jergan tugged at his sleeve.

'If you're going to Nelska then I would ask one favour of you,' the Siren asked in a pleading voice, his violet eyes watching the mage adjust his belt and travel pack impatiently.

'What do you want?'

'If you speak to the dragons, then at least tell them that I'm alive, and not dead. That's all I ask,' whined the man.

Farden nodded and stepped out of the door. The breeze was sharp and cold, but the winter sun was beginning to burn away the drizzle and scatter the clouds. Farden looked back at the decrepit old man standing behind him.

'Thank you, Jergan, for your help. I understand you didn't ask for this, for the life of a lycan, but I hope that you survive it a while longer,' he offered.

Jergan tried to smile, as if it were the kindest thing he had heard in decades. *It probably was*, Farden thought.

'Good luck to you…?'

'Farden, if you must know.'

'Then good luck, Farden. Gods be with you.'

And with that, Farden was gone, jogging across the hills back towards Beinnh and the Arkabbey to the north.

Jergan shut his door and sat back down in his little chair. He looked around at the mess of his little hovel. The wind howled through the crack in the door and rattled the walls, and a single tear ran down the lycan's cheek.

Night had once again fallen upon the streets of Beinnh. Rowdy laughter rang out from tavern doorways and wild yells floated down from the top floor windows of brothels. A light hammering rang through the alleyways, unnoticed or ignored.

The old blacksmith was still hard at work, alone at his forge. The red glow of the fire illuminated his anvil and sparks flew from his hammer as it beat down on a glowing spear point. The thin old man wore a content smile; he had made a good profit on these cheap iron spears. They had earned him a fine bit of gold without too much trouble.

The hammer sent another shower of sparks scattering over his salamander wool gloves. As the smith pondered his next scam he started to whistle, tuneless and croaky. Something moved in the shadows behind him. The hammer fell again and again like a beat to his dissonant warbling, and all the while the something drew closer behind him, creeping unnoticed, treading in the strikes of the hammer.

A hand grabbed the old smith by the neck and shoved his forehead down hard, right onto the glowing spear point. The smith's skin hissed as it kissed the hot metal.

'Aagh!' the smith cried out, dropping to the dusty floor. He rubbed at his skin and howled.

'You lied to me,' the dark hooded figure spread out his fingers and a small lightning bolt flickered over his palm, dancing in an electric blue glow. He grabbed the smith by the wrist and covered his mouth roughly. The old man squirmed as the bolt ran through his bones and rattled his spine.

'Stay quiet, old man, otherwise you might make me do something I'll regret.'

The smith swiftly stifled his yelps and fell deadly silent, eyes wide and terrified. A few muffled questions came from behind his hand.

'You lied to me about the silver mirror, and I warned you what would happen.' The man jolted him again before uncovering his mouth.

The smith panted, bobbing his head. 'I remember yer, I remember! I'm sorry! I'll do whatever you want, er, you can 'ave yer money back I swear! Jus' please don't kill me,' he sobbed. 'Yer not goin' to kill me, are yer?'

The man narrowed his eyes and watched him squirm. 'Lucky for you,' he snorted, 'I'm not. You can keep your life and your money, old thief. But you *can* have your mirror back.'

The fake silver trinket flew from the man's belt and collided with his jaw, cracking his jawbone and snapping teeth from their roots. The smith crumpled to the earth in a flurry of spit and blood and went silent. The mirror skipped and skittered over the dusty floor, colliding with the stone wall with a clang.

Farden pulled his hood down low over his face as he marched out of the forge. Without a sound, he walked down the nearest alleyway and melted into the shadows of the ugly town. Lightning flickered on the horizon as another storm approached over the faraway hills.

chapter 4

Those of special circumstance, can find themselves alone, by the field, the house, the mountain crag, the blood begets the bone.
Friend of foes, and fair thee well, watch out for shadows black, for darkness comes to them too soon, wing'd teeth, bared blades, and trap.
They want what is different, but as all, we want the same, thus blood becomes the birthright, and thy night becomes thy shame.
They judge us by the difference, they judge us from thy teeth. But we watch their necks, we'll string them up, and leave them there to bleed.
Vampyre poem of unknown origin

Durnus was dozing in his loft room, listening to the fire spark and pop as the wet wood burnt away. His sleepy mind was churning over thoughts of war and warriors, kingdoms and traitors, and of the legends of old. He let himself melt into and rove through his thoughts, listening to nothing but the fire, the rain hammering on the stained glass windows, and the wind howling through the dark afternoon. It would be night soon, and there was nothing better than hunting in the rain. He let his eyelids droop some more.

Behind his comfy chair, propped up in the corner of his room, was a tall archway made from black stone and metal scaffolding, strapped to the wall with thick grey rope. It leaned out from the wall and over a wooden lectern holding a thick brown book. The black stone flickered in the candlelight.

The old vampyre turned his head to check on the thing in the corner, as if it might have moved, then turned back to the fire to close his eyes again, enjoying the warmth of the big armchair and the soft upholstery beneath his paper-like fingers. All was quiet in the Arkabbey. Just how he—

There came a banging noise from the corridor outside his room. Durnus sighed, pinching his forehead between his finger and thumb.

The door was thrown open with a crash and in burst a dripping Farden. He collapsed to his knees, palms splayed on the stone tiles, breathing hard and trying to fight from coughing.

'Farden!' The vampyre hauled himself upright and rushed to the mage's side. Through hoarse gaspings, Durnus made out the word "water" and went to a pitcher on the bedside table. He filled a cup and gave it to him. Farden downed the whole thing in one gulp then tossed the vessel aside. He stood upright and groaned.

'That feels better. I've never run that far that fast before,' Farden took a moment to swear before coughing again and seeking the refuge of the other comfy chair by the fire. The vampyre followed him and watched him slump into it.

'You've been gone for almost a week, we were starting to get anxious,' he told him. His friend was still struggling to get his breath back. 'Farden, hold still.'

Durnus spread his thin fingers over the mage's forehead and the tired man went rigid. Farden's eyes shook as his vision burst into colour. He could have sworn his skin vibrated. The vampyre removed his hand and Farden shook his head, blinking and wriggling his jaw experimentally. He could feel himself twitching with the strong spell.

'By the gods, that felt good. Why've you never done *that* before?' said Farden, blinking owlishly.

'Jolting the mind like that too many times can kill a man. Even one as strong as you.' Durnus looked at his old friend. Mud, twigs, scrapes and wounds covered Farden's back and shoulders, his cloak was ripped to shreds and a new sword dangled almost free in the loose strap around his back. Blood oozed from several wounds, some fresh, some old, and his face was a mess of stubble and bruises. He looked as if he had been dragged backwards through a forest and a river, thought Durnus, but at least he was alive.

Farden had regained his breath thanks to the spell and most of the colour had returned to his cheeks, but he still had deep black bars under his eyes and his dark hair was a bedraggled muddle.

'I have news.' Farden cleared his throat again and leaned back in the encapsulating chair.

Durnus leapt back to his seat with surprising agility for someone who appeared so old. 'Well, let's get to it! What happened?'

'I found Jergan on the hills where you said he'd be, south of Beinnh,' Farden paused for another cough. 'And, for a hermit, he wasn't at all shy when it came to trying to kill me. Anyway, in short, you were right. Jergan and the Sirens found our book in the Tausenbar Mountains before the war, in an old elf stronghold, and tried their scaly hands at using it. Jergan was one of the men who studied it, and with their wizards…' He said *wizards* with a hint of superiority in his voice. 'They tried to cast its spells. Apparently the book was some sort of dark elf summoning manual, for bringing creatures over from the other side.'

'They *cast* the spells in it?' The vampyre was shocked.

'That's what Jergan said, and for some reason I trust him. They went through it systematically from cover to cover, and their wizards tested the ghosts and beasts on Skölgard prisoners. Jergan thinks that's why someone would steal the book, to get at the powerful beasts hidden in its pages.'

'But the Arka have fought their fair share of monsters. You were there five years ago, when the minotaurs came out of the Efjar Marshes? Why should this book be any different?'

'He said this book held one spell that the scaly bastards feared so much they never dared to cast it.'

'What spell was it?' Durnus entwined his fingers in thought and stared at the fire.

'They never found out, but it was something that scared the life out of the Sirens and their dragons. A terrifying beast referred to as the "*mouths of darkness.*" They were foolish.'

'Foolish indeed,' said the vampyre, as he watched flames lick at wood and stone.

'Jergan also mentioned that if somebody powerful enough wanted to attempt to summon this thing, that—'

'That they would need a great source of magick, perhaps like one of the dark elf wells?' guessed Durnus.

'Exactly.' The mage smiled at his friend's intuition.

'As far as I know, the last one we found was near Arfell, north of the library and several miles underground.'

'With barely any magick left in it, if I heard right,' Farden added. The heat from the fire curled around him like a blanket. 'And as far as *I* know, there aren't any left in Emaneska, but Jergan seems to think there are a few we might have missed.'

'Indeed. I've spent almost my entire life trying to track them down. It was one of the reasons I came to Albion. This soggy land is littered with old elf ruins. But so far, it's been a fruitless search.' He tapped his thin lips thoughtfully, deciding what to do. 'This is dire news, Farden, especially if the lycan is right about an undiscovered well. If we're assuming that the thief stole the manual to get at the spells, then we have to suppose they intend to release this beast on the world. Why else go to such lengths?' Durnus spoke his words with an ominous tone, a cold voice in a vacuous cave.

'And if Jergan was right about the size and power of this creature, then we could all be in serious danger, and I don't just mean the Arka. Whoever stole that book wants to turn Emaneska upside down.' Farden looked at the vampyre and their eyes locked in a steely embrace.

'We need to get you to Krauslung with all speed.' Durnus leapt from his chair with alacrity that belied his years. He went to the archway and lectern standing in the corner. He flipped the dry pages of the dusty tome on the lectern, his fingers scrolling over the lines of brown ink.

'I'll need most of the night to prepare the quickdoor to the citadel. You need to rest. I can imagine that you've been through enough to get this information, so I advise you just get some sleep, friend,' he said, as his pale blue eyes scanned the writing.

The mage took a deep breath and gathered his cloak behind him.

'What was it like?' asked Durnus, rather abruptly. His finger had stopped on the page.

Farden looked over at the vampyre's back. 'Imagine seeing death in the eyes of a nine-foot-tall wolf.' The mage paused, recalling the blur of a fight with a grimace. Durnus turned to face him, a humorous look in his pale eyes.

'It strikes me as odd, my good friend, that you should ever meet anything resembling death. Every time I fear the worst, you come back to us with no more than a handful of scratches. I envy you, Farden. Out there, face to face with creatures like Jergan.'

'Envy me?' Farden threw him a quizzical look. 'Are you serious?' He lifted his torn cloak up over his breastplate and pointed to the deep groove made by the lycan's raking claws. 'This isn't a handful of scratches; an inch further up and I would be either dead or howling away somewhere out in the mountains.'

Durnus turned back to his book. 'Come now, I know you better than that. You crave danger.' There was a pause. 'That's why I'm always telling you to be careful.'

'Here we go,' muttered Farden, with a mock sigh. The vampyre turned around again as the mage slumped back into the chair. 'No, I'm not going to lecture you.'

'For a change.'

'Fine. All I'm saying is that we've known each other a long time.' Durnus tapped the side of his head with a pale finger. 'I know why you came here to Albion, and what you're trying to hide from, and I've seen how you deal with it. Just remember there are those that care about you, and that even *you* have your limits.' The vampyre crossed his arms and stared at the mage. Farden felt a little uncomfortable, as he always did in these moments, and tapped his vambraces with a fingernail.

'It's not likely I'll find them just yet though.'

Durnus sighed. 'Just don't overreach,' he said. 'And in truth I do envy you, because you're the one who gets to go out there and make a difference, fight the battles and the monsters, uncover the secrets and be the warrior. My days are long drawn out, and my memories are slowly fading, Farden. I can't remember the last time I held a sword. By the gods, it must be at least fifty years ago.'

Farden itched for the opportunity to change the subject. 'That's because you're a historian, old friend. These books are your monsters. I couldn't go out there without your advice and knowledge, Durnus. Have no fear, I'm sure there's still some fight in you yet.'

'Hah! That'll be the day.'

Farden smirked, picked up a nearby book and blew the dust from the cover. He cleaned it with the palm of his hand and squinted at the faded title.

'*Treatises on Shapeshifting*, that's a bit dangerous, isn't it, Durnus? Playing with the old daemon arts?'

Durnus looked at the book and shrugged. 'Just curious. And it's not just daemons that can shapeshift, my dear mage. What do you think I am? Or Jergan for that matter? Both wolf and bat curses have their roots in the ancients,' he said, wagging a didactic finger in the air. 'Did you know that the powers that bind a lycan are completely opposite to that of a vampyre? If a vampyre were to be bitten by a lycan, one of pure breed, then it could technically cancel the two out.'

'What would happen?' asked Farden, but the vampyre shrugged again.

'Who knows? Hence the book,' he sighed. 'But anyway, you need rest. It'll be a while before I'm ready. And please heed my words, Farden, as your friend. I know what your temper can be like.'

'I shall.' Farden walked towards the door and pulled it open. His old friend was right; there were few people in the world that he cared about. He thought of one in particular, an idea blossoming in his mind. 'Durnus, could you send me to the quickdoor at the Spire?'

The vampyre thought for a moment and then nodded. 'I don't see why not. If that's what you want.'

'It'd be good to see old Manesmark before I go to the city.' Farden turned to go, leaving the old man to his books. Durnus could have sworn he heard the mage whisper a thank you before he closed the door.

Elessi was wandering the corridors of the Arkabbey tower. After hearing a rumour that Farden was back, and feeling wounded, she had gone looking for him with angst in her heart.

It was late, and her search of his room and the cavernous dining hall had been fruitless. She was wandering up and down the spiral staircases of the abbey tower, peering in empty rooms, listening to the wooden doors of locked quarters and rooms home to sleeping soldiers.

The maid earnestly skipped up the steps to the training halls near the bell tower, holding her skirts above her shoes. A dull thudding tumbled down the stone hallway on her left and she paused mid-stride.

Yellow torchlight spilled from a door half-closed halfway along, while the rest of the hallway was bathed in lazy moonlight pouring down from a thin arched window at its far end. Elessi crept forwards, running her hand over the rough walls. Her work-worn fingers felt the cracks and pitted surface of the grey stone. The noise grew louder as she approached: a sharp, deep crack of fire against wood.

She reached the door and peered through the gap into the hall. Her pupils shrank in the bright yellow torchlight. Flashes of light and fire skipped over the wooden beams of the yawning roof, and she shuffled around to get a better look at the cause of the noise.

There, standing shirtless and sweating, was Farden, throwing bolt after bolt of fire at a wooden, man-shaped target. The mannequin swung wildly, suspended from the wall and shackled to the floor on short iron chains. It rocked and bucked under the powerful blasts of magick. Farden wore nothing except a pair of black trousers, and in the bright torchlight Elessi could see his chest heaving with deep, arduous gulps of air. His shoulders were bathed in sweat. And there was something else. Elessi's eyes were now fixated on his back.

Lines and lines of thin black script covered the mage's shoulders and lower back, punctuated by swirling elegant lines and spirals clambering over his collarbone, ribs, and shoulder blades. Four symbols ran along his spine, runes with shapes and strange interwoven words.

Elessi couldn't help noticing the dark faces of telling bruises running through the black lettering, and every time the magick surged through his body, the script flashed and glowed. Words sporadically lit up all over his skin, glittering and dancing with a bright white light. The chambermaid was transfixed, locked in a mesmerised stare. She tried to follow the lines of script as they glowed, to make sense of the foreign words.

Farden threw yet another bolt of fire at the target, whose carved wooden face was now charred and smouldering. If a mannequin could look depressed, this one managed it.

The mage paused his onslaught for a moment, clenching his fists. A whirring, crackling sound hummed through the air for a moment, before Farden bared an open palm and sent tidal waves of lightning to wash over the wooden statue. With a crack, the topmost chain melted, and the mannequin fell to the floor in a burst of cinders. Farden cursed and went to find his shirt. Elessi flinched back from the door and ran back down the hallway with mixed feelings of relief and fear.

That night, she dreamed of wounded mages and hulking monsters, of deep caves and ghostly ships made of bones and fingernails, of fire burning under her sheets. Sleep ran from her, and in the morning, she awoke with stinging eyes, dripping with cold sweat.

Farden opened his eyes to find winter sunlight jabbing through his open window. He found he was lying on his front and swiftly pushed himself up and out of bed, stretching with a new-found readiness. He had rested well in a deep dreamless sleep, and now he felt fit and eager to get going. Whatever the old vampyre had done to him had worked, and Farden resolved to ask him about it another time.

He finished stretching and went to find his scattered clothes and armour. He ran a wet cloth over his grimy face and neck, wiping the dirt away. One of his teeth was loose, probably from the fight. Farden tongued it in an investigative way. He pushed a finger into his jaw, muttering something, and the tooth settled back into place. It didn't move again.

Farden moved to the window and let the cold breeze of the morning chill his face. The winter sun was hovering near the horizon behind the trees, lingering behind the leafless branches of the Forest of

Durn. A bird sang somewhere below in the Arkabbey grounds. The smell of baking bread from the kitchens hovered on the breeze. The mage's stomach rumbled, and he hurriedly put on his tunic, boots and armour, and strode out of his room. He would eat in Krauslung.

When he reached the vampyre's room, the door was unlocked. Farden walked straight in. Magick throbbed and hummed in the air; he could feel it washing over him, tingling in his shoulders.

The fire had long burnt out and now only candles lit the dim room. In the corner, the archway of black stone and steel was filled with a haze, as if a silk veil quivered constantly and violently in the centre of the tall doorway. The quickdoor seemed to be open.

Durnus reposed in a wooden chair near a desk, eyes closed, dozing. Farden walked quietly up to him and put a gentle hand on the old man's shoulder. The vampyre stirred.

'Farden. Hmm, what time is it?' asked Durnus hoarsely.

'Just before noon, it'll be afternoon in Manesmark by now. It's time for me to go.'

'Right!' Durnus slapped his knees and stood up, all tiredness instantly forgotten, and headed to the lectern to check on the vibrating quickdoor.

'It's ready, it took me a while to do for some reason, the Albion magick seems to be weaker than normal. The quickdoor in Manesmark is a powerful one though, so it wasn't impossible,' the vampyre rambled away as he leafed through the pages, preparing the next spell.

'You know I don't understand this time and space magick, my old friend. That's your area of expertise, not mine.' Farden smiled warmly.

'It's all about patience, my good mage.'

Farden squinted at the hazy surface of the quickdoor and ran his hand over the archway, careful not to stray too close to the buzzing threshold. The obsidian surface of the stone blocks felt alarmingly hot to the touch.

'Think of it as trying to open and close a window a thousand miles away, with no more than a rope and a long pole.'

'That doesn't really help.'

Durnus thought for a moment, looking at the ceiling. 'No, it doesn't, does it? Well, all seems like it's in order, Farden. Time to travel. Now remember, hold your breath before you step in, and watch your feet. It looks like it's snowing on the other side,' Durnus said, pointing.

Farden gazed at the little flecks of snow tumbling through the foot of the portal, settling in a little patch on the top step of the quickdoor. 'Great,' he said. He had hoped it might have been a little warmer in the city, but apparently he was wrong. The Long Winter won again.

'See you soon, old friend.' Farden shook the vampyre's hand and stepped closer to the portal. Durnus flipped through the pages of his book.

'Try to remember every single detail and be sure in your opinions before you voice them to the Arkmages. You have a meeting with them this evening in the great hall. The whole council will be gathering.' Durnus looked at the sword on the mage's back and sniffed. 'And Farden?'

The mage turned.

The vampyre narrowed his pale eyes. 'I can smell blood on your sword. Who else did you fight besides Jergan?'

Farden lingered for a moment on the best excuse. 'Some people just don't listen,' he said abruptly. He shrugged, eyes searching the wooden floor for an escape from the reprimand he knew was coming.

The vampyre merely sighed. 'Don't get sloppy, Farden. You are an instrument of the Arka first and foremost; a finely tuned weapon of precision and tact. There are rules and there are consequences for poor decisions, mage. Bear them in mind next time you draw your sword. I watched your uncle go down this violent path a long time ago and look where it got him. This is the last time I'll tell you.'

Durnus' gaze was grave, more disappointed than angry, which stung the mage all the more. *There was no need to bring up his uncle*, he thought.

'I won't,' he muttered, before stepping up to the doorway. Farden felt the icy blast of the quickdoor on his skin. As he lifted his foot, the door grabbed him in a vice-like grip, dragging him forwards into a shining white tunnel of light and noise. Wind tried to rip the breath from his lungs and freezing gales attacked his watering eyes as he plummeted through the doorway.

It was over in a blink.

Farden stumbled onto the wet, frozen grass of a Manesmark hillside, putting a hand in a patch of snow to steady himself. Behind him, the quickdoor fizzled shut. The mage shook his head free from the dizziness and rose shakily to find a soldier standing beside him.

The early afternoon sunlight glinted off his steel breastplate, causing the emblem of the Arka, a gold set of scales, to shine and glitter.

Farden nodded to the man, who dipped his helmet in response and wiped the amused smirk from his face. Farden threw him a narrowed look as he wiped himself down.

'I'd like to see you try to land more gracefully,' he said, and the soldier made an effort to stand a little straighter, timidly clearing his throat.

Still dizzy, Farden said no more and walked to look out across the stunning countryside he had grown up in. The landscape was as breathtaking as he remembered.

The tall Össfen Mountains stretched out for miles and miles in all directions, as far as the eye could see, puncturing the wintry sky with their snow-capped summits and scraping at the heavy grey clouds with their rocky teeth. Beneath the jagged peaks and down in the snow-locked valleys, waterfalls played amongst rocks, fjords of ice and farmsteads, like the one he had known as a very small boy.

To the north, he could see the deadly slopes of Lokki, the tallest mountain in Emaneska, towering over the rocky vista. Below him on the steep hillsides, villages and towns sat wreathed in woodsmoke, peeking out of the snowdrifts.

Farden looked down the hill at Manesmark, the traditional home of the Arka's fighting forces. It perched on a snow-draped slope: a cluster of townhouses, inns, and dozens of barracks. The buildings were tall and proud, elegantly built from grey stone and pine, topped with tall, arched wooden roofs of slate. Chimneys belched grey haze and the sounds of a busy afternoon in the market floated across the cold mountain air to Farden's wind-bitten ears.

Scattered memories ran like rabbits through the fields of the mage's mind as he walked across the hillside. Manesmark was the long-established home of the Written, and of the School where every mage studied, where Farden had studied as a child and teenager. He could still smell the strange, ever-present burning odour of the place, feel the rough wood of the floors, the beds, and taste the watery yellow gruel. He could feel the constant thrum of magick from the instructors and classmates.

The School of the Written had been a cruel world of bullying, spells, and constant fear. Many of his classmates had died along the way, victims of an "accidental" knife thrust, or caught by a wayward spell. Vicious competition plagued the prestigious School, and Farden was sure nothing had changed. His class of prospective Written had been whittled down to just three exhausted candidates. Farden had barely made it into the final cut. He remembered standing before the masters on his final day, beaten and bruised, pulsating with magick, feeling blood run down his brow and hearing his name on their stern lips. It had been torture, every moment, but it had made him a man, taught him the true face of magick, and shown him the wild nature behind Emaneska. Farden could still feel the Scribe's whalebone needle carving the words into his back. His Book.

The mage strode up the slippery hillside towards the Spire, a huge black tower that perched on the summit of the Manesmark hillside and climbed hundreds of feet into the sky. Here the Written lived and trained, and slept when they had the chance. As he approached, he could feel the power vibrating through the walls of the tall building, emanating from the parapets and walkways hanging from the Spire. He could feel it like a wind on his skin.

Guards and soldiers swarmed around the base of the tower like ants, and Farden spotted a few Written amongst them, hooded and cloaked like he was, unmistakeable to those who could spot it. A Written walked with a certain assurance; a swagger that only a living weapon can sport.

The magick council had been rebuilding the ranks of the Written ever since the war, and now, even after the skirmishes in Efjar, their numbers were greater than ever before. From what he had gathered from Durnus, there were now almost three hundred mages training in the Spire, and over half of them carried the Book.

Farden reached the foot of the Spire and made for the entrance. As he walked closer to the door, a deep vibration could be heard, like a large bell tolling under a hill.

' 'Fraid you can't go in, sir, too many already in there,' said a short man in uniform who stood at the doorway. He pointed inside with his thumb.

Farden peered through the doorway into the enormous atrium of the Spire, a cavernous hall filled with stairs and corridors running in every imaginable direction. Hanging in the middle of the atrium was a colossal dragon scale suspended in the air by great steel chains. It quivered with energy, making a deep whining sound.

Too many Written mages in the Spire at one time could send the other men mad from the pure power of raw magick. The beaten scale was like a warning bell for the Spire, ringing whenever the magick grew to dangerous levels. It was annoying, but necessary.

Farden nodded in reluctant acquiescence and withdrew to a nearby rock. He watched several people rub at brief headaches and listened to the scale slowly quieten down. The mage shrugged to himself. Krauslung could wait for a little while.

Cheska was standing in her room, watching the messenger hawk flutter around her windowsill. The poor bird was trying to find a place to land amidst the frozen snow on the ledge, flapping and mewing and being altogether useless.

As soon as it came close enough, she snatched the wooden canister from its leg and the bird flew off, back to whomever had sent it. She snapped the tube open and took out the scrap of yellow parchment. Three hastily scribbled words were all she needed to read.

Cheska held the note in her hand and concentrated hard with muttering lips. There was a brief flash of light and the paper note became ash in her hand. She winced, sucking at her singed finger.

The sound of the scale below her reached her ears and she immediately made to leave, checking herself in a polished bronze mirror before opening the door.

A young mage stood in the doorway, leaning against the wall, hand poised to knock. 'Afternoon, Cheska.' Brim smiled a toothy smile and winked at her. It didn't suit him. It made him look like he had a twitch.

'Oh, Brim, I was just leaving,' Cheska said.

'Well, I'm going to the market, we can walk if you want?' he offered.

She nodded, sighed inwardly, and let him walk her to the stairs.

Farden was getting bored. Some sunlight had broken through the heavy clouds, so he had thrown his hood back to soak up the rare warmth, feeling the mountain breeze toy with his dark hair.

A few soldiers he recognised acknowledged him in passing with silent nods. The other Written were mostly courteous, but curious of Farden. The solitary mage had always been quiet around most of the others, preferring his own company, and it was no secret in the Spire that they thought him dangerous and wild. Nevertheless, he had been a hero in Efjar, and that afforded him a bit of respect, though he found it dwindled every year. The mage's eyes scanned the throngs of people milling around, looking for someone in particular. *She must have heard the scale ring*. Then he saw her.

She never ceased to make his mouth hang slightly ajar. Cheska looked as stunning as ever. From his rock, he watched her weave through the crowds with all the grace of a cat, letting her piercing blue eyes rove over the multitude of faces, obviously looking for someone as well. Farden began to smile.

Cheska's long blonde hair escaped from the edges of her hood and swayed hypnotically in the breeze. She always seemed to be smiling, ever since he had first seen her wandering the halls of the Spire, nothing more than a nervous little girl, new to the School. Her skin was paler than most. Like her hair, it betrayed her Skölgard ancestry. Her royal breeding was obvious in her gait and posture. Like him, she wore a dark cloak, with a tight-fitting black tunic that hugged the curves of her body.

It was common knowledge that Cheska was the daughter of Bane, the king of the powerful Skölgard Empire in the northeast. And that made her a princess. For her to be living with the Arka, not to mention practising their dangerous magick, was a massive political step for both countries, and a tough one.

She had been supervised by a veritable horde of Skölgard minders, every step of the way, through every year at the School. One by one she had shrugged them off and immersed herself in the brutal world of magick.

Farden had to admit she was good, better than any he had seen so far. It had made their lives even more exciting and dangerous, as if they weren't enough already. The Written were forbidden to breed; one of the rules all Written had to abide by, or face exile or death by hanging.

Farden let his eyes take in every inch of her. It had been a few months since he had last seen her and a warm, not entirely unexpected, feeling spread across his chest. He spied that friend of hers, Birn, or Bridd, or whatever his name was, following her like a loyal dog hoping to be thrown a scrap. Farden set his jaw with an inkling of jealousy. As her deep, mountain-lake eyes caught his, he got to his feet and grinned.

'Well, well! Look what the gryphon dragged in!'

Cheska smiled as the two came close in a firm embrace. She stood on her tiptoes and threw her arms around Farden's neck. He dared to give her a quick kiss on the cheek and she stepped backwards with a sly look. A rare smile crept over the mage's lips, and he held her eyes a moment longer than was necessary.

The loyal dog coughed into his fist politely, breaking them out of their little trance.

'Oh, Farden, you remember Brim, don't you? He was in the same class at—'

'We've met a few times before. Good to see you again,' Farden clamped the man's hand in an iron grip. Brim tried and failed to return his icy gaze, wincing at the handshake.

'You also, sir. What brings you to Manesmark?' Like all the others at the School, Brim must have heard the rumours about Farden.

'Official business in Krauslung. I have to be heading there soon,' Farden said dismissively, looking at Cheska as she ran a handful of her hair through her fingers. A flash of something red caught his eye. That warm feeling in his chest suddenly turned cold. 'Tell me that's not what I think it is?' he asked stonily.

She laughed, shrugging off his concern. 'You're right.' She pulled back her cloak sleeves and revealed a red band of metal wrapped around her slender wrist. It was a *fjortla*, a traditional bracelet that marked a trainee for being Written. Supposedly the rare red metal brought strength and perseverance to the wearer for the dangerous tattooing process, a three-day ritual that only half of the candidates usually survived. Farden still had his old *fjortla* somewhere back at the Arkabbey.

'We both got chosen. We'll be Written in less than a month!' Cheska smiled and put her hand on Farden's arm to show it off.

'Both of you?' he asked.

'Both of us,' Brim replied, baring his wrist and showing off his own circle of red metal.

Farden found himself filled with anxiety. He couldn't even begin to care about Brim, but Cheska? That was a different matter. Here was one of the few people in the world he did care about, and now she was scheduled for the terrible, gruelling Ritual. Something that could easily kill her.

'Cheska, this is serious…' began Farden, but Cheska shook her head defiantly.

'Don't even start with that vulnerable woman shit. You'll start to sound like my father,' she cursed. Farden glared at Brim for a moment, as if it were all his fault, but then thought better of arguing.

'Fair enough, I won't say another word.' He held up his hands and shrugged. 'Walk with me for a while?'

Cheska smiled. She turned to Brim as she walked away. 'I'll come and find you later, Brim. I'll meet you in the market,' she said.

The young mage nodded, a little confused, and watched the two of them walk off through the throngs of people and soldiers. 'Great,' he muttered, and with a wistful sigh, he turned and headed for the Manesmark market.

❦

'Are you actually serious?' Farden asked gingerly.

'Oh, don't be a hypocrite, Farden. You said you couldn't wait to go through with it when they chose you.' Cheska ran a hand through her pale tresses again. Farden could not help but sneak sideways looks at her. 'What did you think would happen anyway? That I would spend all these years training and then just turn it down?' she huffed, and looked away.

'It's just dangerous Cheska, and you know…' Farden trailed off, thinking of Jergan. His boots kicked loudly at loose stones. They were walking down a quiet path that curved away from the main thoroughfare between Manesmark and Krauslung. Behind them, the noisy bustle of the Spire could still be heard over the sound of flags flapping and birds twittering. Cheska stopped abruptly under a rocky outcrop that bent over the thin path.

'I know what?' she asked.

'You know.' Farden waved a hand dismissively but she caught it deftly and stepped closer to him, that look in her glacier eyes again. Cheska pulled at the red scarf around his neck.

'Still wearing the present I got you?' she smiled. He pulled her closer and they kissed, lips locked in a passionate embrace. Farden's hands snaked around her back and pulled her closer to him, until she stood on tiptoes and let her fingers tangle in his dark hair. He started to kiss her neck, letting her scent dizzy his head, pulling her even closer as his hands moved down her back and legs.

'No, not here, Farden.' She put a hand on his chest and leaned back. He released her reluctantly. 'If we get caught, they'll throw you in the stocks. And who knows what my father would do.'

'They wouldn't dare,' he said with a sly grin. 'You're not a Written yet, why should it matter?'

'Not here.' Cheska kissed him again softly. 'I think I'll head back to the Spire.' She held a finger to her lips as he began to talk. 'I know you're worried, but I can do this, Farden. I've spent the last twelve years training for this, and the gods know I've struggled with my father every step of the way. I'm not going to let another stubborn man get in my way. Just be here for me, Farden.'

Annoyingly she had a point, he thought. Farden nodded and stole another kiss on her cheek, making her laugh as she leapt away from him. Her sparkling eyes flicked to the city in the distance. 'Be careful in Krauslung,' she said.

Farden took her hand. 'Me? Be careful? What are a bunch of bureaucrats and their politics going to do to me?' He laughed and winked. 'I'll see you soon.'

'I hope so,' replied Cheska, turning to walk back up the path.

'Tonight?' Farden hissed, and she looked back over her shoulder.

'I'll find you,' she said.

The mage watched her until she had disappeared behind a little ridge.

'Politics,' he muttered with a shake of his head. 'Politics and rules.' He kicked a pebble for good measure and watched it sail down the mountainside.

About an hour's walk from Manesmark, nestled in a deep valley between the twin peaks of Ursufel and Hardja, lay the immense citadel of Krauslung, capital city of the Arka, home of the Arkathedral and the ruling powers of the magick council.

Farden reached the city just as the afternoon was starting to give way to another dark winter evening. The sky was still bright even through the clouds, but the cold darkness of night lingered on the horizon, ready to sneak through the mountains.

The hooded mage strode over the frozen grass of the valley, staring up at the two steep mountains either side of him. Their sheer rocky faces were dark grey, sprinkled with a few hardy shrubs and pines. They towered over the city walls.

The immense ramparts of Krauslung filled the gap between the two peaks, using their cliffs as a solid foundation for their thick stone defences. Acres and acres of fields stretched out in front of the city, filling the gap between Manesmark and Krauslung. Shacks that were home to hundreds of peasants squatted in the shadow of her soaring walls.

A steady stream of travellers and city folk flowed through the massive main gate, its huge archway dominated by the gatehouse above it that almost rivalled the Arkabbey at Leath in height. Thick stone battlements crested the walls, and from between them a small army of guards watched over the arriving visitors, peering down from their reclusive arrow slits. The long and stiff ceasefire with the Sirens had made the Arka guards wary and suspicious over the years, ever fearing the shadow of a dragon or a Siren spy. Even after fifteen years nobody was willing to forget.

Farden joined the slow-moving throngs of people heading towards the city, boots crunching on the gravel of the wide road. He pulled his cloak around him to ward off the approaching cold.

Merchants at the roadside called out to the passers-by, hoping to make a few more sales before night finally fell. Pigs and goats were being herded in small groups by young children covered in mud. A few dark-skinned men from southern Paraia sat around a campfire beside the road, curved swords at their side, muttering to each other in a low foreign tongue. The smell of exotic spices and meats tickled Farden's nose. A fat man riding a sorry-looking black bear meandered between the people, occasionally whacking it with a thin stick to make it move faster. The beast just grumbled and kept moving at its own pace.

After a short time spent weaving through the ever-increasing crowds, Farden reached the huge archway of the main gates. The thickness of the stone and the massive iron doors never ceased to amaze him, even for one as far-travelled as he. The mage stared up in awe at the murder holes and gigantic stone blocks suspended above his head. The guards eyed him warily for a moment as he passed beneath them. Then, recognising what he was, they looked away quickly to glare at the next person. Farden pulled his hood down even further as he walked under the walls: thirty paces' worth of thick mountain stone.

Ahead of him was the main city, and from his vantage point at the gate he could see the whole of Krauslung spread out like an intricate carpet. The two great mountains either side dipped and fell, giving way to a narrow, sloping valley that ended in a horseshoe-shaped harbour and the Port of Rós, with its legendary shipyards. From there the bay and the cold Bern sea stretched out for many leagues before stumbling across the islands of Skap in the far distance. Their dark blotches stretched out on the horizon like a half-drowned giant.

To the east and west, the Össfen Mountains marched on for miles, steep walls for warding off the bitter waves of the winter sea. The mage could smell the tangy salt in the air and hear the plaintive, hungry cries of the gulls on the wind. He smiled.

Farden switched his attention back to the city. It had been many months since he had last been here. He had almost forgotten the impressive view.

On his right, leaning against the precipitous walls of Hardja, stood the Arkathedral, forged from grey granite and white polished stone from the cliff cities in the west. A great hall perched on top of the colossal tiered fortress, crowned by two thin towers that stood on either side of its domed roof. These towers held the twin bells that shared their names with the two mountains that flanked the city: Ursufel on the left, Hardja on the right. Farden hadn't heard them ring in years, not since the end of the war.

Like the layers of a gigantic cake, the Arkathedral spiralled downward to the city streets, its concentric curtain walls hiding libraries, halls, kitchens, barracks, training yards, and regal abodes for the two Arkmages and the council members. Here was the throbbing heart of the Arka, where the balance of magick was kept in check and the council played out their games with the world.

Farden made his way deeper into the valley and down into the citadel. Night was starting to fall, and the city was buzzing. Down on the streets it was noisy; the gutters were full of water from the winter snows and gods know what else. People leaned out of windows and shouted to others below in the street, while others gambled and bartered in the narrow alleyways. Merchants hawked their wares, bellowing at passers-by, and women painted with gaudy colours whistled and grabbed at some of the finer-looking men.

In Krauslung everyone seemed to live on top or underneath everyone else. The buildings were piled storey upon storey, until each house or shop or tavern seemed to lean against the next, making the streets seem like the darkened arteries and capillaries of some immense living thing. Farden loved it.

In the gutters of the city, nobody paid attention to him; he could melt into the alleyways and market stalls and nobody would look twice at the shady mage. Even the pickpocketing children ignored him, knowing better than to mess with a mage. Farden kept his hood low, staring about the place.

At long last, Farden turned onto one of the main avenues that ran through the city, where the crowds became thinner and slightly more civilised, and a bit more sunlight reached the streets. He looked up at the tallest buildings, at their stained-glass windows and their arched slate roofs, and a few faces peered back at him. From behind the coloured glass, they sipped at delicate goblets and picked daintily at tiny bits of something in their hands. In the city, the finer citizens claimed the upper levels. They had made social class a matter of mere physical height.

Farden snorted and carried on, taking it all in as he walked. He watched some of the more established merchants relaxing at their stalls after a long day of profit, smoking pipes and chewing on tough bread. Arka soldiers stood on every corner. Their polished silver armour shone in the last rays of the day's light. A tavern to Farden's right erupted with loud music as two bards, or *skalds*, rallied the patrons with loud tales of heroes, beasts and magick. The drunkards all sang along, and several spilt out into the streets to slam their tankards together in flurries of brown ale. The soldiers looked on distastefully.

To his left, a group of fine ladies, their faces painted and hair tied up high, ran gloved hands over jewellery and ornaments at a shop stall. A few of the women had pet geese by their side. The fat birds were decorated in the same colours as their owners' dresses and held on thin velvet leashes. They honked quietly, impatiently waddling from side to side. Farden smirked. The fashions of high society females had always escaped him. All he knew was that the wishes of rich ladies always held sway over the coin-purses of rich men.

Farden caught himself staring at one of the blonder women, who looked a little like Cheska, but he pushed her from his mind and kept walking.

Shop windows called out to him with bright colours and signs:

Potions, Lotions and Notions, Magickal remedies for all!

Vigtor Urtt: Purveyor of Blades and Pointy Weapons!

Fine clothes for Fine women!

This last one was accompanied by a little wooden notice that proclaimed: *"No beggars allowed*".

This was how the city was, more so in recent years than ever before. The poor lived below the rich, so close and yet so far, neither crossing the gap between the classes but willing to live in rough harmony as long as their peaceful ways of life were maintained. And that was where Farden thought he fitted in. He was not rich, but neither was he poor, simply somewhere in the middle: an unknown stranger ignored on the streets. Instead he thought himself part of the glue that held the Arka together, a servant of the ruling magick council whose job it was to maintain this balance, this way of life for these naïve people.

It felt abruptly odd to him, lost and unnoticed in the bustle of the city, how thankless this task was, yet somehow he was still stubbornly dedicated to it. It was not as though he was a mere pawn, though. If the world of magick was a game of chess, then Farden would be a knight.

Farden headed north along another wide street lined with houses. He fixed his eyes on the gates of the Arkathedral fortress ahead of him and started the long walk up the sloping street towards them.

chapter 5

"See, I think those Arkmages is sneaky. Why else would they keep us all out of their pretty tower, secretive like. And you know I heard that there Helyard bloke can change the weather? Make it rain and all that? See, now that scares me. If were up to me, I would have us people running things, making sure we're not up to no mischief and all. We're the ones who knows best. What, the war? Well that was all about gold or land or something. Yeah. It was definitely about gold."

Overheard during a conversation in a Krauslung tavern

'Farden!' A loud voice rang out through the marble corridor. The mage turned to see a familiar face creasing with a big smile, and an outstretched hand coming towards him.

'Undermage, always a pleasure.' Farden grinned back and shook the proffered hand warmly and vigorously.

'It's been too long, Farden, too long, and you can dispense with that Undermage rubbish, you know me better than that.' The Lord Vice flashed a smile that was crammed with white teeth and clapped Farden on the shoulder.

'I can see you haven't changed, still playing the politician as usual,' said Farden. They both laughed as they carried on down the corridor. Vice was an old friend and somewhat of a mentor to Farden. He was a powerful mage, and had known Farden almost all his life, ever since his uncle had delivered him to the School, just a young boy.

Vice had been an instructor, and somewhat of a legend amongst the pupils. A war hero.

Over the years, step by step and bit by bit, he had climbed through the ranks of the Arka to sit beside the two Arkmages, the powerful Helyard and the wise Åddren. Rumour had it that Vice was actually doing the council some good. Farden was honoured to have a friend in such high places; someone he could trust in the upper echelons of pompous Arka society.

Vice cut an imposing figure, a good half-a-head taller than Farden and powerfully built, rather than lanky. He had a long ceremonial knife at his hip as a mark of his office and wore a black and green robe that whispered softly against the marble floor as he walked. The Undermage's colours. His dull blonde hair curled and spilt over a tall forehead that was just beginning to show the lines of age and the stress of politics. His dark brown eyes were warm and welcoming, while his defined jaw and high cheekbones gave him a regal air.

Farden knew the raw power that Vice hid behind his usually calm exterior and had seen those eyes flash with furious magick more than a few times. Vice had taught Farden many of his old tricks and spells. However, he wasn't a Written, and he couldn't begin to compare himself to the power of the Arkmages.

As they walked, the affable Vice threw an arm around Farden's shoulders, steering him down the corridor. He spoke in a low voice as a few servants passed. His purposeful eyes flicked between the marble flagstones and the huge arched windows lining the hallway. The sun was starting to set behind the mountains.

'This is a dark time for us, Farden. I hope you have some good news,' he murmured.

'I have news, but whether it's good or not will be up to you and the Arkmages, Vice.'

'The tragedy at Arfell has hit us hard. It's one thing to lose our valuable scholars in such a brutal murder, but to have a dangerous spell book taken from our safe hands is even worse.' Vice shook his head and clasped his hands behind his back.

'I agree,' said Farden.

He paused as several guards swung open a large door and snapped their heels together as the two men passed. They sported short spears and circular shields, and wore the same green and black of the Undermage's position. The mage waited until they had passed through the door.

'Whatever's going on, and whoever's behind all of this, we can't afford to waste time.'

'That'll be your good news, I assume,' said Vice drily. He rubbed his clean-shaven chin. 'We'd better discuss this with the council, they're waiting for you.' He pointed ahead to a wide gilded door, one that Farden had walked through only several times before.

Another gang of guards in full ceremonial armour, gold and green steel, flanked the thick doorway. Their shields were like mirrors and their long spears were so tall they almost scraped the arched marble ceiling. Their golden helmets covered their entire faces, and they nodded to Farden and Vice as they approached. Farden straightened his shoulders and cleared his throat loudly.

'Let's go in.' Vice motioned to the guards and they pushed hard on the heavy doors. They swung open agonisingly slowly.

As Farden stepped into the great hall he tried to keep his mouth from hanging open. It was like stepping into a white and gold cavern. Every time he came here it never ceased to amaze him.

Marble pillars lined the room, tall white columns carved like tree trunks so that their bases spread over the floor like gnarled roots, their tops flaring out across the roof like thick ivory branches, where they entangled themselves in the huge beams and gilded rafters that resembled the ribs of some huge fossilised animal. Light poured through windows that stretched from floor to ceiling, from one end of the hall to the other, fitted with the finest stained-glass that the artisans of Krauslung could ever hope to make.

Farden watched the rainbow light play amongst the ivory branches and golden wood, painting the white floor every colour he could imagine. He scanned the men and women and places frozen forever in the patterns of the coloured glass, their old faces emotionless and regal, staring impassively out from the windows at their successors.

The mage kept walking, following Vice to the front of the great hall. Almost a hundred people stood around them, loitering amongst the pillars and benches, clad in robes and dresses of various hues, talking in low voices and pointing at the mage. Farden ignored them.

In the centre of the great hall stood a statue of Evernia, surrounded by candles. Sitting at her white marbled feet was a set of gold scales, hanging balanced and even, the symbol of the Arka. Two ornate Weights sat in each side, old relics belonging to the Arkmages. High above her head, a huge diamond-shaped window was open to the cold sky, and the cold wind whined across the opening. Through it Farden could see the sky turning a dusty pink with the dying sun. A single star dared to peek through the fading daylight, sparkling gently.

At the front of the hall stood three giant chairs, two equally-sized ones in the centre and a smaller one to their right. Here were the Twin Thrones, and here sat the Arkmages Helyard and Åddren, rulers of the Arka and the heads of the magick council: powerful, wise and beyond contestation.

Vice swept from Farden's side to take his place on the smaller marble chair. Guards hovered in the shadows between the pillars.

Farden stopped several feet short of the three men on the chairs and bowed low to the ground, sweeping back his hood as he did so. Silence fell in the great hall.

'Welcome, Farden, to the Arkathedral. I trust your journey was swift?' Åddren spoke first. He was a short man, with kind blue eyes and a balding head sparsely decorated with copses of grey hair. Åddren was thin and ageing, but the powerful man still wore the long green and gold Arkmage's robe with pride and a strict posture. He hadn't changed one bit since Farden had last seen him.

'It was, your Mage.' Farden rose slowly and nodded with his most courteous smile.

To Åddren's right sat a tall man with a long, sharp jaw and mahogany eyes that roved busily over Farden's clothes and apparel. For his age, Helyard was surprisingly thick-set and muscular, echoes of a long life spent on the battlefield. He sat bolt upright and stern in his marble throne, spine and jaw stiff, his pale hands resting on the broad arms of the chair. Helyard's hair was cut short and was a dirty blonde in colour, with streaks of white beginning to surface through his trimmed curly locks, like worms appearing after a heavy rain. He had a habit of looking down his long nose at the people he addressed, and a love for impatiently interrupting council members he deemed too unimportant to speak.

The austere Helyard sighed theatrically. 'Tell us of your findings then, Farden. If this news is as urgent as I'm told, you'd best be out with it,' he said with a dismissive wave.

'Yes, Lord Helyard.' Farden took a breath. He spoke slowly, with a measured tone, striving to remember every detail, like Durnus had told him. He was unusually nervous in front of these old men.

'The book that was stolen from Arfell is a dark elf spell book, a manual for summoning creatures and beasts from the other side. A few days ago I travelled south into Albion to find a Siren hermit named Jergan. He had been part of the team of scholars that first discovered the book, in an ancient elf fortress in the Tausenbar Mountains. The same team then went on to decipher and cast some of the spells. Jergan spoke of the worst and most powerful of them all, something he said they had called *"the mouths"* or *"mouth of darkness."* They never dared to attempt it, and before they got any further, the Old Dragon had the book banished to a location in southern Nelska, and the Sirens never spoke of it again.'

The Arkmages thought in silence for a moment. Several of the council members murmured between each other conspiratorially, like gossiping maids. Åddren asked a question.

'What of this Jergan? Could he be the one responsible?'

'No, your Mage. Jergan has become a pathetic hermit, nothing but a slave to his curse.' Farden paused as the others threw quizzical looks at him. 'He was bitten years ago by a lycan on the northern ice fields, and since then has lived in hiding, a broken and pitiful man under the spell of the curse. He hasn't left Albion in years and is still hiding on the moors in a hovel. He's innocent.'

'And you're sure about that?' asked Helyard.

'The murders at Arfell were committed by more than just your average magick-user, we know that,' said Vice. Åddren nodded.

Helyard licked his thin lips with a lizard tongue and tried on a smile. 'I hear a rumour that you might be one of the finest Written we have, Farden. Where were you when this book was stolen?'

There was a burst of outrage in the hall, mingled with a few accusing shouts. Åddren banged his fist on his marble throne for quiet.

Farden was shocked, and momentarily speechless, standing there with his mouth open. He tried to think of a careful answer as silence was slowly restored. It hung like lead in the hall.

'Your Mage, I agree that we must examine every possibility, but as for me,' he looked the Arkmage squarely in the eye, 'When this terrible crime was committed, I was in the north of Albion, on a mission given to me by my superior.' Farden paused. The accusation had kindled a little rebellious streak in his heart. 'But perhaps, if I might be so bold in saying, that if we are turning this investigation on the Arka and our own mages, perhaps even the magick council should be considered?'

A few more shouts came from behind him and a low rumble of discontent murmured through the gathered council members. *Arrogant bureaucrats*, Farden thought, making an effort to stand straighter.

Åddren held up his hands for silence. 'No one here is being accused. Farden is a loyal servant and has served us well through the years. Arkmage Helyard is merely being cautious.'

Vice agreed with a murmur, and Åddren changed the subject.

'I'm curious, why did they fail in summoning this creature? Was it purely fear?' he asked.

Farden took the hint. 'Jergan informed me that this spell requires one of the dark elf wells to bring the creature across from the other side. He also seems to think there may be one in Emaneska that we have yet to find.'

Helyard scoffed, and a ripple of laughter ran through the council.

'Did he draw you a map?' shouted a mocking voice from somewhere in the crowd.

Farden stood even straighter. 'He knew something, and I believe him,' he said confidently, looking to Vice for help.

'If what Farden says is true, then I thank the gods that the Sirens didn't ever find a well while they had this book in their possession. Such a force would have made them unstoppable.' Vice mulled over his friend's words.

Åddren held up a solitary finger. 'If the murderers need a dark elf well to summon the creature, then we have no choice but to believe this lycan, and try to find this well before they do. Only then can we catch the ones responsible, and prevent disaster.'

'Yes, your Mage,' agreed Farden.

'Åddren, the wells have been lost to us for years! You cannot seriously believe that one still survives,' Helyard chuckled in mock humour. 'Believe me, I have led many expeditions to find one—'

'As have I, Arkmage,' interrupted Vice. 'I agree with Farden. We need to make sure that this creature, this *mouth of darkness*, is never released. The only way we can do that is beating them to their source of power.'

The Undermage looked Helyard squarely in the eye while he spoke, and the stern man snorted and looked away. Farden could have sworn that Vice flashed him a triumphant wink.

Åddren cocked his head to one side, as if waiting for the answers to come to him. 'How then, if we have been searching for decades, can we find a lost well? Our records simply do not go far enough back in history!'

The others in the hall were silent in thought. A few still sniggered amongst themselves, and Farden contemplated changing their minds with a quick firebolt, but he kept his hands clasped firmly behind his back. And then it came to him, something Jergan had said.

'Some of the dragons could have memories of the dark elves, in their tearbooks,' he suggested tentatively.

'The dragon-riders have been silent for years now, and not a single messenger from Nelska has passed our gates since we agreed on the ceasefire,' Helyard scoffed. 'And that was fifteen years ago. Do you expect them to just hand a tearbook over?'

Farden bit the inside of his lip as he turned to look at Vice.

'Lord Vice?' he asked. Whispers scurried through the council crowd. All eyes turned on the Undermage.

Years ago, in one of the final battles of the war, Vice had bravely led a small group of soldiers through a secret tunnel into the siege-locked fortress of Ragjarak, home of the Old Dragon Farfallen. After a long battle through the ice-tunnels, Vice killed Farfallen and took his tearbook as a trophy. It was one of the few great victories of the war, and the blow had been heavy on the Sirens. Songs were still being sung in the taverns of the great Undermage and his fight with the gold dragon.

Farden had only seen a tearbook once during his lifetime, and that had been half-burnt and half-buried in mud. Tearbooks were large tomes filled with lines and lines of dragon-script, hieroglyphs that held a dragon's memories like a sponge holding a lake. When a dragon's tear was dropped onto a blank page of an empty tearbook, the memories would write themselves over the pages, and the dragon could store his past in one single book to be read as a history of his life, and to stop them going mad. The older the dragon, the longer the tearbook. Some spanned millennia.

'Farfallen's tearbook is empty. It has been for years.' Vice shrugged, and a susurrus of disappointment echoed through the hall. 'Tearbooks fade when they aren't in the presence of their dragon. Eventually their pages go blank.'

Farden thought for a moment, letting a dangerous idea bloom in his mind. He dared to speak up again. *They were not going to like this. Not one bit.*

'Your Mages,' he began, trepidation building inside him. 'What if we took the tearbook back to the Sirens, as a peace offering and a gesture of goodwill to gain their help—'

He did not get any further: the hall exploded into outraged chaos. Shouts ricocheted around the hall.

'Madness!'

'To suggest such a thing is treason!'

'Get him out of here!'

Åddren held up his hands, but the hall raged on. The noise was deafening. Helyard was incredulous. He leaned far out of his chair and gaped wide-eyed at Farden as if the mage had just squatted down and taken a shit on the marble floor.

'How dare you! That is an outrage!' bellowed the Arkmage. His face turned a crimson shade of purple. Åddren banged his fist on his throne and waved his other hand for silence, but none came.

Helyard was still shouting. 'How do we know the Sirens weren't responsible in the first place?!'

Farden looked to Vice for help, but he was busy shouting down another ignorant council member. Farden yelled out over the pandemonium.

'The dragon-riders were the ones who originally banished the book, your Mage. If they see how dangerous the situation is, they may help us in finding the well!'

Helyard slapped his thigh angrily and pointed at the mage with an accusing finger. 'Of course they will, and once we do they'll stab us in the back and summon the creature for themselves! You could start another war with your foolish actions!' he boomed.

'And you could start one with your *inaction*!' snapped Farden. He could feel the magick bubbling up in his chest. He wanted to slam his fist into the Arkmage's nose and teach him a lesson.

'How dare you lecture me!' barked Helyard, his face red and full of indignant veins, his jaw pointed and condemning. Farden could feel the old Arkmage's magick making the air twitch. 'Guards! Remove this f—'

'ENOUGH!' Åddren roared, in a voice quite unnatural for his small figure. Everyone froze, the echoes of angry words hanging awkwardly in the hall. With a snort, Helyard sat back in his throne and moodily drummed his fingers on the marble.

'This is a place of reason and discussion, not petty squabbling and shouting. If you want that then go find it in the streets. I will not have it here. Now, does anyone have anything sensible to offer?'

After a moment of Åddren's earnest glaring, Vice raised a hand and spoke in a measured tone to the hall. 'I suggest that Farden go as an emissary to Nelska and speak with the Siren elders.'

Farden fixed Vice with a wide-eyed look. Vice held his gaze and continued.

'I would rather gain their help than try to face this threat alone. This concerns all of Emaneska now, not just the Arka.'

Farden fidgeted with his hands behind his back, strangely excited.

Åddren sighed. 'Then it is down to a vote. Helyard?' He looked at his counterpart, who still hadn't taken his stormy eyes off Farden. 'Choose your side,' said Åddren.

Helyard was the very picture of rage. Arms folded, he languished in his chair like a spiteful lizard, still boring into the mage's skull with his wooden eyes. 'I say that the dragon-riders are the ones to blame, and we'd be foolishly throwing everything, and I mean *everything*, into their claws. I say no.' The tall man shrugged, shoulders scraping against the polished marble throne.

'Vice?'

'I say yes,' the Undermage said firmly, without missing a beat. 'Farden should take the tearbook back to Nelska.'

Victorious drums started to play in Farden's head. A smile began to creep into the corner of his cheek.

Åddren paused for a moment, and everybody seemed to hold their breath. The suspense verged on painful. He looked up from the marble floor. 'I say yes.'

And here entered the proud trumpets. The council rumbled with mixed opinions. A scatter of applause came from about half of them. Farden saw some of them nodding and smiling to each other, while others shook their heads and crossed their arms. He looked back to the thrones, to Vice and Åddren.

'Thank you, Arkmages, I will not fail you.' Farden bowed his head in a quick nod and put a clenched fist to his breastplate.

'Vice will show you out and find you accommodation in the Arkathedral. We will meet at the west pier of Rós at dawn. May

Evernia bring you a restful sleep tonight, mage,' Åddren said warmly, and gestured to the doors at the back of the hall.

Vice stood quickly and led Farden away from the seething Helyard. The crowded council stared like hawks at the two men.

'Thank you,' hissed Farden, once they were out of earshot.

'Don't mention it.'

The gold doors slammed shut behind them and their steps echoed loudly in the stone hallway, yet somehow the narrow corridor was a relief after the claustrophobic hall. They talked as they walked.

'I've never seen Helyard like that,' said the mage.

Vice nodded. 'Mhm, he's very, what's the word, *passionate*, about his views.'

'And in other words?' Farden grinned, not convinced by his friend's tactful words.

'He's a stubborn fuck,' said Vice, fixing Farden with a serious look. 'He should have been a tyrant or a warlord rather than an Arkmage, it would suit him better. There's no place in the council for people like him. It's time to compromise and open our doors, not to lock them even tighter.'

'It's been a while since I heard you speak your mind, Vice, and I have to say, I prefer it to all that delicate democratic shit,' said Farden, still in a low voice. The corridor seemed empty. He looked over his shoulder to make sure.

Vice nodded. 'And so do I.'

'Åddren seems to know how to handle him.'

'After twenty-five years I would expect him to. He knows things are changing, and he's willing to change with them. The problem is Helyard has many a supporter in the council, so Åddren has to be delicate, and democratic, and find a middle ground.'

'I could never do what you do, sit there and let all the politics wash over you,' said Farden.

'No, you prefer it out there in the wilderness with fire and a sword, where it's up to you and nobody else,' chuckled the Undermage.

Farden patted the sword resting against his shoulder-blade. 'Politics can run a city, or define a nation, but men and magick are still what counts. You can't hammer in a nail with words.'

'No, but you can start a war with them, that's why we still have to be careful with the Sirens,' said Vice, slowly coming to halt. He looked at his friend. 'Can you handle this, Farden?'

The mage stopped in his tracks and crossed his arms. He frowned. 'Straight to the point. What happened to the diplomat in you?'

'I have to ask, Farden. This is bigger than anything you've ever undertaken. You'd be the first Arka, never mind a Written, to set foot in Nelska in fifteen years. I only suggested it be you because, well, who else is there?'

Farden tried to conceal his pride. He shrugged. 'It has to be done. If I'm the one to do it then, well that's that. I go to Nelska.'

Vice slowly shook his head, hiding a smile. 'I always knew you were going to be difficult, the first day I met you. Just be careful, you're no use to the Arka dead.'

The two men continued to walk. 'Please, I get enough of that from Durnus,' said Farden.

'Ah, and how is that dusty old vampyre of yours?' It was Vice's turn to frown.

'He's fine.' Farden tried to skip that particular subject; the Undermage had never been fond of Farden's placement in Albion, nor Durnus. 'Just get me on a ship with that tearbook, and I'll handle the rest,' he said.

'Alright, you heard Åddren. Dawn, at the west pier. And you guard that old tome with your life. Don't let it out of your sight while you're on the ship, or in Nelska for that matter.' Vice wagged a finger at Farden. 'Don't show them the Book either, as in…' He waved his hand towards the mage's back. Farden understood.

'I know. They can't be trusted any more than anyone else can.' He listened to the sound of their footsteps for a while. 'What happened at Arfell? I mean, what really happened?'

They turned a corner, and Vice looked about conspiratorially. 'Three of the old men were so charred and burnt, they didn't even recognise them. The other two were found dead on the floor, slashed wide open with a blade. In the morning the others smelled something burning and saw the blood seeping out from under the door.' He shot Farden a serious look. 'It was an assassination, pure and simple, and a skilled one at that.'

'Fuck,' said Farden. He couldn't think of anything else to say. They came to a small spiral staircase leading downwards into the citadel and Vice stopped.

'I think it's best if you stay somewhere other than the Arkathedral tonight, after what has just happened. There's an inn nearby, on Freidja street, called *The Bearded Goat*, or something like that. I hear it's surprisingly nice, by Krauslung standards.'

'You sound like an old widow,' sniggered Farden.

'And remember, dawn at the west pier.'

'I'm never late.'

'That's very funny.' The Undermage shook his head. 'I won't see you tomorrow, I have to make sure that Arfell is protected. I'll see that the tearbook is sent to Åddren tonight. Helyard has business to deal with in Albion later, and I wouldn't trust him with it anyway. He'd probably burn it,' he said with a scowl.

'Albion?' Farden looked at him questioningly.

'Something with one of the dukes near Kiltyrin, or Dunyra, I forget. Official business.' He shrugged, and his robe rustled. Farden nodded, wondering what the Arkmage could possibly be doing in

Albion. The mage stuck out a hand, and Vice shook it warmly with both of his.

'Thank you, again, for this opportunity. And for how you supported my argument in front of the Arkmages. I don't think they would have listened to me otherwise,' said Farden.

'I think we're doing the right thing, friend, and I'm glad the Arka has somebody like you on our side.' Vice clapped the mage on the arm. 'Now, be careful in Nelska, and remember what I said about words. Diplomacy is sometimes necessary.'

'I'll see you tomorrow, Vice.' Farden spun around and disappeared into the stairwell, taking the steps two at a time.

'May the gods be with you,' the Undermage shouted after him.

Night fell quietly, darkness slipping unnoticed into the streets and roads of the city. Torches sparkled, and the noises of the evening began to fill the cold air. Two figures walked silently through an alleyway, cloaked and hooded, near to where the main wall met the mountain rock. As they wandered further and further away from prying eyes, hands reached out to torches and they hissed and died. The shadows were as thick as black velvet, and the two strangers knew it.

Farden pulled his hood back and held Cheska's hands tightly. She smiled at him through the darkness. 'I told you I'd find you,' she said.

'I'm glad you did,' he replied, barely finishing his words before he felt her lips catch his. Her hands curled around his back as they leaned against a nearby wall. They kissed, hungrily, holding onto each other for what seemed like an age.

Cheska finally pulled away, almost breathless. 'How long are you staying?'

Farden hesitated. 'They're sending me away again at dawn tomorrow,' he said with a sigh. Even in the darkness he could see her disappointed face. Her voice was small.

'When will you be back?' Farden didn't even need to answer; she felt him shrug and shake his head. 'I suppose being Arka's finest has its drawbacks,' she added, resting her head against his shoulder. She was usually excited by his missions. Farden stroked her hair.

'I'll come back, don't worry.'

Cheska nodded. 'I don't doubt you will. You always do, but I just want to spend more than an hour with you before you disappear again,' she said, and kissed his neck. 'I know it's dangerous for us. And now that there's the Ritual, it'll be against the rules.'

'I know.' Farden scowled at the shadows. 'But I don't care, I want you.'

'So do I,' she said, but before she could continue there was a loud shout from nearby, and the orange light of a flame started to creep up the alleyway. Someone was singing.

'Why's it so daaaaark?' sang an off-key voice. Farden growled and moved to stand in front of Cheska. They put their hoods up, letting the shadows cover their faces.

A man appeared from around the corner, holding a candle and tottering from side to side across the cobblestones. He was drunk and being particularly loud. Farden took a step forwards, and the bleary-eyed man noticed the two figures standing in the dark with an expression of overwhelming confusion.

'Whoaaa! Hidin' in the shadows are we?' he slurred. He gave the hooded pair a wide stumbling berth and leered at Cheska.

'Who's your pretty friend, mate? She can come home with me if she likes?' he laughed.

'Quiet yourself, fool, before I do it for you,' snarled Farden. The mage took another step. Cheska put a hand on his arm, holding him back.

'Don't, Farden,' she whispered. He nodded, Durnus' words echoing in his ears.

'Keep moving,' said Farden, and the man did, hollering and hooting with every step. As the light receded, Farden moved back into the shadows and wrapped his arms around Cheska. She toyed with his hair.

'You've always been so quick to anger.'

'I don't much like people,' he scowled, watching the darkness.

'But you like me.'

'You're different,' he said, giving her another kiss. 'You're not like the others. Somehow you can keep me calm. Well, up until now.'

He heard her sharp intake of breath. 'Gods, Farden, you have to stop worrying about this Ritual. I'm ready for this.'

'And what does your father think of it?'

'My father and his precious advisors gave up arguing with me a long time ago. He knows it's what I want and begrudgingly he leaves me to it. As should you. Please stop worrying.'

'Do you blame me?' he asked.

Cheska shook her head. 'No, but we can deal with this when you get back. Not now.'

'Fine,' said Farden.

'I think it's time I left,' she whispered in his ear. She kissed his cheek. 'Please be safe, wherever you're going.'

Farden held her wrist and winked. 'I'd tell you if I could.'

'I know,' said Cheska, then she kissed him once more, lingering on his lips. She ran a hand over his weathered face, before turning away and melting into the darkness. Farden stayed a while, waiting until it was safe, then walked off in a different direction.

An hour later, Farden was sitting in *The Bearded Goat,* quietly sipping his drink and minding his own business. Vice had been right, the inn was loud and full of drunken fools, but the quality of the beverages and food was good, and Farden had found a quiet corner by a fireplace in the dim recesses of the room.

A skald was regaling the rumbustious crowd with stories about the infamous faerie incident. He stood on a table near the door, playing his stringed *ljot*, kicking tankards of beer with his muddy feet and belting out the words at the top of his voice. A few women in thin, frilly dresses lounged about the place, grinning at any man who walked by, beckoning them closer with crooked fingers, nails painted with gaudy yellows and reds. The men cheered and clanged their tankards together, singing along, swinging some of the more sober women around in drunken jigs. The mage watched them impassively. Alcohol worked in mysterious ways.

Farden looked back into the crackling flames and swirled his sweet red wine around in its wooden cup, thinking about his day, trying not to think about Cheska. The fire was warming his cold toes, even through his thick travelling boots, and the warmth and the wine were starting to make him sleepy. He shuffled closer to the fireplace, pulling his hood down over his brow, blocking out the noise. Someone coughed and spluttered nearby, and Farden glanced in the direction of the noise.

Next to him, nearer to the wall and draped in the shadows of the corner was an old beggar, smoking a long, dirty pipe. Farden had seen him earlier, snoring away to himself near the warmth of the fire, but now he was awake and peering about the place with his beady rat-eyes.

The grey man was ugly, unshaven, and unkempt, with greasy hair and dirty, patchwork clothes made from a hundred different garments. Sprouting from his narrow chin was a straggly beard coiled in dirty strands and plaits, with bits of dried stew clinging to it. He busied himself by chewing on the mouthpiece of his curved pipe. Gnarled fingers drummed annoyingly on the arm of the wooden chair he was curled up in. Farden looked him up and down, then went back to his wine. The smell of the beggar's acrid tobacco tickled his nose.

Farden tried to let his concentration melt into the warm fire, but now he could feel somebody's eyes on him. He turned back to face the beggar and met his gaze. His little rodent eyes sparkled with a cheeky glint.

'What do you want?' asked Farden.

The beggar chuckled, his whole body shaking with the effort. His tobacco-smoke breath rattled noisily in his throat. 'Oh nothin', thought I'd look at yer, seein' as yer lookin' at me.' He waggled his pipe in Farden's general direction. 'Yew look like a strong fellow though, don't yer, all quiet and sad on yer own?' he croaked, leering at him with a mischievous smile.

'What's it to you?'

'Oh nothin' at all, friend, jus' makin' conversation s'all. The beggar shrugged and sucked on his pipe. It rattled against his dirty yellow teeth.

'Well, I'd appreciate the peace and quiet if it's all the same to you.' Farden looked away, but out of the corner of his eye he saw the man lean in closer. Smoke escaped from his mouth like thick grey liquid and coiled towards the ceiling.

'Yew that mage? The one I 'eard about?'

Farden didn't move. 'There are a lot of mages in Krauslung old man, I'm not one of them.'

'Heehee, fair enough,' he cackled hoarsely, wheezing and slapping his knee, obviously finding great humour in the answer. 'But I seen yew around, mage: runnin' here, runnin' there. Yer important they say, one of the older ones. I 'eard about yew an' those minotaurs sev'ral years back? Said yew almost took 'em all single 'anded. Saw yer at the Arkathedral, too, an' I can spot those pretty vambraces a mile away.' The beggar winked, nodding to the gold poking from under Farden's sleeve. The mage crossed his arms and eyed the man suspiciously. He wondered if he had seen this old wreck before. He looked familiar.

'Hah, yew 'ave nothin' t' fear from me, big strong lad like yerself.' He paused, taking a drag on his foul-smelling pipe. Farden wrinkled his nose. The man sucked his blackened teeth and held it towards him. 'Fancy a bit?' he asked.

Farden looked at the mouldy pipe and shook his head with a grimace. 'I don't smoke,' he said.

The old man shrugged and looked around furtively with his rat-eyes. His voice dropped to a hoarse whisper. 'How 'bout that, then, and yew look like the manner o' man who does. Maybe you prefer to chew it.' His eager eyes scanned the mage's face and there was an awkward pause.

'I said I don't smoke, and I don't chew tobacco either.' Farden narrowed his eyes threateningly. His patience was wearing thin.

'Wasn't talkin' bout tabaccy now was I?'

Farden stared at the fire. 'This conversation is over.'

'I don't think it is, mage,' chuckled the beggar. He cocked his head to the side like a pigeon assessing bread. 'Yew never smoked it before, 'ave yer?' He leaned forwards confidentially. He looked around at the unfamiliar faces at the bar and sniffed. 'Yer wastin' yer time, only chewin' it. Nevermar's meant to be *smoked*, mage,' said the beggar, and tapped the bowl of his pipe on the arm of the chair.

Farden opened his mouth to say something, then closed it again. He reached out towards the fire and felt the heat creep over his hands. A loud bray of laughter came from the bar. He took a deep breath through his nostrils and let the smell of pipe and woodsmoke fill his head. 'How much?' he asked.

The beggar waved a bony hand and shook his head, as if he had just been insulted. 'Sometimes an old man jus' likes a body to smoke wit', 'stead of bein' on 'is own, see? Makes a change don't it, mage?' The man coughed with the hiss of a man on his deathbed and a waft of bad breath.

'Don't call me that,' Farden warned him. The man shrugged again.

'As you wish,' he said.

Farden's mind raced while he swirled the wine around, making a whirlpool in his cup. Temptation billowed in low clouds over his head. He chewed the inside of his lip. Unwelcome thoughts gathered, memories and dead faces laughed at him. Cheska hovered in his mind, pale, and still. He wanted to stop thinking.

'Fine,' he said, then gulped down the last dregs of his drink in one swift move. 'I'm in number sixteen, if you can count that high, the one with the red door.' With that, he swept up the nearby staircase and disappeared into the shadows of the corridor.

After finding his room in the gloomy hallway, he opened the door and lit the fireplace with a quick spell. He opened the windows to let the cold night air freshen the room and reclined in a nearby chair, impatiently playing with sparks on his palm.

A short while passed before there came a bony knock on the wooden door.

'Come in,' Farden whispered gruffly.

The old beggar shuffled through the door, hunched and crooked. The man might have been tall once, but long years had bent his back and added lines to his face. In the firelight, his skin looked like weathered oak. He now wore a grey cloak—also made of patches—over his rags.

'Have a seat.' Farden gestured to the chair opposite him.

'Give me a moment.' The man ignored the offered chair and squatted in front of the fire. He pulled a few items from his pockets and placed them on the brick hearth. Gnarled hands toyed with them.

Farden pointed to one, a strange pipe, curved but coiled and fat in the middle. It looked like a cross between a snail and a horn. 'What's that?' the mage asked.

'Gim, skiff, redraw, blagg, nevermar, you always smoke it in a pipe, like this 'un,' the beggar muttered. He unfolded a bundle of cloth and started to peel something apart, placing little crumbs of red moss into the bowl of the pipe and pushing it down with his little finger. Once it seemed to be full, the man sprinkled some of his cheap tobacco on the top, and tapped the thing on the edge of the fireplace. He looked at the fire, shook his head, and then cast around for flint and tinder. Then, he had a sudden thought and looked up at the mage. 'D'ye mind?' he said, waving the pipe in little circular motions.

Farden fixed him with a murderous look as he accepted the pipe. 'If I find out that you've told anyone, *anyone* about this, then I will find you, old man, and I will kill you. Understand?'

The old man shrugged and shook his head, trying to portray the image of sincerity and trust. 'Don't know nobody to tell, mage, yew can trust me.' The beggar winked.

'Don't call me that,' said Farden, irritably.

He held the pipe in one hand, and with the other, keeping an eye on the beggar, pointed at the bowl. A little flame appeared on his fingertip, making the stuff crackle and hiss. He felt the acrid smoke burn and scrape his throat. He coughed and spluttered.

'Tastes good, don't it?' chuckled the old man. With great difficulty he got to his feet and placed himself down in the threadbare armchair.

'It's harsh,' Farden groaned. He took another painful drag and tried to relax in his chair, feeling a slight headiness tingling all throughout his skull. He offered the pipe back to the old man, who grabbed at it with grubby fingers.

They sat in silence, listening to the music from downstairs escape into the street below the window. The man watched Farden smoke the pipe with a hungry expression, but Farden didn't even notice. He held the smoke in his chest, feeling the back of his eyes shiver and his temples quiver. His arms felt a hundred feet long and his fingers moved through sickly honey.

They passed the pipe back and forth, and soon enough Farden found himself melting into the chair like an icicle in the morning sunlight.

His mind ran through fields of the absurd, random music scattered between his ears. Strange shapes moved about his room, searching for reality under the bed and behind the curtains. The old beggar shook and bounced, and his jittery bed shifted around in an earthquake.

At some point, Farden looked up to find the pipe in front of him again. The thing glittered like an angry torch, sparking and puffing fumes into the air.

Smoke filled his eyes. His lungs burnt. An intense feeling of dizziness pounded against the inside of Farden's skull. He closed his eyes to watch colours collide and opened them to find he was alone. The old beggar was long gone.

The bed evaded him for a while but at last he caught it, falling into a lake of pillows and sheets. He kicked off boots that were hot and heavy. His tunic was made of thick soup. A pillow hijacked his head and he drifted off into a heavy, drug-laden sleep. Gods danced around his room, and daemons watched from the corners and rafters, quoting something about blood and history. Darkness took him.

The old man slipped out from the mage's room and closed the door quietly with a click. He threw a hood over his greasy hair and kicked at his rough leather shoes as if they annoyed him. With great care, he hobbled downstairs and weaved his way between the drinkers and singers that filled the noisy inn, still worshipping the ale that foamed in their tankards. The beggar shuffled past them, muttering quiet 'scuse me's and comin' through's as he did so, and finally he made it onto the street. He paused to stretch. After a satisfied slap of his thigh, he disappeared down the nearest alleyway, seeming taller and more nimble with every step.

A loud drunk came around a corner and careered down the narrow alley towards the strange beggar. The drunken man leaned into his path, shouting and singing loudly in his face. The smell of his wine-soaked breath was overpowering. The beggar fended off the drunk with a push, but in a fit of anger, the man cursed and swung his arm in a wild punch.

The beggar reacted with a speed that belied his years. A short black knife darted from under his patchwork cloak and plunged into the drunk's side with a thud. He clamped his palm over the man's mouth and threw him hard against the nearest wall, pausing only to viciously twist the knife. The man grunted in pain and shock. Stabbing him twice more in the chest, the beggar let the dying man slump to the cobbles.

Without a moment's hesitation, he pulled his cloak about him and silently disappeared into the night once more. Left to die alone in the cold, muddy street, the drunk gradually slipped away, a bewildered look still plastered across his pale face.

chapter 6

"Dark magick is the scourge of Emaneska. Let no Written ever be involved with it, and all should use full force against those who practise it. Those who wield it should be warned: we will chase you into the mountains, hunt you down, and bury you under the rocks. The council has spoken."

From a speech by Arkmage Åddren in the year 879, addressing the Written after the Neffra Incident

Farden was dreaming again.

He stood in the shadow of a black mountain. He wore only his vambraces. A hot breeze lashed his bare skin, and dust stung his eyes. He could feel the sand between his toes.

The mage looked behind him and saw razor-sharp crags of rock hanging over him, a bare, faceless cliff of jet and obsidian coming straight out of the sand and towering into the sky. Shadows played in the darkness.

The wind whistled through the rocks, making an eerie sound like a faraway horn crying for help, or a wounded animal wailing away its last few hours. Even in the dry heat, Farden shuddered. He looked out, away from the mountain, where the sun shone and the heatwaves danced. He watched the bare earth stretch on for miles, further than even his eyes could see. The horizon shuddered and wobbled.

Farden looked up at the sky, that pure empty sky, and felt a tranquillity he had never felt before wash over him. The mage felt as though he could melt into it; into the vast blueness of it, and never have to wake up again. He could forget about the council, the book, everything, and just melt away.

A black shape fluttered in his peripheral vision, and Farden turned his head. A crow or a raven flapped aimlessly around the rocky ledges of the black cliff, trying to stay out of reach of a skinny black cat that danced below it on its hind legs.

The bird dithered in mid-air, narrowly avoiding the clawing swipes of the mangy cat, desperately trying to find a safe place between the rocks. The cat crouched, watching its prey. Farden tried to shout and scare the animals away, but the hot wind snatched the words from his lips, and he yelled in complete silence.

The cat hunkered down, its haunches twitching and wiggling, choosing its perfect moment until it shot into the air and dragged the bird to the sand. The thing flapped and cried, but the cat was merciless. It pinned the crow to the ground with one paw and sunk its yellow teeth into its neck until its prey moved no more. The bird's head sagged and its beak lay open and silent.

Farden tried to move, to try to chase the cat away from the corpse, but his legs and arms refused to shift. He was glued to the sand. Something flitted from rock to rock above him. A cackle floated on the wind. Farden looked to the cat and saw her staring back at him with obsidian eyes. Blood dripped from her fangs and a black feather hovered at the corner of her mouth. The sand had become a red pool.

She ripped some more flesh from the bird's neck, chewing slowly, staring at him without emotion. She threw her head back, swallowed, then made a howling, whining sound deep in her throat. As quickly as it had begun, it stopped, and the cat took a slow step towards him.

You're between a rock and a hard place, so to speak, it said, an echoing voice in the back of his mind. Farden tried to answer, but no sound came from his mouth. The cat continued to move. Blood decorated her chin. Winged things moved and scraped above him.

They've got you all in a flap.

The sound became a landslide of wings. Black shapes and beady eyes crowded the crags, watching him. Farden struggled in vain to move. He looked at the desert behind him, which had become a plain of fire. The wind blew hot dusty air in his face and whipped his naked skin.

Wings began to fill the empty sky above him and the mountain let loose a whirlwind of black birds. They wheeled and careened through the blueness, cackling hideously.

The cat had come to a halt in front of him. She threw a curious look up at the storm of wings, beaks and claws flooding his dream. They filled every space on the cliff-face, stood on every inch of rock and crag. A thousand of them flapped around him.

It's you they want, just as they once wanted me.

A talon sliced across his back and he felt the drip of hot blood down his skin. Farden winced, trying with all his strength to move. Another claw across his thigh and a beak tore a hole in his side. Wings buffeted his face. Claws ripped flesh from bone.

Follow the dragons, said the voice.

No more than a handful of hours after he had collapsed into his bed, the first streaks of dawn started to stretch across the dim sky.

Farden awoke with a pounding headache. He fell out of bed and collided with the cold wooden floor with a groan. The mage shrugged on his clothes and armour and massaged his temples in a vain attempt to get rid of the waves of pain coursing through his head. He tried to cast a small healing spell but the magick smashed against his skull like a sledgehammer. Farden cursed and flinched, feeling the pain all the way to the tips of his toes. Every movement was a strain.

He blearily looked at his surroundings. The candles had burnt to their bases, and the dim morning light barely illuminated his room. The smell of acrid smoke hung in the air, and the stench made the hungover mage retch.

Stoically, Farden hauled his sword over his back with a wince. He fastened his cloak around him and slammed the door, much to the dismay of his head. He stood in the hall rubbing his temples. All seemed to be quiet in the inn, but something gnawed at the back of his mind, beneath the headache: something that escaped him every time he got close to identifying it.

Shadows of his dream taunted him, not daring to show their true faces. He remembered rocks, birds, or a place with sand. Farden shook his head gingerly and tried to forget the strange nightmare.

The streets of Krauslung were gloomy in the early dawn light. The shadowy clouds hung like a blanket over the mountains and the slumbering city by the sea. Men moved around the streets, cleaning the refuse from the muddy roads while shops and houses started to wake up. A few candles still peeked through the cracks in thick drapes.

'Spare a coin sir?' whined a beggar, who was slumped in a wooden box by the side of the street. Farden looked at him, for a moment thinking him the same beggar. He was not. The mage coughed, winced, and dug a little silver piece from his pocket. He flung it into the beggar's lap and walked off.

The man bit the coin and grinned a toothless smile. 'Gods be with you, sir!' he called after him. Farden wondered why everyone kept wishing him that.

Dawn shone in the east. Chimneys began to belch their sooty breath over the city. Smoke mingled with granite clouds. Squawking, cackling chickens scattered around Farden's legs, and a lone goose wandered through the crowds, trailing a velvet leash in the mud behind it.

People were now beginning to fill the thoroughfares, laughing and talking loudly despite the early morning. A stubby, bearded man, still drunk from the night before, shouted impatiently at the closed doors of a bakery while clinging to a pillar to keep from falling over. Farden watched an attractive peasant girl leave a rich-looking house and skip down the street with a coy little smile. She was still doing up her blouse and wiping smudged makeup from her face when she disappeared around a corner. *Such was the way of Krauslung society.*

Signs told Farden to head right down an alleyway if he wanted to reach the west side of the port. He walked for another half an hour before he came to a short balcony that overlooked a square and the west curve of Port Rós. The mage stood against the stone railings and sniffed the salty air, hoping the fresh breeze could work its charm on his headache.

A cold mist had crept across the sea in the night. Now it lingered in wisps and clung to the edges of the harbour walls. The ships in their docks rolled gently on the calm blue-green swell, crowded side-by-side and tethered by thick ropes. Wooden jetties and gangways ran vein-like through the bay, boardwalk capillaries keeping the ships alive with supplies and sailors. The muffled sounds of the ships' bells and the creaking of the docks was a gentle background noise compared to the shouts and banging of people working around him. The hammers of the shipyards were loud and clamouring. Everywhere Farden looked, cargo was piling up on the jetties. Sailors rushed around their ships and ropes like termites over spindly tree trunks.

Seagulls mewed overhead, catching the morsels thrown into the air by the crowds of people at the dockside. The inns in the city may have closed for the night, but the inns of the port were still thriving with raucous conversation and snippets of atonal singing.

Stalls had started serving fried meat and bread and boiling cheap moss tea for the sleepy sailors. The smells of farska and fish soup, and the infamous sea-serpent pie, were thick in the cold air.

Farden waited in line at a stall, hood pulled low over his baggy eyes, and grabbed a quick bread roll stuffed with cheap greasy venison. He bit into it ravenously, trying to chew in a way that didn't cause sparks to fly behind his eyes. The food tasted like ash in his mouth. A swig of brackish tea just reminded him of the herby charcoal taste of the nevermar.

The mage walked further along the wooden jetty towards the west pier. He munched on his cheap snack as he dodged his way through crowds of bustling dock workers. His sword felt heavy on his shoulders and he swayed drunkenly against the elbows of the men.

He stopped for a moment by the side of a wall to finish his tea. A few deep breaths later, the wave of nausea had passed and Farden felt a little better. He looked ahead and spied a ship flying the golden scales of the Arka. He headed off in its general direction.

Farden was slowly realising how much he was dreading the ship and the turbulent, churning journey that was waiting for him. If he hated anything, it was the open sea, and all of its grey rolling vastness. The excitement of his task had obscured his fear, but now he shuddered.

'Farden!' His own name surprised him. He turned to see Åddren and Helyard flanked by a dozen armoured soldiers. They were heading through the crowd towards him. Farden bowed formally then stood with his hands behind his back. Helyard didn't even look at the mage, but Åddren smiled warmly at him. He had a large sack at his side, hanging by a strap around his shoulder.

'I trust you slept well, Farden?' asked the Arkmage.

'I rested well, your Mage, thank you.' Farden wanted to throw up on his expensive green robe.

'Good. We need you vigilant and well-prepared for this trip. I have convinced Helyard to provide you with fair weather for as far as he can manage,' said Åddren. Helyard just grunted.

Farden had heard the rumours about the Arkmage's power over the local weather, and it had been known that, on occasion, summer days would be surprised with freak snow. That had been before the days of the Long Winter.

Farden looked at the powerful man, wondering why he hated the Sirens so much, but Åddren was talking again.

'Meanwhile, a hawk has been sent to Nelska and the citadel of Hjaussfen to warn them of an emissary from the Arka. I did not mention the true intention of your mission in the letter.' Åddren paused. 'Let me give you the tearbook.'

The Arkmage led the mage away from the others and put an arm around Farden's shoulders. With his other hand, he lifted the travelling sack from his shoulders and handed it to the mage. There was an earnest tone in his voice. 'Keep it safe at all times. Vice hand-picked your crew. These sailors are loyal, as are the soldiers, but greed may change their minds,' he said. Farden nodded wordlessly. Åddren gestured to the others and they walked on towards the ship.

Helyard cleared his throat noisily and spoke up in a hoarse lecturing voice. 'Make sure you read it *first*, mage, and *with* the dragon-riders. Most importantly, don't let them hold information from you, and don't you dare jeopardise this ceasefire,' he growled.

'I think he means don't lose your temper and kill anyone, Farden,' said Åddren calmly. He halted in his steps. Farden tried not to let his eyes betray him. He hadn't expected that the magick council would put any truth to the gossip about his exploits.

'Arkmage, I—' Farden began, trying to conjure a lie, but the kind man held up a hand. He pointed to the ship nestling against the wooden walkway, and the mage looked. It was a low carrack, dark mahogany brown in colour, with tall decks and pine rails. The ship lurched on a wave and brown bilge spewed from the holes on its bow.

Farden looked upward at the tall decks piled on top of each other like an unruly pack of cards. He could see the stained glass of the captain's cabin in the stern, and briefly pondered if he could bunk there, but the sight of the crow's nest made his stomach somersault, and he looked down at the waves. Barnacles and green algae festooned the battered hull, and a sad looking unicorn that had seen better days was the ship's figurehead. A string of sailors hauled boxes of lemons and hard tack bread up the steep ramp, along with an equally depressed goat, which was bleating tediously. Another score worked on the ship, a few already halfway up the mast, others piling up cargo on the decks and making ready to sail.

Farden marvelled at the lengths of rope that seemed to hold the fat ship together, wrapped around its stout rigging and sails like a spider's web on a hedge. He eyed the ominous weather hiding behind the rigging and cast a brief look at Helyard, whose glazed eyes stared at the clouds with a concentrative look.

Cold winter spray splashed over the nearby harbour wall and hissed in the wind. The harsh metallic sea pounded the black granite of the port defences like legions of icy waves drumming eagerly at the gates of the harbour. The mage was thankful that the dock was so sheltered.

Someone was talking to him again. 'Farden, this is Captain Heold.' Åddren welcomed a grizzly old man to their party.

He looked like an ageing pirate, sporting a grey beard that was even bigger than his round belly. He had a kind, weathered face, with eyes as hard as blue diamonds, hiding behind bushy white eyebrows. He looked as though he had been born at sea. He wore a rough uniform of sorts, the green-blue tunic of the navy, with a black cloth hat pulled down over his head.

Captain Heold offered his calloused hand and Farden shook it with a smile. ‘Good to meet yer, Farden. The *Sarunn* is a good ship, we should be in Nelska in about five or six days, travellin’ ‘round the coast,’ he said. Farden had met his type before, a real sea-dog: harsh-spoken, blunt, as superstitious as they came, but a true master of the rocky seas.

‘Excellent. Thank you, Captain.’ The mage struggled to return the man’s vice-like grip, feeling as if he were greeting an overgrown crab. Fortunately, before anything could be broken, the captain released him and turned to shout loudly at his motley crew.

‘Right, let’s step to it lively lads! Prepare to cast off as soon as we can!’ He bowed stiffly to the Arkmages and strode decisively up the ramp, still shouting.

While the accompanying guard made ready to get onto the vessel, Åddren took Farden aside again. The two men walked towards the ship’s gangplank and the Arkmage whispered quietly into his ear. ‘Farden, I honestly wish I didn’t have to ask you to carry out this mission, but if I thought that a mage better suited to the task existed, I would ask them.’

‘Thank you, your Mage.’ Farden didn’t really recall being asked, but he still wanted the opportunity.

‘And you may think that Helyard and the rest of the council are against you in this, but believe me, you are doing the right thing. Not only could we have a chance to stop this malicious plot in its tracks, but we could finally have peace with the dragon-riders.’

‘I know how important this is for our people, Arkmage, and trust me there is no measure I won’t take—’

Åddren held up an interrupting hand. ‘Just be careful mage. Helyard may be rash and swift to anger, but he does have a point. We do not yet know that the Sirens weren’t responsible for the murders,’ he said.

'You think that and still voted yes?' Farden looked at Åddren quizzically. He nodded with a solemn expression.

'There are certain risks that need to be taken, Farden, Vice and I saw that, and that's one of the reasons the Undermage is on the council. Sending you to the Sirens could bring peace to our people, but if Helyard is right and they were behind the atrocities at Arfell then we will find out very soon. It's a gamble in trusting them, Farden, and I regret that you are the tool we must use. But now we must pray to the gods and wait for your message.' The Arkmage looked up at the tumultuous sky and thrust his arms into his robe. 'The old ones still have sway over these lands.'

With a surprisingly brisk jump given his hangover, Farden mounted the wooden boards and steadied the tearbook at his side. 'In that case, Arkmage, let's hope that our gods are stronger than our enemy's.'

'Hope there will be, Written, for the gods and for you. May Njord protect you,' Åddren said, in a louder voice. A few nearby sailors rumbled in agreement, though they eyed Farden like he carried the plague. He sighed inwardly, nodded his thanks to his superior, bowed, then climbed the ship's ramp.

His sleepy brain felt like it was tumbling down a well, unable to put a stop to the journey he was about to take. Nausea groped at his gut as he felt the waves swell underneath his boots. Farden had never liked the sea. He said a swift prayer to Evernia and stepped onto the deck.

The three or four Arka soldiers had found their berths in the under-decks, and the mage decided to go do the same. With one last wave to the Arkmages and their entourage, he ducked under a hatch and went below.

As he descended some stairs into the low, humid belly of the stout ship, he heard the goat somewhere ahead of him. He decided to head in the other direction and soon found an empty stateroom with small windows that looked out from the back of the ship, probably beneath the captain's cabin, with the warm fire and comfortable bed, the fine breakfasts.

Farden paused outside the room, looking around to make sure he wasn't being watched. He grabbed a nearby wooden bucket, swept inside and locked the door.

Farden immediately went to the corner and threw his guts up into the pail. His head lurched with his stomach and the world burst into sparks and leaps. He cursed, slumping back against the bolted-down bed, wiping the mess from his chin.

He knew better but had to try a spell on the chance that the nevermar had worn off already. If this lasted any longer than five or six days he was in trouble.

The most pitiful excuse for a spark of flame flashed on his fingertip for a split second before he doubled up in pain. His head felt fit to explode as tears squeezed their way out of clenched eyelids. Farden slumped sideways to the floor to regain his breath. He had never felt this powerless before. He just lay there breathing.

After a while, Farden felt the ship drift free of the dock, the waves beneath them making the room rock back and forth. The mage fought back bile while the sailors above him sent the ship leaning into the growing wind, clearing the boardwalk and moving out of the port. He could hear their shouts and calls.

After some of the nausea passed, Farden felt a second wind and got to his feet, determined to see the ship leave the harbour. He made sure to lock the door behind him, then tried to negotiate the slippery corridors. He prayed he would not throw up in front of the soldiers or the stout men of the ship. At least he could pass it off as seasickness instead of a life-threatening hangover from a banned drug. *That would make interesting news for the magick council*, Farden thought.

He made it onto the deck, already slick with spray, and headed to the tall forecastle of the *Sarunn*, where he stared weakly at the turbulent seas whirling around the mouth of the huge port. The mage gripped the wood of the railing, feeling the briny spray on his chin and creased forehead. A sailor stood to the right of him, staring at Farden with a wary look. He felt the weight of eyes upon him and turned to face the man. The sailor turned away and busied himself with coiling ropes. He didn't turn around again.

'Mage!'

The mage found Heold briskly running up the steps, coughing steam into the cold wind. He barked a few orders to his men and yelled course directions to the crewman at the wheel. The captain looked at the mage and shrugged.

'Busy day fer us, Farden. We jus' got back int' port last night and were sent a message from the council we 'ad to take you t' Nelska this mornin'. 'Ow are yer accommodations?' Heold grinned, gripping the rails with hands whose skin looked like tanned leather.

'Good, thank you, Captain. I found them, at least,' said Farden. Heold nodded. The ship rose abruptly on a wave, and Farden grabbed at the handrail.

'I guess I can't ask why yer off to the land of the dragons? Nobody's been up there fer years.' He appeared to make blithe conversation, but his keen flint eyes roved over Farden with a powerful curiosity.

'I'm afraid it's a secret,' Farden replied stonily, staring out to sea. The ship was nearing the harbour walls.

'A few degrees to port, Thurgen!' Heold yelled through cupped hands. 'Excuse me. New man on t' wheel today, the other one 'ad the plague, and one o' me mates too, 'ad to replace 'im as well. Sorry t' ask 'bout yer business, Farden. Only the lads are a bit worried 'avin' you aboard. Superstitious lot.'

'I'm not dangerous, Captain, tell your men that. I will be keeping mostly to myself over the course of the trip, so I'd appreciate being left alone,' Farden said, trying to make his words sound kind and courteous. The captain nodded with a grunt and watched the mage go, wobbly on his feet.

'Be some good weather comin' soon, you'll see!' Heold yelled. He pointed towards the breaking clouds in the distance. Farden squinted at the golden sunlight glinting off the waves, but he only shrugged and held his hand to his stomach.

As he went below-decks he could imagine Helyard back on the pier, grumpily agreeing to Åddren's stern orders. The breakers crashed around the bow of the ship again and she lurched awkwardly. Spray decorated the deck as the *Sarunn* loitered on the first few big waves before the helmsman got the hand of the winter swell and set her on course again.

Heold watched Farden leave, a disconcerting cloud of doubt filled his old mind.

Mages were bad omens.

The first two days of the trip were uneventful. The *Sarunn* rounded the west coast and made for the channel between the beaches of west Midgrir and the stunted cliffs of Albion.

The weather remained fine for the first few hundred miles or so, but as they rounded the coastline to head towards the Jörmunn Sea, past the cliff cities of Halôrn, it changed. Clouds began to pile up and darken, bringing squalls and bitter gales to hammer down on the ship.

Farden hid in his room, feeling every pitch and roll of the vessel in his uncomfortable wooden bed. Everything in his cabin was nailed to the floor, which made sword practice impossible, and made everything creak and groan. The bucket had been filled and emptied several times over the first day, but now Farden was finally rid of his massive headache and nausea. His magick however, had not returned in the slightest, and he could feel his tattoo lying dormant on his back like a heavy weight. The mage spent most of his time meditating, trying to get his power back, or absently mapping the stars when the deck was quiet enough.

More than a few times, Farden found himself lying awake on the cold nights, thinking about Cheska, then waking up to find nothing and nobody beside him but faded dreams. Farden tried to ignore the rolling ship and instead stared at the wooden ceiling, picturing her beautiful eyes in his tired mind, thinking long and hard about her body, her laugh, and a hundred other things. Like their future. He wondered what she was doing, where she was, and whether he would be back before she started the Ritual. The ghosts of fear slowly crept back into his mind.

On the afternoon of the first day, a small black cat had found its way into his room. Farden assumed it was the ship's cat, a good luck charm against bad weather, and let the creature wander about his room, investigating everything as cats must do. She sniffed and pawed at his clothes and every corner of the small room for an hour before finally curling into a neat black ball on his pillow.

Feeling a little used, Farden consented to let the animal sleep in his room all day, until it finally disappeared at dinner time. Once, when she had looked at him, Farden had felt something scratching in his mind like déjà vu. Her little brown eyes gazed at him placidly for a while before returning to lick her paws. He dismissed it but found himself watching her and wondering from then on.

Farden walked along the decks during a murky dawn on the third day, accompanied by the lithe black cat, whom he had named Lazy. He attempted to cast small spells in the half-light. Much to his dismay, the magick still rebounded against his head. His study of the stars at night seemed to calm his mind, and his stomach for that matter, though the sea-swell played havoc with him, every now and again.

Later, purely out of boredom and curiosity, Farden took the tearbook from its satchel and flipped idly through the blank pages. They seemed pure and untouched, only yellowed at the very edges. Grey dust filled the cracks in the spine and had settled between the overlapping dragon scales that were a dull, metallic yellow. No trace of any script or writing could be found in the entire book, Farden even tried holding the thin pages up to the light streaming through his small windows. *Nothing*. He gave up with a sigh and replaced the tearbook under his pillow.

Time felt like treacle in the ship and Farden soon grew to hate the constant wary looks from the superstitious sailors. He had already found a greying crewman praying to the old sea god Njord outside his room, trying to attach a cheap-looking charm to his door. Farden had slammed it hard and scowled at the noises of the man nervously scuttling away down the corridor.

Most of the weathered crew were bothered by Farden; all that they knew was that he was responsible for leading them towards a forbidden land, and that didn't make them happy. He was unlucky and unwanted. Everyone seemed to ignore him or stay out of his way, even the soldiers.

They'd made an effort to talk to the solitary mage only once. But Farden hadn't been in the mood to socialise, and his clipped answers had slighted the men. They soon made their excuses and left. What rumours they might have heard about Farden were soon circulated around the superstitious crew. To a certain extent it suited him fine. It meant he was left alone for the rest of the journey.

Only Lazy seemed interested in him. The little thing was happy to curl up beside him at night, purring away softly like a bubbling pot all night until their morning walk.

❦

The next day, dawn found Farden making his way up to the forecastle. He had left the cat fast asleep in his room and wandered across the deck alone. Fingers of light crept along the eastern horizon amongst dark clouds and faraway cliffs. The patchwork sea of blue-green light and shadow foamed and roiled in deep swells. The mage stood at the railing, looking at the skies. A huge bank of storm clouds lingered ahead of them, the shadow of rain falling over the sea.

Someone coughed nearby. A man stood on watch to his right, and Farden recognised him as the man he had seen staring at him on the first day. He stood stiff, back straight, holding his arms crossed behind him.

'Mornin', mate,' the man coughed a rough greeting. He had a thick accent, probably from southern Albion.

'Morning,' Farden replied. He nodded towards the black clouds. 'Weather looks bad.'

The man nodded. 'Looks fairly bad, I agree. Cap'n should ride 'er well.' He was a thin, wiry man, strong-looking despite his size, with heavily calloused hands. He had a square face that was punctuated by a sharp nose. His short black hair was slicked flat to his head. He wore the dark green uniform of the ship's crew. A mole sat on his upper lip. The sailor was a head shorter than the mage, twitchy and energetic in his quick movements. In Farden's mind, he looked like a hawk waiting for his prey. He didn't like the way the man stared at him.

'Good,' said the mage.

'Take it ye don't like the water then?' A smirk curled on the man's face.

'I like it fine.' Farden thought of the tearbook in the sack by his side.

The sailor chuckled. 'Karga's the name.' A hand followed the name, and Farden shook it firmly.

'Farden.'

Karga nodded. 'Aye, I know.'

'You have a fine captain, it seems.' Farden made idle conversation as he listened to the splash of the waves beneath the ship.

The sailor shrugged. 'I wouldn't really know. He seems a fine fellow, but I'm jus' a stand-in for this voyage. Other man got sick.'

'I see.'

'Plague probably. A lot of it goin' around in the east.'

'Mm.' Farden began to feel the conversation dwindling. He nodded to the man and made for the steps. As he was walking away the sailor called to him in a gruff voice.

'Oi, mate, look at this.'

Farden turned and followed the direction of the sailor's pointing finger. In the clouds up ahead something was happening, something that Farden had never seen before.

Between a gap in the immense storm-front, wisps of cloud began to knit together, forming two shapes that towered above the seas. They reared out of the clouds and stood upright to face each other, looking for all the world like two brawny men carved from cloud. And then they began to move. Thunder rumbled, and Farden moved closer to the railing to stare in amazement. One lashed out at the other with a gigantic fist, lightning crackling from its fingers. Wind whipped the waves into foam, and a deafening burst of thunder rocked the ship.

'Storm giants!' yelled Karga, and the helmsman wrenched the ship's wheel away from the stormy duel. Sudden rain lashed the ship, and Farden ran down the steps so he could watch the immense creatures battling.

The giants lunged at each other, throwing punch after punch until the sky shook and the crew cowered around the mast. But as quickly as they had appeared, they died away, and after a few more thunderclaps the giants melted back into the clouds. The sailor at the wheel calmly resumed course, and Heold bumbled out his cabin sleepily to see what all the commotion was about.

'What in the shit is goin' on?' he bellowed, adjusting his wide belt.

Karga shouted from the forecastle. 'Storm giants, cap'n! They're gone now though, disappeared into the storm-front!' Heold squinted at the clouds and frowned. Satisfied that he had missed most of the action and wasn't needed anymore, he headed back to his bed.

'Fine. Wake me in an hour,' he ordered. By the time he had slammed the door Farden was already back in his cabin.

Despite the rocking of the ship and the bad weather, the mage fell into a deep sleep until later the next day. He awoke to find the rain still lashing his window. He groaned and pulled the blanket further around his head. He'd had enough of this voyage. The tearbook nudged his hand from its hiding place under his pillow and he dragged it towards him. The big book propped up his head nicely under the thin lump of cloth. Farden wondered what the council, or the dragons for that matter, would think of him using the tearbook as a pillow.

He let himself doze for about an hour before rising and heading sleepily to the galley. Lazy the cat was nowhere to be seen.

Farden ducked under the doorframe of the ship's kitchen and looked around. The goat was nibbling at grain in the corner of the tiny room while the cook was cleaning dishes.

'All right there, sir?' asked the cook as he wiped a bowl with a dirty cloth.

Farden stretched and stifled a yawn. 'Fine, thanks, I was just wondering if there's any lunch still left over? I seem to have missed it.' He moved forwards and knocked his forehead on a beam.

The man smiled, stifling a polite chuckle. 'Farska's in the pan, or there's some shark 'ere that the first mate caught,' he said, lifting the lid of an earthenware bowl. The smell of the fishy stew filled Farden with ravenous hunger. He dug in with a wooden spoon that didn't look too clean and filled a bowl that had a splintered edge. The mage was too hungry to care. He had eaten worse and from worse.

'There'll be summin' new tomorrow as well.' The cook threw a covert nod in the direction of the fat goat. The poor animal stopped chewing and looked at the two men. There was an awkward silence.

'Well, I'll see you tomorrow then.' Farden smiled briefly and swiftly turned to go. He carried his bowl of fish stew to his room and stared at the steel waves rolling out behind the ship. Farden sighed, consigning himself to another day of feeling powerless and empty from the lack of magick.

It was odd that a strange desire for nevermar had begun to creep into his mind over the last day, a craving to taste that acrid smoke on his tongue again, to feel the familiar numbing in his arms and legs. Farden guiltily pushed the notion from his head, trying to concentrate on his meal.

The shark was salty, and the meagre vegetables floating around his bowl were bereft of colour or taste, but it was food, nonetheless. Farden sipped the hot liquid carefully.

The drug was forbidden for a reason, he reminded himself. Nevermar's magick-numbing power was legendary, and for over a hundred years the council had opposed it with vicious measures.

When Farden had been in training at the Spire, a mage had been caught with nevermar in his room. He had swiftly disappeared and was never even spoken of again. It had been the death penalty for that man, dangling by his entrails from the city gate as an example to all. Farden shuddered.

But it calmed him, made him think less about the dark things in his mind, the fears, the second-guessing. Despite its undesirable effect, Farden had realised that he needed it; that it helped him. Over the years he had been incredibly careful to keep it a secret. The idea of anyone, especially Cheska, finding out was unthinkable, but he was too meticulous, too wary, to be discovered, and so far he hadn't done any harm to anyone besides himself. All that really mattered now was that his magick returned before they arrived in Nelska. He focused on getting through his bland stew and attempted to quiet his thoughts.

On the ship, his mind felt bored and unused. He could feel himself beginning to ramble in his own head, slowly going mad from constantly sitting in his tiny cabin.

With a sigh, Farden resigned himself to going outside, raining or not. He finished his shark, sipped the dregs from the bowl, and threw his hood over his head. He looked at his reflection in the dirty window, thumbing the stubble sprouting from his chin. He would have to shave before they reached Nelska. He relieved himself in the bucket in the corner and left the room.

Farden emerged onto a windblown deck and immediately regretted his decision. Everything had been tied down, and the deck was slick with salty spray and rain. Heold was at the helm, his beard matted and glistening. The big man laughed at seeing the mage.

'If ye didn't like the weather before, ye ain't goin' t' like it now!' he shouted.

As if the sea had heard him, the *Sarunn* dove into a low trough between two waves and yawed sluggishly. Farden's stomach rolled with the waves. He stared at the foam swirling around his boots and tried not to think of the shark stew.

The ship battled on bravely in the roiling carpet of white-capped waves. Overhead, thick black clouds crackled with light and thunder. Daylight was slowly fading, and in the gloom the sailors clung desperately to rigging and ropes, trying to work through the rain and the wailing wind.

'I got bored of my room!' Farden shouted, shrugging at the captain, but Heold was too busy fighting the wheel. A stubborn wish to confront the awful weather made Farden want to go and stand at the railing.

The mage pulled his hood around his face to ward off the stinging rain and headed up to the bow. From there he peered into the storm and tried to make sense of the grey world. He couldn't see any difference between the waves and the granite sky. It was all just one tumultuous mess.

A wave hit the poor unicorn beneath its hooves and the *Sarunn* buried her nose in the surf.

Only one more day to go, Farden thought, remembering Heold's words. He patted his side and realised he had left the tearbook under his pillow in his room.

The mage pivoted on his heel and ran back down the wet steps to the deck. He felt odd, and a weird glow of unrest felt its way into his already queasy stomach. He made his way below and pushed the door to his cabin open with a bang.

The pillow was lying on the damp floor, and Karga stood hunched over the bed, flicking lazily through the pages of the tearbook. The sailor looked up, mildly surprised, and the two men shared an awkward, deadly silence.

'What the fuck are you doing?' blurted Farden.

The sailor stared at the mage with a smirk. 'I knew you wouldn't leave it for long,' he said, looking down at the blank pages. 'He was right; it is empty.'

'Get away from the tearbook,' Farden stepped further into the room. He thought of his sword leaning against the wall behind the door. It was just out of reach, so he took another careful step.

'Whatever you say, Farden.' The sailor held his hands in the air and stepped backwards. 'Whatever you say.'

'What are you doing with my book?' Farden growled. He grabbed his sword from behind the door and pulled it from the scabbard. He pointed it at Karga.

'You have no idea what's going on, do you?' Karga narrowed his eyes and flashed another toothy smile. Farden noticed scars criss-crossing his palms. The ship tilted underneath them.

'Wipe that smile off your face or I'll throw you overboard!'

'I'd like to see you try.'

Farden fumed. 'I think we should see what Heold has to say about this.'

He motioned the door with his sword. Karga didn't move a muscle. Farden burnt with anger. He was confused, thrown off-guard by the sailor's smug expression. There was something very wrong about this.

'Move! Get out!' Farden yelled, but Karga reached out towards him with crooked fingers, palms glowing.

A searing ball of ash and cinders hit the mage in the chest, knocking him straight through the wall of his cabin. Splintered wood and smoke filled the corridor.

Farden coughed and spat and flailed his limbs. He swung his sword blindly and dragged himself around the corner. He felt his skull throbbing as he brushed burning coals from his charred breastplate. Farden's mind raced like a diving falcon as he peered into the smoke.

'Come out here and fight!' shouted Karga. A bolt of lightning tore through the hole in the wall and exploded in the corridor with a screech. Somewhere in the darkness, between the decks, the goat bleated pitifully.

'I'm right here, Karga, come and find me!'

Farden listened to the crunch of boots on the deck, coming towards him. He waited, slowing his breathing and concentrating on not choking, listening intently for the right moment to pounce. Another few footsteps, and Farden spied a shape peering through the hole.

With a yell, he swung his sword at his assailant's head. Karga spun around and held his hands up to block the swing. Just before the blade carved through his fingers, a pulse of energy burst from his palms and the sword rebounded with a clang. Farden swung again, thrusting deadly steel into the man's face, but again Karga blocked and the sword bounced away with a whine.

'Who are you?!' barked Farden.

His assailant dodged another swipe and laughed. 'The man who was sent to kill you!'

He screamed as Farden's blade notched his shoulder. He grabbed the sword with his left hand and sent lightning scattering along the steel.

'Argh!' Farden yelped as the magick shook him. With a purposeful lunge, he slammed his forehead into Karga's nose. The sailor's head snapped backwards. Blood sprayed from his face. Farden followed up with a fist to his stomach, then an elbow into the man's neck. Karga fell backwards against the wall. Some of the sailors had heard the noise and gathered around a nearby hatch.

'Karga!' shouted one of the men. 'What's going on?'

Karga ignored them. He breathed heavily. 'You can't fight me with magick, Farden? What's wrong? I was told you would be fun! A fair match for a sorcerer of my strength.'

Karga's eyes flashed a deep red. *This man had dark magick in him*, thought Farden, *a servant of the forbidden shades of magick.*

Before he could react, Karga clenched his fist and shouted foreign words. The shadows in the dim underbelly of the ship came alive and grabbed at the mage. Farden cried out as a black hand pulled at his face and hair. Shadowy fingers groped around his feet.

Swinging his sword left and right, he dove behind a tall pile of boxes and scrambled deeper into the ship. A ball of hot ashes exploded over his head, sparks showering his hood. A dark shadow snatched at him but he escaped its grasp and ran for the galley.

'Fuckin' fight me!' Karga yelled over the roar of his spells.

Farden dodged under beams and pans and grabbed the sturdy wooden rail of a ladder. Another spell sent cinders flying across the ship's kitchen, singeing the poor goat. Farden pushed the hatch above him, and luckily it came free.

Rain sprayed his face, momentarily blinding him. He leapt up the ladder and onto the deck, where he stood with his sword low. Sailors shouted out to Heold, who was still at the wheel.

'What's goin' on 'ere?!' bellowed the big captain. The sky flashed with white-blue light and thunder boomed. Farden yelled over the howling storm.

'It's one of your crew! Karga! He's been sent to ruin this mission!'

Heold scowled, turning his attention back to the wheel.

The mage wiped spray from his face and tried to catch his breath. *Gods damn that old man and his nevermar*, he cursed inwardly. He needed his magick back. And fast.

A fireball streaked across the deck and struck the mast. The wet sails thankfully didn't catch fire, but the splintered wood creaked and sparked all the same. With fearful cries, the crew ran for cover.

A voice shouted over the howling rain. Karga had found his way to the stairs near the forecastle. 'You can't win, Farden!'

'And you should know better than to interfere with the banned magicks!'

His opponent poked his head above a crate and grinned lopsidedly. 'I just do what my masters tell me!' He shrugged. 'I'm here for you, and you only. That's my payment. The famous Farden, dead at my hands.'

Farden growled. 'Where's the manual?'

Another ball of magma tore over Farden's head and ploughed into the angry sea with a hiss. Karga spat and laughed. 'You'll never find it!'

He sidled along the opposite side of the deck like a hungry eel. Farden crouched behind a wooden skylight, watching him. This sorcerer was strong, true, but he was just a man. Every man can be broken. All he needed was his magick.

Karga called out to him again. 'You're wasting your time! Who knows where it could be by now?' He laughed sadistically.

A sailor with an axe jumped down from the forecastle stairs and strode across the deck to face up to him, holding his weapon high. Karga paused. The storm howled around the two men. Every eye on the ship was upon them, silent and transfixed.

With lightning speed, Karga pounced on the sailor, knocking the axe from his grip and wrapping his hands around his neck. White-hot ash seared the flesh from his bones, and the man gave a gargling scream before tumbling into the green-grey waves.

The crew dissolved into pandemonium. They scurried over the deck, yelling and trying to get as far away from the two mages as possible. Heold shouted from the wheel, trying to rally his men, keeping one eye on the treacherous sea and the other on the danger on his deck.

'Man the mast, lads! Take those sails down!'

The *Sarunn* pitched violently over trough and crest. Farden clanged his sword off the mast as he tried to block a fork of purple lightning. The spell knocked Farden against the back railing, inches from the edge of the ship. He moved away from the sea, taking cover behind a crate. Farden put a hand to his back and winced. Something stirred in his spine, a tingling across his broad shoulders that the mage knew very well indeed. Farden smiled and crouched low, stalking his prey.

It was his turn.

Karga ducked under the railings of some stairs and peered through the pouring rain. Sparks crackled around his fingers as he waited for the mage to show his head. 'Come out, coward!' he shouted. He wiped blood from his nose and spat on the deck.

'Up here,' a gruff voice barked, and Karga looked up to see a boot heading rapidly for his face. The vicious kick sent him sprawling onto the deck with a flurry of bloody seawater.

Farden dropped from the forecastle to the stairs and rested his sword on his shoulder. Karga was ready. Farden swung his blade up, but the man blocked it again, and again, but on the third swipe the blade sliced across his chest and cut a long gash through his tunic. Karga yelled, reeling backwards. Farden was on his feet in an instant.

'You want to see some magick?' Farden ripped his hood back in defiance. His eyes blazed.

At the wheel, Heold's face drained of colour and his shout chilled everyone on board.

'WAVE!'

And with that Farden's world seemed to pause.

His arms lifted through the slowing rain, single droplets sliding over his hands like clear mercury. A lightning bolt tore the sky and froze, stopped in an eternal moment. The air thrummed with magick. Farden could feel the tattoos on his back burning white with heat and fire. He braced himself on the slippery deck, feeling the weight of the spell push him against the wet wood with a squelch in his boots.

The mage took a deep breath and stared into Karga's glowing eyes. There was a look of fear suspended on his face. Farden looked up as flame trickled over his wrists, watching the rogue wave arch over the masthead above them. For the briefest of moments, time stopped and the world around him became quiet. But it was short-lived. As the deck began to shake beneath his boots, the roaring began anew, and time caught up with itself.

With a blast of searing heat, a tower of fire erupted from beneath the deck and ripped through the wood as if it were nothing more than paper. Karga flew from the splintered deck, screaming, swathed in flames, and disappeared into the sea. Farden reeled backwards as the spell consumed the mast and the sails and tore into the wave hanging above. Fire met seawater in an explosion of burning debris and steam, then the wave hit the deck.

Heold's frenzied shouts were drowned out as the wave tumbled onto the ship with the force of a falling mountain. Farden grabbed the rail behind him, clinging on desperately as the vessel rocked under the watery avalanche. The wave washed the sailors from the deck, tossing them into the sea like broken marbles. They shrieked as they hit the icy water.

The mage was almost torn away, but the water receded as the *Sarunn* somehow rode the crest and recovered. Farden was washed sideways across the deck towards a hatch. He grabbed at it. His head pounded, and he felt the sickening dizziness of the spell's wake. Karga was nowhere to be seen, and the charred mast sounded like it was about to snap, splintering into matchsticks around the base with whip-like cracking sounds and a terrible groaning.

'Farden, what have you done?' Heold was on his belly on the top deck, wallowing like a manatee in the salty water.

'It was Karga!' lied Farden. He looked around desperately. The ship was going down fast. Water was now pouring through the gaping hole in the deck. Farden stared wide-eyed and fearful at the seawater gushing into the belly of the ship. The fire spell and the wave had ripped the *Sarunn* almost in two, and now she was floundering, miles and miles from shore in a turbulent sea. Several members of the crew still clung to the rigging, screaming for Njord to save them. Farden didn't expect him to intervene.

He half-ran, half-fell down the stairs, his boots splashing in the rising water. It was icy cold and stabbed like daggers into his waist and chest. He had to get to the tearbook.

Farden ran down the stairs and corridor, diving over broken wooden planks and floating charcoal. He pushed the door to his room open and strode through the flotsam and jetsam. The ship was falling apart quicker than he thought.

'Where are you?' he shouted. Farden was panicking now. The tearbook wasn't on his bed, but he soon found it hiding under the mattress in the water. He tore away his cloak and breastplate and kicked off his heavy boots so that they didn't drown him. Grabbing the sack and the rest of his supplies, he sloshed through the rising seawater and made his way back up to the deck. Once there he tried to get as far away from the water as possible, moving towards the wheel.

Farden shivered in the lashing rain. The *Sarunn* was now pitching on her port side and the ship was beginning to crack in two. Farden found Heold still lying on his front, shouting to his remaining crew, clinging onto the wheel to keep from being washed away. Farden wondered if the captain had broken his back, then he saw his legs. A spar of broken wood had skewered one and smashed the other to a pulp. The captain's shins were a mass of broken bone and bloody flesh.

'Get off the ship, lad! She's done for!' Heold shouted at the mage in a hoarse voice.

'What happened to you?' Farden watched him grimace in pain. 'You have to get off the ship!'

'Cap'n goes down with 'is ship is what I 'eard! Ain't no way I'll make it in the sea tonight!' he bellowed, his face twisted in agony.

'Gods damn it!' Farden cursed at the defeated old man. A few sailors and one of the Arka soldiers, who was furiously shedding his heavy steel armour, clambered over the flooded deck. Farden grabbed a broken hatch cover and futilely threw it into the sea. Then he spied a section of a broken wooden box tied to the railing. He hacked at it with his sword until it came loose, then stood holding it, waiting for the sea to swallow the *Sarunn*.

In heart-thudding panic, Farden watched the hungry waves climbing further and further into the ship with every second. He narrowed his eyes, steeled his reserve, hauled his box to the opposite railing and threw it into the sea. The wind howled around him, threatening to rip the tearbook from his side, but Farden grabbed the strap and yanked it hard.

The mage steadied himself on the railing against the force of the storm and waited for his moment to leap. But from somewhere behind him there came a deep rending crack. Something struck him hard on the back of the skull. Farden fell down into the angry sea and into a dark dream.

part two

FOLLOW THE DRAGONS

Chapter 7

It was at this time that the Scribe came to us, the secret behind a Written's strength, and a great and powerful wing of the magick council came to exist, charged to watch over the dark forces left behind by the elves. The peers of the Arka factions were now under a great duty; to see that the powers of good were exercised in the wild lands of Emaneska, and that direction and order was brought to the people. This was, of course, before the greed of the rich sought to pervert the power of the Twin Thrones, when one by one the members of the council turned their minds from justice and good, and wanted for gold and power instead.

Arkmage Olfar, writing in the year 789

Choke.

Water flooded his nose and ran down his throat like a runaway avalanche of salty black liquid.

The sea pulled at his hands, feet and clothes with ice-cold fingers. His world switched between the roar of the storm and the inky deafness of underwater. Up was down. Water replaced air.

Lightning fizzed in the darkness. Somewhere above or below him the clouds slammed together. Stars swam in his head and invisible gods played with his rag-doll body. He felt like his body was swimming away from him, and he could taste his own blood amidst the salt. The carcass of the drowned goat knocked against him, stuck somewhere in the tangling rigging.

Breathe.

Rain-soaked air, seawater and bile fought for room in his throat. He felt something under his swollen fingers and grabbed it with the last vestiges of strength in his weary body.

Hold fast.

Ropes dragged at raw cuts and lashed him to the crate that kept him afloat. His forehead found a resting place against the salty wood.

Darkness.

Farden shivered in his desert and rubbed at his cold arms and legs. He looked down at his pale naked body, at his wrinkly skin from too much soaking in water, and at the damp patch in the cracked earth under his feet. His vambraces lay rusty and covered in drying seaweed in the dust beside him, one on either side.

Breathe, something said. Farden turned his head to see a skinny black cat, soaked to the bone, sitting near to him amongst the stones. Its ragged fur steamed in the hot sun. A dead, rotting bird full of maggots sat at its feet. Empty eye sockets stared at the sky. Farden looked up, and his pale blue emptiness bubbled and wavered, as if he were looking at the surface of a placid sea. He lifted a finger, and sent ripples spreading out across the vast, cloudless sky. His skin felt wet. There was a rumbling. The sun flashed.

'I am breathing,' he said.

Not for long, replied the voice, and the cat licked its bedraggled paw.

A scout walked alone on the rocky beach. Pockmarked volcanic stones mingled amongst grey shale and pale sand, all crunching under his slender boots. The spear in his hand held him steady against the slippery stones and green seaweed. From under a white hood, purple eyes scanned the grey waves rolling up the beach, while a scaly nose sniffed the salty air. The scout watched the first few shafts of new sunlight pierce the rainclouds, feeling the fresh, westerly wind wrapping around his skin. *Should be a calm day*, he thought to himself, as he breathed deep to let the smell of the salt fill his head.

The scout pulled his white cloak about him and swapped his grip on the spear so he could warm his colder hand in his pocket. He coughed a rattling hiss and walked on, still scanning the beach.

He stopped, crouching by a rocky outcrop. Something had caught his keen eye. A shape lay in the surf.

The scaled man hopped nimbly over the stones, sending sand flying from his boots as he ran over the beach towards the shape. Within moments he reached it, and circled it warily, feet splashing in the shallow water. It looked like a crate, or a door. A mass of ropes and rigging lay useless and tangled in the sand.

Using his sharp spearpoint, he peeled away the matted weed and knotted ropes to reveal the long-dead eyes of a goat, bloated and swollen from the seawater. It grinned at him in death, and its cloudy gaze stared in different directions. He grimaced at the smell of the animal and poked at the rest of the sodden lump.

The scout spied something that looked like a shoe poking out from under a slimy section of wood, and crouched to investigate further. It was a boot, with a foot and leg attached to it.

The scout tore apart the wooden crate in a spray of green weed and water to find a bedraggled corpse lying curled up and half-buried in the sand. Kneeling at its side, he poked and prodded at the face of a beaten man. He looked to be in his thirties, probably from the southeast, with matted dark hair and red-gold vambraces on his arms. He held his spear blade over the man's mouth, and saw a thin mist of breath appear on the shiny steel. The scout slapped the man's face, feeling his chest for a heartbeat. Something stirred there, maybe a faint hint of life.

The scout brought a fist down on the man's chest, at the point where the ribs joined, and the washed-up man began to splutter, retching bile and seawater. He opened his red-rimmed eyes to find a shiny spear blade waving in his face and closed them again to drift back into unconsciousness. With a sigh, the scout seized him by the hem of his tunic and lifted.

'Where'd you find him?'

'On the beach near the southwest corner. Should have been dead, the poor bastard, but somehow there's life in him.' The scout shrugged, trying to rub warmth back into his hands. His white cloak was dripping wet and covered in sand, and brown seaweed tangled in clumps around his wrists.

'Arka, by the look of him.' The healer had the appearance of an ageing crow, and the voice of one, too. He was hunched over the wooden table, murmuring thoughtfully somewhere deep in his throat. His long hair hung in wet strands over his squinting green eyes. His scales were the colour of tree moss. The Siren rubbed his chin as he examined the man spread out on the table below him.

He looked like death, or something very close to it. He shivered convulsively and clawed at the wooden table as if it could give off heat. Like the scout, he was also covered in sand and seaweed, but his skin was pale like paper and as cold as ice. His cloak and tunic were ripped and snagged with splinters of driftwood. He looked altogether wretched. A little black bundle of something lay by his side.

'What's that?' asked the healer, pointing.

The scout carefully turned it over to reveal a dishevelled mess of black fur and whiskers. 'I, erm, think it's a cat. It was near to where I found him.'

'Well, what's it doing here?'

'The thing's still breathing, don't ask me how, but it is. It must belong to him.' The scout gestured to the man with a scaly hand. 'After all the little thing's been through.' He shrugged.

The healer shook his head despairingly. 'Fine, leave it with me. I'll have him taken to my rooms and I'll see who he is, *if* he lives, that is.' He paused, spying something colourful under Farden's torn sleeve. He shifted his long grey hair from his eyes and peered down his beak-like nose. He looked up, a confused look plastered in his face. 'Scalussen vambraces?'

The scout nodded. 'I know. This isn't just some washed up sailor.' He paused. 'The queen might need to hear of this.'

The healer took a moment to think, then waved his hands. 'Yes yes, after I get him back to health. He can't go far as he is. Here, I'll send for my guard to take him to my house, and *yes*, I'll take care of that mangy animal.' The old healer gestured to someone behind him, and a nervous young boy, previously silent in a corner, ran off to fetch help.

'I'll send a messenger to the palace.' The scout turned to go, but the healer held up a hand to stop him.

'*I* will do that, when he is ready to be interrogated. At the moment he is too weak to be questioned. This man is at death's door.'

The scout looked as if he would say something but thought better of arguing. He nodded. 'Fine with me. Good day, sir.'

'And to you.' The healer watched the scout go, then turned back to the wretched man on the table. He poked under the red and gold vambraces, peering down his beak-like nose at the symbols tattooed on the man's wrists. The man's emerald eyes widened. His bony hands scraped at the rotting wet tunic on his patient's back and pulled the fabric aside to reveal something that made the breath catch in his throat.

At that moment the guards knocked on the door, and the healer quickly replaced the tunic. The man was taken further into the mountain on a cart covered by a blanket, headed for a locked room in the healer's house.

That night, the healer quietly padded down the corridor leading to his guest's room, holding nothing but a tallow candle tightly in his hand; a hand that quivered with anticipation and a hint of excitement. His bony fingers fiddled with the key in the lock and he took a few breaths to calm his eager heart. The lock clicked, and he shut the door behind him. The healer lifted the candle high to light the square room.

The man lay prone and unconscious on a wooden table in the middle of the floor. The grey Siren slowly crept forwards and ran his fingers across the man's feverish brow. He put his ear to his mouth and listened to the shallow ragged breaths sneaking in and out between cracked lips. The healer sniffed.

He put the candle down on the edge of the table then pulled a slim knife from under his nightgown. It took all his strength to turn the man over and get him onto his front, but finally he did it, and began to slice through his ragged tunic. Cloth parted, betraying the black lettering hiding underneath. The old healer grinned to himself and squinted. He balanced his little glasses on the very edge of his nose and tugged loose the remaining strands of tunic. Shaking hands moved the candle closer.

After what seemed like hours of reading, he paused to stretch, yawn and rub his eyes. His eyelids felt like they were burning. The yellow light of the dying candle was beginning to fade. As his eyes lingered on the mage's Book, the healer reached to snuff out the flickering flame, but caught it with the back of his hand instead, knocking it to the floor where it spat and dribbled wax on the flagstones. He cursed and bent to pick it up.

He froze.

There was something in the room with him.

A huge shadow fell over him like a blanket and the Siren shivered with sudden cold. He let out a squeak as his throat closed up with fear. He scrabbled for the candle. Whispering voices called his name and he rubbed his eyes again to try to rid of himself of the shadows dancing around him. He wiped his face. Blood from his nose smeared his fingers.

A terrified wail broke from the Siren's throat as he bolted for the door, leaving the candle to die alone on the floor. Breath caught at the back of his throat and his heart jumped in his chest. He groped for the key in the darkness. Terror gripped him tight. All he could do was run. He fled down the dark corridor, listening to the whispers and shrieks biting at his heels.

He skidded and fell into his room, slammed the door, and groped about in the darkness for his bed, his only refuge.

Ghosts threw the fingers of dead men at his door. They scraped at the walls, calling his name as he quivered beneath a blanket and several pillows.

Dark letters swam around his eyes and sleep flew from him like a murder of crows. They danced and fluttered their terrible black wings, swarming his room with cawing and scratching, reminding him of every mistake he had ever made, every bad thing he had ever done. The old Siren sobbed, huddled in a ball under the blanket.

In a dark room down the corridor, a tallow candle finally burnt out on the cold flagstones. A man breathed heavily in the dark. Farden was dreaming his way through a deep, healing sleep, the magick beginning to knit his beaten body back together.

'Why am I here?' Farden asked.

You tell me, said the voice. The cat looked at him with the same deadpan look as always.

'I don't even know this place,' said Farden, annoyed. He looked up, trying to melt into his cerulean sky, trying to leave the aching pain in his body behind.

It's a little of you, and a little of me.

'Well, who are you then?'

I'm trying to help.

'If you wanted to help, you'd get me out of here. You'd help me up and make the pain go away. You'd get me back to Krauslung and you'd help me find the book and save Emaneska.' Farden sighed, feeling the weight of his sky pushing down on him. The heat was unbearable this time. 'I never asked for this.'

The cat yawned and stretched. Its skinny black tail swished back and forth through the dust. *We never do*, said the deep voice in his head. *We never ask for this, nor do we ever complain, we just do what we're told. It's what people like you and I do. We fight for the world and we never ask for anything in return. That is the life of a Written.*

'Who are you?' asked Farden. A wind whined through the desert, a cold cackling wind that whipped the sand into spirals and eddies.

I'm just like you.

'You're nothing like me,' Farden scoffed.

The voice sounded disappointed but earnest. *Keep an eye on the weather, Farden, there's more to this than first appears. You've found the dragons, now listen to them.*

'Leave me alone, I don't need your help. I don't need anybody,' said Farden, crossing his arms stubbornly. The whirling sand whipped his face, and in the spinning dust he discerned faces; faces of Cheska, of Durnus, of Vice, and an old face that he hadn't seen in a very long time. Grit burnt his eyes. Hot tears were stolen by the wind.

As you wish. Keep an eye on the weather.

Something rustled near him. Hay scattered and an animal snuffled. Farden kept his eyes tightly closed. His body ached in a thousand places and his wrists were raw against iron shackles. Straw pricked his back and the wall behind his head was ice-cold. Farden could feel the heat of a fever burning his forehead. Cold chains encircled his wrists. He could tell his vambraces were missing. He was surprised to feel that he still wore his cloak, ripped and torn as it was, but the sackcloth tunic he wore under it felt strange and rough. He idly wondered where his old one was, and who had dressed him, but a ripple of sickening dizziness brought him back to the matter at hand.

He clenched his jaw and slowly, ever so slowly, opened his eyes to peer around the unfamiliar chamber. There was a disgusting stench in the air.

The room was forged from grey granite walls, square and low with a matching floor, and hay was strewn about him. The only apparent entrance was a stout pine door. The source of the smell was an upturned bucket in the corner. Its foul contents lay in a puddle on the floor. A whispering came from his right, along with a nervous rattling of shackles. Farden turned his head gradually. A cackle echoed in the cell.

Chained to the wall, about six feet from him, sat a dishevelled character: a mere shell of a Siren man inside which lunacy had taken up residence. Wide green platters of rapt madness now peered out from the places where eyes used to sit, and a wide curve of yellow teeth half-hid behind dangling tendrils of matted grey hair thick with filth and dung. The Siren cackled and spat; his thin tongue darted like a lizard's.

'The mage! Awake from his dark sleep!' he laughed, cross-eyed.

Farden backed further away from the madman. It was like stepping back in time to a painful memory. He had witnessed this before; in his own uncle the last time he had seen him. The sharp similarity of it made him feel sick.

The Siren foamed at the mouth, grinning and pawing at the mage. It was obvious what had happened. Only a Book could break a man so.

The Book carved into a Written's back was strictly not for reading. The raw magick in the script could warp the mind of a weaker person. There was a reason the tattoo was placed on the shoulders and back, and why the Written were sworn to keep it concealed at all times. It was the reason Farden was so keen to keep inquisitive people like Elessi out of harm's way.

The mad Siren kept reaching out to the mage, rolling his eyes madly. His broken fingernails found cracks in the granite floor and left bloody scrapes on the stone. The resemblance to his uncle was unsettling; a dark memory dug up and dumped at his feet.

'Where'd you go, mage? Where'd you go? Dark dreams you had. Dark dreams indeed!' he hooted, then muttered to himself. 'Dreamdreamdream, stuck in a desert.'

'Be quiet!' Farden shouted.

The man twitched and snuffled. 'Hah! I've read your mind! Felt the lines on your back, felt the writing on my fingers calling to me.' The Siren grinned a smile so wide Farden thought he might break his face.

'Silence!' came a muffled shout.

There was a bang on the door, and heavy bolts slid from their holes. Half a dozen guards burst through the wide doorway and rushed in to grab the two prisoners. One soldier hit the mad Siren around the head with a club and he fell to the floor with a cry.

'Do not move!' another shouted, inches from Farden's face. He froze. Heavy keys jiggled in the locks around his wrists and he fell to the floor in a flurry of hay. Farden was hauled upright and roughly dragged from the room, with the shouts of his raving cellmate ringing in his ears.

'Beware the dragons, mage! They'll steal your soul!' he screamed, before being silenced by a kick.

'Where are you taking me?' Farden coughed weakly. His body screamed out to him in pain.

'Shut it, Arka, He wants to speak with you,' the man hissed through a grille in his helmet. Farden saw a mouth ringed with blue scales.

'Who—?'

The Siren narrowed his eyes. 'No more questions!' He elbowed him hard in an already burning rib.

Farden was silent for the rest of the journey—or more appropriately, *dragging*. He drifted lazily in and out of a feverish consciousness. He was manhandled up steps and through corridors, along bridges and across bustling thoroughfares filled with gawking Siren citizens. Pain from a hundred cuts and bruises blurred with his fever.

He was hauled onto a wide bridge that arched over a massive cave carpeted by rolling fields. The dark walls rose upwards, culminating in a huge ring of rocks like a crater, open to the sky. Daylight surged through an opening high above Farden's head and he could see the snow drifting gently through the cold air. As the party crossed the long road, he managed to glimpse farms and buildings below him. Countless people milled around them like ants, wandering through the furrowed fields and farmhouses, down lanes and curving roads.

What felt like an hour later, Farden's captors dumped him unceremoniously at the top of a flight of stairs. Cold wind tore at his hair. He tried to lift his head up to see what was happening, but a guard yanked him backwards, and the refreshing mountain air was taken away. Farden was dragged again, this time somewhere that swung and wallowed, as if he floated. Somewhere nearby, something creaked.

The mage tried to conserve his strength for whatever was coming, keeping his eyes shut, concentrating solely on staying conscious.

After a jolt, Farden was hauled across a cold, shiny floor and left in a foetal position. All was silent. Behind him, a large door was slammed, and the sound of boots ceased. Light shimmered behind his eyelids. He waited.

'Can you stand?' asked a massive, booming voice, making him flinch.

Farden took a deep breath and let his fingers stretch out beneath him. Shakily, he pushed himself to his knees. Every limb wailed in protest. He cursed under his breath and looked for the first time at his surroundings.

There had not been many times in his life that Farden had felt such awe that it rendered him speechless. This was one of those rare times. The humbled mage felt beyond tiny as he gazed upwards at the colossal domed roof hanging effortlessly hundreds of feet above him. Sheer black rock, with no rafters. A huge skylight punctured the far side of the ceiling, a vast doorway to the snowy skies outside. Around it were gathered a dozen smaller openings, their thin shafts of bright light piercing the smoky gloom of the great hall like spears through a veil.

At least a thousand ledges were carved into the rock walls of the hall: huge sconces carved straight into the stone, like countless honeycombed nests. The candlelight of hundreds of lamps flickered all around him, and in their light he saw dragons. Scores of dragons. They filled the lower ledges of the gigantic hall. They perched in their nests, surrounded by candles and accompanied by their riders. Farden noticed, with unexpected dismay, that only half the nests in the enormous hall seemed to be occupied. The others, dark and candle-less. He wondered what this hall would have looked like before the war.

All around him, the huge lizards shuffled and shifted. The sound of their breathing and their dragon-riders' whispers was deafening. The smell of reptile and woodsmoke was a strange mix, but welcome after the stench of his cell. A half-ring of guards stood behind him, watching him carefully, but the mage's eyes were now fixed on what he saw before him.

There, lying on a huge wooden bed of autumn leaves, spotlighted by a lone shaft of sunlight, was a great gold dragon. The Old Dragon, Farfallen. His bright scales shone with a warm glow, vibrating with an ancient magick Farden did not fully understand. The mage's head swam between disbelief and bewilderment.

Vice had killed the Old Dragon years ago in the battle of Ragjarak, yet here he was, sitting calmly on his nest with his dragon-rider beside him.

Farfallen's rider, the Siren queen, was a tall willow of a woman. Her stern face was like a thin blade, serious and commanding. Her jaw was set and her thin hands were neatly folded behind her back. Her long green dress draped over an impossibly slender body, falling to the floor like a moss-covered tree branch. Her autumn-gold hair was tied back, all apart from two strands that fell in front of each ear, long like the fangs of a sabre-cat. She flared her nostrils every few moments, whether through irritation or habit, Farden could not tell. Golden scales covered her cheekbones and forehead, and they ran in stripes up her neck to meet her chin. As her yellow eyes pierced Farden's, he felt himself blinking weakly even in the low light.

The great dragon stirred loudly behind her and she turned. He stretched out one gigantic gold wing like a huge canvas and blinked each golden eye separately. They were like black orbs flecked with liquid gold and stardust. Farden felt like he might fall into them.

Farfallen finished stretching and watched the quiet mage impassively. A forked tongue graced sharp teeth and flicked over mottled lips.

'Well met and good wishes, stranger. Can you speak?' His voice rumbled like thunder, filling the hall.

'Yes, Sire,' croaked Farden.

'Where did you come from, thief?' spat the queen.

'Be calm, Svarta. Speak, guest, tell us,' Farfallen lifted a huge claw to silence her and then nodded for the mage to continue.

Farden took a deep breath and attempted a shaky bow. 'My name is Farden. I am an Arka mage sent here to speak with the Siren council. My masters, the Arkmages, wish you all kind greetings and express their desire to bring peace between our two peoples,' he told them. Farden was becoming dizzy under the gaze of the dragons. There was a pause as he remembered that the tearbook had been lost. Words failed him.

'You are one of the Written,' hissed Svarta, more of a fact than a question.

Farden immediately grew wary. His mind turned to the raving lunatic back in his cell. 'That is true,' he answered.

'Then you are a danger to us all!' Svarta opened her arms and looked up at the other dragons. 'The magick this man holds in his skin is treacherous. The old healer who kindly brought this mage back from the dead was turned to madness. He lost his mind to whatever spells *you* cast on him.' Her eyes bored into Farden's skull. Some of the dragons murmured in agreement. Others whispered conspiratorially to their riders, as quiet as rustling leaves.

Farden was shocked at such an accusation. 'I have been unconscious for days! The first time I saw that man was in my cell just a moment ago! Whatever he did, he did it to himself and without my help. I'm sure you all know what I am, and what is on my back.' Farden involuntarily pulled his tattered tunic around his shoulders and stood defiantly, still shaky. 'He must have read my Book while I was unconscious. His fate is nothing to do with me.'

'It has *everything* to do with you! A strange man washed up on our shores half-dead and was taken in by a kind healer, who suddenly turns into a raving lunatic? We should have left you for the gulls!' Svarta spat. Farfallen and the council watched on calmly.

'I came here on a peaceful mission! My ship was attacked on the way to your shores, and I was forced to take my chances in the sea. Surely a hawk has arrived with news of my arrival?' Farden explained, exasperated, but Svarta simply huffed and crossed her arms.

Farden met the gold gaze of the Old Dragon, trying to plead with his eyes.

Farfallen took a deep breath. 'No hawk has reached us with any missive from the Arka. We have not had any dealings with your people in years,' he said, letting his eyes almost close, as though a distant thought had just passed through his mind, like a wandering beggar. He seemed tired, dazed, even. 'Who attacked your ship, and why?'

The mage sighed. This was going to be a long story. 'Sire, this discussion might be better held in private, my mission concerns all of Emaneska.'

Another grumble from the other dragons.

Farfallen was about to say something when Svarta jumped in. 'Your *mission*? Did your mission have something to do with *this*?!' She reached behind her ceremoniously and pulled out the tearbook, dry and safe. A collective gasp erupted from the hall like a sudden wind, as if a forgetful guard had left a door open. The dragons flapped in their nests. Some riders perched on their partner's long serpentine necks, leaning to get a better view of the book.

Farden was astounded and relieved at the same time. He was sure that the tearbook had been lost in the waves when he jumped ship, but Svarta held it aloft for the entire council to see. Farfallen was silent, one eye now closed, the other fixed on his tearbook.

'This man was found with *this* in his clutches! Farfallen's memories, long stolen from us and kept by the Arka as a trophy of the battle at Ragjarak—'

'Yes, and if the message had arrived from Krauslung then you would know that I was bringing it as a gesture of good faith! As a peace offering from my people!'

One Siren somewhere in the hall shouted out. 'You're a thief! You stole it from your own people and came here to bargain with us!'

'Liar!' another yelled.

'Enough!' Farfallen roared. For the first time, the Old Dragon reared up from his bed and sat upright with a loud scraping.

Farden found himself gazing up at him. A thick, spiky tail whipped the air and his wings beat like hammers as he hauled his massive weight upwards. The huge golden dragon sat back on his hind legs like a giant cat, his tail waving threateningly. The golden scales covering Farfallen's body undulated and quivered in the torchlight that washed over his shining figure. His wings arched high behind his shoulders, and long horns ran up his spine to meet in a wide crown above his bony brows.

It was the sheer size of him that amazed Farden. The Old Dragon was at least twice the size of the wyrm that had attacked him at Carn Breagh. He spied the long, rippling scar that ran down from Farfallen's throat across his left shoulder. *A blow that should have killed him*. The great dragon flexed his snake-like neck, hinging and unhinging his jaw with noisy clicks. He clacked his talons against the rock floor. Farden's heart thudded hard in his chest.

'I will talk to the mage, but not now and not here. Let him explain himself to me.'

Svarta looked like she wanted to say something, but Farfallen shot her a glance.

'My word is final,' he uttered. She nodded.

The other dragons rumbled their assent, and several leapt into the air, flapping their wings with great whooshing sounds. Farden's dark hair scattered in the wind as the beasts soared upwards through the skylight at the end of the hall. The mage could just about see the snow flurrying in their wake.

'Farden, walk with us.' Farfallen swapped a look with Svarta. The two of them left their platform and headed towards a low doorway in the rock wall.

Farden was ushered along by two nearby guards who grabbed him roughly by the arms. Despite his dizziness, he was beginning to feel strength seeping back into his body; the weakness and fragility seemed to fade with every step he took. He wondered if it was the effect of the dragons' magick.

Farfallen's feet pounded the stone floor ahead of Farden and each step shook his legs. Svarta shot him the occasional glance that spoke of menace and a thirst for justice.

The group strolled around a wide corridor that sloped gently further and further down into the mountain. Farfallen and Svarta were silent as they walked. They would occasionally look at each other as if reacting to a silent rebuke or question. Farden watched them closely, until Svarta chuckled and then eyed Farden over her shoulder. She held the big tearbook tightly under her arm.

They approached the end of the spiralling corridor and stopped in front of a semicircular doorway, locked tight by thick bars of ornate wood. Two Siren guards stood on either side, wearing the expressions of wax dolls. Their bright eyes were rigid and unmoving, the tips of their sharp spears barely quivering, and their lips drawn tight with ceremonious gravity. *Formal would be an understatement,*

Farden thought to himself. Farfallen fixed him with a golden stare, then looked away.

'Leave us,' Svarta called over her bony shoulder, to the guards flanking the mage. They stepped aside, bowed, and scurried back the way they had come. Farden swayed like an old willow on his tired legs.

'Come, Farden, let us talk in private,' said the Old Dragon. He waited for the two guards to slide open the doors, then walked under the gilded arch. The mage followed quietly. He caught one of the soldiers stealing a glance at him as he passed. Their eyes met for a moment and the soldier's head snapped back to position. Farden shrugged as he hobbled into the Old Dragon's chambers.

They were colossal, yet the word didn't do them justice. Everything was built to the scale of a dragon. Long windows running along the side of the room lit the huge space with crisp white light that hurt Farden's eyes. Thick carpets covered the stone floor, wide benches and platforms followed the line of the walls, there was even a resting spot for the huge bulk of the Old Dragon. Wide circular doors led to other rooms and quarters on both sides, and thick wooden bookcases lined one far wall. Another door to a long balcony sat to his right. A fresh arctic breeze caressed Farden's unshaven face, and he could smell the clean, pure scent of snow and mountain air outside.

The dragon shuffled in that direction, and Farden followed like a loyal dog. Svarta lingered by the bookshelves, leaving them to their words.

The brisk mountain air almost knocked Farden over as he stepped over the threshold onto the expansive balcony. High overhead, he could see more dragons circling; coloured shapes whirling through the sky, of all hues and sizes. Scattered snow drifted through the overcast skies, as if the clouds were trying to muster the energy for a blizzard but couldn't quite get there. The thick white flakes were a stark contrast to the granite-grey clouds that rolled and yawned above, a sky so cavernous Farden was sure he had seen it before, though bluer.

When he stood at the railing, he saw the whole mountainside spread below him, but leaning over made his stomach churn, so he looked straight ahead at the dark countryside that stretched out into the distance like a crumpled chart. He held out a hand to let cold snowflakes land on his hot skin.

The citadel of Hjaussfen seemed to be mostly contained within the extinct volcanic shell of the mountain and a few smaller peaks. Towns and villages had pooled together around the mountain's sprawl, linking roads and boundaries to form a suburban carpet of buildings, nestled in the rifts and caverns between the crags of black rock.

Through the scattered snow, Farden could pick out clusters of low circular towers poking from behind volcanic ridges and rugged tors: castles for keeping watch. Farms of dark soil popped up between the rocks here and there, now barren in the winter months. Between them, he could see flat roofs and circular areas lit by wind-blown torches; landing spaces for dragons to use, if they wished.

It was oddly clever, though alien to him, how easily harmony was achieved between these massive beasts and their Siren partners. Everything Farden could see was built for two different kinds of citizens; no road was too narrow, or step too tall. Everywhere he looked he could see the Sirens living in complete cooperation with the dragons. It was the sort of seamless coexistence only several thousand years can breed. *If only the social boundaries of the Arka could be so blurred.*

'We love the snow.' Farfallen rumbled from behind him. The dragon had joined him at the railing. 'Keeps us cool.'

'I've never seen so many of you,' confessed Farden.

'Even in the war?'

'No,' he said, 'that was before my time as a mage.'

'There used to be many more of us in the world, not only in Hjaussfen or Nelska, but in every corner of Emaneska,' the Old Dragon sighed.

Farden thought of the empty nests in the great hall and thought about asking how many, but Farfallen spoke again, so he stored that question for later.

'You must be surprised to see me alive, mage, after the stories of brave Lord Vice the dragon-slayer?' A smirk curled on his scaly lip.

Farden eyed the scar on the dragon's neck.

'It was a good strike, to give him his due, and one that almost killed me. I hear it would have taken nothing but another kiss from his sword to finish the job. But Vice foolishly left me for dead, and I decided it was better to stay that way, at least as far as the Arka were aware, that is,' said Farfallen. His gold gaze was fixed on the horizon.

Farden wondered what Vice would say when he told him. He would not be best pleased, to put it mildly. The mage changed tack. 'There's a lot of reconciliation needed between our peoples, that's for certain, but I'm afraid I'm here for something much more important.'

The dragon dipped his massive spiky head and cleared his throat. The noise was like boulders wrestling. 'You speak of your mission.'

Farden closed his eyes as a wave of weakness came and went. He chose his words carefully. 'I was sent here with ill news, Old Dragon. What I'm about to tell you would be best kept quiet, and between us. I will be honest and say that some in the magick council believe that a Siren was behind it, but standing here now, I really hope that's not the case.'

Farfallen matched his solemn look. He settled down on the cold floor, swishing his tail noisily from side to side. Farden shivered in the wind while he waited, stomach churning.

'Tell me,' said the Old Dragon.

Farden spared no detail. He told Farfallen what had happened in the Arfell libraries, and what had been stolen. Every time Farden feared he was speaking too openly, something in the back of his mind told him he could trust the dragon, and as impassive and as dark as the dragon's eyes were, he saw reliability in them, and so Farden kept talking.

When it came to the subject of Jergan, Farfallen held up a single claw to interrupt the mage.

'Jergan, the lycan?'

'You knew him?' asked Farden, confused.

Farfallen squinted into the distance and tried to think. 'Yes, a long time ago. The memories are hazy, but I remember him, or at least, the memory of him.'

A voice came from behind them. 'I remember when the news came that he had been attacked. Bitten.'

Svarta glided across the balcony towards them, her slim green dress blowing in the wind. She had been lingering near the door, listening in. Farden suppressed a frown.

'He came back covered in deep gashes, soaked by the snow and half-dead from the cold. The healers knew their herbs and spells would be useless. So we sent him away.' Her words sounded cruel and heartless, but Farden knew there was no cure for a lycan's bite; exile was the only answer.

'The wolf-curse is a strong one, and there was nothing we could do for him. He was a danger to us all.' Farfallen agreed, as if reading the mage's thoughts.

'I know. And he wishes you to know that he is alive and well. Sort of. I fought him in the south of Albion about a week ag—' Farden paused. 'How long have I been here?'

'We've put up with you for six days,' replied the queen. She reached for the railing and rested her hands on the cold stone. Her yellow eyes wandered over the view.

Farden counted the days in his head, then realised he had no idea how long he had been stranded at sea. *Eleven, twelve days altogether?* With no messenger hawk, the council would be getting anxious, itchy, and probably fearing the worst.

'I have to send word to the Arka.'

'We'll get to that after you tell us what you're doing here, and why you had Farfallen's tearbook,' Svarta snapped.

'I came here to enlist the services of the Sirens in battling this new, and unfortunately unknown, enemy of ours. If the Sirens weren't involved in this theft—'

'Which we most certainly were not!'

Farden held up his hands. 'From the fact I am still alive, I had guessed as much. Then we must assume that whomever stole the summoning manual wants to use it against all of Emaneska. Both Arka and the Sirens. As I was about to inform Farfallen, only the memories of a dragon's tearbook can tell us where they'll try to summon this creature.' Farden crossed his arms defiantly.

'What creature?' asked Svarta.

'One spell in the manual spoke of a massive, terrifying monster. Something called "the mouths of darkness". This is what we think they're after. If the scholars and Jergan were right, then none of us, not the Arka nor the Sirens, would stand a chance against it,' Farden explained.

'And so you want our help, after all these years?' The sneer that spread across Svarta's face was an oily one. 'The last I heard, the Sirens weren't in favour with your court.'

'If we are to stop this creature from rearing its ugly head then we need to fight together. That's what my "court" decided, Queen. Yes, there were those on the council who accused you of being responsible for this chaos, but it was the ruling of the Arkmages that I was to come here and try to make peace. Unless, of course, your pride will be damaged by doing so?' Farden returned her sneer. Svarta smouldered, words already bubbling up, but Farfallen rested a huge claw on her shoulder and spoke for her.

'We have no objection to peace, Farden, Svarta simply wants what is best for our people, and old enemies are usually far from it. It has been an age since an Arka stood in the palace of Hjaussfen. You must forgive our suspiciousness.'

Farden held up his hands in an earnest gesture. 'Old Dragon, I am here on a mission of goodwill, I swear by the gods.'

'Tell me—if you found a strange, foreign man washed up on one of your beaches with a stolen treasure in his hands and not even a glimpse of a hawk to explain it all, what would you assume?' the dragon asked. The mage had to agree with him. Farfallen rumbled on.

'Friend or foe, I am grateful for the return of my tearbook. Since it was taken, my mind has grown cloudy, unclear. When I try to remember something, it is like grasping at a wet fish. Difficult.' he said, with more than a hint of wistfulness. 'Why are dragon memories suddenly so important to the safety of Emaneska?'

'The spell requires a well of dark elf magick to sustain. Our thinking was that a tearbook could point to one that has survived the years and expeditions, still undiscovered.'

'We have not found one in decades. Jergan and his team were the last to do so, and that one was ancient and empty,' Farfallen said.

'I know, but it is the only way these thieves and murderers can summon the creature. Why steal the spell if they can't use it to its full potential? They must be confident one still survives, or they know more than we do. If we find the well, we find them. And now we have your memories, Old Dragon,' Farden suggested.

'Few scholars have ever been allowed to study a tearbook over the centuries, and never an Old Dragon's,' Svarta whispered, low and strained as though the mage had just uttered a deep heresy.

Farden clenched a fist behind his back. He felt like he was back in the magick council, but this time there was no Vice to help him. He tried to convey the urgency of the situation to Farfallen with his mind. *That seemed to work last time*, he thought.

'My apologies, Queen,' he muttered.

'Say we allow the examination of the tearbooks, delve into our memories and find an old elf well and these thieves. What will you do?' Farfallen asked, turning his face to the wind and half-closing his eyes.

'I'll send the lot of them to the dust myself, and destroy the book so it can never be used again.' Farden's voice was stern and clear, no waver of weakness in it now.

'You're a dutiful mage, Farden,' Farfallen replied.

'I try,' Farden told him, fists clenching harder.

Svarta scoffed. 'And what if you're too late?'

Farden stared right back at her. 'Then it would be an honour to fight alongside the Sirens instead of against them, for once. Then maybe we can have our peace.'

Farfallen and his queen shared a long look, leaving Farden to shiver in the cold and hope his words had conveyed enough weight.

At long last, Farfallen sighed. 'There seems to be no time to lose. I will meet with the other dragons and their riders, quietly. With luck, we can start work on our tearbooks by dawn.'

'I shall summon the scholars,' Svarta grunted. Farden was unsure whether she was being sarcastic or not. She scowled at him once more, then left the balcony. Farden turned back to the Old Dragon.

'You will have to forgive her blunt remarks.' Farfallen sighed, bearing a reptilian smile. His horns rattled as he turned his head into the wind. 'The wind feels good today. The snow keeps us cold, you see.'

Farden refrained from telling the Old Dragon he had already said that and stayed silent.

'Inside we're all fire and heat, so the north always keeps us cool and comfortable. And the weather is better here, too.' He chatted almost conversationally, as if the two were sharing stories and drinks in a tavern.

Farden found himself beginning to like the huge dragon, and he smiled. 'Really? I thought Krauslung was bad, but this is far too cold for me.' The mage shivered even as he said it.

Farfallen laughed his deep, rumbling chuckle. 'For flying, that is.'

'I suppose that's true.' Farden nodded and paused to think. 'I'm glad that you have your tearbook back. Many things happen in war that shouldn't happen, if you know what I mean.' Farden shook his head at his lack of eloquence. He needed sleep.

'I agree. Both sides did terrible things to the other. A king never wants war on his people. If he does, then he is a despot and should not be a king in the first place. Just like the man who sits on the throne of Skölgard. What happened between the Sirens and the Arka is now history, and though Emaneska will never forget it, perhaps we can put it behind us.'

Farden simply nodded, trying not to betray any thoughts of Cheska and her father. He tried to think of a question instead. 'What's it like? Flying, I mean.'

Farfallen cocked his spiny head to one side. 'Exhilarating, and second nature. Dragons are born in the air and we die in the air, so without the rush of the wind beneath our wings we are lost. Think how natural picking up a sword is for you, Farden. You take it for granted. Now think, without your hand, how much you would miss the feel of a sword in your palm.

'I once knew an unfortunate dragon who lost one of his wings during a terrible battle, long ago now. I forget his name, but he said living without flight was like seeing without colours, a wash of grey landscapes and charcoal sunsets. Half a story.'

Farfallen solemnly bowed his head, and Farden felt a deep sadness. 'What happened to him?' he asked.

'If memory serves, I believe he ended up dying from a broken heart. It doesn't happen often to a dragon, but it can. The same happens when we lose a rider we've bonded with. Should they die, we die. Should we die, they live, and from then on, they live like that old dragon, halved.'

'Well, the exhilarating part of it sounds intriguing.' Farden hummed, squinting at the mountainside and the grey clouds and wondering where the colour was in the first place. But he understood what Farfallen was saying, even though his tired mind couldn't manhandle the concept of flight being second nature.

'Ask Svarta, or one of the other riders about it.' It was Farfallen's turn to pause. 'What is it like for you?'

Farden looked confused. 'What?'

'Being a Written.'

Farden was surprised that the Old Dragon would want to know about him and his kind. He tried to put the feeling into words and realised he had never had to explain it before. The Written barely talked about it, even to each other. Even Durnus had never asked him.

'It's difficult to describe,' he began. 'It's constant, in one form or another. It burns hot on your back when you cast a spell, or in the presence of other magick, if it's strong enough. It's heavy. You can feel the sensation of the magick rushing through your veins, ice and boiling water all at the same time. But then at other times it's intangible. The weight lifts, it grows cold, and you can't grab at it or hold it, just like something in your gut, or the wind on the hairs of your skin, or the feeling there's somebody standing behind you. Sometimes you wake up at night with a dizzy feeling when it rushes through your head. It's treacherous, though, and dangerous. It can turn on you quickly if you're not strong enough. Some say that it's more of a curse than a blessing, but we're sworn to strict rules to keep others safe.'

'And what are they?' asked the dragon.

Farden absently clicked his knuckles as he stared at the landscape. 'To serve the Arka and the Arka only. Not to breed, with Written or otherwise. Not to reveal our Books to others, nor allow…'

There was an awkward moment, and the mage looked up at Farfallen. 'And for that I apologise,' he said. But the Old Dragon shook his head slowly.

'It was his own doing. I saw that, as did Svarta. She might not admit it, but there is a lot of blame to be shared between our countries, a lot of steam that needs to be blown off. Please, go on.'

Farden shrugged. 'Whichever way you look at it, we're sworn to a life of service to the Arka. One that ends in death, dismissal, or madness.' The dragon kept staring at him, taking in all he had to say. Farden looked into his giant eyes. He still found himself talking openly to the dragon, as if his tongue had been let loose, or if they were old friends. Farfallen seemed to be a golden rock of common sense, and for some reason he felt he could tell him anything. His lips kept moving.

'My uncle was one of the unfortunate ones. After thirty-three years of fighting for the Arka, his mind started to slip. The magick started making him see things and hear noises. It kept him awake for days on end, slowly turning the screw. He ended up going mad. He convinced himself that there were things in the darkness trying to kidnap him, and he told everyone that there was a daemon trying to control him. One day, he went out into the streets of Krauslung and killed a man for no reason. Ripped him apart and painted the walls with his blood. It was chaos. Later that morning they caught him trying to scale the city walls with a rope. He was stark naked, and had bitten his fingernails off, scratched words into his arms. The last time I saw him, he was being hauled away to the prisons in shackles, shouting and spitting, biting at the guards who carried him.' Farden stared at the snow.

'What happened to him?' the dragon asked quietly.

'He was cast out of the city, banished from the Arka, and sent out into the wilderness with nothing but a blanket and a gold coin.' Farfallen looked confused, so Farden explained. 'When a mage gets to a certain age the council starts to watch him or her closely, to see if they start to act strangely or differently. It happens to about one in every three Written, so it's a risk we all take when we go through the Ritual. If you are one of the unlucky ones, like my uncle was, then you're exiled. Tradition states that you're given a blanket for the cold, and a gold coin to use however you see fit. If an exile tries to get back into the city, then it's an instant death sentence. It's been like that for centuries. It's just the way it is for us. So we fight, and we fight hard and fearlessly, and hope that death comes to us quicker than the madness does,' said the mage. He closed his eyes to feel the wind on his skin.

'It seems like a heavy weight to bear, Farden.'

Farden flexed his fingers and looked at the dirt under his nails, finding Durnus' words coming out of his mouth. 'Sometimes it is. Sometimes I don't even think of it at all. The way I see it, I was born to fight for the Arka, so fight I will. It's just hard when you have so much power, yet have people that constantly worry about what you do with it. People that worry about you.'

He hoped the dragon could not feel the anger under his skin, the rage that burnt there, quiet now, but ever-present. He thought of Beinnh, and the thugs he had destroyed.

'There is one that cares about you more than the others, I take it? A woman?' Farfallen squinted. Farden didn't say anything, careful to keep his eyes straight ahead. 'I don't mean to pry, Farden, and your secrets are safe, but I can feel it burning inside you.' The dragon had indeed spotted a fire in him, just a different kind of fire to what Farden expected.

Farden relented with a nod. 'Any sort of romance, however brief, is against the rules of the Written. So we keep it secret, and hope that one day, if we both live long enough, we can find a way around it.'

'A fire burns more intensely when it is covered up, mage,' said Farfallen. The simple truth of his words made Farden think. But the Old Dragon quickly changed the subject. 'It is strange how different our two peoples are. The way you treat magick, for example. To the Arka, magick is something you can learn through reading a book or a spell, something you can carve into skin. But for the Sirens it's more natural: a gift rather than a birthright. Like you, all our wizards are from long and special bloodlines. But in truth all Sirens have some magick in them, an innate magick that seeps into them from us dragons. It is open to all. Have you ever wondered about why Sirens have scales like us?' asked Farfallen. Farden shook his head. 'Because of the dragons. Living too close to us for too long can change a person, in odd ways.'

Farden nodded, abruptly realising that was why every rider had the same colour scales as their partner. 'I could feel it as soon as I walked into the hall.'

'Not everyone does, but anyone that spends a long time in the company of dragons will feel it eventually, and by the time they realise it, they've already been changed.'

Farden thought about that. 'Maybe that's why our people have been fighting so long. The differences in how we treat magick.'

'Perhaps. I have always been curious at the way you treat it, guarding it as though you have the sole right to it, like it's a treasure to be locked away and given to the chosen. But I suppose, on some level, it works. Your entire country is based upon magick, and through its mastery, you have held your own. Our wizards envy the ease with which you Arka can control and bend magick to your will,' said Farfallen with a sniff.

'I don't think I've ever thought about it like that,' the mage admitted. 'Some say we caught the magick at sea, when the Arka were just a race of fishermen and sailors. Others say it came from our goddess Evernia, and she chose us as her children. But either way, you have a point.' Farden stretched and yawned.

Tiredness seeped into the spaces behind his eyes and even though evening had not yet begun to claw at the horizon, he found himself blinking and squinting in the snowy light. He wondered how it was still so bright when he couldn't see the sun behind the weather.

Farfallen rumbled. 'Down there, to your left, is a small room that our old servant used to occupy. It's warm, and I hear the bed isn't too uncomfortable.' The dragon flashed his reptilian smile again, baring knife-like teeth. 'Rest for now. Tonight I will go to my tearbook. And I think you should see it for yourself.'

He held the mage's gaze for a while longer before turning back to face the wafting waves of cold wind on his gold face.

'Oh, and did you know you weren't the only one to survive the shipwreck? The other is in your room.'

Other? Confused, Farden said his thanks, and headed towards the door between the rock and the edge of the big balcony. It was unlocked, and as he pushed it inwards he heard a little mewing noise, and saw a black shape trotting across the floor towards him. It was Lazy, the ship's cat. Farden was speechless.

He crouched down to let the cat nibble at his fingers and rub itself against his knuckles, watching her intently. He shook his head in disbelief. *Lucky little thing.*

She rattled with a happy purring, watching him remove his cloak and boots. The mage collapsed weakly onto the small bed and into a tangled mess of deep thoughts and cold pillows. Lazy settled down somewhere near him, falling asleep instantly.

Farden closed his eyes, thinking of dragons in the sky, and of flying. He wondered whether dragons slept at all, or if they slept on the wing. He marvelled that they never needed a flint or tinder to light a fire for their rider, and wondered what it must feel like to snort and breathe fire as if it were simply air. Not forgetting, of course, how beautiful it was to watch them fly, how they made jumping into the air seem no harder than picking up a fork. These were true dragons, not the simple wyrms of the wilderness, hunting meat and magick. It was like what Durnus had said years ago, about dragons living for hundreds and hundreds of years; that they just keep going and going and going, like the snowfall outside the window near the door: grey and drifting, like dust on his pillow…

Farden had never slept a deeper sleep.

chapter 8

Never not to understand the beast,
for takes one bite, evermore curs'd to feast.
All morality and goodness, thieved by silver moon,
For evil take thee, wolf claws and doom.
The Lycan Curse

A banging awoke him. A persistent, resolute knocking that stubbornly shook his door. The blankets tugged at him to get up, and his eyes snapped open to see a boring stone ceiling. It told him to stop staring and answer the door, so he did.

Svarta stood behind it with her arms crossed. Night had descended on Hjaussfen, and the yellow light of a nearby torch cast angular shadows across her face, accenting her stern expression of impatience. 'I have been knocking for a long time,' she said.

'I'm sorry, I was asleep. Look, by now you must know I'm not here to harm anyone, so why can't we just forget that you want to lock me up in a cell and start over?' The Siren merely stared at him, frowning. 'Do you want to come in or something?' he asked.

Svarta snorted and turned around to walk away. 'We don't have time for your games, mage. Follow me, and be quick about it.'

Farden smirked to himself and adjusted his rumpled clothing. He smoothed his hair back into something more socially acceptable and rubbed the vestiges of sleep from his eyes. He noticed his sword and Scalussen vambraces had been returned. He decided against taking the blade but slid the pair of vambraces onto his wrists. The metal contracted around his skin with a metallic whispering, like a snake wrapping tightly around a tree. Farden smiled. *His old friends.*

A new pair of surprisingly comfy boots had been left by the door, so he put them on. His red scarf, however, was nowhere to be seen. He wondered if Cheska would mind that he had lost it. He had been through a shipwreck, after all. Farden turned, ruffled Lazy's ears, and slammed the door with a bang.

'Who's *we*?' he called after the Siren queen.

Farden followed Svarta through the Old Dragon's huge room and out into the cavernous corridor once again. They meandered through seemingly endless, identical hallways that curved through the mountain like the tunnels of some monstrous rabbit warren. Farden felt completely lost after the third turning, but held his tongue as he walked behind Svarta. She was silent, brooding, occasionally throwing him a look to check that he was still in tow.

After a long and silent journey, they reached a tall set of iron doors. Svarta stopped abruptly and swivelled on one heel to face the mage.

'If it were up to me, you would still be asleep and we would be doing this alone, as is proper. But Farfallen thinks there is some sort of good in you, and for some reason, he wishes you to be here for his re-bonding. Me? I think we should shove you into a rowing boat and point you south. *If* it were up to me, of course.' Svarta narrowed her yellow eyes.

'But it's not.' Farden shrugged.

'Don't be clever with me, mage.'

'If I had wanted to hurt anyone, then believe me, I would have done it already. If Farfallen trusts me, maybe you should, too.' Farden stared defiantly into those eyes. Her lips curled into a reptilian snarl and she spun back around. She pushed against the doors and they swung open with a creaking scrape.

A few torches glimmered in the shadows, trying their best to light the cavernous hall with their meagre light. As the doors closed with an echoing thud, Farden blinked his eyes to adjust to the gloom.

Between the spots dancing in front of his vision and the yellow flickering of candles, he could discern a massive shape at the end of the room. Farfallen crouched in the shadows, eyes closed and still, like an elaborate statue.

He felt Svarta close to his ear, whispering. 'Unless somebody asks you a question, you are to be silent in this room.'

Farden nodded and took his place a dozen paces in front of the silent dragon. He looked up at the stone ceiling held high above them by a ring of thick stone pillars. The hall was bare, with no decoration or carvings, and no furniture besides a low stone table and a shrine against the back wall, behind Farfallen.

It was an alabaster effigy of a god that looked as though he were half-man, half-dragon. Arched wings sprouted from his back and a spiny tail curved around the stone clouds that formed his pedestal. Small candles hid in niches or danced gleefully in their metal holders, sparkling for their deity, Thron, the Siren god of weather.

'Bring the book!' Svarta called to the shadows, and a small man shuffled from the darkness, holding the tearbook. He looked for all the world like a shrivelled vole, with glasses set deep into his wrinkly face.

The man placed the tome on the stone table under the dragon's chin, then backed away into the darkness. As he did so, Farfallen opened his eyes. Svarta moved forwards to the table and grudgingly beckoned the mage to follow.

Farden moved silently, abruptly aware of a low hum that seemed to be emanating from the dragon, like the rumble of a distant avalanche.

Svarta pried the old book open and turned straight to the last page, which was as blank as all the others. Farfallen flicked one eye to look at Farden.

'Tearbooks go backwards. The start is the first memory a dragon has, the last pages are the most recent,' he rumbled.

A single tear rolled from his golden orb of an eye and coursed its way down his scaly face with agonising slowness. The tear quivered on the end of his chin for a moment before dropping soundlessly onto the book.

Farden looked down at the pages and saw them begin to quiver with energy. Nothing appeared at first, then slowly, as Svarta closed her eyes and lifted the page ever so slightly, a rune materialised in the bottom right hand corner. It was swiftly followed by another, and another, until the page was completely covered. The strange foreign lettering kept writing itself across the next page, then the next one after that.

The letters danced over themselves, every invisible quill-stroke scuttling across the pages, glyph by spidery glyph. As the script moved faster, so did Svarta's page-turning. Farden could see the dragon's eyes twitching as he tried to follow the pace. He wondered when Svarta would slow down, but her practised hand movements only sped up. The sound of her hand on the pages grew into a flurry of papery whip-cracks that echoed around the hall.

She stopped. The writing slammed to a halt, letters bunching up messily on the first page as their momentum carried them onwards. As slowly as she had opened the book, Svarta closed it and locked eyes with her dragon as she did so. He gave a deep rumble and her neck twitched involuntarily. Then she clicked her long fingers high above her head. Once again, the old man came shuffling out of the shadows. With the same careful deliberation, he hefted the tearbook, turned, and disappeared once more.

Farden was confused. Svarta fixed him with her usual condescending stare.

'Feel privileged, mage. Never before has an outsider watched a dragon re-bond with his tearbook.'

'I'm honoured.' He directed this to Farfallen.

'I can feel the memories flowing through me again. I had not realised how much had been lost to me: names, places, kings and queens, all coming back to me now. Bit by bit.' The Old Dragon drew a long breath in through his nose and closed his eyes.

Farden watched him as he held the breath in his lungs for an impossible time. When he finally exhaled, a blast of red-hot fire burst from each nostril. The air rippled like the heat from a blacksmith's forge.

'A long time has passed since I last breathed fire, Farden. Far too long a time for a dragon.' He pushed himself up so he could sit upright, making his scales move hypnotically in the candlelight.

Rearing his spiny head, Farfallen took a deep gulp of air and spewed forth a stream of searing fire that curled around the pillars and licked at the granite ceiling.

Heat bathed the two standing at his side and Farden's eyes went wide with awe. Svarta even looked happy for a change, clasping her bony hands together in what the mage could only guess was delight. Farfallen roared and Farden had to cover his ears to escape the pain. The echoes clattered around the chamber for almost a minute afterwards, like winter waves crashing on a shore. The Old Dragon closed his eyes once more and was silent.

Svarta tugged at Farden's sleeve and headed towards the door. She whispered to him while they walked. 'Come, I'll show you where the kitchen is. I assume the Written eat?'

Farden's eyes burnt with the after-image from the bright fire and he rubbed at them to get rid of the dancing dots that swam through his vision. 'We do eat, yes, but only live children.'

'Very funny,' came the curt reply. 'Enough of your nonsense. Let's go.'

'How long do you think it will be before you realise I'm not a spy? I probably have a few more days left here, but I really can't stick around to prove you wrong.'

'Good. She closed the tall doors with a bang. Svarta's fists were clenched by her sides, her chin held high, pointing the way ahead like the scaly bow of a narrow ship. She led him down another long corridor that looked like all the others. Farden had no idea how anyone managed to find their way around this place.

'If you think you can toy with me, then you're mistaken. Just because Farfallen has taken a liking to you doesn't mean I have to,' she snapped.

'What is your problem with me? What else must I do to prove I'm not going to murder all of you in your sleep?'

The Siren queen shot him a fierce look over her shoulder. 'There's something dark inside of you, mage. I can feel it even if the Old Dragon can't. I won't be comfortable until you're far from our lands.'

Farden shook his head, wondering how far he could push her. 'Well, what am I supposed to do then, while I stay here?'

'Stay in the confines of the palace, and no one will harm you. No Arka has set foot in the citadel in more than fifteen years, so wandering around the streets is out of the question. I don't want some angry, over-zealous citizen deciding to pick a fight with you. Who knows what would happen, with your power.' Svarta looked him up and down with a flick of her head.

'Thanks for being so concerned with my safety,' Farden said dryly. As he spoke, he caught the stare of guards standing in alcoves.

Maybe Svarta was right: the ceasefire had always been shaky at the best of times. 'Fine. I'll stay out of sight. So what happens to the tearbook now? Where is it being taken?' Farden asked her, remembering the Arkmages' orders.

'Like the Old Dragon, it must rest,' said Svarta. Farden could hear the effort to stay calm in her voice.

'When can we start reading it?'

'Soon, mage. But enough with this questioning.' She glared at him. Farden scowled.

'Where can I go, then? Is there anywhere I can train?'

Svarta stopped in her tracks and whirled around. 'Are you joking?'

Farden set his jaw resolutely and matched her stare. 'No, I'm deadly serious. I've been unconscious for a week and I need to regain my strength.'

'You want me to agree to you practising your dangerous Arka magick in the palace of Hjaussfen?' She was incredulous.

Farden nodded 'Yes, if it's not too inconvenient.'

'By the gods,' Svarta closed her eyes tightly for a moment. She exhaled heavily and her words came flying with her breath. 'I will speak to Farfallen.'

'Thank you, Svarta.'

'Don't thank me, thank Farfallen. His word is law.' She resumed her marching, shooting him a look that would have killed a lesser man.

There was an awkward silence, broken only by the smart tap of their footfalls on the rock floor. Farden was slowly realising there was a lot about the Sirens he had never been told. 'Why Farfallen, why is he king and not one of the others?'

Svarta sighed. 'He's the oldest and goldest of them all. The longer a dragon lives, the golder he gets, much the same as we go greyer with age. The golder a dragon is, the greater his right to rule. The goldest of all of them is crowned the Old Dragon, and he rules until he dies. A few of the elders in the council are close to his age.'

'How old is he?' Another boyish question.

'We have been bonded for three hundred years, but Farfallen is close to a thousand years old,' she said.

'You don't look older than forty,' replied Farden. It wasn't supposed to sound like a compliment, but it did, and Svarta glared.

'Whatever power the dark elves left behind gave our ancestors extremely long lives, hundreds of years longer than you Arka,' Svarta said snidely.

'Us peasants are lucky if we get to eighty.' Farden narrowed his eyes at her. 'Speaking of the Arka, I need to send a message to the magick council.'

'You can do that after you eat.' No sooner had she spoken than the two emerged into a long room that roared with the sound of conversation and the business of eating. Steam rose from pots and stoves along the far wall, in between cauldrons, trays of food, and busy cooks. Farden's stomach growled as the smell of broth, bread, meat, and all sorts of other victuals hit him.

The tables filling the room were crammed with soldiers and servants. Svarta stood to his right with her arms crossed, apparently her favourite pose. She leaned close to one of the guards flanking the door and whispered something. He threw a quick look at the mage behind her and nodded.

'If anyone should take a disliking to you, these guards will see that you are escorted back to your rooms. I'm warning you Farden, I want no magick whatsoever while you're here in the palace.'

'Fine.' Farden saw several Sirens lift their heads from their bowls, watching him. A hush crept across the room until almost everyone was staring at the strange Arka mage standing in the doorway.

'I'll be in my room if you need me.' Svarta sneered as she left, leaving him standing alone in the unfriendliest room he had ever encountered.

Farden sighed, steeling himself to walk towards the food spread out at the back of the room. A hundred pairs of suspicious eyes followed him as he walked, watching their uninvited guest navigate his way through tables and chairs. Farden had never felt so unwelcome in all his life. Wandering through the towns of Albion was bliss compared to this.

Still, he persevered until he reached the back wall. A cook fixed him with a disgusted look before shoving a plate into his hands. It was followed by some roasted fish, a dollop of watery stew, and a brown bread roll. Farden nodded his thanks at the silent cook and turned around. Everyone was still staring at him.

'What?!' he shouted.

It seemed to work. Most of the Sirens returned to their meals and carried on their noisy conversations. Farden sighed and found a place to sit, up against one of the walls. The Sirens nearest to him cast a few wary, untrusting scowls in his direction but Farden just busied himself with his plate of food and tried not to cause any further disruption to the mess hall.

The fish was oily but tasty, and he found himself ravenously tearing at the bread with both hands, previously unaware of how hungry he had been. He finished his whole plate in double the time than was polite and, after deciding against licking the plate clean of stew, he reclined against the wall and attempted to relax. A torch fluttered above his head, and Farden let his rambling thoughts mingle with the flickering flames until he was staring blankly into space. Tiredness crept over his body like a snail, and he could feel the warmth from the fire and the torch seeping into his bones. *He was getting too old for this business*, he thought.

Farden could still feel unfriendly eyes watching him from the tables nearby. Conspiratorial whispers reached his ears. *Gods damn that Svarta*, he cursed mentally. Leaving him here alone amongst soldiers that hated him was a sure way to get him into a fight, or worse. Farden would not be baited, not this time and not by her. He refused to give her the satisfaction.

In his peripheral vision, he saw a tall figure stand up from a bench and make his way slowly through the chairs and tables crammed with Sirens. Farden lowered his head, trying to ignore the stares.

'You're the one they found on the beach,' a deep voice spoke up.

Farden looked up to see a tall man in a floor-length brown robe standing with arms folded into his deep sleeves. The man had lost an eye some time ago: a long silver scar ran across over the space it used to be, carving its way down his stubbly face to his neck. His hair was curly, dark, and hung in coiled tendrils over his remaining eye and forehead. Scales decorated his temples and neck, grey and dun-coloured like the granite walls of the palace. There was something about those scales and the look in his one eye that was different to the other Sirens in the hall. He considered Farden with a solemn, unreadable expression.

'The Arka mage?' the stranger asked again.

'I guess so.' Farden put his empty plate on the floor and rubbed his cold hands together. The man towered above him. He must have been at least a head and a half taller than the mage and bulging with muscle.

'Follow me,' the man said, nodding towards the door. The Siren's voice was unnaturally deep.

'I'm fine here, thank you. I don't want any trouble.' Farden closed his eyes again, letting his head rest against the wall behind him. He heard the man crouch next to him and lean closer. Farden could smell the cheap wine on his breath. Magick thrummed at the base of the mage's skull.

'You've come to the wrong place if you want to be left alone, Arka. I suggest you come with me if you don't want to find yourself in a brawl with some of the more unrestrained men.'

Farden opened his eyes and looked at the nearest table of Sirens. They whispered and pointed at the mage. One of them brandished a fork menacingly. Farden considered his options: follow a big stranger or stay in the room with a score of unfriendly soldiers who, with utmost certainty, all wanted to cave his head in.

'Lead the way,' he sighed, curious why his decisions always seemed to be made for him, like riding a wild beast over which he held no power or sway. Durnus had always said that was the way of the Written.

The Siren stood up and headed for the door with Farden in tow, much to the displeasure of the murmuring men clustered around the table.

Farden followed the big Siren silently, picking bits of fish from his teeth. He rubbed his chin and wondered where he could find a blade to shave with. His sword would probably be rusted after all the salt water.

The air was cold outside the warm hall, a refreshing change from its stuffy, uncomfortable atmosphere. Farden contemplated going to find Svarta and giving her a piece of his mind, but he honestly couldn't be bothered with her foul mood. He coughed to clear his throat and the big stranger turned around questioningly.

'I've heard a lot of rumours about you, Arka. People say you sent one of the healers mad,' he said.

'People seem to say a lot of things about me in this place.'

'We haven't seen an outsider in years. Some of the other riders and soldiers are scared of you, or instantly hateful of you because of the war. The dragons just seem curious.'

'It's the magick in my blood,' Farden said as they jogged down a tall flight of steps.

'Only wild dragons hunt magick, Arka. Not the old ones,' the stranger corrected him.

'Are you a rider then?' Farden asked.

There was a lengthy pause and Farden wondered if the stranger had heard him. He watched water trickle from a little rock-pool on his left as he passed it.

'Yes. I am,' the big Siren finally answered.

Farden couldn't think of any reply besides an acquiescent hum, so he turned his attention to where they were going and his surroundings.

The corridors were starting to close in, becoming narrower, rockier and distinctly less grand. The air was thickening with humidity. Springs of water bubbled up out of little rock-pools in the floor. Some hissed at the two men, and others gave off clouds of steam that filled the hallway. Their boots splashed quietly on wet steps.

When they came to an archway, the stranger pushed open a low wooden door set deep into the wall. A strong gust of air sent Farden's cloak billowing wildly about his legs and snow scattering around his boots. He followed the man out onto a long balcony, much like the one in Farfallen's chambers.

The sudden cold felt particularly bitter in comparison to the hot corridors inside the mountain. Snow swirled out of the darkness to sting his face. Above him, the sky loomed dark and heavy, streaked with low ashen clouds, the kind that always seemed to hang listlessly in the sky, somehow never moving despite the powerful wind. Stars struggled to find space amongst them. A flaming torch flapped and fluttered nearby, turning the flakes into a swarm of yellow flies that melted immediately in the darkness, or on the wet stone.

The stranger headed straight for the railing and stood, shoulders hunched, staring into the night sky. Farden just pulled his cloak around him as he stood by the door, watching the big Siren with a wary eye.

His new friend pointed a monstrous hand at the sky and Farden followed its direction with his gaze. Above the clouds, in the very darkest parts of the sky, streams of coloured light danced across a black canvas. Blues, dusty greens, and charcoal whites; the faint colours wavered and surged through the stars like long grass dancing in the wind.

'The Wake,' the Siren told him. Farden could barely hear him over the sound of the wind, so he walked forwards. 'The First Dragon is out flying tonight.'

'They're beautiful. Now, what do you want with me?' Farden asked. The Siren's good eye was fixated on the swirling lights above them. He spoke without looking at the mage.

'Tell me. Have you killed dragons, mage?'

Farden mentally tensed. 'Only wild ones, on occasion,' he said, choosing his words carefully.

The Siren made a sucking noise with his teeth. 'That alone is reason for the soldiers to hate you,' he paused, still looking at the sky. 'Farfallen has asked me to watch out for you. Svarta may be his rider, and my queen, but he knows she isn't fond of you.'

'*Not fond* isn't actually the phrase that best describes it.' Farden leaned his back against the railing, facing the door. The huge mountain slope towered over him, a jet-black silhouette against the cloud and colour-strewn night sky. Torches shone from a thousand windows and ledges, making the huge mountain look for all the world like a solid island in the sky, covered in a myriad of campfires.

'She wants you to prove her right: that you're dangerous and need to be locked away. So by sending you into the sabre-cat's den, as it were, she was hoping you'd provoke a reaction from the other soldiers and guards.'

'I am dangerous, but not to anyone here in Hjaussfen. I'm on a peaceful mission for once,' replied Farden, with a humourless chuckle at the back of his throat. He turned to look at the murky darkness of the slopes spread beneath them.

'Mhm. Farfallen's told me,' the big Siren nodded and wiped the snow out of his curly hair.

'Who are you, anyway?' Farden asked.

'My name is Eyrum, partner of Longraid.' The man bowed his head and put a hand to his chest in a formal greeting.

'Good to meet you, I'm Farden.' The mage returned the bow and smiled at his new ally.

'Well met and good wishes, Farden. The Old Dragon speaks highly of you, which is, needless to say, strange under the circumstances of your arrival. They say you were washed ashore after a storm and a shipwreck?'

'I was.'

'Then it's a miracle that you survived the freezing waters. The weather-god must hold you in high favour,' Eyrum said in a deep, solemn tone.

A distant flash amongst the low clouds caught Farden's eye. 'Another storm?' he asked, pointing at the sky. Eyrum squinted upwards as another flash of light appeared on the horizon.

'No, something else entirely. Wait,' he said, putting a finger and thumb to his wrinkled brow. He nodded and smiled. 'Give him a moment.'

Farden was confused, but as he scanned the skies, he discerned a jet-black shape darting under the low clouds. 'Is that your dragon?'

Eyrum just wiped snow from his face. Farden hoisted his hood over his wet hair and shrugged the precipitation from his shoulders.

The dark shape swooped down to glide over the foothills and crags far below them. Farden watched, holding his breath as the dragon dropped further and further until it seemed to be flying only a few inches above the jagged black rocks of the mountain. The Siren stepped back from the railing and Farden felt he should do the same.

There was an anxious moment of silence as the shape disappeared from their view entirely, then a gigantic gold dragon tore past the balcony with incredible speed. The thunderclap from Farfallen's massive wings was deafening and the violent blast of air almost pushed the two men to the ground.

The dragon climbed further into the night sky to pirouette on one wing tip. Just as Farden thought he would tumble from the air, the Old Dragon somersaulted and dove for the balcony, tucking his wings in tight to his flanks, like a falcon.

The mage backed away towards the door, but Eyrum didn't move. It looked like Farfallen would plummet headlong into the rocks, but at the very last moment, his wings flared open and the dragon stopped in mid-air, letting his whole huge weight come to rest on the stone railing with all the gentleness of a feather. His claws scraped on the stonework as they retracted. Farfallen flashed a smile and a tiny flame escaped from one nostril.

Farden grinned, moving closer to the dragon. 'You seem happy. Looks like that tearbook has done you some good.'

Farfallen chuckled and scratched his spiky chin with a claw. 'Maybe it has, mage, and I have you to thank for bringing it back to me. It has been many a year since I felt this good. Like a power I have not tasted in too long.'

'It was the magick council that agreed to send me here with it.' Farden said quietly, thrusting his cold hands deep into his pockets.

'And I wonder who suggested that the tearbook should be returned in the first place?'

Farden was dumbfounded. 'How did you—?'

'There are many things about dragons you have yet to learn, Farden,' Eyrum said from beside him.

The mage had already realised that there was a lot more to the Sirens and their dragons than he had assumed. They were nowhere near as barbaric as the Arka had portrayed them in the war. They were fierce warriors, agreed, and had fought with tooth, nail, and flame in battle, but now he could see that they were older and wiser than the Arka gave them credit for.

'Have you found anything in the tearbook yet?' he asked.

'My memories are many, and stretch far back, Farden. Once the tearbook is ready, it may take many days for our scholars to find the location of an elven well, if one even exists at all,' Farfallen said.

'We can't rule it out. What happens if you're wrong and the creature is summoned? Even if the Sirens and the Arka fought it together I still doubt we—'

Farfallen shook his head. 'So you have said, Farden, but the scholars have a thousand years of my life to sift through. Needless to say it is not a quick process.'

Farden found himself frustrated and impatient, but he knew Farfallen was right. 'Gods damn it,' he cursed.

'Come, Svarta told me you wanted to train. Maybe it'll help you blow off some of that steam we mentioned.' Farfallen smiled again.

'Hmm, and speaking of Svarta—' Farden began, but the Old Dragon interrupted by holding up a claw.

'I am aware of what she did, and I will talk to her in good time. You must remember she is doing what she thinks is best for our people.' Farfallen said.

'Luckily you had the foresight to send Eyrum here to keep me out of trouble.' The big Siren to Farden's right nodded slowly.

Farfallen edged closer to the railing and began to stretch his wings out with a satisfied groan. 'Eyrum will take you to a room where you may practice your magick. I will meet you there shortly.'

With that, he flapped his huge golden wings, threatening to blow the two men from the balcony, and launched himself into the dark sky. Eyrum headed towards the doorway and Farden followed him back into the steamy corridors.

'One more time. Keep it the same level.' Farden grinned, wiping sweat from his brow and bracing himself against the wall.

Farfallen took another deep breath and crouched low to the floor. The great dragon closed one golden eye and sent a thin stream of fire exploding from his jaws.

Farden threw open hands out to meet the blast. An invisible wall slammed into the fiery onslaught, stopping it mere inches from his fingers. The ferocious flames swirled around him, licking at his boots, but his shield spell held strong. Farden clenched his teeth as he pushed harder, making the fire recede a few more inches.

Farfallen ran out of breath and drew himself up to laugh heartily. 'Impressive, mage!'

Farden ran a hand through his sweaty hair, panting hard. He flexed his fingers, sending cinders flashing across his skin. *It felt good to have his magick back*, he smiled to himself. *Even if he was a wreck.*

'How many Written are there?' asked Eyrum. He was standing behind them, arms folded at his back. His face was as expressionless as usual, and he cocked his head to one side, as the Sirens seemed to have a habit of doing.

Farden thought. 'About a hundred, I think, maybe more. Not everyone who goes through the Ritual actually survives it. About half the candidates die.'

'And are they all as powerful as you?'

'Some are,' the mage shrugged. When compared to those of the Arkmages or Vice, Farden knew his spells couldn't compete. They were the masters, and Farden, even thirteen years after his Ritual, was still learning. But out of the Written, he was one of the best. If not *the* best.

Farfallen turned his head to look at Eyrum. 'I think our tall friend here has a few tricks of his own. Perhaps you would like to see?'

The quiet Siren shook his head and mouthed a refusal, but the dragon was not to be discouraged. 'Come now, friend. Show Farden that it is not just the Arka who are skilled in magick.'

'Sire, it has been years since I have tried,' Eyrum mumbled as he looked around in an effort to avoid the dragon's golden stare.

'And I am sure it will come back to you.' Farfallen looked at Farden and winked again. 'It's just like riding a dragon: you never forget.'

'My knowledge of wizards' spells is limited,' admitted Farden. 'It would be interesting to see Nelska magick.

'I suppose you never fought any in the war? Only dragons?' Eyrum's tone grew icy.

'I never fought in the war; I was still in training.' Farden replied, trying to smile around his words.

With a harrumph, Eyrum untied the belt on his brown robe and cast it aside. He walked to the centre of the hall and crossed his arms. He issued his challenge. 'Well then, send one of your fire spells at me, mage, and you will see some Nelska magick.'

'Are you sure?' Farden noted the serious look in the Siren's eyes. Eyrum nodded.

He did relish a challenge, it had to be said. 'Alright.'

Farden stepped back to his spot against the wall and slammed his wrists together with a clang. He held his hands out in front of him, curled fingers forming a cage around nothing but air. Then, a spark ignited and a spinning sphere of fire bloomed between his palms. The wider he held his hands, the bigger it grew, until it raged and spat like a trapped sun.

With a swift movement, Farden spun on one foot and hurled the fireball straight at Eyrum, who stood dead still about forty paces from him.

Just as the fire spell was about to blast the Siren into charcoal, Eyrum moved. He did it without any obvious movement at all, simply becoming a blur of a man, sliding sideways across the stone floor to dodge the spell. He did it all in the space of a blink.

The fireball exploded against the opposite wall with a crash and a roar, cracking the stone.

Farden was stunned. Eyrum now stood about fifteen feet away from his previous location, still with his hands clasped behind his back. A satisfied grin threatened to creep across his scarred face.

Farden raised his hands again. Sparks danced along the mage's arms and a fork of lightning tore through the air.

With no more than a mutter, Eyrum side-stepped again. He ended up a dozen paces to the left, his bulk blurring as he moved.

'Speed magick,' Farden said, with an impressed smile. 'One of the few schools of magick that we Written never learn.'

Eyrum nodded again and looked to Farfallen. 'In truth it is not Nelska magick. It comes from the nomadic people in the east, far off in the deserts of Paraia where they learn to catch strange, tall deer that can run like the wind. My dragon, Longraid, would fly there to dodge through the dunes and canyons for sport.'

'She said that the creatures there tasted better than anything else. She loved to hunt the desert cats, too, and the sand worms,' Farfallen rumbled, eyes distant.

A moment of silence followed. Farden sensed something deep and sorrowful in the room. He could only try to imagine what it must be like to lose a dragon, or a rider. He felt a surge of sympathy for the man.

'I'm sorry, Eyrum. For your dragon,' the mage offered, feeling awkward.

The Siren looked at him with a surprised expression, then bowed his head low in gratitude. Farfallen chuckled with a low growl.

'Did I not tell you, Eyrum, that not all the Arka were as heartless and cruel as you thought?'

chapter 9

When the elves left, Emaneska was left to fend for itself amidst the darkness and chaos that remained behind. And it was at this turbulent time that three great nations appeared amidst the Scattered Kingdoms. The first and greatest, the warlike Skölgard, seized the lands of the northeast. For a hundred years, they carved out their vast empire, ruling all from Gordheim, the City of Waterfalls, on the northeastern lakes. The second, the small sailing nation of the Arka, finally chose to settle in the Össfen Mountains. They used their trade routes and seafaring abilities to grow rich and powerful, meddling in the matters and affairs of magick.

The third, and most mysterious of them all, was a more ancient and proud race, born from the dark vestiges left by the elves. These were the dragon-riders, the Sirens, a strange civilisation bonded to the great dragons of the north, reptilian in their appearance and just as fierce. They built their capital in the ice-locked fire lands of Nelska, tunnelling deep into the mountains to carve out their cities. Their magick was of a different ilk, more natural than that of the bold and flashy Arka.

What was strange about these three great nations? Was it their wild differences, their abilities, and cultures? No, Emaneska has never longed for simplicity. It was how quickly these simple peoples managed to rise above the Scattered Kingdoms, to become unified and powerful, a force beyond even the most hopeful dreams of Halôrn, or the Dukes of Albion, or even Rassmuen. These mere kingdoms and fiefdoms will remain subdued and quiet, servants to the whim and machinations of these three great nations.

Taken from *The Scars of Emaneska*, by the critic Áwacran

Farden had gone to bed early that morning, just as the first fingers of dawn were reaching over the mountainous horizon. In the candlelight of Farfallen's cavernous hall they had sipped warm wine and dark spirit under the gaze of the half-man, half-dragon weather-god, Thron.

They had talked for hours. Farfallen had regaled them with stories of battles and great dragons far into the small hours. Quiet Eyrum had become almost jovial. Farden had not been able to tear himself away from the Old Dragon; his tales and deep tones had been engrossing. But finally, they had retired to bed, the mage quietly managing to dodge Svarta when she rose to go about her morning business.

The curtains in Farden's room had done their best to keep the bright sunlight out, but now, as the fiery disc began to reach its zenith, the thick cloth glowed with pale yellow light.

The mage turned with a groan and threw a pillow over his eyes while sleep began its slow retreat. His mouth tasted like dried wine and he found himself ravenously hungry again. A small voice inside his head said something about trying to find some nevermar before he left for Krauslung, but he told it to be quiet. Lazy yawned at him, twitched her whiskers, then went back to sleep.

After a few minutes dozing, Farden hauled himself out of the sheets and stumbled out onto the balcony. Sunlight burst through an almost cloudless sky, stinging his eyes. The white glare of newly fallen snow covering the wide ledge didn't help matters.

He scooped some up in his hands and spread the cold ice over his face and neck in an attempt to wake himself up. As his eyes slowly adjusted to the brightness of the day, Farden covered his brow with a cupped hand and stared up at the reptilian shapes wheeling overhead like massive vultures, black against the dazzling sky. The dragons trumpeted and bellowed as they called to one another, and Farden thought he could hear the muffled shouts of their riders even from far below.

Farden wandered back into his room and found a fresh tunic had been left for him in one of the wooden cupboards. He changed and polished his boots before leaving.

Wind tugged at his cloak as he walked across the snowy balcony. Farden was curious to find out if this country ever grew warm. It was the Long Winter after all, he reminded himself. He rubbed his hands, knocking his gold and red vambraces together with a muted clang.

Once inside, Farden found a big bowl full of fruits laid out on a dining table. Some of them were strange and foreign to him, but he tried them all the same, with a few slices of bread that had also been left on the side. *Perhaps Svarta poisoned the food before she left*, he pondered as he chewed, but he was too hungry to care, and munched on. As he pulled his cloak about him, he decided that if he wasn't allowed in the citadel, then he should at least wander through the palace.

Farden spent the rest of the afternoon aimlessly ambling through the long, identical-looking corridors carved into the rock of the huge mountain.

The citadel of Hjaussfen seemed to be a complex warren of polished stone hollowed out from the volcanic leftovers of the mountain and foothills. Every arched hallway was tall and wide enough for the biggest of dragons. Walls ranged from glossy black marble to flecked and veined granite, and here and there Farden let his hand run over the surface of the smooth stone. From some of the windows, he found he could peer down into the craters and crags of the outlying districts and watch the hustle and bustle below.

Long roads spanned the wide gaps, suspended high above the houses and streets. Towers of black stone watched over the noisy thoroughfares crammed with Sirens, cattle, goats, and other strange beasts for sale. The bright colours of the houses and the markets stood out against the drab greys and blacks of the rock. Farden's keen eyes picked out a few sabre-cats gnawing at their cage bars with long, deadly teeth. He could hear their roars even from high above in the towering mountain.

The mage saw a few dragons wandering through the paved streets. They shone like jewels in the sunlight. Every Siren bowed out of their way to let the dragons pass. Their riders sat atop their scaly hides, just behind the base of the neck, lounging backwards against their rippling shoulders and saddle, nodding solemnly to the citizens passing by.

Farden found some food in a smaller mess hall that was mostly empty. The few cooks that were there stared at him with the usual mixture of fear and curiosity. The mage tried to ignore their gazes and took his lunch with him to eat while he walked.

Most of the other Sirens in the citadel just ignored him, but there were more than a few angry glances from the soldiers at the guard posts. They let him pass nonetheless. None of the other soldiers, scribes, slaves, or riders that he saw bothered him in any way. *Svarta's new orders, obviously*, he smirked to himself.

The palace seemed to be abuzz with activity. Farden had no idea what was going on, so he carried on eating the bread and cheese he had scavenged from the kitchens and kept walking.

Farden soon found himself in the same colossal great hall to which he had been dragged a day before. The sound of Sirens working and talking was a dull roar. A few dragons perched in their nests high up on the walls, their greens, blues, and reds sparkling in the sunlight that streamed through the holes in the roof. Tables had been brought in, filling every available space. Groups of men and women in white tunics and robes crowded around them or dashed about with parchment clenched in their fists. Farden had never seen such madness.

A white and yellow dragon flapped into the hall through the huge window and hovered high above them near the ceiling. It spun into a slow, spiralling descent, coming to rest gently beside the mage. Still holding his plate in one hand, Farden watched the dragon fold its wings away and bow its head. It then closed its eyes and spoke with a low, gentle voice.

'Well met and good wishes, Farden. I am Brightshow, partner of Lakkin. The Old Dragon, in all his wisdom, has gathered all the scribes and wizards in the citadel to search through every historical account we can dig out of the libraries. Some of the older dragons have loaned their tearbooks to be scrutinised, in the hope that we can find this dark elf well of yours,' she said. Her white-gold flanks glittered like liquid whenever she moved.

A little overwhelmed, Farden bowed. 'Good to meet you, Brightshow. I take it Farfallen isn't worried about keeping this matter a secret then? What if there are spies amongst the scribes or helpers?'

'Farfallen has seen to that, my good mage. Some of our dragons have spent decades honing their skills at reading the hearts and minds of men. Those ones above us, you see? They watch over all these scribes and the soldiers, making sure that they are all as loyal as they should be.' Brightshow pointed to the three dragons perched above them with a claw. Farden shook his head with a smile.

'You dragons never cease to amaze me,' he confessed.

'We may be an ancient race blessed by the gods, Farden, but it is you men who will inherit Emaneska when we are gone.' She grinned as she stretched a patchwork wing. 'But not yet,' added the dragon.

Farden smiled politely. 'So,' he said, as he finished off the last of his meal. 'What now?'

'For now, we let the scholars do their work, and we can get you a hawk to send a message to the Arka with all speed. Unless, of course, you can read dragonscript and feel like helping?'

'Hah, not me. I can barely read my own writing,' Farden laughed.

'Then allow me to fetch one of the scribes to get a messenger bird ready for you.' She waggled a claw to the few soldiers nearest to them and they clattered off into the corridors to do the dragon's bidding.

Farden watched the chaos of the great hall with a growing sense of bewilderment. At the end of every desk and table, piles of useless or unhelpful scrolls were slowly growing. Pages and parchments covered every available surface, rustling like a forest during a gale. Hundreds of scribes poked at books, scrolls, maps, and, of course, tearbooks. Even some of the nearby soldiers were trying to make sense of the spidery dragonscript. Somewhere in the forest of tables and scrolls was Farfallen's tearbook, slowly revealing its lost knowledge, or so the mage hoped.

A splash of colour caught his roaming eyes. Decorating the smooth granite walls between the nests and the many archways and corridors leading from the hall were numerous frescoes and wall paintings. Farden wondered how he hadn't noticed them before.

Most were faded with age or sunlight, but some were still perfectly colourful. Beautifully chiselled, they depicted great battles, heroic-looking dragons, and great landscapes of ice and snow that seemed as real as looking out of a window. There were also strange, ancient beasts immortalised in intricate detail, some of which Farden had never seen before.

The mage left his plate on a nearby stool and made his way through the tables to the nearest painting. He ran his hands over its cold, dusty surface. Huge grey and brown beasts moved across the frozen scene, tusks and trunks towering over the tiny specks of men at their huge feet. Farden remembered seeing such creatures during a voyage to the south long ago. The men in that foreign land had called them bastions, and their feet had shaken the ground like thunder.

In the next painting, sabre-cats, long wingless wyrms, daemons, giant manticores, and huge rats were locked in an eternal battle, faces snarling and claws reaching. In yet another, Farden recognised gryphons, giants, minotaurs, and more dragons. They were swarming across a field, surging into battle against gangly, grey men-like creatures with long black swords. *Elves*.

As Farden walked on, the epic scenes seemed to fade and age, illimitable years stretching over rock. Durnus would have given anything to study these pictures.

Brightshow rejoined him and stared over the mage's shoulder. 'This is the history of the world.'

'I've always wanted to talk with a gryphon,' said Farden.

'There are still some, in the northern wastes, or in the east I think, but like most of the other beasts on these walls, they have long abandoned Emaneska, heading east to the far realms.' A hint of wistfulness crept into the dragon's voice.

Farden pointed at a picture of a winding, horned sea serpent with ridges of spikes sprouting from its head. It was blue, like the surrounding waves, and covered in barnacles. In the mural, its gigantic tail was drowning a boatful of the same tall grey men, and there was a hungry look in its row of eyes. 'I saw one of these once, in the Bern sea. It sank a ship in the blink of an eye, then just disappeared under the waves,' he said.

'Leviathans. Good meat if you can get at them. Now these are, or were, phoenixes, distant cousins to the dragons. They were the first of us all to learn how to breathe and live with fire, but the dark elves hunted them all down, in the name of sport.'

Brightshow gestured to a flock of red and orange bird-like creatures. This mural seemed to be one of the older ones. The fiery colours of their wings had dimmed long ago, but Farden could still see the coiled flames trailing through the sky in their wake.

The mage contemplated the history of the world spread out before him, picture by picture, one mural at a time. In just a short walk along the wall, Farden had travelled at least two thousand years back in time, long before the ice had started to creep across the lands, when simple man was just a nomadic, pathetic race, lost in the new world.

Unlike the Sirens, the Arka had always hidden their histories in libraries and temples, away from the commoners; purely for the enjoyment of scholars and the education of the upper classes. But here in front of him he could see the old days: the great days of magick and monsters, when the elves ruled and the Arka were no more than an idea in the back of some goddess' mind. Brightshow was right: men would inherit the earth, but only long after the last of these ancient creatures had left or died.

Farden was filled with a deep sadness. The world he knew now seemed like a faded painting; a leftover from greatness and power that had now flaked and rusted away. His fingers traced the chiselled grooves of the mural as he tried to imagine the older days. The dragon broke the silence.

'The world is constantly moving, Farden,' Brightshow said softly. He could barely hear her over the roar of activity in the hall. 'In another thousand years it will all have changed again, and another like you will be standing here looking at pictures of ancient men and lost dragons. The world moves on. It is the way of things.'

Farden nodded, vaguely recalling Farfallen saying something similar. Emaneska had been here longer than anyone could remember, and it would still be here a thousand years from now. Farden wondered idly if anyone would ever paint a picture of him on a wall, and why. Shadows clouded his mind.

'Come, let us send your message.' Brightshow put a huge claw on his shoulder, surprisingly gently, and nodded towards a large doorway across the hall. Farden shook himself from his trance and followed her.

They walked out of the hall, and up a spiralling set of lofty stairs that led into a tall pinnacle of rock. Light and snow streamed into the room through tall windows carved out of the stone. Their ledges were wide and strewn with blankets and comfy-looking pillows. It seemed this area was for Sirens only: Brightshow barely fit into the small space. She crouched by the bigger stairwell, murmuring uncomfortably.

Arranged in a circle was a score of cages sitting on high stilts. Birds of prey of all shapes and types preened and screeched amongst themselves. They wore little leather hoods with bells on, covering their eyes and keeping them calm. Feathers covered the stone floor, along with patches of white shit. Farden wrinkled his nose at the stench.

A greying Siren bearing a wide-gapped grin emerged from behind a desk at the back of the room. His wispy grey hair was like a wild shrub, growing in all directions. He looked Farden up and down without a hint of fear or anger. The mage wondered how long he had been left up here, alone with his birds. Maybe since before the war.

The Siren never seemed to stop moving, not even for a moment. He nodded enthusiastically to Brightshow.

'Well met, friends! The guards said you might be coming up, so I have prepared a hawk for you.'

He rushed back to his desk with a hobbling gait, beckoning Farden to follow, shooing a few tame sparrows that were perched on a table. The small birds jumped into the air with a flurry of annoyed chirping. The old man grabbed a small piece of parchment and a hawk-feather quill from his cluttered desk, handing it to Farden and tapping the wood.

'It's been a while since we sent a message to your kind, sir. Been a long time indeed,' said the Siren, eyes constantly flicking about the room.

Brightshow hummed in agreement as she surveyed the hooded birds of prey in the cages. They had grown quiet and shuffled nervously. They had caught her reptilian scent on the breeze.

Farden voiced a question. 'By the way, is there a quickdoor in Hjaussfen?'

With a vigorous nod, the old Siren pointed out of the window, beyond the rocky foothills. 'Down by the south docks. It's an old one, but I hear it still works.'

'That is, if you don't want to fly.' Brightshow grinned, revealing rows of pointy teeth.

'Maybe one day.' Farden returned the smile. He spread the scrap of rough paper between his finger and thumb and dipped the quill. He scratched a brief message in red ink and tiny letters. It stained his fingers as he wrote.

ARKMAGES,

SAFE AND WELL IN THE NORTH. SIRENS PEACEFUL. SEARCHING FOR THE WELL NOW. RETURNING TODAY OR TOMORROW BY QUICKDOOR WITH NEWS. BEWARE SPIES IN MIDST, SARUNN WAS DESTROYED BY A DARK SORCERER AND ALL HANDS WERE LOST. TRUST NO ONE.

FARDEN.

There was no room for ceremony or formality in the message. The Arkmages would hopefully understand and get the quickdoor ready for his arrival. Farden purposefully left out the news of Farfallen still being alive. He had decided to tell Vice in private rather than in front of the entire council. He didn't want his friend's reputation to be tarnished.

'These birds will get your message there fast, sir, have no worries. They're a lot faster than your southern hawks, I can tell you that.' The grey Siren winked at him. His scales hung from his jaw line like dark brown lichen on a tree.

'Is that so?' Farden humoured the funny old character.

He winked. 'They're fed on a strict diet of rabbit meat and lightning, makes them fast you see.' The Siren grinned at his own joke.

Farden handed him the scrap of parchment and, with a deft little movement, the grey Siren coiled it up into a small tube and twisted the ends tightly. He dipped each end in a pot of green wax that bubbled above a nearby candle. Each end of the scroll was stamped with an ivory signet ring on his finger, in the shape of a feathered wing. Then he whistled piercingly to his birds. Like an arthritic hunting cat, he prowled along the front of the cages, looking for one bird in particular. He stopped when he came to a still, composed hawk that was calmly preening its feathers.

'Aha, here she is, finest and fastest of the lot.' The Siren thrust his skinny arm into the wooden enclosure and reached for his bird. The bell on her hood jangled as she latched onto his scaly arm with her talons, flapping her wings for balance. Her plumage was a soft russet brown, flecked with dark spots, with snowy white feathers on her underside that shone in the daylight.

'Come here then, come on.' He spoke softly to the hawk as he brought her out into the light. 'If you don't mind, I have to face her away from you, madam, in case she gets scared,' said the Siren to Brightshow. She nodded.

Farden looked at the proud bird of prey, perched so gently on the old Siren's arm despite her razor-sharp talons. The hawk sat tall and still while her hood was removed, then shrugged her wings and looked around. Deep yellow eyes blinked in the sunlight as she stared at the mage indifferently. Two long feathers, like those of a heron, stood out behind her head, and when she spread her wings the mage saw her long dark pinion feathers. They quivered, as though she were eager to get going. She screeched once, clear and piercing.

With a slender piece of twine, the old Siren fastened the waxy scroll to the bird's yellow leg, wrapping it over and over in a criss-cross pattern until it was safe and secure.

The last thing he did before letting the hawk go was to whisper into the feathery place where her ears were hidden, then he flung her from his arm and out of the window. The bird screeched another thin, piercing wail before disappearing into the grey sky.

'Thank you,' said Farden.

The Siren bowed, practically wriggling with excitement. 'My pleasure sire, always nice to be of service.' He bowed again. Farden shook his wrinkled hand.

'Please let us know if and when a reply comes from the Arka,' said Brightshow.

'I will, Madam, good wishes to the two of you,' the grey Siren dipped his head once more, then wrung his hands until they left, as if he were unsure of what to do with himself.

Brightshow and Farden went back to the hall, where Farfallen, Svarta, Eyrum, and a few other dragons had gathered in the centre of the huge mass of tables. Svarta seemed angry, but then again Farden had never seen her look any different. Farfallen looked disappointed and pensive.

As they emerged into the light, the Old Dragon beckoned them closer with a silent wave of his great claws, careful not to interrupt the heated conversation between his rider and one of the scholars.

'What do you mean, *weeks*?' Svarta demanded. The man opposite her was tall, blonde, and freckled, and had obviously drawn the short straw. He looked nothing short of terrified of the Siren queen, blushing through purple scales, constantly fidgeting with a quill in his hands, and smoothing his blonde hair down against his forehead anxiously.

'Even the oldest of the tearbooks don't go back as far as the Old Dragon's. So far, er, your Highness, none of the scrolls or parchments we've read mention a well. Therefore, I—*we* think it must be…' Here he faltered.

'Must be what?' Svarta snapped. Her hands were fixed to her hips.

'That a clue has to lie in the Old Dragon's memories,' the young scholar added quickly. 'And that's the problem, your Highness. Translating those is taking far longer than we anticipated.'

'And you're telling me it would take *weeks* to search through Farfallen's memories?'

The young scholar looked behind him, seeking back up from his cluster of colleagues, who all bobbed and nodded frantically. One held up a hand and answered for him.

'It seems so, my Queen. The older the memories are, the more ancient the translation, and the more difficult they are to read. They are detailed, condensed, crossing over with memories of former Old Dragons. It is taking us far longer than we thought, and so far we haven't found anything at all.'

Svarta huffed, but Farfallen spoke in his deep booming voice. 'If it will take weeks, then it will take weeks. These men are trying their hardest and we must give them the time to finish their task.' The blonde man visibly relaxed.

'However!' Farfallen held up a claw, flashing a look towards Farden. 'Understand that we are all in great danger, and your lives depend on finding this well before it is too late. Do you understand me?' Farfallen looked around with a raised brow. Every single scribe, scholar and Siren in the room bellowed loudly in agreement and scrabbled to get back to work. The hubbub rose afresh.

When the Old Dragon turned to depart, the blonde scholar was left looking relieved, if not a little shaky. He turned back to his gang and breathed a heavy sigh, fetching a few pats on his back for good measure.

Farden followed in the wake of the group of dragons and riders as they left the hall. Farfallen led them down a wide corridor to a long room that was missing a wall, leaving it open to the sky on one side. Cold wind swirled around the bare space, and the dragons gathered in a group at the end of the room.

'Well, what now?' Farden asked loudly as he walked towards them, arms spread wide.

Farfallen looked at him, cocking his head on one side like a giant cat. 'Now, Farden, you go home. We will continue to search through my memories, and we *will* find this elf well. And when we are successful, I will send our fastest dragons to Krauslung with the news. You have an Old Dragon's word,' Farfallen said.

Farden shook his head, thinking of Helyard's warnings. 'But you said yourself that it will take weeks,' he objected. 'It could be too late by then.'

'Maybe so, but if I and Svarta and the others help them search,' he replied with a confident air, 'then you shall have your answer within a week.'

The other dragons rumbled in loud agreement and gazed calmly at the mage with their colourful eyes.

'My memories are slowly flowing back to me, like a trickling stream, but soon they will burst their banks, and become a great torrent in my mind. That will help the scholars. We can't rush this, Farden, and we need to be careful.' As if sensing Farden's concerns,

Farfallen added, 'And yes, mage, we are aware of the lack of time. We want this as much as you do.'

Farden looked down at the stone floor and fought off a deep sigh. 'Then I will return to Krauslung. The Arka will need to be ready, just in case,' he said.

The Old Dragon smiled. 'Hopefully it will not come to a fight, my good Written. But if it must, then the Sirens will stand beside you.' He looked to the other dragons before continuing. 'And tell your Arkmages that they can once again call us allies. The war ended a long time ago, and I think it is time for us to open our gates.'

Svarta shot Farfallen a disbelieving glance and then, catching herself, turned to face the mage with an expression of poorly hidden anxiety.

Farden smiled and crossed his arms over a chest that was swelling with pride. 'Thank you, Farfallen.'

'Towerdawn here will take you anywhere you want to go.' Farfallen nodded to a stocky red dragon on his right, and the muscular beast bowed his chin to the floor. His scarlet scales rippled in the sunlight and the dark wine-coloured crest running along his spine rattled.

Farden bowed in return, but shook his head. He was curious about flying, of course, but now was the time for speed. 'Again, thank you, but I've learnt there is a quickdoor at the docks that I can use to get back to Krauslung.'

Farfallen nodded. 'Of course. It is ancient, but I know it still works. I shall have one of the wizards open it immediately.'

'Then I will need to pack.'

'Svarta will have some provisions brought up to your room.' Farfallen said. Svarta nodded tiresomely. Farden bowed and Brightshow followed him out of the door. When they had left the room and were walking back down the corridor, the dragon sighed in mock annoyance.

'Well! It seems we've only just met and you're already leaving.'

'It is a shame.' Farden smiled. 'But I have to be getting back to the Arkmages as soon as possible.' He had decided that he would miss Nelska and its dragons.

'I've heard one of your elders has spells that control the weather?' the dragon asked.

'Helyard, yes.' Farden murmured thoughtfully, surprised that Brightshow would know that about one of the Arkmages.

'He must have the blood of the daemons in him then, one of the nefalim,' the dragon whispered, as though it were heresy in Hjaussfen to say such words. She sounded like one of the superstitious sailors from the *Sarunn*.

Farden found himself laughing out loud. 'Hah! Now that, I would find very hard to believe. He's a powerful mage, yes, but not some kind of half-daemon. Just an angry old man.' Farden shook his head, chuckling quietly.

'A man who controls the weather should be careful with his anger. He sounds dangerous to me.'

Farden could not help but agree. He had long feared a traitor in the midst of the magick council, and more than once the name Helyard had crossed his mind. It would be dangerous, but he would talk about this with Durnus, and Vice, when he got back. He could trust them at least.

'He does, you're right,' Farden mused for a moment before changing the subject. 'Do you think that Farfallen and the others can find that well in a week?'

'If Farfallen gave his word, then it will happen. The Old Dragon doesn't often disappoint.'

'Good, because we'll need all the help we can get to stop those behind all this. I'm just praying they don't already know where a well is.'

'We would know by now if they did,' Brightshow countered.

Farden grunted. 'I hope you're right.'

'And here we are,' said Brightshow. They had come to the large door to Farfallen's rooms, where they paused.

'It was a pleasure to meet you,' Farden said with a smile. Brightshow's huge yellow eyes had the same kind gaze as the other dragons. He caught himself slowly getting lost in them.

'And you also. It's time for me to go and find my rider, Lakkin, so sadly I won't be able to see you off at the docks.'

'Well, perhaps I will see you in the days to come.'

'Perhaps. Well met and good wishes, Farden.'

The dragon turned and the mage ducked as her long white tail swung high over his head.

Farden went to his room to gather up the rest of his clothes and armour. The only problem was that the people of the palace seemed intent on knocking on his door, continually delivering provisions and supplies from the Old Dragon.

After two hours, the mage stood surrounded by parcels of bread, cheese, meats, and fruit; haversacks filled with a mealy cake thing; a small oil lamp; two fresh tunics and a new black cloak; a length of red rope; various maps; a small book entitled *Flight for Beginners;* and an ornate vial of melted snow, for his health, of course.

As soon as Farden dared to assume he had seen the last of the servants, another dull thudding shook the mage's door. With an exasperated sigh, he leapt to the door and yanked it open, only to find Eyrum standing outside. The big Siren said nothing and the mage gestured for him to enter, ushering him out of the wind. Eyrum had to stoop to avoid hitting his head on the doorframe.

'What brings you to my humble room?' asked Farden.

'I have a parting gift for you, before you go,' Eyrum replied solemnly. The mage guessed he wasn't used to this sort of sentimentality and nodded for him to go on.

He took a breath and cleared his throat. His eyes wandered around the room and over the scattered supplies strewn over the bed. 'Seems like you've had enough from Farfallen as it is. That dragon really has taken a liking to you.'

'Gods know why,' chuckled Farden, as he gathered up folded clothes and packets, ready to stuff them into his travel bag. The supply belt around his waist was already full to bursting.

'Even so, I thought you would appreciate this.' Eyrum held out a big fist and slowly opened his fingers to reveal a small glittering object curled up on his palm. The Siren lifted the shiny pendant up by its thin metal chain and offered it. Farden accepted it gently, holding it up for closer inspection.

It looked like a thin sliver of a dragon's scale, sandy orange in colour and sparkling as though encrusted with gold dust. There was a warmth to it; a glow that Farden could feel only if he held the scale tightly in both hands. As he was turning it over in his fingers, Eyrum explained.

'When a dragon dies, their scales soak up and hold on to their luck. So if you wear this around your neck, it might bring you good fortune in the weeks to come,' the man told him quietly. He had hardly moved since first entering the room; he just stood like an obelisk, his big hands now back in his cloak pockets.

Farden was shocked, honoured, and confused at the same time. He handed the scale back to the big Siren. 'I can't take this Eyrum. It's your dragon—' But Eyrum pushed his hand back, closing his fingers around the pendant for him.

'I have a feeling you need it more than I do.'

Farden didn't know what to say, so he just stared at the pendant. A gift was a gift, after all. 'Thank you, Eyrum.' Farden looked fruitlessly around his room to find something to offer the tall man in return. 'I have nothing to give you.'

'No need, mage. It has been good enough to meet you, and to see your impressive display of magick last night. I hope that we have both learnt something while you were in Hjaussfen,' Eyrum said.

Farden smiled. 'I think that a lot of my opinions have changed since being here, and not only about dragons. If only the rest of the Arka could see through my eyes, they'd understand there's something deep and ancient about you scaly lot.'

Eyrum managed a small smile. 'Indeed. Then I think it is a good thing that you were washed up on our shores.'

'Maybe.' Farden mused, noticing that fate had once again manoeuvred his life without his control or blessing.

Eyrum moved towards the door. 'I will see you at the docks, Farden. The quickdoor should be ready within the next hour.' He opened the door, letting a cold breeze in.

'Thank you again, Eyrum, for the gift,' said the mage, as he looped the chain over his neck and slipped the scale under his tunic. The big Siren said no more, and shut the door behind him with a click.

An hour passed, and Farden managed to squeeze most of the stuff into the haversack and decided to eat whatever he couldn't fit in.

Lazy stretched and yawned, then got up to sniff around the packages. She looked at Farden with an all too human expression, as if she wasn't fond of change, before sitting on the corner of her bed to lick herself.

Farden was munching on an apple and a slice of some dark dried meat, which was a bit too fish-flavoured for its colour, when yet another visitor knocked on his door.

Still chewing, he opened it to find Svarta standing with her arms crossed, her face displaying its usual irked expression. Farden waited to finish his mouthful of apple before speaking. 'I'm sorry, were you waiting for long?'

'Are you ready to go?' she asked pointedly.

'Almost, come in.' Farden walked back inside the room and she followed. Svarta looked around at the mess of packing. She eyed the cat with a curious look, then turned back to the mage, pointing a long finger at him.

'Where did you get those vambraces of yours?' she asked. Her voice was quiet and controlled, as if she were forcing herself to be civil with the mage.

Farden looked at the red and gold metal covering his wrists and forearms, deciding whether to lie or not. 'I won them years ago, when I was hunting in the far north with some of the other Written.'

Svarta crossed her arms. 'Won them? Gambling?'

'Sort of. There was an argument that I couldn't win a fight against the champion warrior of some village. These vambraces, a family heirloom, were his wager. The skin from my back was mine.'

Farden could still remember that fight like it had been yesterday: every blow, every scuffle, every shout of the crowd, even the smell of fear on his opponent. All of it was painted as vividly on his memory as the murals in the dragon hall. *A story for another day.*

'I take it you won,' she said dryly.

'Clearly.' Farden said no more about it, busying himself with the heavy sack of supplies and his bulging belt. Tucking the last of the meat back into his pockets, Farden swung his newly cleaned sword over his back and strapped it tightly to his chest.

Svarta still stood with her arms firmly crossed. Her two blonde strands of hair framed her frustrated face quite perfectly. Her lips were drawn thin and she held her weight on one foot, tapping the other in some test of patience. Her long dress was a shimmering blue that day, crystallised like a frozen waterfall, and the thick leather jacket on her shoulders was dusted with fresh snow. Her face was white from the cold, but the deep yellow smudge of golden scales running over her cheekbones and neck were bright and shining.

Farden gave her a questioning look, and she finally let her restraint snap.

'Look, if you think for a moment that I'm going to let the rest of the Arka traipse all over Nelska again, you're sorely mistaken!'

Farden laughed out loud. 'You can't let it go, can you? This was Farfallen's decision—'

'That doesn't matter,' Svarta snapped. She clenched her fists and her dress rustled. 'It may have been before your time, mage, but my people still haven't forgotten the war, even if the Old Dragon has. It will be a while before we open our gates wide enough for the Arka.'

'I couldn't care less about that. All I'm concerned about is finding this well before the others do. Farfallen has given me his word,' said the mage.

Her face hardened as though Farden had challenged her honour. 'And that unfortunately stands for both of us, for his word is mine also.' The Siren queen shook her head. 'You have proven your good intentions to the Old Dragon, and if he trusts you, then maybe one day I shall, too.' Her last remark stung as she said it, he could see that much, but Farden knew she was trying her best.

He pulled at the straps of his haversack and Svarta moved to the door. Farden ruffled Lazy's sable ears, looking into the cat's brown eyes. 'Look after my cat, if you can,' he said, and the queen sighed.

'Fine.'

Farden briefly entertained a feeling of excitement at the thought of seeing Cheska again, and perhaps, if he was lucky, getting some well overdue time alone with her. But the cold snow that whipped his face stole away his thoughts, and he pulled the hood of his new cloak over his eyes.

'Well, you can relax now that I'm going back home,' he shouted over the noise of the wind. He could just about hear Svarta's grumbling behind him.

'Unlikely, I have a tearbook to scour through,' she snorted, slamming the door behind them.

Down at the docks the weather was no more gracious. The earlier sunlight had vanished, replaced by another front of bad weather from the west. The rimy sea-spray stung the faces of the huddle gathered on the solitary pier. The sea beyond it was grey and as hard as flint. White crests swiped at the frenzied snowflakes falling from iron clouds before crashing against the rocks in huge fountains of foam.

As he shuddered in the cold, Farden wondered if Krauslung was any fairer this day. The dragons seemed to be loving the foul weather, pointing their snouts into the face of the wind and letting the water and ice lash their scales. *The fires in their hearts must be keeping them warm*, Farden thought.

The mage stood beside Farfallen. In front of them, the pier stretched out into the waves. Halfway along, two slender spurs of black rock formed the gateway of the quickdoor, which thrummed with energy as sea-spray fizzed into steam on its hazy surface.

A wizard, his long red cloak plastered to him, was calling out words from a spell book that looked very much like the one that Durnus used. The scribe at his side was no more than a boy, shivering through wet clothes while trying to turn the pages for his master.

'Is it ready yet?' one of the dragons called from behind them. Farfallen repeated the question to the old wizard, whose face was almost completely covered with blue scales. The man shook his head and carried on shouting over the wind and thundering waves.

Every time a grey wall of water struck the rocks under the pier, a cloud of spray soaked the group. Farden was growing more and more eager to dive through the quickdoor with each passing minute. He turned his head to look up at the black mountain towering above them. The docks were in the shadow of the mountain's steeper slope, and wet granite cliffs soared high into the air, leaning over them like the prow of some gigantic black ship. Farden could imagine them toppling at any moment.

'What did Eyrum give you?' Farfallen's deep voice broke through his reverie.

'A dragon's scale.' Farden plucked the tiny pendant from under his cloak and showed it to the gold dragon.

Farfallen hummed. 'That is quite a gift for a rider to give,' he said. 'That is a scale from his dragon, Longraid.'

Farden nodded without saying anything, staring at its ochre surface. He thumbed it and thought about trying to give it back to Eyrum. He was about to take it off when Farfallen shook his head.

'He wanted you to have it, and it is highly inappropriate in the Siren culture to return a gift, Farden. Just keep hold of it for now.' He winked. As he did so, the Siren wizard shouted and threw his hands in the air.

'It's ready!'

'Good! Now, mage, are you ready?' The Old Dragon shouted so all could hear. Farden looked around him as the others gathered to watch. Svarta stood as still and silent as always, but for once her face held no anger or venom. Eyrum stood at the back of the group, hood high up over his head so that half his face was hidden. Farden nodded to the big Siren and Eyrum raised a hand silently. He turned back to Farfallen.

'I'm ready.'

Farden picked his way carefully over the slick stones with the dragon and stood in front of the quickdoor. The portal throbbed with a low rhythmic beat and he could already feel the pull of the vortex on his cloak and boots. He looked back. 'I expect to see you flying over the Össfen Mountains in less than a week,' he shouted at the Old Dragon.

'You just concentrate on getting the Arka ready. We will do our bit.' Farfallen exposed his fangs in a wide smile as the mage tensed his body, ready for the journey.

'Gods speed you, Farden!' the dragons called to him as he stepped over the threshold, then everything melted into one white blur in front of his eyes.

The breath burnt in his lungs. His ribs were squashed as he flew through a tunnel of white ice. He fought to keep his eyes shut. His legs felt like they would be ripped from his body any second, and wind roared past his ears like a hurricane. Farden clenched his teeth, struggling to keep his body upright for the landing. He braced himself.

chapter 10

Remember also the manner in which a dragon may read your soul, and speak silently to its rider. Remark at the startling resemblance a rider displays to his dragon! The scale colours are almost always the same hue, and he or she may share the same temperament, or physical features. They boldly sit astride these enormous savage beasts, as if they were no more fearsome than a simple cow, riding into the cold sky with them like birds. The Sirens are truly odd!

From *Inside Nelska: A Warning Guide* by Master Wird

For once, the sky was clear over Krauslung. A few idle wisps of cloud streaked the crystal blue like the accidental brush strokes of an indolent artist. There was a crisp coldness to the air, the type just after snow, and the people in the streets burrowed deep into their coats and cloaks for warmth. Clouds of breath rose from the crowded citizens gathered around market stalls and tavern doorways. A distant bell tolled in the Port of Rós, breaking the stillness of the frozen city.

Vice watched the crowds milling around from far above. The towering fortress walls of the Arkathedral were sheer, so he could lean out over the window ledge to watch his people rush around below, bundled up in coats and hats, thick scarves wrapped tightly around their heads. They looked more like ants from so high up. A man's voice broke through his trance.

'Undermage, the quickdoor is opening,' a soldier called. Vice spun round to face his small group of guards.

'Stand back and give him some room. Get that blanket ready, man!' He waved his hands about and the men hurried to obey him. The soldier holding the thick woollen blanket over one arm stood to the side of the quickdoor and unfolded it.

Vice stood with the other men, half a dozen paces back from the quickdoor, watching intently. The small room grew hot and sparked with electricity as the archway began to hum and shake. A slight haze started to spread across the doorway, rolling and undulating like a translucent veil of energy. Several flashes of light dashed across the door and a low rumble came from somewhere deep inside.

Without warning, a pulse of light and a gust of air pushed all the men a step backwards. Farden came flying out of the quickdoor backwards and fell heavily to the floor, crumpling into a heap.

The mage shivered convulsively, pulling his legs from the portal just as it began to close. The soldier threw a blanket over him as Vice strode forwards to help him up.

'Give him a hand over here,' he ordered, and the soldiers scurried to help the mage to his feet. 'Glad to have you back, old friend,' laughed the Undermage. He grabbed Farden's hand and shook it warmly with both of his. 'No doubt you have a story to tell me?'

'Just get me some warm wine, Undermage, and I'll tell you any story you want.' Farden had managed to stand on both feet, but his teeth chattered over his gasping words.

'Hah! You heard the man, get him some wine, and some *mörd*, too!' Vice called. Two soldiers ran from the room.

'Come on, let's get you to my chambers.' The Undermage put an arm around Farden and guided him on.

❦

'Drink your wine, Farden, don't just stare at the fire,' said Vice, leaning back into a deep armchair with a chuckle. He tossed another log into the fireplace. It landed in the flames with a burst of sparks. Steaming wood cracked and spat at them.

Farden shook his head and blinked. He was perched on the edges of his own luxurious chair, leaning forwards to get closer to the roaring fire. He sipped the steamy concoction from the silver cup in his hands. It was warm and sweet: mulled wine mixed with the infamous Arka moonshine called *mörd.* Or *piss,* as it was more commonly known.

It was a soldier's drink, devastatingly strong and as clear as ice water. He had heard many of the older veterans arguing long into the night about its magick healing powers, and Farden was inclined to agree with the bunch of gap-toothed brawlers. It was like drinking fire, but not altogether unpleasant. The steaming liquid warmed his throat and burnt in his belly like the wood crackling in front of him. He was starting to feel better again. Farden squinted as he looked around.

Vice's private chambers were vast, decorated in the finest styles. Couches, tables, bookcases, desks, and chairs filled almost every available space. The difference between the Undermage's rooms and Durnus' was startling, but they were just as warm, and Farden was just as happy to be there. They hadn't changed much since his last visit, but he still found himself looking around.

Trophies and paintings of Vice's victories covered the walls, jostling for space between the long windows that stretched across the far wall. The sun was just about to disappear over the mountains, and the clouds were beginning to gather again as the weather from Nelska travelled southwards. Farden turned his head to watch the red orb sinking into the sea behind the distant islands.

'I knew this weather wouldn't last,' he said.

'It's been bitterly cold since you went away. Helyard's been in a foul mood. Maybe that's why.' Vice shrugged.

'What's wrong with him now?' Farden sighed. He still harboured suspicions about Helyard but had decided to hear what Durnus had to say before telling Vice.

'Your disappearance, my good mage! The whole council has been in uproar over the apparent loss of the tearbook. It was only when your hawk arrived that Åddren finally managed to bring peace to the council, and I was sent to get the quickdoor ready for your arrival.' Vice leaned back even further into the massive chair and smiled at Farden. He entwined his fingers, humming thoughtfully.

'Well, it wasn't all fun and games for me either, but I can assure you that the tearbook is safely back in the hands of the dragons. They have promised me that within the week we will have our answers.'

' "Safely back in the hands of the dragons." Is this you talking, Farden? I thought we agreed they couldn't be trusted?' Vice spat.

'I wasn't treated so kindly at first. The Siren queen, Svarta, wanted to lock me up and throw away the key.'

'But what about the message we sent to them warning them of your arrival?'

'It never got there. I think it had something to do with the sorcerer on the ship.' Farden stared into the flames again. The cup was warm in his hands.

'Right, I'm completely lost. Start from the beginning.' Vice scrunched up his face as if the confusion physically hurt him.

'Sorry.' Farden laughed before shuffling his chair around to face the Undermage. 'A few days before the end of the journey I caught one of the sailors in my room trying to steal the tearbook. I thought he was just a thief, but he was a sorcerer, and a dark one at that. It turns out he had been sent by the same people who stole the summoning manual. I managed to fend him off, but a wave hit the ship and she went down.' Farden was glad Vice wasn't as good as detecting lies as the dragons were. He sipped his *mörd*.

'So, how did you get to Nelska without a ship?' asked Vice.

Farden shook his head and thought hard, something he had spent many hours doing in Hjaussfen. *By all rights he should be dead.*

'By some sort of miracle, I was washed up on the beach near the palace and a guard found me. And let's just say that there were some complications after that.'

'Tell me,' Vice said, leaning out of his chair to listen more carefully.

Farden had hoped to skip this particular matter entirely. 'One of the Siren healers read my Book while I was unconscious, so they locked the poor lunatic in a cell with me. When I finally came to, half a week later, they dragged me in front of the dragons and interrogated me. They weren't the least bit happy after that debacle.'

'It was his fault, not yours, if you were unconscious.' Vice scowled.

'Either way, the queen, Svarta, was overruled and they let me stay in the palace, free to wander around and train,' said Farden.

'You can't be serious,' Vice scoffed, sceptical.

Farden nodded. 'I swear to the gods. I told them the Arka finally wanted peace, and after seeing the tearbook they were convinced I wasn't there to cause any trouble. I was as surprised as you were. There's a lot more to the dragons than we've come to assume, Vice.'

The Undermage scowled again before quaffing his drink. He put the glass down on a nearby table with a sharp tap. 'That's another matter for another day. What will happen to the tearbook now?' he asked.

'It will stay with them for the time being, and within a week we will have the location of the well. They have every scribe in the city working through every old scroll and historical account they can get their claws on. And now that Svarta and the other dragons are working beside them I have no doubt; if there's an elf well left in Emaneska, they'll find it.' Farden matched Vice's intent gaze. 'There must be so much knowledge in the dragons' memories. So many lost things, places, people…' The wine stole the mage's words, and he sipped some more.

Vice nodded slowly. 'That's why Helyard never wanted Farfallen's tearbook to leave Krauslung, even though it was blank, the stupid fool. He was worried it would give them lost secrets. An edge.' He paused, looking over the rim of his cup. 'Did the script reappear, once it returned to Nelska?'

'As a matter of fact, it did.'

'I'll inform the Arkmages. Helyard will no doubt be soured by the news.'

Farden kept his face in his cup, staying quiet. He would tell Vice of Farfallen soon, but not now.

Vice continued. 'If you can trust the Sirens, then so shall I. I just hope you know what you're doing, Farden. As does the council.'

'I have their word,' said Farden.

'And how much is that worth? If the dragons are too late, then we must be ready to fight this creature ourselves. I don't care how many men it takes—we cannot let this thing survive. Åddren and Helyard share my sentiments, and I'm sure the Sirens feel the same way about the matter.'

'They do, and they have sworn their assistance should the situation grow that dire,' Farden assured him.

'Good. Then by tomorrow night, the whole army will be ready to march. I will leave it to you to gather the Written, old friend. You will have all the hawks you need at your disposal, and I will send word to the Spire that you are to lead the others. It is about time the Written had a good captain.'

'The Captain of the Written? Vice—' Farden began, but Vice held up a silencing hand.

'No, Farden. I don't want to hear another word. It's about time you had your own command. I can't think of another better suited for it. It's time to put all the rumours and gossip behind you and stop playing the hermit.'

He was about to protest again, but Vice cast him a look that said, 'my word is final.' Farden resignedly swilled the last of his wine around the bottom of his cup.

'For now, you will rest, Farden. I will have a room set up for you.' Vice rubbed his hands together as he stood up.

Farden gulped down the last of the warm *mörd*, letting an idea unfurl in his head. He smiled. 'Thank you, friend, but there is a comfy bed in a comfy inn that has my name on it.'

'Hah, so you like the *Goat* then? I told you. It's one of the oldest taverns in the city,' he said, pushing himself up from the chair. Vice strode across the room, leaving Farden to gather his things. The supplies given to him by the Sirens still threatened to burst out of his haversack, but at least he would not have to pay for dinner tonight.

Farden watched the Undermage shuffle some scrolls on a desk and hum to himself. In many ways, Vice was very similar to Durnus: both of them knew him too well and cared too much. He was starting to realise how much he needed such friends.

Farden snorted to himself; wine always made him think too much. Vice waved a hand at him dismissively.

'Be gone with you, you hooligan. Be here bright and early tomorrow. I'll inform the Arkmages tonight that we must assemble the council,' Vice said, joining the mage at the door. They shook hands warmly and the Undermage looked his friend in the eye. 'It is good to have you back with us. I was worried.'

Farden winked as he turned to leave. 'It's starting to look like you'll never get rid of me.'

'I damn well hope not,' laughed Vice. He watched the door close behind the mage, then stretched with a yawn and went to find the rest of the *mörd*.

❦

An hour later, true to form, the glassy skies above Krauslung became crowded with billowing grey clouds rolling and piling on top of each other, blotting out the first stars of the evening.

The city was starting to sparkle with candles and glow with torches. The cobbled streets were as cold as the early evening sky. Farden wandered through the streets towards his favourite inn.

A spot of rain landed on the back of his hand and he licked it, tasting the cold water on his burning tongue. The *mörd* was like fire in his veins, warming him from tip to toe. He tilted his face to the tumultuous sky to feel the soft, cold rain on his sweaty skin. Thankfully, there was no wind to chase the raindrops, and Farden found himself in good spirits. Even though he missed the dragons, it was good to be back in his city again, no longer under the untrusting eyes of Siren soldiers. Just another hooded stranger in the street. He felt good, and strangely calm. Whole. However brief, his stay in Nelska had done something to him. The mage allowed himself a private smile.

Farden quickened his pace, striding briskly through the rain and the darkness. The gloomy puddles in the street rippled with orange light under the flickering street lamps. A few passers-by coughed and shuffled on the wet flagstones, but they paid him no attention and the hooded mage continued on through the night.

❦

The Bearded Goat was lively that evening. Farden could hear its noise echoing through the dark alleyways from several streets away. At first he had thought a fight had broken out, as there were several city guards standing in the road, leaning on their spears, but Farden soon realised it was singing that he had heard, not fighting. Though *caterwauling* would have been a more accurate term.

The guards laughed at the drunkards of the inn. Farden kept his hood down, passing them silently. Rain splashed in the puddles, soaking the city to the bone.

A man had collapsed in the gutter outside the inn, still clutching his ale, singing random lyrics in varying bursts of energy and volume. One of the guards tried to move him on with the butt of his spear, but the drunk refused to be uprooted from the wet cobbles, arguing loudly about how sober he still was. He would probably still be there in the morning. Farden chuckled to himself as he peered through the windows at the commotion inside.

Had Farden wanted a meal and a drink in the bar he probably would have cared a lot more, but seeing as all he wanted was to get to his room, he greeted the chaos with a bemused grin.

Not one, but two skalds had arrived that night, and both were belting out old songs and *eddas* to the bustling crowd gathered at the bar.

The mage managed to make it through the door and squeeze past the drunken men towards the stairs. He threw a sympathetic look to the innkeeper as he passed the bar. The man looked stressed, furiously doling out tankards of ale and wine in every direction. Silver and copper coins clinked together in his bursting pockets.

At the end of the bar, the two skalds danced on a tabletop, getting faster and louder with every note, each trying to outdo the other, tales of war and heroism as their weapons. The drunkards sang the bits they knew, shouted the bits they didn't, and drowned out the ljots with the banging of bottles and tankards on wooden tables. The whole inn was a deafening cacophony of noise, music, and laughter.

Farden could not help but admire the mayhem with wonder as he shook his head.

To his right, a man was trying to cook a half-eaten sausage on the roaring heat of the fireplace, while another skinny fellow was half-hidden under a table, throwing up in a hat. The gentleman whose hat it was laughed and pointed, then, outraged, demanded another beer to compensate for the vomiting. The skinny man kept at it.

A few soldiers were leaning against each other on the stairs, long off-duty but still in armour. They stank of cheap wine and sang their own songs over the chaos, cheering as Farden nudged them aside with his elbows, calling for him to join them. He ignored their offers, skipping quickly up the stairs to the first floor. They would be in for a surprise in the morning, he thought, when Vice called the army to assemble.

Once his door was shut, drowning out most of the noise, Farden threw off his wet cloak, dropped his pack, and sank into a nearby chair with a tired sigh. The chaos was a muffled roar under his floorboards, and it permeated the walls and windows. Rain dripped and splashed onto his windowsill from the overflowing gutters above. Farden stared at the wet evening outside his room, thinking of the dragons and the last few days.

It was a blur, to tell the truth. He now wasn't quite sure whether it had really happened. He rifled through his bag, inspecting the things the Sirens had given him.

Most of it was still dry. He held the vial of ice water in his hand. It was still freezing cold. The little book on flying looked interesting, even if it was in a strange dialect. The illustrations were detailed, depicting diagrams of how to hold onto a dragon, and how a dragon moves through the skies. He tossed it on the bed to read later.

Farden shuffled into a sitting position and threw a bolt of fire at the cold hearth. The dry wood burst into flames with a snap and a crackle and began to burn. The mage stretched out his hands to feel the warmth of the sputtering logs and threw his cloak over the nearby chair to dry. Farden perched on the edge of the bed, leaning towards the fireplace, and wondered what the hour was. His head still swam with warm wine. He could feel himself growing tired. The bed and its blankets behind him looked inviting, and he contemplated melting into it. With a grunt, he allowed himself to lean back and sprawl across the mattress with his boots still on the floor.

Farden let his mind rove through the dizzy sleepiness of alcohol. Nights like this were usually spent worrying and thinking too much. The last night he had spent at this inn, he had met the grubby old man with the pipe. But Nelska had calmed his thoughts, and the idea of nevermar seemed distant and useless. Just what the dragons had done to him, he had no idea, but something was different, and he was grateful.

Farden played with the dragonscale amulet around his neck, wondering what it would feel like to lose a dragon, or any loved one. He thought of a familiar face, of her skin, and her mountain-lake eyes. Farden sighed. *He would lie there for a moment longer, then unpack his things, then head to the Spire to see the girl that had been stuck in his mind ever since he had left the city*, the mage told himself, stretching. He would get up in a moment, he mentally repeated as he closed his eyes.

There came a quiet knock at the door. With a huge amount of effort Farden shook his head, blinked, and sat up. He looked around, blearily, then the knock came again, louder and more impatient. The mage hauled himself from the bed and went to the door. He lifted the latch cautiously and peered through the gap.

In the dark hallway stood an extremely cold, extremely wet Cheska, hair bedraggled and dripping, coat gripped tightly around her. She was shivering violently, yet her eyes sparkled and she managed a smile.

'Hello,' she said, through chattering teeth

Farden's heart lurched. 'Cheska! Come in. You look like you're freezing,' he said, ushering her through the doorway. He took a moment to glance up and down the corridor to see if anyone was watching, then locked the door behind him.

'Expecting someone?' Cheska asked quietly, pulling her thin leather coat tighter around her shoulders. Farden turned and looked at her, realising in that moment just how much he had missed her. Her voice sounded like joyful bells in his ears.

Farden smiled and shook his head. 'Definitely not you,' he said, grabbing a blanket from his bed and wrapping it around her shivering frame. They perched on the edge of the bed in silence, both feeling awkward. The mage's eyes could not help but rove over her, and she stared back, waiting.

'I was going to come see you at the Spire tonight,' he said. Cheska made a face. She looked around, at the crackling fire and the book and the rumpled bedsheets.

'I've been waiting for hours, Farden, ever since I heard you were back.'

He inwardly chided himself. 'Vice and I had things to go over. There was wine. It's going to be a difficult day for us tomorrow,' he made his excuses, reaching out to play with a strand of her hair. Cheska batted his hand away and started combing her wet tresses through her own pale fingers.

'My Ritual starts tomorrow,' she said, waving her fjortla in front of him. Farden hesitated, searching for something appropriate to say, but all he wanted to do was to put his arm around her. She didn't push him away this time, and they let the noise of the fire and the rain fill the silence. For a moment Cheska did nothing, then she rested her head on his shoulder. They both knew what the other was thinking, but neither wanted to voice it aloud. It had been a long time since the night in the alleyway.

'I thought you were dead,' she said finally, barely a whisper. She fiddled with the edge of the blanket. He rubbed her shoulder with his hand, trying to inject as much humour into his brief chuckle as he could.

'You know me better than that,' he said, but the awkwardness didn't die as he'd hoped. Cheska stared at him, and her serious expression made him look away. He stared into the bright flames and sighed.

'I'm sorry,' he said, searching for something else to add. He had always been the emotionless one, and now he struggled to put his feelings into words. Cheska nodded knowingly and looked away. Another moment of silence. 'I haven't stopped thinking about you,' Farden told her. 'About you and tomorrow. I just hope you know what you're doing, Cheska.'

'Farden,' she said, turning his head towards her with a gentle finger. Her blonde hair hung over her crystal-blue eyes but Farden couldn't miss the determination burning within them. 'You know I do.'

That was all he needed to hear. Since that day outside the Spire, he had tried his hardest to ignore the possibility that he might lose her to the Ritual, and up until now he had succeeded. It was another shadow in his mind that he didn't need, and it threatened to cloud his new-found calm.

'I hope so,' he hugged her tightly, sighed, then ruffled her hair affectionately. They said no more, and Farden buried the matter under hope.

Cheska's serious face soon warped into a tiny smile. 'See, you do care about me.' Farden narrowed his eyes.

'Hmm, don't flatter yourself too much,' he muttered, and she playfully slapped his arm. She stood up and went to the window to stare out at the rain.

'So, what was Nelska like?' she asked.

Farden scratched his head. 'Nelska was…' He tried to search for the right word. 'Difficult.' He settled on that.

'What happened?' she asked. Farden sighed. He had no idea where to start nor how to explain it, but the beginning felt like as good a place as any.

Farden told Cheska about the sorcerer on the ship, the cold of the northern waters, and how he had been unconscious for almost a week, flitting in and out of sleep and dark dreams. He told her about Svarta, but not Farfallen, trying to loosely explain why it was so important that they find a dark elf well. He trusted her, but some things could be left until this was all over. She was silent and engrossed while he talked, as if trying to imagine every detail.

When Farden had finished, Cheska nodded slowly, as though her mind was still trying to order and catalogue the flood of information. She came to sit next to him on the bed again and took a long breath. 'So, we're at peace with the Sirens now, and they're helping us find a magick well?'

Farden shrugged. 'If all goes to plan. And now Vice has ordered me to get all the Written ready to fight.'

'You? The captain?' Cheska was taken aback, but then put a reassuring hand on his. 'Not that I think that's a bad thing, but out of the Written, everyone knows you're the outsider. And after, well…' Her voice trailed away. 'What happened with your uncle.'

Farden had to admit she was right. He nodded, scratching an imaginary itch on the back of his hand. 'I know that, and Vice knows that, but for some reason he thinks it's a good idea.'

'Maybe it is.' Cheska offered. He shook his head.

'I don't think so, it's been years since I lived at the Spire. Half of them probably don't even know who I am, aside from the rumours.'

'Then they will soon enough. If the Undermage thinks you're capable, then so should you.'

'Perhaps.' Farden left it there, listening to the rain on the glass. 'All that matters is stopping the people behind all of this. I can't let them get away with it.'

'You always make it *your* fight, don't you?' Her voice was distant, like she hadn't realised she was speaking aloud. He nodded. Cheska looked at him with a strange expression. 'It's always got to be your fight and yours alone, ever since I've known you. Why do you put so much weight on your shoulders all the time?' she asked. Her hand was now resting softly on his leg. Farden could not help but stare at her.

'Because someone has to,' he said quietly.

Cheska shook her head. 'Then why you?'

'Why any of us? We're the Written, we do these things because we're the only ones who can. I've never failed a mission yet and I'm not about to start now.'

'But it doesn't always have to be you, Farden. What exactly are you trying to prove?'

'Yes, it does, and I have everything to prove.' Farden shook his head stubbornly.

She threw up her hands, exasperated. 'There's a whole tower in Manesmark filled with people like us. Like you, Farden. You don't have to prove yourself anymore, don't you understand that? It's why you don't want to be in charge of the other Written, because you still think you can do this on your own. The lone wolf. Farden saves the day again. Is that what you want?' Her questions were like arrows. He knew she cared, just like all the others, but the edges of her words still cut.

Farden looked deep into her eyes, clasping her delicate hands between his. 'I know what I'm doing, and right now I can't take another lecture about how I need to be careful. I get enough of those from the rest of them,' he said.

'It's because of your uncle, isn't it?' she ventured, knowing how touchy the subject was. 'That's what you're trying to fight,' she said. Farden's face clouded over.

'No,' he said. 'I'm nothing like him.'

'I didn't say that. I meant his legacy,' replied Cheska. 'Farden saves the day. Proves he's not mad Tyrfing. Well, you've already proven that, Farden. Time and time again.'

She must have seen the fire in his eyes, because she left the matter to die away. With a frown, she looked away. 'One day we're going to give up trying to convince you, and one day it'll be too late,' she said, with a slow shake of her head. A shiver shook her body.

'You're cold,' said Farden, changing the subject. He got up from the bed to add more wood to the fire. The mage picked up two logs from a box by the window and held one in each hand. Flames trickled along his fingers and the dry logs began to hiss. As the bark started to burn by itself, Farden dropped them gently into the fire with a shower of sparks.

Cheska rolled her eyes. 'That was unnecessary.' She was now sitting cross-legged on the bed with the blanket gathered around her like a shroud.

Farden tidied his things and smirked at her slyly, glad to have escaped the previous conversation. 'But it's why I'm so good; I'm always practising.'

Cheska raised an eyebrow. 'I could give you a run for your coin.'

'There's a reason we've never duelled, Cheska. I'm scared I'd hurt you.' Farden leaned against the fireplace and crossed his arms triumphantly.

'Afraid to lose?' came the snippy reply.

'Hah! We'll see in three days' time.' Farden smiled as she looked for a pillow to throw at him. But joking about it didn't make it any better, and he tried to force his mind away from shadows. 'What did you choose anyway?' he asked.

'Illusion and spark.'

'Interesting. What about your friend, Burg? Brine?'

'You know it's Brim. Shadow and vortex.'

'Interesting *and* original then,' he said mockingly.

'Oh, be nice.' She held out a hand for him to join her. He sat on the edge of the bed facing her. They kept hold of each other's hands. 'Brim actually looks up to you, Farden,' said Cheska.

The mage shrugged. 'I can't imagine that, he's so protective of you.'

'He's probably just a little jealous. You should teach him some things.'

'I don't even know how to begin to teach someone. That's for the masters at the School. Leave it to them,' Farden snorted.

Cheska shuffled closer. 'You could take any one of them.'

'Probably.' The mage nodded reflectively. He lost his train of thought when she started to lean into the warmth of his neck. Her voice sounded small from below his chin.

'What did you choose?' she asked quietly.

'You already know, fire and light,' he said.

There was a pause, then she put a hand on his warm chest to feel his heartbeat. 'What about the other two runes?'

Farden shook his head, irritated. People were too eager to gossip about things that didn't concern them. 'Who told you about that?' he muttered. 'Or have you looked?'

'Wouldn't dare. We all know the stories about Farden the minotaur-slayer.' Cheska chuckled. 'What are the others?' The mage sighed and looked up at the ceiling. Tonight had been for forgetting, not dredging up the past. His calm was being put to the test.

Every Written's Book contained certain runes that gave power to certain schools of magick, like water or fire, gifting a mage with enhanced abilities in those particular skills. Back in the earlier days, when Farden had still been in training, the Scribe could write as many as four runes into a tattoo. But, in light of a few certain incidents, his uncle included, the council had ruled that using so many runes was dangerous for a candidate, and more likely to dissolve their minds like wet sand. They were unfortunately right; the more magick that was forced upon a mage, the less they could hold onto reality as the years went by. Farden had been the last to receive four runes, and it had been a highly-guarded secret. Until now. Rumour had it that Farden's uncle had five runes in his Book.

'Spark and quake,' said Farden quietly.

Cheska tutted. 'There's no tact to you, is there? As subtle as a house.'

Farden wagged a finger mockingly. 'A Written isn't meant to be delicate and quiet, Cheska. You can't win a fight with shadow magick.'

Cheska shrugged. Farden looked down at her, and she up at him. They held each other's gaze for a while. There was no sound but the dripping rain on the windowsill and the muffled caterwauling from downstairs. Cheska looked down at her nails and searched for some way to say it.

'I'm scared, Farden,' she said, but Farden put a hand to her cheek and, before she could go any further, he kissed her. Their lips met and she let his hands wander across the soft skin of her neck, up into her hair. She threw her arms around his shoulders in an enveloping embrace and Farden felt her heart beat hard against his own. She was intoxicating.

The mage didn't stop her hands exploring inside his tunic while they kissed, fingers running over his chest, blindly tracing ridges of old scars. He let Cheska pull him backwards onto the bed and wrap the blanket around them. In a flourish of blonde hair, Farden pulled her shirt over her head and began to remove the rest of her clothes. They landed in a heap on the floor, swiftly followed by Farden's tunic.

Cheska bit gently into his shoulder as she kissed him. Her nails dragged softly over the tattoo on his back and with one hand he entwined his fingers in hers and held her down on the bed. He ran his hands over her breasts and the rest of her naked body. He let his tongue rove over her skin, listening to her moan and sigh. Her beautiful skin shone pale in the dying firelight, and her eyes sparkled with the reflections of the flames. Farden had never seen her look so beautiful. They stared at each other for a moment, then kissed again.

He explored every curve of her body and felt Cheska's hands doing the same to him. Her fingers floated across his skin, moving slowly further down his torso to his waist. Farden shifted to be closer to her and they pressed themselves against each other rhythmically, feeling their heartbeats quicken and knowing nothing but each other's skin. His was rough, weathered. Hers was impossibly smooth.

Cheska pulled Farden close and moved his hands between her slender legs. Her breathing was loud in his ear, and her scent filled him with animal lust. She smelled incredible. She was the mountains, the sky, the crystal lake, everything, and her sharp nails raking across his back only made him want her more. The shadows burnt away from the corners of his mind and he forgot everything except her. She was a bright island, a candle in his darkness.

His fingers moved up and down, gently at first, then faster, sliding in and out of her until she wrapped her legs around him and took him in her hands, drawing him closer, pulling him in, until they were one and the same. Farden held her hands above her head, pressing her into the covers and letting himself melt into every part of her, forgetting everything else in the world except her, letting the shadows burn away until only they existed together in the darkness.

Soon they were both tangled in the sheets, panting breathlessly as they writhed back and forth. Once, she screamed his name, when she was on top of him, hands in her hair and head thrown back. The noise from downstairs drowned out the sounds of their own commotion, and by the time they finally collapsed into a deep sleep, the fire had long burnt out.

Farden's dream was made of darkness. He could feel the heat of the day failing around him; feel the hot wind dying on the horizon as it chased after the receding sun. But it was dark, impenetrable, like black hands had covered his eyes and stolen away every scrap of light. He was standing. He could feel the ground under his bare feet. He moved his toes and felt sand crunch between them. Hot sand. Farden looked to where he felt was up, and blinked.

Ever so slowly, as if the stars were forming for the first time, pinpricks of light began to puncture the blackness above him, like white knives through black fabric. He could hear their rumbling as they burnt and throbbed and shook themselves into being. Farden couldn't tear his eyes away.

One by one, the stars appeared, and the mage lifted a finger to trace their familiar shapes in the sky. A ribbon of light began to sparkle above him, like a milky river across the vastness, and with it he could hear the roar of countless voices, yelling and moaning and crying, whimpering, and plotting. Convoluted whispers of ten thousand times ten thousand. The shapes moved, and the sounds of battle clashed against the shadows. The old gods galloped across the skies as they shouted and twirled. Yet more stars grew, then suddenly, as quickly as it had started, the sky froze, the chaos halted, and earth and sky fell from the havoc.

Farden heard something shuffle nearby, and he spun around. Nothing there but the thick darkness. Impenetrable. It circled him, scratched, sniffed, yowled at the night sky. The stars cast no light, illuminated nothing. The thing kept circling the mage, and Farden followed it with his ears, waving his unseen hands around him.

There's more to this than first appears, said a familiar voice.

'What do you want from me?'

Whoever they are, they're not who you think. That's how they got me, came the reply in his head.

'What is this place?' he asked. The voice paused, as did the scratching.

It's where you want to be, Farden, not I. And something here feels wrong, different, ruined.

'Show yourself!' shouted Farden, whirling around. In the corner of his eye he saw a shape move in the sky: the shape of a man holding a bow, with a sword at his hip. Wild dogs followed in his wake. With a mighty heave, he leapt across the sky, sweeping a third of the stars with him, then pulled the string of his bow to his cheek.

Farden felt paralysed, cornered. He looked for somewhere to run but saw only darkness and the hunter. He loosed his arrow, and his stars began to fall. Gold, silver, purple, and scintillating white they fell, ripping the sky like torn skin, bruising the mountains with fire. The noise was deafening.

This was how it all started, mage, when the stars fell. The gods and giants of old.

'This doesn't make any sense. Why do you keep bringing me here? If you want to tell me something, then just tell me and stop all this nonsense!' Farden yelled. He tried to run, but his feet melted into the hot sand around him.

Be careful, Farden. Something stirs in Emaneska tonight.

'Who are you? Show me your face!'

I'm just like you, which is all the more reason to be careful.

'I told you, I'm nothing like you! Leave me alone!'

Not this time. It's only just beginning. Just promise me you'll stay alive.

The stars buried themselves in the ground around him. In the flashes of light Farden could see a man standing with a cat, and a thing with wings.

'SHOW ME!' bellowed the mage as a flaming rock struck his hand. He felt his skin sizzling in the place his arm used to be.

Keep an eye on the weather, Farden. It's not worth dying for.

chapter 11

"The rumours of a fierce, ravenous vampyre in our forest are completely ridiculous! Why would such a beast settle in our quiet countryside, and hunt such kind people? These goings-on are just plain and simple accidents, nasty trips and falls, or perhaps a rogue wild dog! Pardon me? No, I don't know anything about the bite-marks. Now, if you'll excuse me..."

The Duke of Leath speaking to the townspeople after alleged "vampyre sightings" some years ago

The wind was bitingly cold, tearing at the black cloak of the figure standing in the darkness on the shore, like the teeth of a thousand rats, invisible and hungry.

It was a moonless night, and the clouds were spinning across the seething sky, trying to find calm after the storm earlier that day. The jagged rocks of the beach were slippery, wreathed in tangled seaweed that had been ripped apart by the waves and left to lie like dead soldiers on the shoreline.

The sea crashed noisily on the rocks behind the man, and he could just about catch the shouts of the people in the small wooden boat, furiously paddling against the surging waves. They were loud fools. They would wake up the whole mountain if they weren't careful.

The huge face of the fortress of Hjaussfen towered above him. The black granite cliffs were almost invisible against the dark sky, but yellow torches glittered from a handful of windows, betraying the lower levels. To the quiet man standing alone on the beach, the weather was perfect. He smiled a wolf's smile.

The wind howled, and the figure trudged on, thick black boots crunching the grit and scraping on the wet pebbles. Knives clinked softly at his belt.

In the darker shadows of the cliff-face, a Siren stood guard, spear held firm and low by his side. He cleared his throat, blinked, and peered into the windy darkness. Standing near the mountain afforded a little shelter, but the cold still crept inside his cloak, stealing his warmth. His red eyes watched the clouds racing overhead, unable to spy a single star in the dark sky.

A strong hand slipped over his mouth, jerking him backwards. A sharp pain shot up his spine, and a slender silver blade slid out from his chest. The soldier looked down in bewilderment at the knife protruding from his thick leather tunic, gawping as he felt the blood draining from him.

There was a crunching sound as the blade was yanked free: the scrape of bone and armour. Blood bubbled in his throat. The pain began to spread, but darkness was already gathering at the corners of his scarlet eyes. By the time he hit the ground he was dead.

The assailant wiped his knife on the Siren's body and sheathed it slowly. He bent to grab his legs and then hauled the body into the shadows.

Halfway up the cliffs, at the top of a winding staircase, there was a small doorway cut into the rock. A lone soldier stood against the jamb, beneath a wind-harried torch. He shivered in the cold, stamping his feet as he tried to keep warm. Someone had taken his cloak from his cupboard, meaning he had only his leather armour to shield him from the weather.

The butt of his spear rattled against the stone as he trembled. He thought again about going inside and stealing a blanket from one of the other guards, but the sergeant probably wouldn't take too kindly to that, so he decided against it.

A stone slipped from its perch somewhere on the path to his right, just at the top of the stairs. It clattered noisily as it fell. The Siren lowered his spear and blinked against the cold, his watering eyes narrowing at the darkness. Nothing. *Probably just the wind.* He huddled deeper against the doorframe, trying to feel the warmth of the barracks inside.

Another noise reached his keen ears over the howling wind, the sound of boots on stone. The guard peered around the corner of the small door to see a tall stranger, hooded and cloaked, carrying a spear low at his side. The guard shuffled forwards, hands still deep in his pockets, and opened his mouth to hail him.

The man dropped the spear and darted forwards. The Siren guard panicked. While he struggled to get his other hand free of his pocket, the stranger's hands began to shimmer with a strange blue light. A yell caught in his throat as a bolt of lightning slammed into his chest, throwing him backwards with a crack of thunder. The door splintered into pieces beneath his back. Ribs pierced lungs as he collided with the wall at the far end of the dark room. The shouts and cries of the others sounded distant and muffled from where he lay crumpled on the floor. Blood oozed from his ears.

A man-shaped shadow filled the shattered doorway. Light glowed in his fingers, blinding the half-dozen Sirens as they fell out of their beds and scrabbled for their weapons. Their yells filled the space.

A flaming knife flew across the room, dispatching a bewildered guard as he crawled across the floor. A gurgling cry and a crash of furniture rang out. The stranger held his hands wide and sparks began to gather and spin. The crackling lightning grew, spitting light and fire inches from his crooked fingers.

With a grunt, the man tensed and the spell exploded from his hands, flicking from guard to guard, searing and choking them as it burnt a wicked path across the room. Cries were drowned out by the roaring thunder and, one by one, the Sirens fell limp and smoking to the floor.

The smell of burning flesh and smouldering wood choked the air, making the darkness even blacker. All was silent apart from the hoarse breathing of one or two, still clinging on. The dark stranger went to each one, plunging a knife into their hearts to make sure they saw their way to the other side. When his work was done, he sheathed his blade and left the room, scurrying out of a low door into a gloomy corridor.

Deep in the mountain, a flickering torch fizzled out, clasped between quiet fingers. The spreading shadows hid the cloaked figure as he stepped lightly on the flagstones, creeping higher and higher into the citadel.

Around a corner, a guard stood attentively at his post. The man pressed a palm flat against the wall, and the stones rippled outward with a low rumble. Just as the guard turned his head at the noise, the wave reached him. The wall beside him burst apart in a cloud of bricks and stone. The man was knocked flat, blood dripping down his head. He tried to get up but the figure dashed forwards, ending his life with a vicious slash across the throat. Dark blood poured over the dusty rubble.

The stranger ran on, taking every staircase he could find. Soon enough, a bell began to ring from somewhere deep in the mountain, and the corridors began to fill with soldiers, swarming like ants. They surged through the lower levels, yelling vengeance, but the stairs slowed them, and the murderer was far ahead, high up and near the palace.

Before long, the hooded man stood in front of a tall set of iron doors, looking up at the high arch of the doorframe. He strode forwards and pushed on the metal. The door creaked in protest, but swung open slowly, letting the man slip into the cavernous hall. He dodged furtively from pillar to pillar, making his way to the statue of the winged god at the end of the hall, and the little stone table sitting before it. The tearbook and a flock of papers sat there, barely illuminated by the flickering candles huddled around the shrine.

The stranger dashed to the table and seized the tearbook with hungry hands. He slipped it into a satchel under his cloak and stuffed the papers alongside it. The sounds of bells and horns began to shake the fortress around him.

It was time to leave.

The man reached inside his tunic and brought forth a golden object that glittered brightly in the dim candlelight. He gripped it in both hands and headed for the door.

The bright corridor was full of the sounds of armour and clanging weapons. Just as he emerged from the dark hall, a group of soldiers appeared around a corner. Shouts rang out, and the man broke into a sprint. The roaring Sirens gave chase but the man was too fast. He had already reached the end of the corridor and disappeared.

More soldiers joined them, pouring out from adjoining hallways, spurred on by the shouts. In minutes, the entire palace was snapping at this intruder's tail, following the trail of dead bodies left on staircases, in doorways and slumped against walls. The Sirens wanted blood. The stranger knew that, so he darted between rooms and corridors, leading the pursuers a merry chase towards the outside of the mountain. The palace was a warren, and he was slowly losing them.

No sooner had he thought this did he turn a corner to find a swarm of armoured soldiers blocking the corridor, teeth bared, scales flushed, tall shields forming a wall. The man skidded to a halt and stared at the angry Sirens. They growled at him, waving spears and blades threateningly. This corridor was the only way out of this section on the palace. But the man had one more card to play.

He looked at the gold disk in his hand and lifted it closer to his face, lips mumbling the incantation etched into the shiny surface. Footsteps clattered behind him. A soldier rushed forwards, brandishing a short sword. The man ducked and spun, flinging out the hand that held the disk and catching the Siren in the face with the hard metal edge. The soldier let out a cry as his feet flew from under him, hands clasped to his bloody nose. The others charged to their friend's aid, yelling war cries and screaming for revenge.

The stranger held firm, holding the disk straight out in front of him as he muttered the last few words of his spell.

At the very final moment, before the spears and swords cut him into pieces, before the hands encircled his throat, before his limbs were hacked away, the stranger swung the disk in a wide circle and vanished. There was a thunderclap, and the air in the hallway wobbled like a plucked string. The Sirens skidded to a halt, stumbling over each other amidst shouts of surprise and rage. They looked about them, bewildered, for any sign of the intruder. He was gone.

Back on the beach, the wind howled, and the rain lashed the stones and shale. The crew in the boat had done well to bring her into shore again, and they now crouched by the pale hull of their wooden vessel, waiting in the stormy darkness. They did not have to wait for long.

Further up the beach, a pile of pebbles began to shake and jitter, rocking back and forth as the air began to hum. There was a sound like the cracking of a whip, or a tree branch snapping in half.

The air split in two with a flash of light, leaving a hooded man standing in the darkness. He looked down at the gold disk in his hand, now caked in blood, and turned it over. Shouts rang out from the cliffs behind him, and he heard the sound of arrows against the wind. A few barbed shafts slammed into the gritty sand next to him. He started to walk briskly back to where the waves crashed on the shore. The men and the boat were only a short distance away, but the archers were slowly getting used to the range. He wiped rain from his face and threw a quick look behind him.

There were soldiers running along the beach from the west, and the black shapes of dragons were circling the darkened summit of Hjaussfen. Their eyes could pierce the darkness like an owl hunting a mouse, so the stranger doubled his pace, running towards the sea.

The men beside the boat had already pushed it into the water, and were testing their oars against the turbulent seas. The stranger was getting closer by the moment, hopping from rock to slippery rock to dodge the buzzing arrows. His hands were numb from the cold, and the wind constantly buffeted him, tearing at his cloak.

As he reached the shoreline, he looked back at the Sirens dashing after him across the rain-lashed beach. A rancorous smirk crept across his lip, and he looked down once more at the bloodied disk in his hand. With a chuckle, he flung it towards them. It clanged against the slippery stones, bouncing between the rocks, metal singing.

Lightning flashed above him as he leapt into the boat. Oars and paddles dug deeper into the dark water, and the vessel lurched across the roiling waves with the wind gnashing in its wake. The hooded man stood upright in the bow of the ship, peering back at the shore, holding firmly onto his hood. A member of the crew pawed at his heel, shouting a question over the howling wind.

'What?' snarled the man.

'Where d'ye want us t' go, your Mage?!' the man asked again.

'Around the coast, to the north. And be quick about it if you don't want to be speared by the Sirens or caught by a dragon!' shouted the man. The sailor nodded, blinking as another wave splashed against the side of the boat. He made to turn around, but his master grabbed his shirt sleeve before he got away. The man reached inside his cloak for the satchel.

'Put this somewhere safe,' he ordered, and with a flick of his wrist he tossed it at him. The sailor caught it awkwardly, narrowly avoided dropping it into the roiling sea, and clutched it to his chest.

An arrow thudded into the hull of the boat, causing the crew to immediately row faster with urgent, hissing shouts. Perhaps it was the current and the wind that pushed them, or perhaps it was something to do with the mage at the front of the boat, raising his hands to the skies, but either way they sped across the choppy seas and into the stormy night, untouched.

Snatches of words, fuelled by rage, could be heard on the wind. Yells and the banging of weapons on shields. Dragons roared with fury. Bells and horns shook the mountain of Hjaussfen.

The men rowed on, watching the dark skies with wary eyes.

part three

YOU ONLY COME ALIVE IN THE DARK

chapter 12

As a whole, the people of Albion are, without a doubt, utterly dim-witted, displaying an idiocy only just surpassed by the foolish pomposity of their so called "dukes". The citizens of this drab land seem to spend their time standing on street corners, scratching themselves, gambling, or gawping at the rest of the world flying past without them. In all my years I've never met a more dull set of people. But then again, it's probably why I enjoy hunting them so much. They're as slow as their cows.

From the diary of Durnus Glassren

Farden awoke when the bright sunlight climbed over the rooftops and pierced the darkness of his room. The rain had stopped in the night, and now an early morning mist filled the streets and fogged the dirty windows.

The mage, however, hadn't noticed any of this yet, and closed his eyes tighter against the offending sunshine. The fading tendrils of the dream hovered behind his eyelids. They confused him, annoyed him, and had ruined his sleep.

They were dreams without meaning and Farden tried to dismiss their strange words as nonsense, but he could not help but wonder why the voice sounded so familiar, why he felt as though he should pay attention. He shuddered as the hazy memories of the darkness and the sand and the falling fire came back to him. He would keep an eye on the weather, he decided, whatever that meant.

Rolling over, Farden reached out for the beautiful girl in his bed but found only empty space next to him. He shrugged. He had expected her to disappear during the night, careful to keep their secret a little longer.

Farden had often pondered what would happen if they were discovered, what the magick council would do, what would happen to them, and more importantly, what her father would do. Cheska was a princess, and very soon she would be a Written. That would make her by all reasons and definitions, *forbidden*.

A wave of anxiety washed over him, but faded just as quickly, replaced by a glimmer of hope; the feeling that his luck would pull through. That it would all turn out fine, somehow. Farden felt the small dragonscale amulet tapping against the skin of his neck, and thumbed its rough surface contemplatively. *From now on*, he said quietly to himself, *things would get better.* Then, just for once, he let his mind go quiet, and let the problems fade away.

Farden smiled to himself as he put his hands behind his head, still refusing to open his eyes and admit it was daytime. He let the events of last night wander through his head. With a smile, he stretched and his hand knocked against something small and metallic on the pillow beside him.

Farden grabbed at the object and held it in front of him, blinking his sleepy eyes into focus. It was Cheska's fjortla, left for him to keep until she had passed through the gruelling Ritual. He gripped the bracelet so hard that it hurt his hand, then forced himself to sit up. He muttered a quick prayer to the gods to keep her safe before getting up to gather his scattered clothes.

The bar area was filled with snoring, unconscious men, most of whom were sleeping either under or on top of tables. Most were covered in vomit. Others lay flat about the stone floor, swollen bellies rising and falling laboriously with deep, drunken breaths.

The two skalds had fallen asleep leaning against each other, voices and fingers likely raw from performing. The innkeeper had disappeared. He was probably nursing his own throbbing head somewhere upstairs.

Farden had to step over a huge man in a guard's uniform who lay blocking the doorway. His beard was still wet with ale and his chest rumbled like a storm cloud. Farden could smell the alcohol on his breath as he passed.

The streets were buzzing. Everyone seemed to be rushing around. Even though it was still early, the roads were packed with noisy, bustling crowds. Farden pushed his way into the street, joining the throng of teeming citizens. Carts pulled by donkeys crowded the thoroughfares, their drivers yelling angrily for people to move and give way. The whole city seemed in uproar.

Farden hoisted his hood over his head, weaving through the crowds, easily pushing people aside. Everywhere he looked he could see guards frantically running back and forth, spurred on by shouts from their captains and sergeants. *Vice and the magick council have been busy this morning*, Farden thought. He dug out a piece of dark, dried meat from his belt, the same fishy stuff he had eaten in Nelska, and nibbled as he walked.

Even though he was but a short distance from the Arkathedral, it took him the best part of an hour to reach the tall gates of the fortress. Even there, people clogged the roads and gathered at the foot of the walls.

Farden squeezed through a crowd of citizens that were yelling angrily at the squad of soldiers standing at the gates. The armoured men repeatedly shook their heads at the people while their captain pushed them back with a short wooden stave. Farden elbowed his way to the front.

'What's going on here?' demanded Farden, once he was close enough to the officer.

'Get back from the gates!' the soldier shouted at him.

Farden yanked his hood back and held up one of his wrists. The captain looked at the mage, then at the symbol on his skin, and bowed immediately. 'My apologies sir, the citizens are demanding refuge in the Arkathedral, but we're under orders from the Undermage not to let anyone in besides soldiers or mages.'

'Why?' Farden looked at the man quizzically.

The man shrugged. 'They didn't say, but orders is orders and I does what I'm told. You're better off askin' them inside,' he nodded towards the tall gates.

'This city is a madhouse,' Farden muttered, and the soldier laughed without any humour.

'If you think this is bad, then you're not going to like it in there.'

Farden nodded grimly and the man bowed, calling to his men to let the mage through. Their ranks parted. Behind him, Farden could hear the captain poking and shoving the people away with his stave.

'Back! Get back I say!'

Farden walked under the massive gateway and quickly realised the soldier had been right: the whole Arkathedral was alive with activity, buzzing loudly like a hornet's nest. The mage groaned. It was as if war had broken out while he had been asleep. A chill crept up his spine.

The grand marble atrium was crammed with all sorts of people. Servants scurried this way and that through clusters of workers, their arms full of supplies and boxes or pulling little carts behind them. Soldiers ran back and forth, lugging armour and bundles of weapons, yelling, 'Move!' and, 'Mind out!' as they pushed others to the floor. Guards gathered at every doorway and entrance. Everybody was shouting and rushing around.

Only a handful stayed relatively still amongst the disorder, gathering in the corners of the marble hall, hooded and conspiratorial in their small groups. Several of them noticed Farden standing alone in the gateway, watching the chaos. One in particular, a willowy man with white-blonde hair, broke away from his group and waded through the masses towards him.

The man proffered a hand, which Farden shook warmly with a smile. The symbols on their wrists flashed for a moment as their skin touched.

'Modren, at least there's one sane person amongst this mess,' said Farden.

The other Written nodded. 'Good to see you again,' he said quietly. Farden could barely hear him over the cacophony of voices.

The thin man seemed to sway gently, like a sapling in the breeze, yet his eyes were a deep green that watched everything with the intensity of a hunting cat. He wore a long red coat, and a sword on either side of his belt. His whitish hair was short and waxed back. A black ring hung from his left ear.

'Whatever's going on here, it's all gone to shit, I'll tell you that. Thialf and the others are over there. Freidd is coming soon. Word came to the Spire that we were to gather here as soon as possible.' Modren paused, giving Farden a strange look. 'The order sounded like it came from you,' he said.

Farden inwardly sighed as he attempted to appear confident. He matched Modren's look. 'The Undermage has put me in charge of the Written for now. We have something very dangerous to deal with.'

Modren shrugged, nodded, then grinned, showing off a set of perfect white teeth. 'Sounds like my kind of fight,' he said with relish. 'And if you're the captain now, well, so be it. Couldn't think of anybody better suited to the job. Better one of us mages than some bureaucrat.'

Farden nodded, 'Let's hope the others feel the same way.'

'Doesn't matter if they don't, Undermage's word is law.'

'What's this I see? Emaneska's most dangerous hermit is out and about for once!' a voice laughed gruffly from behind them.

They both turned to greet a stocky mage with a shaven head and tribal tattoos covering half his face. He smiled lopsidedly at Farden. 'It's been a long time,' said the man. Farden nodded silently, smiling back.

Modren held out a hand to the muscular newcomer. 'Good to see you, Ridda,' he said. Ridda chuckled as he shook it. He still hadn't taken his eyes off of Farden.

'So what brings you out of your cave, then?'

'The usual,' replied Farden, 'something needs killing.'

Ridda made a humming sound, then laughed again, clapping Farden on the arm. 'Ain't there always.' He rubbed his hands together as a servant flew past with a pile of books in his hands. 'What's all this about then? Any ideas?'

Farden looked around at the bustling hall with a slow shaking of his head, marvelling at the sheer volume of people. 'I've never seen the Arkathedral so busy. How many of us are yet to arrive?' he asked. Ridda scratched his chin.

'A score or so are off in the east dealing with the wyverns, but there's at least sixty here and a few dozen more in Manesmark,' he answered. Ridda's voice was incredibly deep for a person of his stature. The brawny mage barely came up to Farden's shoulder, but he was as wide as he was tall, with an ever-suspicious gaze and mischievous smile.

'Good,' said Farden. 'Hopefully that will be enough. I need everyone here before nightfall, ready to march and ready to fight.'

Ridda looked at Modren, then back at Farden, wearing a quizzical expression. 'You in charge now?' he asked.

Farden hesitated for a moment, then cleared his throat with an air of authority. He nodded. 'It looks that way, according to the

Undermage,' he replied. Ridda looked confused at first, but his face soon broke into a wide grin.

'Fuck. Out of his cave for a couple of days and already he's causing trouble. Fine with me, better you than an old greyhair who's never cast a spell in his life,' he chuckled.

Modren nodded and clapped his hands together loudly. 'That's what I said. We'd best get to it then!'

Farden tried to hide his groan of relief as he leaned in close to the others so they could hear him over the noise. 'Get Neffra and a few others to the hawk-houses. Send word to every Written that's more than a day's march away. Tell them to come here, that they're needed to protect the city. Then order the rest to get their weapons and anything else they need ready by tonight. We'll meet in the great hall an hour after sunset.'

'I'll deal with the hawks,' said Ridda decisively. Without another word, he slapped Farden on the shoulder again and strode off into the crowds. Modren turned to Farden with a mock sigh.

'Let's go and see what all this madness is about,' he said.

'Agreed.'

The two mages spun smartly on their heels and strode purposefully towards the main stairs. They jostled with soldiers and servants for space, dodging around workers and equipment that was gathering, for some reason, on the steps. They walked in silence for the most part, glaring at anyone who got in their way. Their looks sent more than just a few people scuttling away with muttered apologies. Nobody wanted to get on the bad side of a Written.

The mages walked side by side up the endless stairs and through the maze of corridors that would finally lead them to the great hall and the root of all this commotion. Farden was eager to find Vice.

Modren chose to break the silence, leaning close to whisper to Farden. 'Rumour has it you were up in Nelska recently.' It was a question hidden within a statement. Farden nodded. The blonde mage watched his friend from the corner of his eye with a knowing smile. 'I take it I shall find out later then?'

'You never did have much patience.' Farden smiled.

'Never,' said Modren. 'In all honesty though, Farden, I haven't seen this sort of mayhem since the year those faeries escaped and got lost in the city. This has something to do with the murders at Arfell, doesn't it?'

Farden looked warily about them, waiting until a group of people had passed. 'It does, but it's something much more serious than just a few dead scholars.'

Modren fell silent and ran a hand through his bright hair. 'About time we had a wind to blow the dust off of us,' he muttered.

It took the mages a good half an hour to reach the marbled hallways at the peak of the Arkathedral. There was a massive throng of people gathered outside the gilded doors of the great hall, but a line of soldiers in gold and green armour barred their entrance with tall shields.

Modren began making his way through the crowd. 'Move aside there, let us through!' he barked, pushing people aside mercilessly. One haughty scribe prodded him as he passed, referring a little too loudly to the blonde mage as a bumbling oaf. Modren rounded on him, fixing him with a stare that could have frozen a sun.

'If I were you, scribe, I'd keep your mouth shut and your fingers to yourself, otherwise you just might lose one of them.' Modren punctuated his threat by clicking his fingers. Sparks flashed over his nails. The scribe fell deadly silent and slipped away into the massed crowd. Modren huffed, pulling his long coat around him to avoid it getting trampled.

'Good work,' chuckled Farden.

Modren nodded. 'I thought so. Let us through, gods damn it!'

Farden reached the armoured soldiers and located the man in charge. The sergeant looked the mage up and down with a wrinkle of his nose and an imperious sniff.

'State your business,' he shouted over the noise.

Farden glared at him. 'We're here on direct orders from the Undermage, I need to speak with him immediately.'

The soldier shook his head and pointed to somewhere beneath his feet, as if the answers lay on the floor. 'He ain't in the great hall, sir, and I'll doubt you'll find him with the Arkmages. Try his rooms, one level down.'

'What are all these people here for?' Modren called to the soldier.

'Everybody and their brother wants to see the Arkmages today, but we can't let 'em in until the council meeting has finished,' he shrugged, his polished armour clanked noisily.

'What the hell is going on?' Farden asked as he looked around at the chaotic crowd.

'Haven't you 'eard?' The soldier looked confused, a serious expression hovering over his face. The two mages shook their heads as one. 'The dragons are comin' to Krauslung!' the man said, wide-eyed.

Farden's jaw dropped. He turned to Modren, who also looked completely baffled.

'Did he just say—?' Modren began, but Farden cut him off.

'Yes, he did, now come on. We have to find Vice!'

They began barging their way back through the crowd towards the relative space of the white marble hallway. As soon as they had room, they broke into a run and Farden led them left and down a wide, curving staircase. They narrowly avoided knocking down a terrified-looking man carrying a bundle of arrows, dodging artfully around him before skidding to a halt outside the tall oak doors of Vice's rooms.

Farden banged loudly on the door and waited, breathing more heavily than usual. Modren was adjusting his clothes and smoothing his ruffled blonde hair. Farden crossed his arms and drummed his fingers with impatience.

There was a clanking noise and the door was opened by a slightly-built servant with a kind face. He looked them up and down. 'How may I help you, mages?'

'We need to find the Undermage, right away,' Farden said hurriedly.

'He is dealing with council matters, sir.' The servant shook his head slowly, as if it were in danger of falling off. Farden snorted with frustration.

'My lord is due to return soon, if you would like to wait?' The servant opened the door a little wider, gesturing for them to enter the huge room. As he did so, a huge spider crept from behind the doorframe and sidled around the wall. Farden watched the black, spindly beast scuttle silently into the hallway and disappear under another door. The man seemed not to have noticed the arachnid, and he looked back and forth between the two mages.

Farden shook his head. 'No, thank you. When you see the Undermage, tell him Farden is looking for him.'

'Of course, sir.' The wisp of a man bowed, quietly closing the heavy door with no more than a barely audible click.

Modren walked to a nearby window to look down at the crowds in the streets. The noise of the people bellowing could be heard on the chilling breeze. The sky was crystal clear once again, the clouds banished behind the pale blue of the mountain sky.

'This is mad,' Modren said quietly, as he leaned forwards to watch the guards at a gate below.

Farden put a hand against the marble wall and stared at the floor. He chewed at the inside of his lip. *Something was wrong.* If the dragons were coming to Krauslung then it meant that they had found the dark elf well, but if that was so, why was the city so full of fear and panic? Something was niggling at the back of his brain, but he couldn't grasp it. *And just as things were starting to go right for a change, too*, he thought.

A booming voice echoed down the corridor. 'Farden!'

He spun around to see Vice standing at the end of the hallway, arms spread questioningly, one foot on the bottom step of the staircase. He was wearing the long formal robe of his position: black cloth trimmed with green. A long, curved sword was at his side, hanging from a golden belt. That was unusual.

'Where have you been?' he bellowed. His expression was stern.

The two mages jogged to meet him and bowed quickly. Farden pointed behind him at the door. 'Trying to find you, Vice,' he said. Modren nodded furiously behind him. The Undermage snorted and stormed up the stairs with loud heavy steps.

'You did a fine job of that, didn't you? Follow me,' he said. They leapt after him.

Farden marched at his side. 'The guard at the great hall said the Sirens were coming here?'

'And you heard right,' Vice replied. He seemed furious. There was a bubbling anger simmering underneath his pale skin. He took the steps two at a time, fists clenched white by his sides. Farden hadn't seen him like this in a long time.

'Those bloody Sirens are up in arms about something, and they won't tell us what until they get here, which is any minute now. They've threatened war, Farden.' Vice threw him a serious look. The mage's eyes went wide. He lowered his voice and moved closer to the Undermage, struggling to keep up with Vice's long strides.

'War? So this has nothing to do with the well or the tearbook?'

'All I know is they're on their way, and whatever it is, that Siren queen of theirs is not at all happy. Somehow the news of their arrival got out early this morning and everyone started to panic.'

'Gods' sake,' Farden shook his head. They emerged into the long white corridor outside the great hall.

'The Arkmages are furious,' said Vice. 'As am I, Farden, with *you.*' Vice stopped abruptly in the middle of the hallway and rounded on Farden with an icy stare.

'With me?' the mage spluttered. Modren stayed quiet and tried not to get involved, staring at the marble decor.

Vice narrowed his gaze. 'Why didn't you tell me about the Old Dragon?'

Farden mentally reeled. In all the confusion he had forgotten about the matter completely and was utterly at a loss for an answer. 'I thought it would be best to tell you in private.' Farden groped for an explanation.

'Well, it would have been, Farden, when we had the privacy of my chambers! No wonder the tearbook came back to life. Imagine my surprise when I was told by the Arkmages this morning that the old fiend is still alive. Helyard accused me of being in league with them!' Vice was fuming. His hazel eyes aflame.

Farden held up his hands. 'He knows that's not true. I can explain it all.'

'And so you shall. Right now!' Vice spun around so fast that his long robe billowed out like a sail. Farden was left behind, eyes wide. Modren put a hand on his friend's shoulder.

'Better you than me, mate,' he whispered.

Farden was about to launch into a sarcastic retort, but Vice flashed them a frosty glare to see if they were following.

'Fuck's sake,' he muttered, running to catch up.

When they reached the great hall, the Undermage pushed his way into the crowd as if he were tackling a troll. One of the guards spotted him and immediately began laying about with the butt of his spear. 'Let the Undermage through! Move out of the way!'

Farden and Modren followed in Vice's wake, elbowing their way through the noisy ranks of people until they were standing up against the gilded doors. Holding their shields with both hands, the soldiers braced themselves against the crowd, keeping them back while the doors were opened just enough to let the three men slip through. The doors slammed behind them, shutting out the masses. Sadly, the scene outside paled in comparison to the uproar that was the magick council. It was absolute chaos.

All around them, council members argued at the top of their voices, throwing opinions back and forth while the Arkmages sat on their tall white thrones, talking agitatedly between themselves. Colourful patterns from the stained glass windows played on the walls and floors, painting angry faces all sorts of strange hues.

The three mages walked into the middle of the room and stood beside the tall gold statue of the goddess Evernia, her feet still surrounded by a score of candles despite the bright daylight streaming in from above. As soon as Åddren noticed them he held his hands in the air authoritatively. His normally kind eyes pierced the room like blue icicles. Nothing happened, and the roar continued unabated.

'SILENCE!' Åddren's voice was like thunder. Loud words and arguments froze on the lips of the council, and an awkward stillness fell upon the hall. Men and women meekly shuffled to the spaces in between the tree-like pillars.

Helyard scowled about the hall. 'I hope to the gods you can offer us some sort of explanation for this chaos, Farden! Your meddling ways have caused us enough trouble already, and now you've brought those despicable dragon-riders down upon us.' The Arkmage looked down his nose at the mage with his usual disdainful air.

Farden walked across the marble floor to stand closer to the thrones. The council whispered like autumn leaves around him.

'Your Mages, I have no idea why the Sirens are on their way to Krauslung, or why they are threatening war.' The whispering increased, 'When I left Nelska, they assured me that our two peoples were at peace.'

'So we heard from Lord Vice this morning, when he gave us your report—' Åddren started, but the stern Helyard swayed forwards in his throne and wagged a bony finger.

'*Which*, we might add, left out the most important fact that the Old Dragon Farfallen is still alive! I'm assuming that neither you nor the Undermage can explain this omission?' he said.

Farden looked to Vice, then back to the Arkmages. He nodded slowly. 'The Undermage is no traitor, Arkmage Helyard, and it is no fault of his that Farfallen still lives. I admit that I was reticent, but I thought it best that I tell the Undermage in private, and hadn't yet had the chance to do so.' Farden eyed Helyard defiantly as he spoke, but the Arkmage snorted and looked away.

Åddren opened his mouth to speak but was interrupted by the wailing cry of distant horns ringing out along the walls of Krauslung. The magick council murmured nervously.

The dragons had arrived.

Every eye turned inexorably to the huge, diamond-shaped skylight in the roof. Farden slowly retreated to stand with Vice and Modren, who had now moved further back towards the doors, necks bent upwards, eyes scanning the blue skies. A nervous hush descended on the hall. Ranks of soldiers slowly took their places in between the marble pillars. Archers in their dozens stood above them on benches, arrows notched and ready.

The pale blue sky hung above them, crisp and empty. The cold breeze blowing across the skylight was the only sound. But soon, from the ramparts and the tall towers of the fortress beneath them, came the long moans of the warning horns. The twin bells of Hardja and Ursufel tolled ominously. A few shouts rang out from the walls below them, and a huge shadow scattered over the stained glass windows on the eastern side. A roar echoed through the valley.

Farden took a deep breath, standing stiffly, his arms by his side. He glanced at Vice and the Undermage nodded slowly at him with a look that conveyed a sarcastic, 'Well done'. To his right, Modren clicked his knuckles one by one, staring up at the skies.

Farden tried to relax. He turned back to watch the roof as the deep sound of heavy wing beats rocked the air, as if the clouds were tumbling down the mountains.

A collective gasp came from the crowded hall as a scarlet dragon dropped like a gigantic stone through the ceiling. The great red beast folded its wings so as to fit through the gap, then blew a whining snort that made the nearest bystanders scurry.

It landed on the floor in front of the statue of Evernia with a heavy thud, extinguishing more than a few of her candles with a flap of its crimson wings. It looked like the dragon Farden had met briefly in Hjaussfen, Towerdawn. He solemnly bowed his head to the Arkmages, then moved aside with ponderous steps that made the floor shake. His rider was a short woman with copper-coloured hair that cascaded over her dark metal armour like a rusty waterfall. She looked around the room with slow, measured turns of her head and flicks of her tawny eyes.

The next dragon to drop into the hall was Brightshow. Her pale white and yellow colouring glittered in the sunlight and when she bowed her head her horns shone gold. Her rider, Lakkin, if Farden remembered correctly, sat tall and straight in his saddle at the base of her neck. He wore black and silver armour and a long sword was strapped between his shoulders. His black hair had been slicked back by the wind, and his keen yellow eyes roved over the gathered council members.

Farden watched more Arka soldiers slowly manoeuvring around the council members. Tension hovered in the hall like a taut bowstring. They all waited for the last dragon to arrive.

The hall was abruptly shaken by a massive roar from the skies above them, and Farfallen descended through the skylight with a flash of golden scales. He landed on the floor with a bang, then reared up to his full, intimidating height as he tucked his wings behind him.

Svarta sat tall and straight on Farfallen's neck, with no saddle beneath her and a small bundle of cloth in her hands. She jumped from her dragon's back and stood imperiously by his side. She wore a grey leather tunic with leather and mail trousers that clung to her long legs. A black knife hung from her side. The blonde strands of hair that hung beside her flinty face flicked from side to side as she paced back and forth with twitching, cat-like movements. Svarta cast a glance behind her and scowled at Farden. *Nothing had changed there, then.*

Farfallen took a deep breath and flared his nostrils, puffing smoke. He looked at the Arkmages, who were now standing up in front of their thrones. Farden felt the swelling of their magick.

'Well met and good wishes, Arkmages. It has been a long time since we last met, and it is with regret that we must meet again under such dark circumstances,' said Farfallen.

Åddren bowed low and cleared his throat. 'It seems to be the destiny of our peoples, Old Dragon, to have war constantly hanging over us,' he replied. Farfallen nodded sagely.

Vice folded his hands behind his back and took a few steps. 'Your message did not mention the purpose of your visit,' he commented. He watched Farfallen avidly, and Farden could see his eyes flicking to the scar on the gold dragon's chest.

Svarta completely ignored the Undermage. Her harsh tone bounced off the walls like pieces of shattered ice. 'We are here for an explanation, Arkmages, as to why you have attempted to betray us.'

'Betray you—?' Åddren started, but the Siren queen cut him off.

'Don't play games, Åddren. Last night, Farfallen's tearbook was stolen from us, along with the translations we had been working on to help *you*, Arka! More than a score of Sirens were slain and the murderer disappeared into the night along with the tearbook. And now we have come here to demand retribution!' Her face was pale, lips pursed tight with barely restrained fury. Whispers filled the hall. Svarta looked around her, glowering.

Åddren held up a hand and spoke in a calm voice. 'Your accusation makes no sense, Queen Svarta. Why would we send you the tearbook only to steal it back again, at great risk and cost? And why are the Arka being so readily blamed for these crimes?'

Svarta sneered. 'You should know, Åddren. After all, it was one of the Arkmages that committed this crime,' she said.

The hall erupted with angry shouts and hoots of derision. Farden could see the soldiers tensing. Towerdawn snarled, rattling his spikes. Brightshow bared her teeth.

Vice stormed forwards. 'This is an outrage!' he bellowed, and the crowd yelled with him. The Undermage stared straight at the golden dragon and Svarta as they whipped around to face him. Farfallen growled deep in his throat and Farden could see flame in his eyes. Vice showed no fear.

'How dare you accuse the Arkmages of such a crime! What proof do you have, if any, of this *ridiculous* accusation?' he shouted. His face was flushed, his fists clenched.

Svarta laughed contemptuously. She waved the small bundle in her hands. 'You want proof, Vice? Arkmages? Here is your proof!' She held the cloth package at one end and shook it out.

A blood-stained gold disk tumbled out of the fabric, falling to the floor with a metallic clang. It bounced noisily on the marble as it spun to a rest, directly in front of the Twin Thrones. As it fell silent, so did the great hall. Everybody stared at the dried blood, and the lettering, and turned pale.

Vice's face dropped. He was visibly shocked. Svarta tossed the bloody cloth to the floor and crossed her arms contemptuously. Modren looked to Farden, but he was watching Helyard's face closely.

The Arkmage sat perched on the edge of his throne, gripping the arms with white knuckles. His face was struggling to remain calm and composed. Farden could see the sweat starting to gather at the roots of his dirty blonde hair. Watching the tall man's face, his suspicions about the Arkmage were suddenly thrown into sharp, painful reality. With the truth looming in front of him, the mage felt a sickening feeling of betrayal, as if the floor had just given way under the hall, and the Arka were falling into dark waters below. Farden looked down at the disk.

It was a Weight, the enchanted symbol of office carried by all Arkmages since anyone was able to remember. Just as there were always two Arkmages, there were two Weights; one for Åddren and one for Helyard. Together they balanced the scales sitting at Evernia's golden feet, and it was where they normally sat during a normal council session. Farden cast a furtive look at the scales hanging awkwardly askew, surrounded by the remaining lit candles.

The Weights were essentially quickdoors, though much smaller and infinitely more elegant than their unwieldy cousins. Relics of an age of finer magick, when gods had walked the earth.

Farden squinted, trying to see the lettering hiding under the dried blood. Engraved in the gold were powerful spells that allowed the user to travel to anywhere they wished in moments. But it wasn't that simple: Weights are dangerous, and almost impossible to use. For any mage who isn't strong enough to use one, there is rarely a second try.

Farden had heard more than his fair share of stories about mages getting the spell wrong and appearing on a mountain top, or, worse, partly in, partly out of a wall, broken and dead. Only the Arkmages could use them, and only fools tried.

Uncertainty scurried amidst the awkward silence, and there was a terrible feeling of dread in the hall. More than a few of the council members exchanged fearful looks. Svarta looked about victoriously, challenging anyone who met her gaze with scowling eyes. Farfallen was silent and looming, waiting for someone to respond. The other two dragons said nothing, but Brightshow wore a concerned look, and Farden watched her shuffle her clawed feet from side to side.

Vice looked to his superiors, the first to speak. 'Your Mages?' he asked. The Undermage's voice sounded strangely loud after the awkward silence. Everyone watched the two men on their tall thrones.

With a terrible slowness, Åddren lifted a hand and reached inside his gold and green robe. Every single eye was upon him, and he looked whiter, paler, suddenly old and frail. With shaking hands, he pulled forth a gold disk from under his robe, one that was identical to the disk lying on the floor. He lifted it high for all to see. Åddren then turned to his old friend and fixed him with a stare that could have spoken a thousand different words.

'Helyard?' Åddren said with a cracking voice, 'I think an explanation is needed.'

Svarta sniggered and looked to the two riders flanking her and Farfallen, waiting.

Arkmage Helyard's jaw was set, eyes fixated on the Weight on the floor. 'This is ridiculous,' he croaked, and licked his lips.

Svarta cocked her head. 'Excuse me?'

Helyard's mahogany eyes flashed with anger and Farden could have sworn he heard him growl at the Siren queen. 'I said that this is *ridiculous*! Gods damn it, can't you hear how absurd this accusation is, Åddren? I was here in Krauslung for the entire evening, ask my servants! This is nonsense!' His eyes were narrowed, his expression that of a venomous snake caught between a spade and the heel of a boot.

'I wouldn't call the death of a dozen Siren guards and the theft of the tearbook nonsense, Arkmage,' Farfallen warned. The tension was growing, like a bowstring being drawn tighter and tighter. Farden looked up at the skylight and noticed the clouds gathering above the great hall, marring the crystal clear morning. Several other dragons were wheeling high above, colourful specks on a greying backdrop.

Helyard thumped his fist against the marble throne. 'I am innocent of this crime! How dare you try to blame *me*, an Arkmage! I can't believe these lies are actually being listened to!' He was furious, scrabbling weakly at explanations, constantly looking to Åddren for help. Farden could see the guilt in his eyes now, and the mood in the hall was slowly turning from uncertain fear to righteous, indignant anger. Council members whispered and pointed, nodding and shaking their heads, all thinking the same.

Farden felt his own anger welling up inside. He contemplated dragging Helyard from the hall himself.

'I am not a traitor!' shouted the Arkmage.

'THEN EXPLAIN THIS!' yelled Svarta. With a snarl she kicked the Weight against the foot of his throne.

'Lies! It was stolen and—' Words caught in his throat. He blinked, wide-eyed. His mouth hung open. The clouds were darkening, and the other dragons were soaring on the approaching gale.

Svarta spread her arms wide and cast an accusing look around the hall. 'Stolen?! From one of the Arkmages? Even if it had been taken from you, who else can use it, Helyard? Who?'

Several of the council members shook their heads at her as if they were actually being blamed.

'I didn't think as much,' she said. Farfallen cleared his throat loudly, shooting Svarta a warning look. She retreated to her dragon's side, simmering with righteous anger.

Helyard continued to splutter, shaking with rage. He looked to Åddren again, but the Arkmage was now slumped in his throne with his head resting in one hand. His own Weight lay in his open palm. Vice walked calmly forwards until he stood beside the Arkmage, then leaned down to whisper confidentially to him. Farden wondered how much privacy they could muster under the watchful eyes of the dragons and the rest of the hall. Helyard stared on, eyes wide and furious.

Ears were pricked. Vice seemed to ask a question. Åddren shook his head once or twice, then nodded with a look of sad resignation at the Undermage, his blue eyes looking as if they would shatter like glass at any moment. Vice bowed his head and stepped back, folding his hands in front of him calmly, even though he shook with anger and disappointment. Farden watched his friend carefully, and like everyone else in the great hall he waited, boiling with tethered, indignant fury. He shared a look with Modren. His friend was wide-eyed and unsure.

Åddren's voice sounded like a snapped twig in a silent forest. 'Guards.' He paused there, and an expression on abject horror pasted itself on Helyard's pale face. The clouds above were now heavy and ominous. The verdict was in.

'Remove the Arkmage from the hall,' managed Åddren in a quiet breath. Vice sighed and snapped his fingers at the armoured men standing behind the pillars. There were no shouts of protest, no whispers from the magick council this time. Everyone in the hall just watched, and glared.

'This is *impossible*!' Helyard shouted, his voice now high-pitched and his eyes like saucers. The soldiers approached him gingerly and tried to uproot him from his throne. Helyard rose stiffly, face still like thunder, mirroring the dark clouds gathering above.

Fearful of touching the Arkmage, the guards escorted him across the hall. Farden half-expected Helyard to try to fight his way out, but he stayed silent until he passed Evernia's shrine, where he started to protest at the top of his voice. Only once did he try to move past the guards and get away, but the armoured men formed a ring around him and used their shields to move him along. Condemning shouts of, 'Traitor!' and, 'Snake!' came from the council. Helyard's fists pounded the air, eyes wide with rage. He pointed at Svarta and spat venomously.

'This isn't over, Siren! I'm warning you! Åddren, this is madness!' Helyard's words echoed around the hall until he had disappeared behind the golden doors with a bang.

Vice turned to Svarta and Farfallen. 'Are you happy now?' he demanded.

'Not in the slightest,' the Siren shook her head.

'You've got what you came for! Helyard has been exposed and will be punished accordingly,' said Vice, walking swiftly to take up his own seat near to Åddren.

But Svarta wagged a finger at him. 'Not so fast, Undermage, we came here for answers.'

Åddren exploded with anger. 'And what answers would they be!?' he shouted. His face was drained of colour and his hands were shaking with fury, or grief, Farden couldn't tell. Åddren slammed his palm down on the marble arm of his throne with a loud slap.

'You've brought this magick council to its knees and had one of the Arkmages imprisoned for treason. What more could you possibly want? Do you want *me* hauled away as well? The cloak off my back? My throne? Here!'

Åddren tore wildly at his gold and green robe, ripping it from his shoulders and throwing it over his head. He slung it to the marble floor next to the bloody disk and stood with his arms wide, half-naked, eyes burning. For once, Svarta remained silent.

'I just watched a man thrown into prison for murder and betrayal. A man whom I have known for years. A man I trusted implicitly! And yet, under my very nose, he has plotted and he has schemed against his own people! When have you known such betrayal, Svarta? Tell me how you think that would feel!' Åddren's eyes glowed with fire as he waited for an answer, but the Siren queen kept quiet, staring at him impassively. Farden had never seen the Arkmage like that before, and neither had the council.

Farfallen took a deep breath. 'I think we have argued enough for one day.'

His deep voice seemed to calm Åddren, and the Arkmage slumped wearily back into his seat. The gold dragon continued.

'But the question still remains whether Helyard was working alone, or if we should still ready ourselves for the summoning of this creature.'

Vice stood. 'I agree. Farden was attacked by a dark sorcerer while on his way to Nelska, so we must assume that there are others involved.'

Brightshow piped up. 'But without Farfallen's tearbook we have almost nothing, not even the translations.'

The whole council sighed, feeling the first icy tendrils of failure creeping over them. Farden wracked his brains, trying to quell the anger inside him so that he could think straight. Cheska's words from the night before echoed in his head.

Vice clicked his fingers as an idea came to him. 'Albion,' he said, looking around.

Åddren seemed confused. Farfallen narrowed his eyes at the Undermage. 'Albion?'

'Helyard has been travelling there at night for the past few weeks. We thought nothing of it until now.'

Farden recalled a memory and spoke up. 'He went to Albion the night before I left for Nelska. The sorcerer on the ship also had an Albion accent.' The pieces began to click together.

'He said he had business with one of the dukes,' added Åddren. Vice nodded.

'He went to Kiltyrin two nights ago, and Fidlarig before that. This has to be what we're looking for.'

Åddren put a hand under his chin and quietly muttered his agreement. The council members talked amongst themselves, wagging their chins and fingers. Everybody seemed to agree.

'While our scholars continue to look at the tearbook, we can have dragons searching for the well in a few hours,' Svarta said decisively.

Farden walked forwards confidently. He resisted the urge to knock the Siren queen with his shoulder and stood in front of the thrones. He looked to Vice.

'The Written can travel by quickdoor to the Port of Dunyra, Undermage. I can have all of us there before sunset, ready to fight,' he said.

Svarta looked disgusted at the thought of an army of Written, but Vice was smiling.

'We will need all the help we can get,' said Åddren. Behind them, the Old Dragon settled down to sit on the floor and rumbled thoughtfully.

'Now that Helyard's been exposed, his friends are likely to spring their trap early,' he warned.

'That's assuming they've already found a dark elf well,' Svarta added.

Åddren raised a hand and spoke in a calm measured tone. 'We cannot afford to take that chance. They may know what to look for in the tearbook. Who knows what Helyard has been up to all these years, what powerful friends he might have?' he couldn't suppress a disappointed sigh. 'Vice, you will take the army to the Port of Dunyra by ship or by quickdoor, find that well, and destroy it. I will not allow these traitors to summon this creature and have their victory. It must be killed at all costs!'

The council murmured, and a few yells of support could be heard.

'I agree,' Farfallen growled. 'I will send my fastest dragons to Albion within the hour, and if you are willing, the rest of us will remain here to guard Krauslung for the time being. Our army will be ready to leave Nelska by the morning.'

'Please accept my hospitality,' Åddren bowed his head with a friendly, though wary, gesture. Farfallen flashed his reptilian smile and Svarta cleared her throat in some sort of icy, indifferent thank you.

The Arkmage rapped his knuckles on the side of his throne. 'The council is now dismissed. The dragons and their riders may stay, as can you Farden.' Åddren pointed to the mage.

The council drifted out of the door and out into the now hushed corridor. Soldiers and important citizens peered over the heads of guards like eager chicks in a nest, trying to see into the great hall. It wasn't every day an Arkmage was hauled off to the dungeons. Modren made to leave, but Farden beckoned to him and he joined him in front of the thrones.

Soon the hall was empty and the doors were locked shut from the outside. Vice sighed loudly, eyeing the scar on Farfallen's chest. 'Farden and I will go and ready our forces. There is much to do.' His eyes flicked to the mage, and Farden nodded quickly.

Åddren spoke. 'I will talk with the mage for a while. I want that Weight hidden in your chambers, Vice, keep it safe and out of sight.'

The Undermage stood up and went to the blood-encrusted Weight on the floor. Using the cloth, he picked it up and gripped it tightly. 'I'll meet you outside, Farden,' said Vice, leaving the hall.

After he'd gone, Åddren beckoned to Farden. 'Come here,' he said. Farden came to bow in front of the throne.

The Arkmage held out his own Weight. It caught the light and glistened like the sun. Åddren spoke slowly. He sounded tired.

'It seems you have proven your worth once more, Farden, and I am glad to have you back in one piece. Because you have been loyal to the Arka in the face of such betrayal, I want you to hold onto this, so that I may be exempt from any blame. After tonight I will remain in my chambers, and the council will be suspended until I say different.' Åddren looked towards Svarta and narrowed his eyes ever so slightly. 'Vice has done well to choose you to lead the Written. I know you will not disappoint.'

Farden felt truly honoured. For the first time he felt as though he had stepped out from the shadow of his uncle's legacy; that his dedication had been noticed. That he was no longer a piece, but a player.

Farden bowed once more and thanked the Arkmage. He took the Weight, marvelling at its lightness, and slipped it inside his cloak. As he turned, he looked to Farfallen, who blinked slowly and hinted at a smile, then made to leave. Svarta watched him go suspiciously.

As he reached the doors, Farden stopped and turned, an idea forming in his head. 'If I might ask a favour of the Sirens, your Mage, I would request that Brightshow fly me to the Arkabbey in the Forest of Durn, in Albion, if she and her rider are willing?'

Modren looked aghast at the notion of dragons and flying in the same sentence.

'And what is the purpose of this diversion?' Åddren inquired.

'My superior at the Arkabbey, the vampyre Durnus.' At this Svarta looked even more appalled. 'He is one of the finest historians and scholars the Arka has. He has spent decades studying dark magick and Albion, and I think he would be invaluable in helping to find the elven well,' said Farden.

Åddren thought for a moment, then nodded. 'It makes sense, and I see no problem with it. Be quick though, Farden, we have no time to waste.' Åddren waved for him to go, managing to offer the mage a weak smile. Farden could see that the day's events had hit him hard.

'I'll meet you in front of the main gates outside your city, Farden, as soon as night falls.' Brightshow said. Her rider gave the mage a formal, polite smile. Farden smiled at the dragon, bowed again, and left with Modren in tow.

Vice was waiting outside the door. The people had been ushered downstairs and swiftly out of the citadel at the behest of the Undermage's sharp tongue. His soldiers now stood at every door and corner in the fortress, green and black armour clanking loudly as they patrolled around in pairs.

'There you are.' Vice scowled at them. He hissed at Farden as the door banged shut. 'What did the Arkmage say?'

'He said you did well to choose me as the captain of the Written, and thanked me for all I did in Nelska,' replied Farden.

They walked as they whispered, meandering through the corridors down into the fortress below. Modren remained a few steps behind, too overwhelmed to say anything.

'Helyard all along,' Vice mused, rubbing his chin with a hum. He smoothed his hair as he spoke.

Farden shook his head, clenching his fists. 'He's been against our every move since the start. I should have realised earlier when he tried to pin it on me.'

'None of us could have predicted that the traitor would be an Arkmage. Not even in our wildest nightmares.'

'I always knew there was something strange about him,' muttered Farden. 'He's always been the more powerful of the two. I half-expected him to try to fight his way out of there.'

Vice agreed. 'Well, he's locked away now, and I'd like to see him try to break his way out,' he said. 'Those prison doors are bound with spells for a reason. I designed some of them myself. Even air couldn't escape those cells.'

Farden and Modren nodded. The prisons were legendary. Every criminal's nightmare.

Vice looked at the two mages. 'Are the Written going to be ready in time? As much as I distrust that golden lizard, Farfallen is right: whoever Helyard was working with could release the creature at any time now they have the tearbook. We're still working on a guess.'

Farden lifted his chin authoritatively. 'I'll assemble them now and get them through the quickdoor to Dunyra as soon as possible. We'll be at Fidlarig by midnight.'

'Good. You're in charge now.' The Undermage paused. 'So don't let me down.' Vice threw him a sideways look and softened the warning with a smile. Farden retorted with an arrogant smirk.

'Never been a problem before,' he said. They jogged down a flight of steps two at a time, boots echoing on the stone. The noise from below was getting louder. 'I almost forgot,' Farden said, 'I'm collecting Durnus from the Arkabbey before I go to Dunyra.'

Vice looked confused and annoyed. 'Why?'

'That old vampyre has been sitting in a study for the best part of two hundred years, poring over history books and old maps. He knows more about Albion than anybody. If we want to get to this well as quickly as possible, he's our best bet.'

'Fine, bring him,' acquiesced the Undermage. 'I'm staying in Krauslung. Someone needs to be here to stop it falling apart. Åddren is deeply shaken, and I doubt he'll be thinking clearly, so I want to be here in case anything goes wrong. Those dragons need watching.' Vice moved closer to whisper in Farden's ear. 'I see what you mean about that Siren bitch.'

The three of them descended into the depths of the Arkathedral fortress, their steps getting faster and faster with each flight of stairs and every corridor, as if success depended on their haste. In what seemed like no time at all, they reached where the crowds were at their busiest.

Vice paused on the steps. The noise was deafening, bouncing off the marble walls and floors, so he had to shout to be heard. 'I will join you in a few days. Don't let me down, Farden! Remember, you're in charge now.'

'If there are any problems, I'll send word immediately, so keep the quickdoors open!' Farden shook Vice's hand, and Modren bowed low. The Undermage gripped Farden's shoulder tightly, then turned away and headed for a bustling group of his guards.

'May the gods be with you!' he called back to them.

Once Vice had left, Farden sighed and shrugged at Modren. His blonde friend shook his head, breathing out an exasperated, exhausted sigh. 'You've got a lot of explaining to do.'

Farden rolled his eyes. 'Tonight, when I get back from the Arkabbey, I'll tell you everything,' he said. 'This day has been fucked up beyond all recognition.'

'This whole situation is fucked up! Morale's going to be terrible when word gets out about Helyard,' Modren cursed.

'I know, but we've got more dangerous things to think about now, and places to be, so get a move on. I'm going to get my things and get ready, then we'll meet back here at sunset, like I said.'

'Fine,' said Modren, and the two mages strode purposefully down the corridor.

No one would ever suggest that the Written are out of control, but they seem to work best when we leave them to their own devices, and we know that. They act in pairs or they act alone and as long as the job gets done, then the council turns a blind eye to the method. But thank the gods that we ruled against the third and fourth runes. Some of the older Written are almost as skilled as I am.

From pages found in Arkmage Helyard's rooms

Within half an hour, Farden was back at *The Bearded Goat* and quenching his thirst and nerves with fresh, cold ale. The drunks had been turfed out and the inn was being slowly cleaned by a set of weary-looking staff. The innkeeper barely said a word to the mage. He had deep purple bags under his eyes and his hair resembled a dishevelled haystack.

Farden paid the man for his room and his drink, then went upstairs to gather his things. It was just past midday, and there were at least four or five hours until sunset. He slumped onto the bed, quickly falling into a deep sleep.

When he awoke, it was no more than an hour later, yet he felt refreshed and eager. The sun was beginning its slow fall towards the western slopes, and the city outside his window was still crowded and turbulent. He was glad he had kept the window shut. Farden stretched, yawned, then got out of bed. Most of his clothes were already packed, seeing as he hadn't quite *unpacked* yet, but his sword was blunt and his boots were looking just a little too worn. He checked his supplies, of which he had plenty, thanks to the Sirens.

The vial of ice water sparkled blue in the sunlight. The maps the Sirens had given him didn't make much sense, but they could prove useful, so he packed them as well. The book followed, as did Cheska's fjortla, then he was ready to go. Farden grabbed his cloak from the chair and flung it around his shoulders. Something solid knocked against his shoulder, and he pulled a confused face, rummaging around in the pockets until he found the culprit: the Weight.

Farden brought it out into the light and ran his calloused fingertips over the gold, feeling the ridges and dents of the script. The words were strange, foreign, like the old spell books he had seen on Durnus' shelf. Farden handled the disk as if it might explode at any moment, as if it could whisk him away to some unknown place just by holding it. He carefully put it back in his pocket, making sure it was safe. Then he slid on his vambraces, cool against his warm skin. They gripped him tightly, making Farden smile as they always did. With that, he was done. He hoisted his pack and his sword onto his shoulders and once again, the mage was ready to go.

Farden left the *Goat* in a jog and headed towards the nearest market. People were beginning to barricade doors and windows with planks and boxes. Somebody had left an old cart in the middle of the road, and a man had clambered on top of it, yelling at the top of his voice that war was coming. There was a bottle in his hand, and he swayed back and forth as the cart rocked.

Soldiers stood on every street corner and patrols meandered through the crowds. They seemed on edge, and Farden didn't blame them. There was an undercurrent of fear running through the city streets, mingling with all the sewage and bustling feet. He looked up at the sky. No dragons now, but the clouds were still gathering, as they had been since that morning. No doubt Helyard was up to something, even sitting shackled in his cell. Shadows scuttled over the city as clouds passed over the sun, and the light of the clear day began to fade. As Farden strode briskly through the streets, he kept an eye on the weather.

The mage found the market. Crammed as it was with people, he managed to make his way to a blacksmith's forge. Weapons were piling up on the tables, in front of a backlogged queue of soldiers who stood impatiently tapping their feet and fingers. Their expressions were of irritated boredom, yet they were all silent, waiting for their turn.

Farden approached the line of men. He could feel their eyes on him. As he went to join the back of the queue, they moved, one by one, out of his way, gesturing for him to move up. Farden nodded, smiling awkwardly as each man silently shuffled aside. Word spread fast in the city. He was the Written captain now.

When he reached the front of the line, a skinny young boy took his sword and unsheathed it, testing its edge. He couldn't have been more than ten years old, but he swung it around him once or twice, nodded, then gave it to the man at the grindstone. The blacksmith looked at it, thumbed the blade, then spun his wheel. A shower of sparks flew from the steel, which hissed and whined as the metal moved against the rough grey edges of the stone. Farden waited, running his hands over the armour and shields on display.

The blade was soon finished, and the boy handed it back to the mage. Farden could see the boy's eyes widen hungrily at the sight of the red and gold metal around his wrists. Farden smiled and tapped his vambraces with a finger.

'Not for all the coin in the world, boy,' he said with a wink, and walked off, nodding his thanks to the line of soldiers as he left.

Replacing his boots took a while. It seemed difficult for any of the merchants at the stalls to find any pairs that fit him. After an hour or so of looking, he found a pair of black travelling boots that matched his black cloak. They hugged his feet comfortably. Once they had been "blessed" by the owner of the stall, a strange and twitchy young man, Farden headed back towards the Arkathedral.

He gathered a few more supplies on his way, but just as he was about to escape the clutches of the busy market, he saw a tiny little stall, no more than a banner and a tall box, hiding under the porch of an old building on the corner of the street.

A tall woman, almost taller than him, stood behind the stall watching the passing commotion with a calm, expressionless face. He didn't really have time to spare, but there was something about her wares that caught his eye. Spread out on the top of the dusty box was a white cloth, dotted with stones and gems of all different kinds. Farden walked a little closer to take a look.

Some stones had smooth surfaces, some were rough and spiky. One in particular glittered in the fading light, shining with every colour imaginable. Another looked like a lump of gold. The rest were collections of deep molten purples and greens, metallic, mottled oranges and veiny crimson reds. Farden could not help but examine each of them in turn. All the while, the tall, serene woman watched him calmly.

'Would you like help, sir?' she asked, and Farden looked up at her. She was pale, unnaturally pale, with long jet-black hair that reached her hips. Like her face, her limbs and fingers were thin, as if her whole body had been stretched and drawn out. The woman's eyes were strange almost seeming to move independently of each other. They were dark, inky and inexpressive, like two rockpools of glassy water.

Farden pointed to the small cabochon stone that was nearest to him. It slowly changed colour, back and forth between green and red.

'What's this?' he asked, and she leaned forwards as if noticing the stones for the first time.

'The bloodstone heals feuds and protects against injustice.' Her voice was small and without accent, strangely monotone. 'Many women come to me for it, to heal homes and lovers.' She pointed to a grey stone that shimmered like steel. 'This, too, they buy,' she said, then cocked her head to one side, much like a bird looking at a worm. 'Are you here for a woman?'

Farden quickly shook his head. 'No, well, yes, but just a present for my, er, sister. She's gone away for three days, and I wanted to get her something for when she returns,' he said, with a brief smile. 'Which she will,' he added.

The woman grinned back at him, but it was a tight expression that bore no emotion. 'Well then, Written, this would be a fine and useful present for her.'

Her long fingers moved over the cloth slowly, finally coming rested on a brass-coloured rock. It looked like a lump of tarnished gold, full of angular facets and sparkling edges. 'These fall from the stars in the south, usually in the morning hours. Some, like the Paraians, call them firestones, others call them daemonstones. But they show the truth of things hidden, give hope, and make an excellent present for a loved one.'

'My sister,' said Farden.

The woman nodded and smiled again. 'Of course.'

Farden rubbed his chin. 'How much?' he asked.

'Only two silver for my trouble,' replied the skinny woman. He had never really bought a present for anyone before, but it seemed nice enough, and Farden reached for his coins.

He placed two silver bits on the cloth and the woman snatched them away before wrapping the small rock in a sheet of waxy brown paper. Her fingers moved rapidly over the package, creating a crackling sound, and soon enough Farden's gift was waiting in the thin woman's hands.

He smiled again, uneasily, reaching for it. From the way the corner of her mouth curled upwards, and the way she stared at him, he half-expected her to pull it back and ask for something more, but she didn't move a muscle. The mage stuffed the paper package inside his cloak and made to leave.

The woman looked to the grey skies with her glassy eyes and muttered to herself. 'Rain's on its way, it seems,' she said.

Farden looked up at the clouds gathering overhead, their dark bases heavy with precipitation. The Arkmage was hard at work indeed, and it was time to meet the rest of the Written. He nodded to the strange woman and left her stall, feeling her strange gaze upon his back.

The gem knocked against his chest with every step, and every time it bumped him, he thought of Cheska. Farden would keep it for her, while she was in the Spire, and afterwards, once she was rested and healed, he would give it to her. He could already see her face lighting up in his mind.

He took a deep breath, and seeing as she had kept him safe so far, he threw a quick prayer to the goddess Evernia and made his way towards the Arkathedral, just as the first heavy rain drops began to fall, and as darkness gathered in the corners of the wintry skies.

Almost an hour later, Farden reached the Arkathedral gates. Heavy raindrops splashed on the walls, soaking everything to the bone, making buildings creak and swell, drowning the city in the downpour.

With the outbreak of rain, the streets had soon emptied. The angry crowds had dispersed, and the people had gone home for the evening to lock their doors and pull their curtains. There was no shouting to be heard, no revelling. The news of the Arkmage's incarceration had spread fast and the blow had been mighty. Farden looked around as he walked, listening to his boots splash in the bubbling puddles. Krauslung was strangely subdued that evening.

Modren was waiting for him in the rain, hood up, grinning like a fool. He watched Farden striding across the cobblestones towards him and raised a hand as he shook with an audible shiver.

'Brrr. Getting cold out here,' said Modren.

'You *are* standing in the rain,' replied Farden.

The mages walked to stand by the sputtering torches hanging from the Arkathedral walls, where they could shelter for a moment under the curve of the archway. The mighty gates were slightly ajar, and a loud clamouring could be heard behind them; a roar that rose above the noise of the rain. Bright light poured onto the street and the guards at the gates looked deeply unsettled.

Modren whispered behind a cupped hand. 'You wait until we get inside, mate. I haven't seen something like this in a long time.'

Farden threw a quizzical look at him, then realised what he was talking about. He could already feel the magick.

His heart began to beat harder as the guards pushed the heavy doors open. The bright torchlight momentarily blinded the two mages as they stepped inside. The roaring slowly ground to a halt, and as Farden blinked the spots from his eyes, more than a hundred faces turned to look at him. His stomach bubbled with sudden fear, or maybe it was stage-fright. Farden couldn't tell.

Modren had been right. The main atrium was crammed to bursting with Written. Farden didn't think he had ever seen so many of them gathered in once place in his lifetime. His chest swelled with pride, his head thrumming with the pressure of the combined magick.

Each and every Written was armed to the teeth and eager to fight, eyes blazing with the anticipation of battle. Farden looked over the multitude of different faces, picking out a few he had fought with many times, and others he had never seen before. Fresh-faced, overly confident youngsters stood beside grim, hardened men, standing battle-scarred and proud.

Every Written wore the same smile, the one that Farden himself had flashed countless times. Self-assured mettle that blazed on their faces as well as their backs.

Farden stood as tall as he could. He tried to look authoritative. He tried to act like he belonged to this crowd. He tried to forget that they all knew about his uncle. He wanted to be everything everyone was expecting. *If the Undermage thinks you're capable, then so should you.* Cheska's words echoed through his mind.

Farden spoke clearly, with a commanding tone. 'Listen up!' He could hear his name being whispered around the marble hall. He ignored them. 'I'm sure you all know me, and for those who don't, then I expect you soon will.' He waited for the muttering to die down again before he continued.

'I have no doubt that you've heard about Helyard, and the traitors who killed the scholars at Arfell. Word has always travelled fast in these parts.' A few people chuckled, others nodded. There was more whispering.

'I'm not going to waste precious time talking, so here's the problem. The ones who killed our old scholars stole a book, a powerful summoning manual from the times of the dark elves. With this book they want to release an ancient monster that will tear Emaneska to pieces. It would seem that the Arkmage Helyard was behind this plan, and now that he has been thrown in the dungeons the council have no doubt that whoever he was working with will accelerate their plans. The only chance we have to stop this creature is to find a dark elf well before they do.' He let that settle in for a moment. 'And that's why we're headed to Albion tonight, to the Port of Dunyra.'

Farden took a breath and looked at the calm faces of the crowd, simply waiting, staring at him, not even the slightest bit fazed.

'We all know that we're the best at what we do because we've spent our lives proving it, time and time again. Well, it looks like we have to do it one more time. The safety of Emaneska rests on our shoulders, and we're going to put a stop to this, the only way the Written know how. So let's go do our job, and as always, let's go do it well!'

A hundred fists punched the air along to his words. The accompanying roar that echoed throughout the great marble hall was deafening.

Farden turned to Modren standing by his side and grinned. Modren puffed out his skinny chest and returned the smile. Farden laughed out loud. Shouts continued to fill the hall as the mages began to form long, noisy lines, facing the stairs. There were a few more yells and calls, then they started stamping their feet with impatient eagerness, warming themselves up.

Farden turned to Modren, shouting in his ear to be heard over the commotion. 'Get them to Dunyra, and meet up with the dragons there, if they've arrived. Don't waste any time! You're in charge while I'm gone.'

Modren nodded. 'You going to get that vampyre of yours?'

'Durnus, yes. I should be back by morning, but just make sure that if it comes to the worst, don't hesitate, understand?' he shouted. Modren nodded fervently.

With a grunt, Farden tightened the straps on his pack and clapped his friend on the arm. Without another word, he turned and left. Modren watched him disappear behind the edge of the gate, leaving the zealous Written to themselves.

Outside, Farden paused for a moment on the rain-slicked cobbled street. He took a deep breath, letting it out slowly through his nostrils as steam.

Rain splattered against the gutters and swirled around the drains, making a rushing din as it collided with the world. Dusk was quickly approaching, sneaking along the horizon like a hungry cat. Farden waited for a moment, waiting for his heart to calm itself, then he was gone again, off into the evening and towards the city gates.

It took him a while to reach the main gates. When he got there it was dark, and the downpour had only gotten worse. The guards had taken shelter under the thick arches. They saluted the mage as he approached, hurrying to open an iron door set into the huge gates.

Once he had stepped through, Farden stood in the shadow of the wall, blowing hot breath into his cold, wet hands to warm them. A rumble of thunder rocked the gloomy sky, and lightning split the darkness. The mage spotted Brightshow standing further up the road. She was shiny with rain and blinking water from her great eyes. She smiled toothily.

'Well met once again, Farden!' she called to him over the roaring downpour.

Farden smiled as he approached the dragon. 'And good wishes, no doubt!' he said as he reached her. 'Thank you again for agreeing to take me to Albion.'

'It is my pleasure. Lakkin has left his saddle on so it'll be easier to hold on in this weather. I wouldn't really recommend barescale your first time riding a dragon.'

Farden had to agree. Brightshow flicked her white and gold head to the leather seat strapped behind her at the base of her neck. Farden clenched and unclenched his fists in a last effort to coax some heat into them. He looked up the hillside towards Manesmark, where the lights of the Spire shone brightly. The mage drew a deep breath.

'You scared?' laughed Brightshow, her voice breaking into his thoughts.

Farden shook his head firmly. 'It's nothing. Maybe a little,' he confessed with a nonchalant shrug.

Brightshow winked. 'I don't blame you, our riders train for years. But it's much more fun than a quickdoor, or so I hear.'

'I'm sure it is,' Farden replied. Rain poured off the edge of his hood in tiny waterfalls. 'Shall we go?' he said.

Brightshow nodded. 'As you wish. Climb up then, before this storm gets any worse!'

She bent her shoulder to the ground, extending the edge of her wing to make a ramp up to the saddle. After a moment of uncertainty, Farden clambered up her wet scales and tried to balance for a moment while he slipped a boot into the leather loops that hung from thick straps. He teetered for a moment before regaining his footing, swinging his other leg over so that he was sitting astride the dragon. Once he had strapped the leather belts securely over his thighs and feet, Brightshow stood up and spread her wings like a huge umbrella over his head. Farden made sure his supplies were all in place and not likely to fly away, then yanked the strap that held his sword to his back.

'Are you ready?' she shouted to him.

Farden blew rainwater from his face and smiled grimly as Brightshow turned her head to look at him. 'As I'll ever be!' he called, and she flashed a mouth full of teeth.

'Then let's go!' she cried.

The pale dragon crouched for a split second, just long enough for Farden to regret his decision, before exploding upwards into the sky with one giant leap.

Rain and wind pressed his body flat against her rough scales. The air howled around him as white wings beat the air with huge whooshing sounds, like trees falling. The mage bounced up and down in the saddle with each lurching stroke. The tight straps protested but they held, thank the gods.

Brightshow shifted her body until her head pointed to the sky and Farden found himself strangling the leather horn at the front of the saddle, holding on for dear life. He swallowed nervously as he caught a glance of his city spread out below him like an intricate model, getting smaller and smaller with every flap of the dragon's mighty wings. Somewhere in the back of Farden's mind it was exhilarating to see the ground fall away beneath him, if not more than a little terrifying. His teeth chattered with excitement as well as the cold. The knuckles that gripped the saddle were so white they looked like bone.

Farden crouched low to match Brightshow's streamlined shape, beginning to feel the dragon's body moving through the wind, noticing how the delicate twitches and swerves of her tail kept them steady in the face of the terrible weather. The Össfen Mountains looked like scattered rubble beneath them. Farden pulled his cloak around his head to shield his eyes from the stinging, biting wind.

chapter 14

The deserts of Paraia are indeed a wild and fearsome place! Behold, the monstrous coelo, with armour for skin and enormous horns placed atop its nose. And the bastion, that towers above the endless sandy plains, legs like trees and tusks that could skewer almost four cows at once! And of course, beware the wily faun, a desert creature hardly ever seen, but infamous for its treachery and lies. Brave travellers beware!

From *Perilous Paraia* by the infamous Master Wird

Jarrick had been on watch for the last twelve hours, and he was starting to fall asleep at his post. He shook his head and sniffed, trying to keep his drowsy eyelids from closing completely. *Ganlir should be here soon*, he thought to himself. *Not soon enough.* The guard shrugged in his heavy gold-plated armour.

Jarrick eyed the corridor: a dark hallway untouched by the light of the flaming torches near the door. Further down that corridor was another door made of thick steel and strong oak. Behind that slept the traitorous Arkmage Helyard, locked away in a windowless room with nothing more than a bed of straw and a scrap of sackcloth to keep him warm. *Just as the traitor deserves.*

The Arkmage had been brought in at the start of Jarrick's shift. It had been a surprise to say the least. Helyard, who minutes before his arrival had been a proud ruler of the Arka, had been reduced to nothing more than a snarling, angry old man, spitting curses and threats like a common thief on the way to the stocks.

Helyard had pounded on his cell door and hollered for hours. He had given up when night fell, and finally all was silent in the prisons of Arkathedral.

Jarrick watched the shadows of the corridor and sniffed. At least he was warm, rather than out on patrol in the pouring rain, he thought. Reassured that nothing was amiss, the sleepy soldier turned back to his staring spot on the wall, counting the bricks and patches of lichen hiding between them. His eyes closed briefly, but he shook himself awake again and changed his grip on his tall spear. He concentrated on the weapon in his palm and tried to stay vigilant… *Where was that blasted Ganlir anyway*? He yawned.

A minute later, Jarrick was leaning against the cold wall, asleep on his feet, his armour grating softly against the stone as his chest rose and fell. A low snore escaped from his open mouth, and his eyelids fluttered in the throes of a dream.

He did not notice the door on his left slowly creeping open. He did not see the shadow sidling into the room, cloaked and hooded. Jarrick was completely lost in his dozing.

With careful movements, the intruder pushed the door shut and reached for a set of intricate keys dangling from a hook. They jingled softly in his hand.

Above him, a torch hung from a bracket in the wall. Using his free hand, he stretched up to touch the flames. The fire seemed to flow into his skin, plunging the corridor into total darkness. The cloaked man listened to the shadows, but all that could be heard was the rise and fall of Jarrick's snores.

The figure crept on down the hallway, quickly finding his way to the sturdy oak and steel door. It had been barred and bolted from the outside with a series of intricate brass cogs and latches. The keys jingled again as he felt their jagged edges. With a scraping sound, he slid the shapes into their respective holes.

After a whine, something within the door came loose. The figure reached for the handle but felt something still holding it tight. A face frowned in the darkness. The man ran his fingers over the surface of the door, feeling the cracks and contours of it, searching. He pressed his palm flat on the wood, near the keyhole. There was a dull thud, and a pulse rippled across the oak. He paused warily, then pushed the door gently. It moaned but shifted an inch or two.

With a bit more persuasion, it swung open into a cell that smelled like sweat and frustration. The bitter scent of urine made the figure wrinkle his nose as he stepped over the threshold and closed the door behind him, locking it with a spell of his own.

From somewhere in the darkness came a quiet snuffling and a rustle of hay. A flicker of flame pierced the gloom, sending the shadows running. The fire burnt in the intruder's open palm, which he held high so that he could peer around the cell. Orange light scattered around him, illuminating piles of straw and a rickety cot in the corner made from driftwood and sackcloth. Curled into a ball on the uncomfortable bed was Helyard, groaning as he scrunched up his eyes in the light. The Arkmage was covered in dust from head to toe, his robes stained and wet.

'What do you want from me now?' he demanded gruffly.

The man took a step forwards. Thick travelling boots scuffed the stone as he bent close to the Arkmage's face. 'I have come to set you free, your Mage,' he whispered.

Helyard peered into the gloom, but the darkness of the figure's hood completely obscured his face. 'Who are you?' he asked quietly. The man stepped back and gestured towards the locked door.

'A friend,' came the reply.

Helyard sat up with a tired groan, trying hard to steady his legs underneath him. The old mage ran a hand through his dirty blonde hair. Mahogany eyes gazed at the hooded figure standing tall between him and the door. There was a tinge of sadness in them.

'Those seem hard to come by these days,' he coughed, and stood up with a sigh. The Arkmage waved an impatient hand. 'Well, whatever it is you want from me, let's go.'

The stranger just stood there. Helyard crossed his arms and waited. 'Well?'

Beneath his hood, the man smirked. Then he grunted and jabbed forwards with hands held like blades. The air thrummed, knocking the Arkmage hard against the cell wall. His skull cracked on the stone and he reeled, blinking pain from his eyes. Helyard must have been stunned, but he was quick enough to throw up his hands as a lightning bolt flew towards him. The spell withered against an invisible wall about a foot in front of the old mage.

Sparks crackled angrily against his magick shield, but he stood firm, eyes blazing defiantly. Helyard stamped his foot on the stone floor with an almighty thud, and a wall of air expanded outwards. It rippled through the floor like a grey wave crashing on a beach, smashing the cot into splinters.

The man was thrown backwards against the metal door, but quickly recovered his footing. He made a claw-like shape with his bony fingers and his whole arm started to convulse. He cursed, choking on the words of the spell as if they scraped at his throat like blades.

Helyard went stiff, eyes bulging from their sockets. His legs dangled beneath him as he was lifted into the air. His arms thrashed wildly, tearing at an unseen hand that squeezed his throat in a vice-like grip. Vertebrae audibly crunched. The Arkmage gargled as the life was slowly crushed from his neck.

The man dropped his clawed hand and Helyard was lowered inch by agonising inch, feet and arms still frantically flailing. His breath came in ragged gasps.

Abruptly, he was released. The Arkmage collapsed in a heap on the cold stone of the cell, unmoving. With a contemptuous snort, the hooded man strode forwards, drawing a long, wicked knife from beneath his cloak. Helyard's eyes were frozen shut, screwed up in agony. The man leaned down close to the Arkmage's face, holding the knife high above his prey, ready to strike like a snake.

The Arkmage was waiting for him.

With speed that belied his ageing frame, Helyard grabbed the stranger's arms and let loose a guttural battle cry. Green light surged from his fingertips, sending the man flying into the air with a yell. He crashed into the ceiling with a shower of broken stone and dust. With a hoarse, wheezing cry, the man fell back to the floor. Chips of stone flew in all directions.

'Thought you could get rid of me quietly, did you?!' shouted the Arkmage. 'Thought you could come in and murder the old man in his sleep, hmm? Who are you? Answer me!'

He wiped stone dust from his eyes and grabbed at the man on the floor, kicking him roughly. The mage snatched at the hood, tugged it back and cast a light spell to reveal his assailant's face.

The knife was nothing but a silver flash in the dusty air as it buried deep inside the Arkmage's chest. Blood appeared at the corner of Helyard's mouth as he blinked and gasped with confusion. The man fixed him with an intense, hungry stare, enjoying every emotion that crossed the mage's face, every twitch that he would make in his last few moments.

'*You*?' Helyard croaked, squinting.

'Since the beginning.' He slowly released his grip on the knife and the Arkmage fell to his knees. Helyard leaned back on his heels, his eyes never leaving his murderer's face. Blood was running down his chest, pooling in his lap, but he couldn't wrench his gaze away. All he could do was watch the curl at the corner of Vice's lips: an arrogant smirk that lifted his cheek to meet the victorious look in his eyes.

'Since the—' Helyard gasped weakly. He rocked back and forth on his knees, swaying like a plume of smoke on the breeze.

'The beginning. Yes. I have been planning this since before you were Arkmage, Helyard. Since before the war,' chuckled Vice, eyes as hard as volcanic glass and just as sharp.

Helyard took a sharp breath. 'Wh—why?'

'Why what?' Vice chuckled. He watched the old mage's life gradually slipping away, pooling in front of him on the stone floor. 'Why you?' he pointed a finger. 'You were just a diversion, Helyard, a parlour trick. Sleight of hand to keep all eyes on you while I went about my business. You were just too easy to imitate, old man, ridiculous for someone of my skills. Stealing the precious Weight from your chambers was nothing but child's play. The scholars and the Sirens had no idea,' he snorted sardonically.

Helyard swallowed blood. 'You'll never win, Vice, that creature and your plan will be thwarted by our army—'

'Your army will be several hundred miles south of where they need to be, you fool. You forget that with you gone, I alone command our men. Once I'm finished with them, the Arka and their new Siren friends will be nothing more than a forgotten song on the lips of dead skalds.' Vice sneered. 'There's not a single person who can stop me now, old man. By the time they find you dead, I'll have disappeared, and my plan will be too far gone to be stopped.'

Helyard shook his head, attempting to raise himself up, but his eyes were slowly, inexorably closing. 'You've betrayed your people,' he wheezed: half-laughing, half-coughing. Dark blood spattered his chin. 'The so-called Undermage is nothing more than traitorous scum after all. I always knew you were a snake. Now look at you.' Helyard showed rows of bloodstained teeth. 'May the gods curse you.'

Vice's eyes blazed with murderous fire. He grabbed the Arkmage's head with both hands and brought his lips to the old man's ear. The handle of his knife was pressing against his chest and he could feel Helyard writhe in his grasp as he held him tightly.

'The sad thing is, old friend,' he said, leaning harder and harder on the knife, 'they're not my people!'

Vice wrenched Helyard sideways, throwing him to the ground. He heard a snap and the Arkmage did not speak or move again. He simply stared into nothingness, forever still.

Vice stood and looked down at the lifeless body at his feet, its head tilted to one side. 'Let the gods curse all they want,' he muttered. 'They hold no sway over me.'

Outside, over the city, drop by drop, the rain came to a halt.

Jarrick had slept right through the banging and muffled sounds of commotion from down the corridor. He snored on as a dust-covered figure slipped silently past him through the door.

Vice left without a sound, and the soldier slumbered on, dreaming of nothing in particular.

chapter 15

There are many faces of Evernia, many facets to her magick. In her kindness, the goddess provided the world with a multitude of powers: schools of fire, lightning, earth, and wind. It is these legacies of the goddess that we Arka strive to protect. But the daemons perverted her gifts and tainted them, soiling her magick for the elves' use. Their despicable children, the giants of old, the half-breeds, did no better. They were the ones who forced the gods to leave, not us. And now we pray and wait for their return, for the day that the old ones walk our shores again and rid the world of its evil leftovers for good.

From *The Matters of Magick* by Arkmage Legrar

Seven hundred miles away, a white and gold dragon crashed to the leafy floor of a dark forest clearing. The impact sent stones and earth flying in all directions, crushing a small sapling in the process. Her wings slumped to the ground with exhaustion and the mage on her back rubbed his head where it had collided with the dragon's scaly neck.

'Sorry about the landing, Farden. My legs are cramped up after the flight,' she apologised with a tired smile.

Farden rubbed the graze on his forehead. 'That's fine,' he said, managing a polite grimace. Assessing whether there was blood on his fingers in the dark wasn't working, so he clenched his other fist and a light spell burnt through the clearing. Their distorted shadows mingled and danced with the gloom under the pine trees.

Brightshow's enormous yellow eyes shrank in the light as she looked around. 'How are you feeling?' she asked.

'Well, my face feels like it's frozen solid, but apart from that I'm good.' Farden smiled wryly. His extremities felt like ice.

'It's a shame Lakkin didn't have any spare riding clothes,' said Brightshow with a shrug.

'Mm,' Farden hummed, preoccupied with untangling the leather straps around his thighs. He tried to hop down from the saddle, but got his foot trapped in the leather stirrup and fell awkwardly to the ground. Red-faced, he freed himself clumsily and brushed the twigs and leaves from his black leather cloak. Farden jiggled his sword, checking it was safe and sound, then massaged his legs to try to revive some feeling in them. Brightshow didn't manage to hide her laugh, but she composed herself and took stock of their surroundings while she caught her breath.

The Forest of Durn swayed gently in the calm night breeze. Grey trees whispered at the edges of the clearing, their bony branches knocking together gently. The sounds of the trees were like those of some great animal, as it hauled itself through the loam.

Farden's light spell filled the clearing with a clean, white glow that fell in speckled patterns and narrow shafts. They could just about make out a goat path path leading into the dense black undergrowth to their left, to the west.

Brightshow sniffed the air and looked up. The air felt icy in her nostrils. The cold sky above them was empty of clouds. Tiny stars sparkled overhead, distant and lonely, straining to pierce the night with their weak lights. A sliver of white moon lingered above the treetops, dangling quietly, unassuming.

Brightshow dug at the mouldy loam beneath her with her claws, searching for nothing in particular except something to fill the silence.

Farden adjusted his tunic again. ‘Right, I’m ready,’ he said, patting his belt. ‘I’ll see you at Kiltyrin later tonight, hopefully before sunrise.’

Brightshow turned to face him. ‘Hopefully your vampyre will be able to help us.’

Farden chuckled and shook his head. ‘Durnus knows more about Albion than the dukes do, have no fear.’

‘Well then,’ she said, stretching her wings out once more. ‘I’d better be going. Good luck, Farden, and be as quick as you can.’

‘We’ll be fine,’ he replied, and they said no more. Farden watched the dragon circle the clearing before taking off. Then with a toothy smile and a blast of air she was away again, flapping through the darkness and leaving the mage standing alone in the darkness. Farden could hear the sound of her wings fading into the distance as he disappeared into the thick forest.

It wasn’t long before Farden emerged from the scraping branches and stepped onto the neat lawns of the Arkabbey. The silvery light from the moon and the pale stars had turned everything a different shade of grey; a bleached monochrome version of the night. The wind rippled across the lawn and through the trees, bending a pillar of smoke which rose from a nearby chimney.

The Arkabbey slept on peacefully, untouched by the distant problems of the Arka, ignorant of the danger that waited in the southeast.

Farden moved silently across the grass towards the abbey. There was no guard at the door. It was unlocked, so the mage went straight in and headed for the bell tower.

When he reached Durnus' room, he saw light creeping out from under the door, so Farden knocked loudly on the oak and waited. There was a pause, followed by some rustling and a bang.

'Just a minute,' came a muffled yell.

After a few more scuffling noises, the door was unlatched and swung open. Firelight spilt into the dark corridor, framing the vampyre in an orange silhouette.

'Farden!' cried Durnus. His face creased into a wide smile as he moved to embrace his friend. 'By the gods, you are alive!'

Farden clapped him on the back and grinned. 'Apparently so,' he replied.

'Come in, come in!' Durnus beckoned for Farden to enter and he followed the vampyre into the warm room. Candles flickered lazily in their holders and a strange smell hung in the air, like that of flesh or uncooked meat.

Durnus was wearing a long robe of dark blue and green that brushed the floor, rustling against the stone as he moved the chairs around the fire. He rubbed his hands together and turned to the mage.

'You must excuse me, Farden, you've caught me in the middle of my evening meal,' he said quietly.

'Anyone I know?'

'As always, no, but you can rest assured that the bothersome Duke of Leath will be most confused by where his new butler has disappeared to.' Durnus chuckled. With a sigh he lowered himself into his comfortable armchair. The vampyre looked tired.

Farden nodded grimly and followed suit, taking his own chair in front of the crackling fire. The subject of Durnus' dinner habits had always made him slightly uncomfortable. But there were other things on his mind.

'There is much to discuss, old friend,' Farden started, 'and we don't have much time at all.'

'Apparently so. I received word from a hawk that Helyard has been thrown into prison for treason. Tell me this is some sort of sick joke?' Durnus' face was grave.

'Sadly, it's not. Helyard went to Nelska last night, murdered a dozen Siren guards and stole Farfallen's tearbook.'

'Wait, I thought that Vice had the tear—'

Farden waved his hands. 'There's so much to tell you, Durnus, but we don't have time to talk about everything.'

'Report, mage. I need to know.'

He sighed. 'I was sent to Nelska to negotiate a peace between our peoples, and to enlist the help of the dragons. The Arkmages sent the tearbook with me as a gift, in the hope that they could find the whereabouts of a dark elf well in the dragons' memories. Somehow Farfallen survived the Battle of Ragjarak, which is fortunate, as the clues to the location of the elf well may well hide in his tearbook. Now, he and his queen are in Krauslung.'

Durnus looked dumbfounded, but Farden continued. 'Last night, Helyard went to Nelska to steal the tearbook, and in the process killed half the palace guard. The Sirens threatened war, but Åddren and Vice managed to calm them down and forge an agreement. Unfortunately for Helyard, he dropped his Weight in Nelska, and now he's locked up in the Arkathedral prisons.'

Durnus took a moment to mull the information over, his pale eyes wide. 'And how is Åddren dealing with all of this?'

'He's a broken man. He trusted Helyard implicitly for years so he's taking his betrayal harder than any of us. And now that Helyard's traitorous nature is public news, the city is at breaking point. You can feel it walking down the streets. An awkward silence,' Farden explained. 'The presence of dragons does not help.'

Durnus rubbed his forehead with both hands and took a long breath. 'With Helyard gone, Åddren will stand alone, and he'll be hard pressed to keep some of the more radical members of the council in check, even with that friend of yours, Vice, there to help. There are some that won't be too keen on this agreement with the Sirens. Some who want to see nine more years of war.' Durnus wagged a cautionary finger.

'You said it yourself: Vice is there, and I trust him to stand up for Åddren. He also has control of the army and right now they're gathering at Dunyra, ready to face this creature.' Farden paused. 'If it should come to that.'

Durnus looked confused. 'I don't understand.'

Farden waved his hands. 'Helyard has been travelling back and forth between Krauslung and Albion for the last few months. We think that this is where his conspirators plan to release the beast. Vice and the dragons suspect there may be a dark elf well here, somewhere we've never thought to look before now.'

Farden could see the intrigue sparkling in the vampyre's eyes.

'I—Where?' he asked.

'Between Kiltyrin and Fidlarig.'

Durnus banged a fist against his knee. 'I damn well knew it! I've always suspected there was a well hiding in Albion, and here it is, right under the dukes' noses!' He stood abruptly and rushed over to the desk in the corner, stepping over something on the floor as he did so. He rifled through various maps before jabbing his finger at one of them. 'Several ruins on the side of a hill, on the border of the duchies. They've been explored but not deep enough. Could be your best shot. Or there's a barrow here. There are a few possibilities.'

Farden got up from his chair, making for the door. 'You'd better bring that with you then. We don't have much time.'

Durnus looked up, an uncertainty on his face that Farden hadn't seen before. 'Me?' he asked. 'What are you saying?'

'I'm saying we need your help, old friend,' replied Farden.

The vampyre looked down and began to shuffle the papers and parchment, shaking his head. 'I haven't left this duchy in years. I have responsibilities here. I… Oh, what would I know, anyway? I'm just an old bookworm! I belong more in Arfell than Albion.'

'Durnus!'

'No, Farden. You can do this without me.'

'You've always said how much you envy me! This is your chance to get out there and make a difference,' urged Farden. Durnus stayed silent and stared at the maps on his desk. The mage kept talking. He knew his old friend better than that.

'*Lost by dark ones all forgotten, lakes of magick below paths untrodden*. You taught me that old Dust Song. None of us know the dark wells like you do, we need your help.'

There was a moment of silence as Durnus considered his plea. When he finally looked up, Farden could have sworn he saw a twinkle in those pale blue eyes.

'It has been many years since I left the comfort of this abbey, but if the fate of Emaneska is in the balance, then I suppose I must acquiesce.' He smiled.

'It *was* technically an order from Åddren,' added Farden.

Durnus shrugged and began to roll up his map. 'Well, in that case.'

'Good man.'

'There are still a few hours before sunrise. I will prepare the quickdoor for us. Did you say Dunyra?' Durnus walked to the corner of the room where the quickdoor sat dormant.

'Yes, near the port. It's where I ordered the other Written to gather. By the time we get there they should already be searching the hills,' Farden said.

Durnus froze. 'You? Ordered?'

'Well.' Farden started to shuffle towards the door. 'Desperate time, desperate measures. Vice saw fit to promote me.'

The look on the vampyre's face was one of absolute pride, barely contained behind a smile.

'Then let us not waste a minute more, Captain! Give me an hour, and I shall be ready to leave.'

Farden nodded and left his friend to it. Shutting the door quietly behind him, he set off wandering through the dark corridors. He had no time to catch up on sleep, so decided to make his way into the kitchens and satisfy his growling stomach instead.

The kitchens and dining hall were dark and eerily silent. Everybody was fast asleep.

Farden crept around the kitchen under the orange light of the stove until he located some bread. He found a pot of cold soup to dip his bread in, following it with some of the dragon-riders' chewy travelling biscuits and a weird brown fruit that tasted like a sour apple. Farden walked as he chewed, heading towards his room for a quick lie down.

His room seemed cold and bare compared to the dishevelled yet cosy atmosphere of *The Bearded Goat*, but it felt good to be back in familiar surroundings. He dropped his supplies to the floor with a thud and stretched out his arms. The mage walked to the window to stare out at the grey forest. The neighbouring owl hooted somewhere in the trees. Farden chewed his biscuits and listened to the night sounds.

The room was dark, so he reached for the candlestick that sat on his bedside table. As he clicked his fingers over it, he knocked it clumsily to the floor with a dull clunk. Farden muttered to himself in frustration and cast a light spell instead. As he bent down to pick the candlestick up, a small bark-cloth bundle caught his eye. He froze.

Lying on the floor was the scrap of nevermar from all those weeks ago. The hazy memory of hiding it inside the hollow candlestick slowly drifted back to him.

Farden made sure the door was closed and crouched down, listening for any footsteps in the corridor. He put aside his biscuit and grabbed the bundle. The nevermar smelled old, dry, and there was only a small bit left. Farden clenched his fist around it as he let his mind wander. He ground his teeth together, feeling temptation prodding him as it always did.

Something knocked against his collar-bone: the amulet around his neck. Farden scratched at it. He could almost taste the smoke on his tongue. He closed his eyes and gnawed at his lip.

Let it go, said a voice. The voice from his dreams.

Farden shook his head defiantly.

With a grunt, the mage stood up and left his room. He ran quickly and quietly down the stairs until he reached the ground floor. He made for the door, still gripping the bundle tightly in his hand. Farden emerged into the shadowy gardens and strode across the damp lawn without a sound. He reached the edge of the forest and ducked under a branch, wary of any sounds behind him, then crept into the trees.

Farden walked until he was a safe distance away from the Arkabbey, careful to mind snapping twigs. Deep in the woods, the night was impenetrable. The only sounds were the trees shaking their bare branches and the screeching of the distant owl.

Farden leaned up against a tree trunk. He lifted the bundle to his nose and smelled the earthy, sickly-sweet scent of the nevermar again. He peeled back the cloth and pinched the dry moss between his fingers. Saliva filled his mouth in anticipation as he twirled the nevermar between his fingers and rolled it into a tiny ball. He felt a fire spell stirring in his hand.

'What are you doing?' said a voice from behind him. Farden jumped, dropping the bark-cloth and the nevermar. His hand flew to his sword handle and a light spell pierced the gloom. He whirled around to find Elessi holding her hands over her eyes.

'Farden, it's me!' she cried.

'Elessi?! What are you doing out here?' Farden released his sword and blew a substantial sigh of relief.

'I could ask *you* the same question,' came the snippy reply. She was wearing just a nightgown and sandals. Her curly brown hair spilled over her shoulders. Despite her defiance, her eyes were wide and nervous. She was upset or scared, or both, Farden couldn't tell.

'It's none of your business,' he said, immediately irritated.

'You've been gone for weeks, I was startin' to worry about you.'

Farden shook his head. 'You always worry about me, Elessi, but I'm always fine,' he hissed. He looked down, surreptitiously trying to spot the bundle of the nevermar amongst the leaves.

'How can I help it, Farden, when I see you sneakin' off into the forest in the middle of the night? I haven't seen you in days!' Her voice was full of emotion, but Farden wasn't listening.

'Where is it?' he mumbled to himself.

'What's wrong with you?' She sounded like she was about to cry.

Elessi followed his gaze and spotted something by her sandal. Before he could stop her, she bent to pick it up and held the cloth bundle in her hand. She peered inside. The sickly-sweet smell was unmistakable, even for her. Tears sprang to her eyes and Elessi looked up at Farden with a quivering lip.

'Tell me this isn't yours, Farden, please,' she said, shaking her head as if she couldn't—or wouldn't—believe what she had just found.

The mage ground his teeth in annoyance. 'I was getting rid of it, Elessi. Just give it to me,' he muttered quietly, holding out a hand.

'No,' said Elessi. She fought back tears as she clasped the nevermar to her chest. Farden wasn't sure if he had ever seen her cry before.

'Elessi, give it to me,' he repeated.

'No, I won't. Not till you explain what's going on here. You know this is against the rules. How could you do this to yourself?' she said, unable to hold back a sob any longer. Her face scrunched up and her wide eyes glistened with tears.

Farden clenched his fists by his side. 'I don't have to explain myself to you,' he growled through gritted teeth. His words sounded foreign even to him. Her expression said everything. Even without words, her face screamed disappointment.

Elessi sniffed loudly, shaking her head at Farden's cruel words. 'Maybe not, but I think Durnus would want an explanation!' she cried.

She stumbled as she turned to run into the forest. Farden grabbed her arm before she could get any further.

'Wait a minute!' he snapped. He pulled her close and put both of his arms around her to make sure she couldn't get away.

'Let go of me!' she shouted. She thrashed futilely against his chest, pounding her fists like a child, sobbing and straining to get away. Farden held tight.

'Listen! Elessi, stop struggling!' He winced as a blow caught his chin.

After a few more punches, she gave up and buried her head in his tunic. Farden whispered in her ear as she sobbed against him.

'I won't hurt you, Elessi, but you need to listen to me. Durnus must not know about this, understand? I can't let him find out. I can't disappoint him,' he said. His words flooded his heart with guilt.

'Is that all you care about? What about me?' she choked, punctuating her words by thudding her fist against his chest. 'What about you? They will hang you for this.'

Her words were like darts, sending Farden's heart sinking into his stomach. He sighed heavily and rested his chin on her head. Farden looked around at the dark forest, trying to find an explanation in the shadows that surrounded the two of them. He was speechless, bereft of excuses. 'I kept it secret, didn't I? I can deal with it,' he said quietly.

'Alone, and without help,' Elessi sniffed. 'And you, of all people,' she muttered, accusingly. Her words ricocheted around Farden's head, and somewhere deep down he realised it was because of who he was that he started using nevermar in the first place. Elessi was right. He had always hidden it. *Alone*. The mage lifted his head and met her teary eyes. He had never seen her so sad.

'I came out here to burn it, I swear to you. I'm finished with it.' Farden paused. 'Please believe me.'

Elessi blinked, thinking for a moment, a moment that felt like forever to the mage. 'Fine, but you go back on your word and that vampyre will be the first to hear about it. I swear to the gods.'

Her voice was hard like granite, and Farden believed her. She awkwardly thumbed away a tear, suddenly embarrassed. She slapped Farden one more time on the chest for good measure.

Slowly, he let go of her and took a few steps back. Elessi cleared her throat. In the light of his spell and the moon, he watched her blinking the last of the tears away. Her eyes were still fearful, but she tried a weak smile and Farden held out his hand for the nevermar.

At first she shook her head resolutely, but he took a slow step forwards and met her gaze, trying to convey as much trust as possible through his eyes.

'Please,' he said, in no more than a whisper. Elessi sighed and reluctantly handed over the bark-cloth with pursed lips and wary eyes. Farden closed his palm around the little bundle. A burst of orange light flared between his fingers and smoke curled around his hands like grey liquid. As the sickly smell of the drug reached Farden's nose, a pang of regret shivered across his chest, but he shook it off and threw the burning mess into the bushes. *She was right.*

'I suppose that's the first step, then,' Elessi whispered. She clasped her hands in front of her.

'Thank you,' he said.

She shook her head at him. 'I've watched you for years and I never suspected a thing. You've come too far to ruin it now, and I… Well, we care too much about you.' The maid sniffed. '*I* care too much.'

Farden looked up. A stray cloud had momentarily covered the moon. 'You always have,' he said.

Elessi still wore wide eyes. 'I can't help it,' she said. 'I lo—'

Something moved in the shadows, and Farden swiftly covered Elessi's mouth with a hand.

A twig snapped under unseen boots. The metallic whisper of swords sliding from scabbards floated on the breeze to Farden's keen ears. The twang of a bowstring sang out from somewhere behind them and with the speed of a pouncing wolf, Farden threw out a hand. A burst of white light burnt the arrow to cinders in mid-air. Elessi screamed. Farden grabbed her roughly and pushed her into the undergrowth, back towards the Arkabbey. She was making enough noise to wake an army. Farden kept pushing.

'Move Elessi! Go!' he yelled at her, as he turned to face the attackers. The forest came alive with shouts and cries. Dark men with hidden faces swarmed through the trees towards them, waving blackened swords and curved knives.

Farden crouched to the loam and put his fist to the cold ground. He shuddered as the spell ran through him. It jolted his arms but he held his stance and concentrated.

As three men burst from the bushes closest to him, a wall of rock and earth sprang from the ground. It collided with them like a wave of dirt. Their cries were cut short as thick soil filled their open mouths. Both roots and armour cracked noisily under the spell's force.

They scrabbled to their feet, spluttering, but the mage was already gone. Farden grabbed Elessi by the hand and sprinted back through the forest, leading them a twisting path between trees and bushes. Elessi cried out as branches whipped her face and scratched her arms. Farden kept going, weaving through the darkness, ignoring the threatening cries from behind them.

'Just keep moving!' Farden yelled.

When they stumbled onto the short grass of the abbey lawns, Farden pushed Elessi in the direction of the kitchen door. She hesitated, but he waved his arms frantically for her to flee.

'Go to Durnus, he'll get you out of here!' he shouted.

Elessi's eyes were wide, flicking nervously between the forest and the mage. 'But—' she stuttered, clinging to her nightdress.

'GO!' Farden yelled. The maid said no more, scurrying off into the darkness with her sandals slapping against her feet.

Farden turned to face the invaders, planting his feet wide. His hands shook with magick. Their stealthy approach ruined, the attackers now bellowed their war cries as they crashed through the forest towards him. Their shouts had woken the Arkabbey from its peaceful slumber, and a handful of soldiers tumbled out of the main door, still struggling with their armour as they wiped tiredness from their eyes.

The moon and stars bathed the abbey grounds in a pale glow, revealing dark shapes swarming in the forest. The trees shook with movement. The sound of men and metal clattering through the undergrowth grew louder by the second. The Arkabbey bell began to toll.

'Stay together!' Farden shouted to the bewildered soldiers. They clattered to his side and readied their weapons, forming a line halfway across the lawn. Arrows burst from the trees, thudding into the grass just inches from their feet. They held firm, their courage bolstered by the powerful mage standing with them, pulsating with magick.

Farden stretched out his hands to either side and a strong wind sprang up to flatten the grass around the group. Dead leaves scurried around their feet and their cloaks fluttered, cracking like whips.

'Hold on!' Farden bellowed to the others. He began to push his hands forwards, inch by blustery inch. The wind howled wolfishly around him.

Two men emerged from the trees and rushed forwards, only to collide with a wall of air. Farden pushed his hands further out, shaking with effort, and the men were plucked from the lawn and thrown backwards into the forest. Three more ran yelling out of the undergrowth, but the wind ripped the swords and shields from their hands and sent them tumbling into the bushes.

As Farden wound the spell down, a flash of light caught the corner of his eye.

'Watch out!' A shout rang out as a streak of fire tore through the night towards them. Farden spun, throwing himself flat to the ground. The fireball exploded against the chest of a soldier standing behind him. Flames consumed his face and neck and he crumpled to the ground, choking. The poor man frantically beat his scorched chest as the others ran to quench the fire.

Farden didn't waste a moment. He leapt to his feet and threw several of his own fireballs back in the same direction. He found himself barking orders at the men.

'You two, take that man back to the kitchens and help him there. You, guard the main door. The rest of you, follow me!' The soldiers sprang to do his bidding without hesitation, dashing off into the night and dragging the wounded soldier with them.

Farden's eyes roved over the bushes and trees, watching for any sign of movement or a glint of metal. Aside from the pealing bells, all had become quiet in the grounds. There were no shouts now.

With his soldiers, Farden jogged towards the north side of the Arkabbey. The men at his back breathed noisily and their armour clanked, but they were ready enough. They kept moving.

As they reached the corner of the north wall, a shout split the silence. A blast of lightning struck the lawn in a shower of dirt and charred grass. The men ran for the cover of the wall and crouched low in the flowerbeds.

Farden slammed his vambraces together and a ball of fire began to spin above his palms, growing larger and hotter with every second. The soldiers shuffled backwards, eyeing the mage warily. Farden, deep in concentration, muttered one word at them. 'Ready?' They all nodded eagerly, and Farden stood up.

Another fork of lightning flashed across the lawn as he emerged from behind the wall, the spinning fireball balanced in his hands. A dozen yards ahead, two hooded men crouched between a fallen tree and a stone bench. They yelled, pointing at the mage, but it made no difference.

Farden lifted the searing fire above his head. It pierced the night like a miniature sun. It took all of his strength to hurl the spell. It careened through the air in a dazzling yellow streak and crashed against the tree trunk. With a boom and a blast of heat, the trunk shattered into a thousand pieces, sending splinters of wood flying through the air like furious hornets.

He held up his arms in defence and a bubble of air pulsed from his hands with a dull thud. The flaming daggers of wood ricocheted to the ground and sizzled out.

Farden blinked, clearing the white spots from his eyes. He assessed the damage he had caused. A smoke cloud rose like a gigantic mushroom above the crater where the tree had been. The stone bench lay on its side with a new crack through its middle. Behind him, he could hear the soldiers gawping at the flaming scene.

A coughing came from behind a section of the shattered tree and Farden dashed over to investigate. He found a hooded, masked stranger lying just behind the broken bench. The man's chest was punctured by three thick chunks of wood, buried deep in his ribcage. Every breath seemed to be a battle for him, and he was losing. Blood was pooling in the scorched dirt under his back.

Farden crouched down beside him. 'Hey! Who sent you?' he growled.

The man attempted to laugh but ended up coughing instead. 'You think you scare me, Farden? A hermit like you? You're a lost cause.'

That voice! With a flick of his hand, Farden tore away the mask covering the man's face. His stomach flipped.

Ridda grinned at him through a mask of blood and whispered his last few words. 'Think you can run, Farden? Run from the likes of *him*?'

'Tell me who you work for, you traitor, or I swear to the gods I will make you die in agony,' Farden's eyes were like flint. Blue sparks fizzled threateningly in his palm. 'Is it Helyard? Speak! How did he get his orders to you?'

All Ridda gave him was a wheezing chuckle, sending blood trickling down his chin. He shook his head and mockingly wagged a weak finger. 'Helyard…' He paused to gulp down blood. 'Is only the beginning.'

Farden fumed. Nauseating dread clutched his heart with the icy fingers of a corpse. He shook Ridda to keep him from slipping away too soon.

'Who do you work for?' Farden's hand hovered over Ridda's leg, letting a spark loose. Ridda flinched, yelping, then winced as the wooden splinters twisted inside him.

'You're a—'

Farden jolted him with another spark. His eyes had already started to close.

'—dead man,' he croaked, for the last time.

Farden clenched his fists and roared with frustration. He staggered to his feet and kicked the dead mage, swearing through gritted teeth. The nearby soldiers looked at one another, swapping nervous glances.

At that moment, another masked man emerged from behind the splintered tree and tried to limp away, but Farden's anger quickly found him.

In a flash, Farden's hand flew to his sword handle and wrenched it from its scabbard. The blade flew through the air and impaled the man between the shoulders. He fell to the floor with a crunch and didn't move again.

The Arka soldiers moved to make sure the man was dead but waited to touch him until Farden joined them. When he reached the body, Farden tore the sword and the bloody cloak from the man's back, ripping his tunic apart until he found the dead man's bare shoulders. His dirty skin was unmarked. The soldiers muttered amongst themselves as Farden simmered with anger.

A smash of glass came from above them. They all turned to see a limp body land in a small bush at the foot of the wall with a grotesque crunch.

Farden looked up to see Durnus standing at a broken window, gazing down at them. His face was smeared with dark blood and his fangs were bared, eyes wild with the fire of battle. He shouted to the mage.

'Farden! They're inside!' he yelled, but the mage was already running towards the main door.

The soldiers could barely keep up with him. He slid to a halt in front of the tall oak doors and darted into the darkness of the abbey.

A man ran at him from the shadows, wielding a long knife. Farden dropped to his knees as light pulsed from his open hand. The man stumbled backwards, blinded by the brightness. Farden punched him hard in the midriff and he crumpled to the floor, winded. The mage's knee collided with his forehead and knocked the life out of him. Farden took the knife and ran on.

He leapt up the nearest staircase, taking the steps two at a time. The clanging of swords rang out above and below him but he kept running, heading for the vampyre's room at the top of the tower. The bells were still ringing.

A young maid ran screaming from a doorway, followed by another figure in a hood. He snatched at her arm but she managed to escape him, and cowered by the wooden banister.

Farden sprinted to plunge his blade into the man's chest. He was dead before he hit the stone. The girl stared in horror at the corpse, then ran off into the shadows whimpering before Farden could stop her.

He sprinted on, the sounds of fighting growing louder with every step he took. The Arkabbey was now completely overrun by hooded and masked men.

Servants and soldiers were being mercilessly cut down in the darkness of the corridors. Shouts and curses echoed off the stone walls. A haunting wail came from somewhere below. Farden's head spun.

Another man appeared in a doorway, snarling, poised to fire an arrow at the mage. Three broken ribs and a shattered skull later, the stranger lay on the floor, gasping through crushed lungs, choking on the dust from Farden's boots.

Up in the far reaches of the abbey tower, Durnus pressed himself against the door as the men outside charged for the tenth time. Elessi wrung her hands frantically while she paced back and forth in front of the fire. Her nightgown was shredded; covered in dirt and flecked with blood.

The vampyre growled, shoving the door again to keep it closed. He could hear blades hacking at the wood from the other side.

'What on earth we going to do?!' moaned the maid, pulling agitatedly at her curly hair.

'Calm down, Elessi. Farden will be here soon, then we can leave!' Durnus licked his lips as he cast a glance at the humming quickdoor in the corner. The fire crackled noisily in its hearth. The tolling of the bells above made the room vibrate.

There came a splintering as a spearhead wiggled its way through a gap in the planks. Durnus yanked the blade with a forceful twist. The shaft split, eliciting a cry from the other side as someone tried in vain to retrieve their weapon.

The vampyre yelled through the door. 'Leave this place, before I kill you all!'

Laughter floated in from the corridor. 'We just want to talk, old man, let us in!'

'I am no man!' Durnus spat blood through the gap in the door. His lips and face were covered in dried crimson and the look in his pale eyes was as frosty as the ice fields of the north. He licked his deadly fangs and thumbed the sharp nails of his fingertips. The door was pounded again, but Durnus steeled himself against it. He would wait for his friend.

'Let us in, old man!' came more taunts from outside.

Something snapped inside Durnus. 'So be it,' he whispered. This was the fight he had waited decades for.

With a burst of inhuman strength, the old vampyre ripped the door from its hinges and jumped headlong into the group of men with a snarl. A knife raked his arm and fists collided with his body, but Durnus felt strength and speed he had not known in years flowing through his dusty veins. He moved like a deadly shadow, claws ripping through cloth and flesh. He was a blur of animal rage, whirling in circles, sinking his fangs into anything that moved.

The men started to back away, trying to surround the vampyre. Durnus breathed in gasps, hissing like a cornered swan. He now bled from a dozen deep scratches, painted in blood that wasn't all his own. His keen eyes could pierce the darkness better than his enemies, and he waited for them to pounce.

'Durnus!' A shout echoed down the narrow corridor, followed closely by a fireball. It ripped through the group and exploded against the wall.

Seizing his chance, Durnus jumped on the nearest hooded figure, sinking his fangs deep into the soft place under the chin.

'Get him off me!' screamed the man, convulsing. He crumpled under the vampyre's weight as Durnus bore him to the ground.

Chaos erupted in the hallway. Farden appeared amongst the men, striking left and right with his knife, hacking indiscriminately at arms and legs. All around him, men fell awkwardly, crying out in pain.

One landed a blow on Farden's shoulder, but he pivoted sideways and stabbed the man in the groin. His face scrunched in pain as Farden grabbed his throat and sent a stream of lightning coursing through his bones. The man shook like a rag doll, turning limp and lifeless when the spell stopped his heart.

'Farden!' Durnus called out. He was pinned to the floor, trying to stop a dagger from getting any closer to his throat. The man on top of him shook with effort as he pushed his entire weight into the handle. Durnus' eyes were wide. The blackened steel tip tickled the papery skin of his neck.

Farden leapt forwards and kicked the attacker in the ribs with the toe of his boot. The crack of bone was audible and the man collapsed instantly. Farden kicked the dagger aside and slammed him against the nearest wall. He tore away the face cloth, but it wasn't a face he recognised.

Fury bubbled up inside Farden, like one of the volcanic springs at Hjaussfen. He shook with rage. A deep growl burnt the back of his throat. Fists clenched white, the growl became a guttural roar as he struck the man hard in the jaw. Once. Twice. Thrice.

Knuckles bloodied, Farden let the corpse slump to the cold floor, face crushed. The corridor fell silent. Just like the bells above.

'Argh!' Farden pulled at his hair in anger.

'Let's get out of here while we still can! Come on!' The vampyre tugged at the mage's cloak as he ran limping back through the broken doorframe to his room. When Durnus reached the pedestal by the quickdoor, he paused.

'Elessi? Elessi!' he shouted. The maid was nowhere to be seen, then a shaking hand emerged from behind one of the huge armchairs.

'Can we go now?' asked a high-pitched, terrified voice.

'Yes, now get up and come here!' Durnus snapped. He began to flip through the spell book's pages, murmuring the incantations and spells.

'Farden?' Elessi crept out from behind the chair and looked around for the mage. Farden still stood in the corridor, boots in a pool of blood, silently fuming, staring down at the dead stranger.

His mind churned through every possibility, pulled apart every piece of information, and still nothing offered an explanation. He felt useless in the face of such treachery, confused and bewildered. *Lost*. Farden flinched as a hand alighted softly on his shoulder. It was Elessi, her eyes full of fear.

'Durnus is making his door thing work, it's time to leave,' she said softly.

Farden nodded, still looking at the fallen bodies around them. Some were still groaning with pain. He wanted to sink a blade into every single one of them, just from spite.

A hoarse shout came from inside the room. 'Farden, I swear to the gods, I will carry you through this door myself if you don't hurry up! It's almost ready!'

With a grunt, Farden hopped over the splintered mess of door and helped Elessi to do the same. The air in the room crackled with the quickdoor's energy. There was a low, familiar humming. Durnus whispered words into the pages of his hefty tome.

Farden led the maid forwards and stood her next to the vampyre. 'Keep your arms and legs tucked in, close your eyes, and try not to think too much,' he said, speaking in what he hoped was a calming voice. Elessi was still shaking and had started to bite her nails with agitation.

'And hold your breath, too,' Durnus slammed the book shut with a forced grin. 'You'll be absolutely fine, my dear, do not worry. Come, you first.'

'But—' She raised a finger in protest, but Durnus ushered her to the doorway. The wavering, translucent surface hissed at her. She flinched. The cold wind from the other side was starting to blow through the room. It ruffled the curtains and pulled at the fire.

'No buts, Elessi, we need to go, now,' urged Farden.

'But… Does it hurt?' she asked. The vampyre sighed with impatience. Threatening shouts echoed down the corridor.

'Not as much as I will hurt you if you don't move that backside of yours through that door. *Now*, Elessi!' Durnus shouted, sending her flying with fright. She half-stepped, half-tripped through the fizzing surface. Her scream trailed off like a distant echo.

Durnus looked to Farden. 'Was that a bit much?'

Farden shrugged. 'Maybe. You'll find out on the other side.' He looked behind him as the sound of a blade on stone rang out.

Durnus put a hand on his friend's shoulder. 'Thank you Farden, for coming for us. I don't think I would have made it if—'

'Nonsense, old friend, you finally got the chance you were looking for,' Farden replied. 'This is a conversation for later, Durnus. Go, before it closes!'

The vampyre moved forwards, but hesitated on the threshold of the quickdoor, bloodshot eyes still fixed on his friend. Farden kicked an armchair aside and braced himself in front of the broken doorway, fire starting to crawl over his fingers.

'You have time!' cried Durnus. 'Farden! There's no shame in running to fight another day.'

'I need to find out who's behind this. Go! Now! Before it's too late and we're both stuck here.'

Farden met Durnus' gaze. The look in his eyes was now grave, but he nodded and jumped into the quickdoor. The moment he disappeared, the arches shook and with a gurgling sound the portal vanished. Farden gritted his teeth and smiled at the corner of his mouth. *He would make these bastards pay.*

The first man through the door received a fireball to the face and ran around the room screaming. Farden ducked an ambitious sword-swing from the next before winding him with a punch to the stomach. Farden's forehead smashed into his nose, making him drop his weapon. Before the men could recover, Farden had already disappeared down the corridor.

The mage careened around corners and flew down stairs, jumping entire flights in windmilling leaps. Screams and shouts now came from every corner of the abbey and bodies were piling up in the corridors and doorways.

Righteous anger pounded in Farden's chest as he ran to where the sounds of fighting were loudest.

'Jus' tell us where 'e is an' we won't af to 'urt you, will we, my pretty?'

The man's leering grin made the young maid shake with terror. Half a dozen other servants kneeled around the statue of Evernia in the main hall, cowering and frightened. A score of men stood around them, holding blackened blades and bedecked in scruffy armour and raggedy cloaks. The flickering candlelight threw grotesque shadows across their faces.

'Where is 'e?' asked the man again. The servant girl shook her head. Her lip quivered as he ran dirty fingers along her chin. The man was hideous, with a scar on his brow and a broken nose. His hand moved across her breasts and down to grip her thigh, but another man, hood still up and mask still on, whacked him hard on the shoulder.

'Control yourself. There'll be time for that later,' he said. With a grunt, the man retreated to stand with the others.

Moving deliberately between the prisoners, the hooded figure looked at each one of them in turn, choosing the next victim. He grabbed a young soldier with a black eye and a nasty cut along his forehead. He lifted him up by the throat and a strange green light shivered across his gloved hands.

'Where is Farden?' the man whispered from behind his mask.

The boy panicked, trying to wriggle out of the iron grasp. 'I—I told you I don't know, he comes and goes, we never see him!' he choked.

With a snarl, the man threw the soldier back on the floor and pointed a finger at the others. 'If I don't start hearing the answers I want to hear, people are going to start dying all over again, understand?' Renewed sobbing broke out amongst the captives.

The scarred man spoke up again. 'One of yer must 'ave seen the bastard? Eh?' When nobody answered he shook his head. 'By the beard of Jötunn, this is useless!' he cursed.

'Be patient. He'll come to us.'

'You'd better 'ope so, mage, my men are gettin' restless…' His voice trailed off, realising what he had just said.

'Is that a threat? Because if it is, I can always leave you and your men to explain to my employer why you returned *without* Farden's head in a bag.' The hooded man let his words sink in for a moment. The others around them muttered amongst themselves in the candlelight.

'No? I thought not. Now get the fuck out of my way and do what you're paid to do.' He barged them aside and walked off towards the main door, leaving Scar-face to clear his throat and try to save face in front of his thugs.

The man strode through the shadows towards the doors, cursing the Albion reprobates he had been forced to work with. *Give him a handful of mages and this Farden would have been trussed up and stuffed like a boar by now, if only he—*

A knife cut off his trail of thought, weaving its way between his ribs with a crunch. He looked down in amazement at the steel poking from his chest. He could feel the blood pooling in his lungs, and as the blade twisted, the shadows leapt up to greet him.

Farden hauled the body further into the gloom and pulled aside the man's tunic to get a look at his shoulders. In the dim light, he could see black script etched into pale skin, weaving across his back between bloodstained runes and symbols.

Two runes meant new blood. Farden didn't recognise the man, but he was Written, Arka born and bred, and that made his blood boil all the same.

Farden gritted his teeth and strode boldly into the middle of the hall where a single shaft of moonlight pierced the shadows.

'Oi!' he yelled.

All eyes turned upon him. Farden grinned and shouted at the top of his voice. 'If you want me, come and get me!'

A scarred man went purple with rage and began to wave his sword in wide circles.

'After 'im!' he bellowed. He broke into an ungainly run with the rest of his men close behind him, baying like a pack of wild animals.

Farden spun on his heel and dashed off in the opposite direction, leading the attackers away from the prisoners and out into the cold night.

part four

AND IT ENDS WITH FIRE

chapter 16

Beware the monster behind the door, watch out for the spiders all over the floor.
Be brave like your father, proud warrior and all,
Something is gnawing at bones in the hall.
Maybe you'll run, or maybe you'll fight,
Maybe sleep soundly all through the night.
Never you mind, now close your eyes,
Pray you sleep well, not be food for the flies.
Skölgard nursery rhyme

Someone was screaming in the locked room at the top of the Spire. The cries of pain were chilling, accompanied by the howling wind that pawed at the windows and battlements.

Two soldiers stood guard with spears at the top of a lofty set of stairs. Their gold and white ceremonial armour glittered in the light of the flickering torches as they stared straight ahead, silent and still, seemingly oblivious to the screams coming from the door behind them.

Behind that door was a small chamber and another door, and through that was a circular room, windowless and plain, with nothing but two wooden stools and a bench for furniture. The walls had been painted pure white, like a new canvas waiting for an artist. Scores of candles in glass jars were spread over the cold stone floor, making the room and the walls dazzlingly bright. Perfect for keeping a candidate conscious through the Ritual. Dotted all around the room, gathered in little clusters, were tiny bottles of thick black ink, sealed with cloth and wooden stoppers.

In the centre of the room sat the two stools, and upon one sat a wizened man, snow-white with age, boasting a beard so long it was tucked into his belt. His head was bald and freckled while his shoulders were hunched like the wings of a wet crow. On his pointy nose balanced a set of intricate lenses made of stacked slices of crystal. They made his dark, beady eyes look ridiculously huge.

The old Scribe was fixated on his work, his wrinkled, skeletal hands weaving to and fro, pricking the pale skin in front of him with a long, delicate sliver of whale-bone. He hummed in a deep drone as he worked, singing long-forgotten tunes and songs of magick to help the ink settle around the needle's point.

In front of him, on the other stool, sat Cheska. Tears rolled down her face, dripping onto a floor that was already soaking from two days worth of crying. She was hunched over and shaking. Her knuckles had turned an unnatural, whitish-purple colour from gripping her knees so hard. Her arms and legs shook uncontrollably, as if she had just been pulled from a frozen lake.

She stared with bloodshot, hollow eyes at a spot on the floor, mentally clinging onto an imaginary place where the pain could be kept at bay. Cheska willed herself to feel the cold breeze of the shore near her father's palace, the smell of the pines by the lake, the sound of the waterfalls roaring past her window. But the needle kept dragging her back to the white room.

Her back stung in a thousand places. After two straight days, the needle felt like a burning knife point. Feverish sweat streamed into her eyes but she blinked it away, allowing herself a hopeful look at the hourglass at the end of the room, slowly dripping sand through its tiny waist. *It can't be long now*, she prayed, to whichever god might be listening. Her face scrunched up in pain and she let out another chilling cry.

Outside the Scribe's room, in the first chamber, Brim sat on a low wooden bench between two elderly servants. They wore robes bearing the rare symbol of the tattooing art of the Written: the scales of the Arka weighing a feather quill. The two men had long flowing beards and calm eyes, silent and still. The torch-shadows danced across their wrinkled faces.

These servants were the only people ever allowed near the Scribe. They were his eyes, his ears, and his mouth in the outside world, often charged with passing messages to the Arkmages in measures of absolute secrecy. Nobody knew where the Scribe or his servants had come from, or even how ancient they truly were. There were some who whispered that the Scribe was a man from the old times, part-elf maybe, or perhaps a man of Servaea who had escaped before it sank into the sea. But whatever he was, the withered old man was an ancient mystery shrouded in secrecy; the hidden treasure of the Arka.

Brim was trembling. He wished he could put his hands to his ears and block the sounds of his friend's screams. He chewed anxiously at his lip while fear squeezed his stomach. The young mage smoothed his white and gold ceremonial tunic for the hundredth time and ran his dry tongue along the back of his teeth.

'May I have some water, before I go in?' he asked, looking to the aged men on either side of him. They didn't move a muscle and continued to stare at the opposite wall. Brim sighed, and tasted blood coming from his lip.

Outside the chamber door, on the stairs, the two soldiers exchanged glances as they heard heavy footsteps coming up the stairs below them. They shuffled forwards and peered down the steep flight of curving steps, waiting to see who came round the corner. One of them lowered his spear in readiness. It was forbidden to interrupt the Ritual.

A tall man in a flowing black and green robe appeared, striding purposefully up the staircase towards the soldiers. At his hip was a long knife in an ornate golden scabbard. When he noticed the two men ahead of him, he smiled amiably and held up a hand.

'Good evening, gentlemen,' he greeted them. His dark brown eyes were warm and welcoming.

'Lord Vice, an unexpected honour!' replied one of the soldiers. He saluted with his spear and the other hurriedly followed suit.

'Your Mage, the first candidate should be almost finished,' added the second soldier, not wishing to be to left out.

'Good, good,' replied the Undermage. Vice made it to the top of the stairs and smiled. He folded his arms behind his back and paused.

The first soldier ventured a question. 'To, er, what do we owe the pleasure, sir?'

The words had barely left his lips when the Undermage grabbed the knife from his belt and buried it hilt-deep in the man's neck. The soldier sank to the floor with a crash, choking on steel. Vice finished him off with a bolt of fire that shattered his armour like molten glass.

'Murder!' the other soldier shouted, aghast and shocked. He made to run but Vice kicked out and caught him squarely in the breastplate. The soldier staggered backwards and tried to fend off the Undermage with his spear. A firebolt ricocheted off the soldier's shield and Vice cursed the magick in the golden metal.

He dodged the jabbing spearpoint like a cat. The look in the soldier's eyes was one of pure panic. Vice grinned at his prey and the man visibly gulped. The Undermage took a step forwards, letting lightning flow from his fingers. The spell struck the man in the hip, catapulting him into the wall behind him with a despairing cry. Vice advanced on him immediately, hands still buzzing with sparks.

The soldier hauled himself up only to find iron hands circling his neck. Vice slammed the poor man back against the wall and the crunching sound of bone and steel against stone was nauseating. Vice shocked him again. The man went limp in his grip, neck charred and smoking.

Behind the door, Brim nervously wrung his hands, over and over, desperately wondering what the loud bangs and crashes had been. The two old men swapped concerned glances. All was silent now, no shouts. Even Cheska's screams had died. Brim's fingers twitched nervously.

Inside the white room, Cheska lifted shaking hands to her face, wiping away her tears for the final time. Her back was on fire, and the smell of her own sweat made her gag. The pain was starting to recede from the edges of her eyes, and the pounding in her head seemed to soften.

The Scribe had finally stopped humming and had turned to watch the door behind him. His needle was on his lap, wiped clean and unmoving now; the first time it had rested in three days. Sniffing like a rat, he wrinkled his freckled nose and squinted through his thick glasses.

Cheska was still blinking dizziness from her eyes. The bright room stung her vision. She tried to stretch her back and sit upright but the sensation of her skin moving made her feel as though she were lying in a pit of burning coals. The magick swirled around her body, dizzying her. Instead, she stayed put and tried to stop her heart from racing.

Brim cried out in alarm as the door burst into fragments. He fell to the floor, frantically waving his arms to keep the burning splinters from his eyes.

The two old men rose sombrely from the bench, as if they had barely noticed the door exploding. Moving as one, they pulled aside their white robes and drew long swords from hidden scabbards. Their blades were etched with unknown words and symbols. They stood tall, silent and ready, swords held in front of their faces. Brim cowered at their feet and tried desperately to remember his spells.

There was the briefest moment of uneasy silence before a man in full ceremonial armour flew through the smoking doorframe and crashed to the stone floor. Brim tried to cast a shadow spell but his lips were shaking too much. The incantation bounced around his head uselessly.

A tall figure stepped through the smoky haze of the doorway. Without a sound, the two old servants walked to meet him. As they raised their swords above their heads, the figure began to laugh contemptuously. Fire danced in his hands, a deep red and orange flame that crackled angrily.

The two ancient men did not stand a chance. Flames jumped from the man's hands and consumed them in a flash of light and black smoke. They crumpled to the floor like burnt paper and lay there smouldering, their swords forgotten in their hands. The room filled with acrid smoke, smothering the torchlight. Brim crouched low to keep from choking.

All was deathly silent. Slowly, as if emerging from some hazy nightmare, the tall man stepped out from the smoke with wide eyes and a grin. With horror and confusion, Brim recognised the black Undermage's robe.

Vice strode calmly towards him, a menacing knife held low at his side. Brim slowly backed up against the wall, mentally scrabbling to invoke any spell he could think of that might save him.

'Any profound words in your last moments, young mage?' The Undermage sneered.

Brim couldn't manage even one word, he just gaped and stuttered. Cold steel pressed against his throat and he stared helplessly into Vice's eyes with utter disbelief.

Cheska tried not to vomit for the third time as she focused on stopping the room from spinning. The throbbing in her head had evolved into nauseating pain, and it felt like her stomach was trying to punch its way out of her belly. And now she could smell smoke.

Through bleary eyes she could make out the Scribe packing away his tools. He looked agitated, and Cheska dazedly wondered if there was a fire.

Her thoughts were interrupted by a bang from behind the door. Cheska swallowed bile and fell to her knees. Her back burnt with excruciating pain and the sound of the stool hitting the floor sent shockwaves through her skull.

The Scribe dashed to her aid, pulling her nearer to the bench at the side of the room. Glass jars scattered under her shaking limbs and candles hissed out but the Scribe urged her on, making her crawl as far under the bench as she could. The look in his dark eyes was urgent and grave.

Cheska's head swam. Wearily, she pressed her forehead to the cold stone and watched the Scribe from the corner of her throbbing eyes. He was rushing around the room, blowing out the tiny flames. The room was plunged into darkness, candle by candle.

There was a deafening crash and the Scribe spun around to see the door fly inward under a shower of sparks. A man strode through the splintered doorway and stood in what was left of the candlelight with his arms crossed defiantly, ignoring the orange flames that licked at his boots and robe.

When he spoke, his tone was cold and formal, yet there was an odd familiarity to it, thought Cheska.

'I take it all is in order?' he asked quietly.

The wizened Scribe clicked his neck to one side, then removed his spectacles and polished them slowly with the sleeve of his tunic in small, circular motions.

'Three, just as you required.' His voice was like the rasp of files on glass; hoarse as though he had spent an age in silence. The dark newcomer nodded slowly. Their eyes were now locked in a strange battle. Both seemed to be waiting for the other to move. The etiquette before the first strike.

It never came. Cheska waited, shivering in her hiding place. She squirmed, trying to calm her writhing stomach. It was too quiet.

'Who have you truly come for, Vice?' asked the Scribe.

'Who do you think?'

The Scribe slowly turned his head to look at the figure cowering under the bench. 'Given your precious experiments, I would say just her, but the look in your eyes speaks differently,' he said, cocking his head like an inquisitive bird.

Vice lifted his knife and casually examined the blood-smeared blade. 'It's a true shame that you have worn out your usefulness,' he offered with a shrug.

The Scribe shook his head, anger flashing behind his black eyes. 'The sons of Orion will get what is coming to them in the end.'

'I beg to differ,' began Vice, but the Scribe turned his back and snorted.

'It matters not. The decision, it seems, is already made.' The Scribe seemed to let go of a heavy weight then, his shoulders visibly sagging. Cheska held her breath. Fire licked at the walls.

The Undermage lowered his knife. 'I take no pleasure in doing this,' he whispered.

'You can't fool me, Vice, I have spent several hundred years listening to you lie,' he said with closed eyes.

Vice sneered as he grabbed the back of the Scribe's neck. 'That you have,' he replied, in a voice as cold as ice.

There was a metallic crunch and the old man slumped to the floor at Vice's feet. Cheska tried to melt into the shadows of her hiding place. When she opened her eyes again, a shadow stood over her. He looked down at her, smiling wickedly, brandishing a dripping knife in his hands.

The mage Farden is to be commended for his outstanding efforts in the battle of Efjar. Without the aid of this brave mage our men would surely still be deep in the marshes fighting the minotaur clans. It has been a long time since I have seen such a skilled mage in our proud ranks, not since the days of his unfortunate uncle. Let us hope he does not follow the same path as Tyrfing.

Letter to Arkmage Åddren from Lord Vice in the year 884

Nothing lived on the Dunwold moors. Nothing. If one were to find themselves standing on the rolling hills and downs of Albion's eastern coast they would find nothing but rocks and wet grass with no living thing to accompany them. Dunwold was bare, cold, and agonisingly empty, stretching on for miles and miles around as far as the human eye could see. Here and there, a few stunted trees stood amongst the rocky crags and boulders, clinging to whatever life their geriatric roots could find between the grey stone and pale lichen.

After running for two days straight, Farden had finally collapsed between two boulders in the shadow of a low hill. His heat spells had worn off and now the cold was slowly seeping into his bones. Farden had slept fitfully. The dreams hadn't returned and no voices had spoken to him, and he wondered if they had left him for good. He threw a cursory look at the grey skies. *Nothing*.

Farden shifted and winced with pain. He could feel the barbed tip of the arrow in his side working its way deeper into his flesh.

Blood covered the grass beneath him and caked his hands and clothes. The exhausted mage put a tentative hand to his ribs, not daring to touch the broken arrow shaft. Pushing with his elbow and grunting, he managed to prop himself up to peer over the edge of the boulder at the grim countryside.

Dawn was slowly creeping across the edges of the moors. The cold wind toyed with the frost-choked grass, flipping it this way and that like a cat with a dead mouse. Farden's tired eyes roved over his surroundings, watching for movement. His pursuers were nowhere to be seen.

After halving their numbers the day before, he had outrun the men at some point during the night, and now it was daylight once again. The mage had intended to circle back on himself but after losing his sword, his way, and his temper in the marshes, he had lost all hope of making it back to the Arkabbey. Farden hadn't seen or heard anything of the men since nightfall. Their parting gift was still stuck in his ribs.

His heart was heavy and his head pounded. And, as he had left his supplies at the Arkabbey, he was also now ravenously hungry.

With shaking fingers, he peeled some of the moss from the boulder and ate it. The taste was bitter, but he hoped the foul stuff would stop his stomach from complaining. Farden kept his eyes on the horizon while he chewed. His instincts told him he hadn't seen the last of Ridda's cronies, and that the only way to get back to the Arka was going back the way he had come, or…

He quickly pushed that thought away. Even so, his hand strayed to the circular object hidden safely inside his cloak. *Åddren's Weight.*

Farden had contemplated using it that morning, shortly before he had collapsed in a heap between his two rocks. For anyone except an Arkmage, using the Weight was almost as good as suicide. He had heard the stories. Without the necessary power or skill, a user could easily end up crushed inside a mountain, or at the bottom of the Bern Sea. Farden wasn't willing to take that chance just yet.

The mage forced himself to his feet with more willpower than he knew he had. He swayed as the world performed a cartwheel, but he swallowed and blinked the nausea away. Farden's hands were shaking and he could feel the blood seeping down his leg. He longed for the comfort of *The Bearded Goat*. The warmth of a fire, hot wine in a cup, or a sip of mörd with Vice in his opulent chambers. He longed for the feel of Cheska's warm skin against his. The brisk wind tussled with his hair and made him squint.

Next to him, a pool of water had been trapped in the rock, and he bent down to look at his haggard reflection. A stranger with red eyes and thick stubble greeted him. Perhaps it was the clouds hanging overhead, or maybe it was the rock beneath the almost-freezing water, but Farden's skin looked deathly pale: grey and wan like a ghost's. His face and neck were covered in scratches from the claws of trees, his skin was red and blistered, and his dark hair hung in matted locks over his hollow eyes. Farden decided he looked like hell.

He looked down at the arrow sticking out of his ribs. He had snapped off the feathered end last night but the shaft still protruded a good few inches. The wyrm wound from all those weeks ago was now a silvery scar winding through the crusted blood. He touched the arrow gingerly and the spark of pain made him twitch. Farden tried to get his thoughts in order. Without a healer, the arrow would work its way into his lungs or stomach sooner or later, and no amount of magick could save him from that.

'Fuck this,' he cursed, and put the thick collar of his cloak between his teeth. With a deep and heavy breath, he wrapped his fingers tightly around the blood-caked arrowshaft and yanked. Hard.

Light exploded behind his eyes. He choked on pain and fell heavily to the wet ground, but the arrow was out and lying beside him. Blood flowed freely from the gaping wound like a swollen red river.

Farden groaned and clamped a hand to his ribs. He summoned the last of his energy for a healing spell, then darkness swallowed him once again.

❦

When Farden awoke, the sun was just passing its zenith, peeking out from between the thick clouds that covered Dunwold and its moors. His breath caught in his dry throat as he shook himself into consciousness, coughing violently. He quickly realised his painful error as his ribs screamed in fresh agony.

It took another hour to summon the strength to even sit up. The arrow wound looked as ugly as sin. Even though Farden had removed the arrow, he had seen wounds like this catch the rot and fester in a day, especially in the wilds.

Farden sighed as he scanned the moors. Even armed with his spells, he was exhausted and heavily wounded: an easy target for his pursuers. *If the bastards were still around*, he thought grimly. An instinctive voice told him they were. Farden nibbled at some more lichen with another sigh.

In his mind it was like all sense of control had flown away and disappeared beyond the gloomy horizon. Whatever semblance of order and purpose he had felt leaving Krauslung had now crumbled. Ridda had been a loyal and respectable mage. *So what had made him turn so readily*? Whatever it was, Farden knew there was a great evil behind all of this, perhaps more than just Helyard. He just hoped that Durnus and Elessi were safe in the south.

Farden's heart clenched as he remembered the last time he had seen Cheska; skipping around the edges of sleep, face covered by her golden hair, glowing in the dying embers of the fireplace. Farden had run his rough hands over her skin and marvelled at the softness beneath his fingertips, and thought how much he didn't deserve her. He remembered the three words he had whispered to her that night while she slept. She would be finishing the Ritual by now. Either that, or she—

He cut that trail of thought off and hid it like a coward. Farden glanced down at his reflection in the rock-pool once more. The image shattered as he dashed the water away with his hands. A determination flushed through his veins. Whatever it took, he had to get back to Krauslung and find Cheska, and, even if it killed him, he would see an end to this betrayal once and for all.

Farden hauled himself up with a defiant grunt. The stubborn mage took a few deep breaths and stretched his muscles with a new-found resolve. Durnus may have been right after all, he thought. Only he could get himself into such ridiculous situations as these. *Such is the life of a Written*, he smirked wryly, before breaking into a limping jog.

Some time later, Farden was leaning against a mossy boulder in a narrow gully, trying to catch his breath. The wind howled through the rocky culvert, blowing strands of Farden's sweat-soaked hair into his eyes like tiny whips. He was breathing steadier now, but the wound on his side felt as if a rat was gnawing at his ribs. His lungs burnt like hot tar.

The mage froze as the wind moaned again, blowing southeast, in the direction he was heading. A faint sound hung on the stiff breeze for a moment, then fell. Then another, louder this time.

A shout.

Farden started to run again. There was no time to waste. As soon as he was out of the gully, he would be in open view and, with the wind behind his pursuers, in range of their bows. *But then again*, he grimly surmised, *he didn't really have a mountain of options*. His tired feet pounded the frozen earth below him. It was better to run than to be caught hiding.

Farden reached the end of the gully and burst into plain sight, hobbling his way across the moor like a wounded stag. He heard the angry shouts on the wind and snuck a brief look over his shoulder.

Six men were charging towards him over the rolling mounds, waving various sharp objects in the air. They were still about half a mile behind him, but were swiftly catching up, caked in mud and faces furious. Spending two nights in the stinking marshes looking for an invisible mage would drive any man to rage, thought Farden.

Inch by agonising inch, the six men closed the gap. He tried to speed up but his ribs cried out painfully. Their orders had been long forgotten; this was now a personal feud.

Farden stole another look over his shoulder. At their front was the scarred man. He ran as though the wind snapped at his heels. His five cronies slavered at his side like rabid hunting dogs. His eyes were wide and red, starved of sleep.

A rasping shout ripped from his throat. 'Come on lads! 'E's got nowhere t' hide now! I want 'is head on a stick!' Cries went up from the rest of them and they redoubled their efforts, feet pounding on the frozen moors.

Farden could hear their baying getting closer. Rocks and shrubs flew past him, snagging at his cloak. Ahead, the moors stretched out for miles, barren and hopelessly open.

He could feel his lungs sticking to the inside of his ribs. His legs were starting to seize up and slow him down. Specks of colour gathered at the corners of his eyes, and Farden could feel the fatigue trying to drown him.

A heavy object banged against his side and made him wince. *The Weight.*

Farden skidded to a halt and turned to face his pursuers. He grabbed the gold disk from his cloak pocket and looked at the symbols and lettering on its surface. He recognised about half of them.

The mage thumbed the raised lettering and tried to think straight. In his peripheries the shapes of running men were slowly but surely getting bigger.

The Weight felt hot against his sweaty palm. Farden's heart pounded as his mind raced over options. He had to get back to Cheska and warn Åddren and Farfallen. And Durnus, Elessi: he had to protect them as well. But this contraption in his hand was dangerous beyond belief, and he would be no use to anyone if he dead dead.

Farden gritted his teeth, clenching his fingers around the Weight. He tried to block out the fear filling his mind. He tried to remember every book of foreign spells in the Manesmark library; everything Vice had ever told him about the Weights; everything that Durnus had ever taught him about quickdoors. How they were like liquid. *You just have to pour in the right direction.*

The Weight was burning his hand now. The old vampyre said it was about connection: where you could be at one second is where you can also be in another place.

Hot tears sprang to Farden's eyes as he muttered the words he knew. The magick bit him. He held the Weight out in front of him and the gold disc shook and buckled, sending waves rippling through the air, splitting the icy atmosphere of Dunwold as though the very air itself were a broken mirror. An arrow whistled past his ear, but he held firm. The mage planted his tired feet into the ground and tried to bend all his being into seeing one place. *No thoughts, no distractions*. The glowing Weight fractured the air, searing Farden's hand as it split the sky.

Everything stopped.

An arrow poised motionless in the air in front of him, dangling, slowly inching forwards like a dagger through treacle.

The sound of feet pounding on grass and clanking armour rolled on forever, repeating, looping like a dull drone. A shout caught on the wind.

The mage watched it all for a split second, frozen like the wave hanging over the *Sarunn*, like a painting that seemed all too real. There was a deafening crack and Farden was dragged into the darkness, down into oblivion.

The mage vanished into the shivering air and the arrow dug into the cold grass with a useless thud. The ugly man came to a grinding halt, skidding on the grass, breathless and stunned. The others kept running, looking around frantically.

The man's mouth hung open with a confused yet pained look, as though a ghost had just punched him in the stomach. It took a few moments for him to sink to all fours. Slowly, very slowly, his face began to turn a shade of purple, and he shook with frustration. The surrounding men cautiously backed away.

With a guttural scream, he slammed his knife into the grass. 'Aaaaagh! Curse yer, Farden! Curse yer t' all the gods!'

Hundreds of miles to the east, the air whip-cracked and split in two like a jagged gap in a window pane. There was a whooshing sound, then the shape of a bedraggled man appeared out of nothing. He flew through the air and crashed into a nearby wall with a terrible crunch.

Farden gasped for breath, trying to ignore the pain that had set his body on fire. *What genius put a wall here*? he asked himself, nursing bruised ribs and an already sizeable lump on his head. His arm throbbed and he panted as he tried to lift himself to all fours.

Farden scrabbled around at the base of the wall. It was getting difficult to breathe through the pain and fatigue. He slumped to the warm grass and rolled onto his back. He opened his eyes and stared at the horizon.

Nauseating dread gripped his heart when he couldn't make sense of the upside-down mountains, but when he managed to focus his eyes, he found himself looking at the familiar countryside of Manesmark. Farden breathed the biggest sigh of his life.

He rolled over and lay spreadeagled. Blearily, he watched the flakes of ash land on his vambraces and open hand. He watched the flickering orange and yellow glow set the metal aflame, and he wondered where Cheska was.

Ash.

Farden pushed himself to his shaky feet. He collapsed at first but the second time he found his balance and made it to his knees. A roaring sound grew loud in his ringing ears and he rocked back on his heels, craning to gawp at the orange sky.

Flames consumed the Spire, licking at the stonework and battlements of the blackened tower. They leapt from beam to beam. They burst through walls and stone like paper. They tore at the night sky with orange fingers.

Farden was frozen in shock. Although the heat seared his face and the light hurt his tired eyes, he did not move. He simply stared, watching the Spire burn. It was only when a section of the nearby wall fell inwards, sending a cloud of sparks and ash belching into the sky, that Farden moved.

He rolled onto his side and dragged himself away from the blistering heat. Covering his face with his hands, he crawled as far as he could before running out of breath. Above him, dragons circled the tower, hauling blocks of ice and barrels of water into the sky to drop onto the burning tower. The clouds behind them were black and ominous, swollen with smoke. Ash fell like snow.

Farden stood aghast. Hot tears stung his eyes. The shouts of countless voices could be heard from all around as survivors and bystanders were hauled out of the way. Farden could see water and ice mages standing in line near where the main atrium used to be, where the fire burnt fiercest and roared like an army of daemons.

The mages were painted black with smoke, yet stubbornly they battled on, throwing spell after spell into the inferno. Somewhere within the blackened walls of the once-great Spire, amidst the firestorm, the dragonscale bell clanged mournfully in its death throes.

Farden watched, horrified, as another floor collapsed inwards. A young soldier ran past him with a leather bucket of water but Farden grabbed him before he could get away. The boy, barely old enough to be in the army, froze as the bloodied, bruised stranger seized him by the neck.

'What happened here?' bellowed Farden.

The confused boy stuttered nervously. 'Er, the fire, sir?' he managed.

Farden shook him again. 'Tell me what happened, gods damn it!'

'No one knows, sir! It started at nightfall, several hours ago!' Words escaped the boy as he stared fearfully at the mage's ripped clothes, wild face and red-rimmed eyes.

Farden's heart froze over. 'Was there anyone inside? Quickly, boy!'

'E—Everyone sir! All those who didn't go to Albion with the others!'

He released the boy and sank to his knees. The young soldier hesitated for a moment before running off towards the fire with his water, leaving the mage alone and silent on the hillside.

Farden let the orange and yellow flames burn into his eyes, let the prickly heat wash over him, hoping the flames of the Spire would distract him from the fiery pain that burnt inside his chest. *Cheska would have been in the very top room.* Where Farden had been all those years ago for his Ritual. *Where every Written went.*

Farden felt the tears running down his cheeks. He put his head to the scorched grass and began to sob uncontrollably. Images of Cheska trapped in a burning room, surrounded by fire, sprang unbidden into his head. They taunted him with sick, cruel reality. Farden could see her beautiful blonde hair, scorched and charred, just like her face. He could hear her smoke-choked screams.

Farden knuckled a tear away with a shaking hand and saw a small group of people nearby, supposedly the lucky ones that had been pulled from the fire. Their skin and clothes were black from smoke. Fierce red patches of skin showed where the fire had kissed them. Healers moved amongst them, tending burns and handing out pitchers of ice water to stop the coughing.

Even though sobs still shook him, a desperate urgency was stoked inside Farden's chest, and lifted him from the ground. He broke into a limping run, hauling himself towards the pitiful group. Muttering nonsense, he went from person to person, grabbing them by the shoulders and glaring into their faces, praying all the while for a glimpse of bright blonde amongst the black and char.

His hopes were dashed soon enough. Nobody resembled her in the slightest. But Farden wasn't finished. He circled the entire tower twice before he gave up. Defeated, he slumped to the grass. The roar of the fire filled his ears as grief gripped him with its cold fingers.

High above him, the dragons fought on bravely, swooping in and out of the plumes of smoke. Farden gazed upwards through his tears, watching the flames dance over iridescent scales, making the huge beasts sparkle with oranges, reds, and bright yellows.

He saw Farfallen drop an immense block of ice onto the towering pyre, watched it crash through the blackened beams, sending bricks and planks spinning through the air. The Old Dragon shone like liquid gold in the light.

A scream turned his head. A water mage near the Spire had been swallowed by flames. His cries would have been stomach-churning, on any other day. A handful of the others dashed to his aid, beating him with wet, steaming cloths. Another mage showered them all with a waterfall spell, barely keeping the raging inferno at bay while they dragged the smoking body from the fire. Still, they fought on.

It was useless. The fire had already won.

Farden closed his eyes. He let the roaring, screaming and crashing wash over him, as though he were an island in a boiling sea. Grief and rage tore mercilessly at his heart. His only reason to keep going had been cruelly taken away, scorched to nothing, left as ash in his hands. Farden's breathless sobs returned and he buried his face in the grass.

It was a grey morning when Farden awoke. It was freezing. He felt like his limbs had been fused together at the joints. He was unable to move, painfully numb, and he could feel the wet coldness of his clothes. He croaked as he moved an icy hand to wipe his face. His fingers came away black. The ash was still falling, though lightly.

'I didn't think you would wake up for a few more hours,' said a deep female voice, from somewhere behind him.

Farden jumped, turning to find Brightshow staring down at him with a concerned look. She sat like a cat, her wings folded back neatly, and her thick tail wrapped around her clawed feet. The spines running down her neck and back were limp, leaning to the side like the branches of a willow.

'At least I did wake up,' he muttered darkly. The dragon pretended not to hear him. Instead she looked away and up at the blotchy sky. Farden pushed himself up from the dirty grass and sat straight, feeling his back crack in a hundred different places. The wound between his ribs flared with pain. 'How long have you watched me?' he asked.

'Since we found you in the early hours of the morning,' she replied. Still she did not look at him.

The Spire was now a smouldering skeleton of its former glory. Barely a single floor high, the tower walls had fallen in and the wood had burnt away to nothing, leaving only the dead husk of a once-proud building. Cracked, blackened stones littered the hillside, while the bigger bits of burnt wood and charcoal were slowly being piled up by tired, scorched workers. Somewhere beneath the rubble the fires were still burning. Telltale wisps of smoke continued to rise into the overcast sky.

Farden watched the people mill around. Some absently picked up burnt artefacts as if they would bring back those who had perished in the fire. Others scattered mountain flowers. Everybody looked the same: covered in soot and burns, tears running in rivers down ashen skin.

A dragon had died in the flames. Perhaps caught in the collapsing tower, or suffocated by the smoke, Farden didn't know. The green beast lay still and silent amongst a pile of rubble, where a few people had laid flowers and wreaths for the Sirens. A rider lay prostrate on the ground next to her, a single hand pressed against the faded emerald scales of his cold dragon.

Farden looked to Brightshow, whose eyes were gold-flecked orbs of sadness and solemnity. 'Did you know anyone? In the tower, I mean?' she asked.

Farden didn't have any more tears to shed. 'The only person I cared for,' he replied hoarsely. Brightshow looked at the people gathered around the smoking ruin.

'There could still be a chance—'

'She's gone. I've looked.' The reply was stony and cold, so Brightshow let the matter drop. Farden cast a look at the dead dragon lying amongst the stones. 'I'm sorry.' was all he managed to say.

'We're all angry, Farden, and some of us lost more than others,' she said.

The mage looked at the lonely rider kneeling by his dragon's side. Farden nodded, trying to understand, but all he could see in his mind was Cheska. His only love trapped in a burning room at the top of a tall tower. Farden stubbornly swallowed the pain, getting to his feet with resilience he didn't know he had.

Something golden caught his eye and he turned to see Farfallen with a smaller black dragon striding across the grass towards them. The Old Dragon looked sombre.

'Grave times are upon us, mage, and it is with a heavy heart that I greet you.' He bowed his golden head, eyes closed, and sighed. 'I sense a deep sadness in you, Farden. I wish I could help.'

Farden said nothing in reply. Farfallen looked to Brightshow and she shook her head. If a dragon could shrug, that's what Farfallen did. He lifted a claw to point to the lithe dragon at his side. 'This is Havenhigh, one of our youngest.'

The mage nodded to Havenhigh and turned back to Farfallen. 'What happened here?' he asked.

'She will tell you, if you can stand to listen. There is an ill will behind the cause of the fire.'

The bells rang in Farden's head again as he looked to Havenhigh. The black dragon had scales like mottled silk, sleek and dangerous. Her back was dotted with curved spines and two long, black barbels hung from her chin, like those of a carp. Her forked tail swished back and forth restlessly. As she spoke, Farden could see the rows of teeth lining the inside of her narrow jaw.

'This morning I saw two bodies in a pile on the other side of the Spire. They were scorched and burnt with something more than just fire; the holes in their breastplates told me as much. I spoke to one of your men, a soldier, and he said they had been pulled from the tower early in the evening, but by whom he didn't say,' Havenhigh said. Her voice was sibilant, and her words rattled strangely.

'What does this mean?' Brightshow asked.

'It means—' the Old Dragon started, but Farden cut him off.

'It means that somebody started this fire,' he said, eyes downcast, searching the ash-black grass. His cold words were like rocks dropped from a cliff. 'Are you sure about what you saw?' he asked, fixing the black dragon with an intense stare.

Havenhigh nodded. 'The bodies of the two men should still be there. Your people haven't cleared anything away.'

Farden was already walking. He marched across the wet grass towards the other side of the Spire. Storm clouds made of dark thoughts gathered in his mind. He could hear the dragons following close at his heels. They were as silent as he was and just as purposeful.

Within minutes, they came upon the first pile of bodies, heaped shoulder-high, grotesquely positioned at the base of what used to be the Spire. Their pace slowed a little as they saw the broken corpses. The mage surveyed the grisly collection with a knot in his throat.

Some were charred beyond recognition, others were wax-like, their eyes open and faces painted black and grey. Even Farden's battle-hardened stomach twitched. Mingled with the acidic charcoal taste that lingered in the air, the smell of death was sickening.

'Havenhigh! Where are they?' he called.

The lithe dragon scanned the dead faces and pursed her lips. She took a few moments to move around the piles, looking for a glint of armour. 'Here!'

Farden was the first to reach her. He stood by the dragon's side and looked down at the two bodies on the ground. They barely resembled men at all, but Farden only saw the jagged holes in their armour. Kneeling, he ran a finger across the scarred, molten surface of the breastplates, noticing how the gold was puckered and cracked. He stood up, rubbing his face. *This was no accident.* It was the next notch on the mysterious blade behind all of this. Farden just wanted to find the invisible hand that wielded it.

'This one on the left was hit by a firebolt. The other there, see how the hole is less charred and smaller? That's spark magick,' Farden said quietly.

'Then this was murder, and the fire was no accident,' Farfallen voiced what all the others were thinking. The great dragon sighed. 'We must take this to Åddren immediately.'

Farden looked at the dead guards lying in the wet grass. Their eyes frozen wide in their last moments. 'I think I know someone that could tell us what happened here, if we asked him right,' he growled.

Keep an eye on the weather, he thought. He would do more than just keep an eye on it.

Farden let a moody flame burn in his palm for a moment before extinguishing it in a clenched fist with a hiss. He looked Farfallen in the eye. 'You go see the Arkmage, I'm going to pay someone else a little visit.'

Without another word, the mage was off, hobbling down the hill in a limping run, heading towards the dark clouds that were gathering over the city. As the dragons watched him leave, Farfallen sighed deeply.

The mood in Krauslung was sombre and downtrodden. The city mourned its deep loss. The atmosphere was taut like a bowstring. Every door was closed, every window latched. The taverns and drinking-holes of the city were unusually quiet, and as Farden lurched past them he watched the men in the candlelit windows, looking at their yellow melancholy faces as they sipped at cold ale. Farden trudged on.

He felt the first patter of rain on his shoulders, then heard the heavy thwack of several drops landing on his dirty hood. Rain was just what the city needed. Half of Krauslung was covered by the cloud of smoke and ash that still rose from Manesmark. It hung above like a gravestone, and just as heavy. The pain needed to be washed away.

Farden zig-zagged through desolate streets, fists clenched in his pockets, his hood pulled low over his fiery eyes. His gaze caught a flash of colours between two rooftops. Gold, white, red, and black: four dragons heading for the great hall. Farden walked even faster, ignoring the pain in his side. All he could think of was Cheska.

The guards at the citadel gates were wary of Farden. They looked at him with anger in their eyes, as if he were somebody they could blame. But they did not challenge him, and Farden limped on past.

The stairs made his wound scream with fresh agony, and the long hallways seemed endless. Farden drove himself on.

As he made his way deeper into the fortress, the white marble and gold trimmings of the Arkathedral disappeared, gradually replaced by drab granite and gloom. Windows became stone walls and thick iron doors hid in the dark recesses of the corridors. Guards stood quietly on every corner. They did not bother Farden either. They just stared at him blankly as he hurried past, deeper into the mountain.

Like Hjaussfen, the prisons were like a warren, a labyrinth of cells and hallways designed to slow the escape of anyone who dared to try. But Farden wasn't escaping. He knew exactly where he was going.

Soon, he came to another thick iron door. At some point in the past somebody had painted it blood red, but the colour had long-since flaked away, leaving the metal brown and rusty. Farden kicked at the door and it swung open, startling a young guard standing on the other side.

'State your business!' he demanded. Farden found a shaky spearpoint waving in his face. He held up his hands.

'I'm here to see the Arkmage,' he said.

The young man shook his head resolutely. 'Nobody's to go in there. Lord Vice's orders, under pain of death!'

Farden's patience was wearing dangerously thin. 'I don't have ti—'

'I'm sorry, sir, but you'll have to leave!' The spearpoint got closer as the guard took a nervous step forwards.

Farden grabbed the spear shaft and broke it in two. He pushed the stunned guard backwards until he collided with the wall, then sent him sprawling across the floor with a deft kick. Dazed, the young guard cowered where he landed.

Farden grabbed him by the collar of his breastplate. 'I said I don't have time for this! Now, where's Helyard?' he bellowed, every word making the man jump a little more.

The guard pointed a shaking hand down the dark corridor, to a passage leading left. 'Down there, sir!'

'Good man,' muttered Farden. He lifted up a clenched fist and a light spell burnt the shadows away, half-blinding the young man in the process.

Anger bubbled inside him, and even though he had no idea quite what he was about to do; somehow he sensed either vengeance or answers were close at hand. Farden would have at least one tonight.

He tried to calm his breathing. The magick ran like boiling water though his veins. He thought only of Cheska.

Farden found the cell door and spread his palm over the cold steel and oak, letting his fingers creep inquisitively over the metal. The symbols under his vambraces burnt white with angry fire. The mage had no time for subtlety. He could feel the magick rebounding through his forearm but he held firm and pushed again. The iron buckled under his hand. The door shook with a terrible wrenching sound. Farden clenched his jaw even harder, pushing with every ounce of his strength. Sweat dripped from his forehead.

With a metallic squeal, splinters flew from the metal brackets. Another shove and the door flew open in a cloud of white dust. Farden did not waste a moment. He burst through the haze into the room, fists clenched and fire trailing around his wrists. His heart pounded as his eyes roved around the room.

Then the smell hit him. That sickly rotting smell that nobody could ever forget once they had experienced it. Farden saw the body on the floor surrounded by a dark, sticky pool of blood. His heart fell in his chest like a cold rock in a colder sea.

Farden walked slowly and knelt down by the corpse's side. It was Helyard. The old man's head was twisted at an ugly angle and his body lay in an awkward position. A knife was buried hilt-deep in his chest. The Arkmage's bloated face was ashen, frozen in horror. He looked surprised, pained, and Farden stared into his glazed eyes. He wondered what he had seen or what he had been thinking. *Who he had faced.*

Farden gingerly lifted Helyard's chin, trying to restore some sense of decorum to the old man's posture. He had died not a traitor, but a victim of the same conspiracy that sought to bury Farden.

With a gentle hand he closed Helyard's eyes for the final time, and like a bucket of ice water, a renewed sense of loss washed over him.

Farden looked around at the room, staring at the pockmarks in the walls and the splintered remains of what looked like a cot. The floor and ceiling were cracked and blistered, like the armour of the unfortunate guards at the Spire.

Without a sound, Farden stood up and left Helyard in peace.

All he could think of was Cheska.

chapter 18

I am not becoming someone different. I am simply getting to know the person I already am.
Old saying, origin unknown

For once, *The Bearded Goat* was quiet. A few people were scattered around the bar, not bothering anyone except themselves, sipping ale and drowning their thoughts as though there was not going to be a tomorrow. Even the sound of the inn's creaky sign, swinging outside in the breeze, was louder than the muffled sound of conversation.

The fire crackled quietly by Farden's side. Someone coughed. He swilled warm wine around his mouth. After leaving Helyard's cell, he had gone straight to find Vice, but the Undermage was nowhere to be found. His rooms had been empty and his servants clueless. He had gone to tell the Arkmage and the council but Åddren had merely slumped deeper into his throne, staring blankly into space without any words of wisdom or comfort to offer. Nothing. Farden had been furious.

To make matters worse, talk of his daughter's death had reached Bane, the King of Skölgard. He had dispatched a dozen hawks with news of his imminent arrival to Krauslung. Bane wanted an explanation as to why his only daughter and heir to the throne had died in the care of the Arka.

Bane had demanded retribution for Cheska. He had even gone so far as to threaten war on the magick council. They only had days before Bane and his army arrived.

The mage could not help but think that somehow it all rested on his shoulders. Even though he should have been in Albion with the other mages, he needed time to think.

Farden took a bite of the lonely piece of bread that lingered on his plate. A mixture of anger and grief flushed through him and he shuddered. Farden tore at the bread with his teeth, sending a shower of crumbs scattering across the table. He narrowed his eyes and tried to think, tried to figure out this mess once and for all.

That evening, the city was filled with lights. As night fell, the stars battled with the thick cloud for a place in the darkening skies.

Torches crept into the streets and candles appeared in windows. One by one, people left their houses, carrying candles in glass jars, or tall blazing torches, or little whale oil lamps for the children. The countless lights made their way south towards the sea, meandering through the winding streets of the city like swarms of fireflies. They mingled and gathered, their bearers silent and sombre, and all together they quietly proceeded down towards the shore.

An Arkmage had died.

Gradually, the lights assembled by the sea and lined the piers, boardwalks, and rocky beaches. The people gathered in complete silence, letting the sea's sounds fill the wordlessness. Innumerable shoes crunched on the sand and shingle. A myriad of candles, lamps, and torches sparked and hissed in the cold night breeze. The water lapped gently at the shore, rocking the ships in the port. Their bells moaned with muffled clanging.

Within an hour, the entire city had gathered at the water's edge, and every single one of them remained deathly quiet. People stood in their thousands, anywhere they could find the space to do so. Peasants rubbed shoulders with aristocrats and fine ladies stood with battle-scarred soldiers. Sailors stood at the railings of their ships alongside their captains. Even in their thousands, nobody made even the faintest sound. The silence ached.

Åddren stood alone at the tip of the longest pier, at the front of the crowds. He looked out over the calm waves that rippled the Bay of Rós, rolling out towards the Bern Sea. The dark waters were glasslike, mottled like obsidian, and every now and again the frothy tip of a wave caught the bright torchlight and shone orange. Åddren let a slow, sad sigh escape from his pursed lips. The night breeze made him shiver.

At that moment, a lone horn rang out from somewhere in the port and nine small boats began to drift out to the mouth of the harbour walls. Another horn cried: a long, high-pitched wail that floated across the cold air. Everyone just watched and waited.

With the breeze behind them, it did not take long for the boats to reach the gap in the stout harbour walls. Lashed loosely together, they bobbed on the growing waves, thudding against each other with dull knocks.

Another larger boat, a skiff, had followed them out. Standing in it was a man holding a bow and a quiver of rag-bound arrows. Slowly, with a great deal of reverence and ceremony, the man lit a torch with flint and tinder and touched an arrowhead to the crackling flames. He raised his bow, took aim, and fired. The blazing arrow ripped through the air, a yellow streak in the darkness.

The first boat, its sad cargo liberally doused with oil, burst into flame. The man in the skiff fired eight more times at each of the boats in turn, then let them be, watching them drift out into the bay. A final horn signalled a farewell.

The thousands gathered on the beaches and ships bowed their heads and whispered their prayers to their gods. When they were finished, they snuffed out their torches or candles. The port was gradually plunged into an eerie darkness, until the only lights burning were those of the nine boats drifting out into the Bern Sea.

Far away, on a distant Manesmark hillside, a hooded figure sat watching the ceremony with his arms resting on knees.

He was as silent as the rocks around him.

Farden's keen eyes had long since adjusted to the darkness, and now he stared raptly at the tiny twinkling lights in the distance. He let the breeze tug at his hood, breathing slowly, listening to his mind wander through dark places.

While he thought, Farden absentmindedly twirled something between his fingers. It was Cheska's fjortla. He had toyed with it for hours, but the red metal was still cold to the touch. The fact that she could have died during the Ritual and not in the fire was no comfort. He looked at it a hundred different ways and the outcome was always the same.

Cheska was gone.

The night was cold, and the mage was numb, feeling as lost as ever. More than once that evening he had contemplated throwing himself onto the rocks below the hill but somehow he knew the fall wouldn't have taken his problems away.

Farden's morbid thoughts were interrupted once again by the sense of duty that incessantly poked at him. Whether he felt it was his responsibility, or it was just his craving for revenge, he didn't know, but something was trying to keep him going, stoking the angry fires deep in his heart. At the same time, an overwhelming desire to give up and wallow in grief tugged at him from the opposite direction, and he was caught in the middle of both feelings, undecided and confused.

Farden was tired. As the very last of the lights disappeared on the horizon, he got to his feet with a grunt and strode into the darkness.

❦

The walk back into Krauslung took almost two hours, and as Farden walked under the huge city gates it began to snow. The flakes were few and lazy at first, gently drifting down from the black sky, but Farden could feel in the sharpness of the air that a blizzard was approaching.

As he descended into the streets of Krauslung he looked up at the dark clouds between the buildings. In the orange light of the torches the snowflakes looked like grey flies floating on the growing breeze, swarming around gutters and windowsills. Farden pulled his cloak about him and coughed, watching the hot breath escape from his lips. The cold was doing wonders for his arrow wound.

The city was quiet again. Now that the funeral was over, the citizens had gone back to their homes and locked their doors for the night. Snow soon covered the streets, blushing orange and yellow in the torchlight, making the edges of alleyways and buildings glow.

Farden could barely see ten yards in front of him. He made out a few people wandering towards him through the thick snow. The figures looked faint and misshapen. They passed without a sound, and like Farden, their hoods were pulled low and their hands deep in their pockets. They made a funny sight, their heads and shoulders covered in a layer of white, huffing and puffing steam like chimneys as they hurried home. Farden must have looked the same.

Somewhere in the streets, a mother shushed a whining child. There was a peal of boyish laughter and two more children wrapped in scarves bounded out of the whiteness.

A few moments later, another fatter child raced after them, carrying two sizeable lumps of snow in each chubby hand. Farden shook his head and allowed himself a hint of a smile, even though the expression felt foreign in his current mood. *They were so oblivious, so innocent and carefree*. The mage felt a pang of jealousy, wishing he could go running off into the snow and forget everything.

Farden came to a familiar corner and heard the muffled squeak of a familiar sign. He sighed with relief; all he wanted to do was sleep. The mage made his way to the brightly lit doorway and stamped his feet hard on the steps to shake off the snow. *The Bearded Goat* was quiet once again, subdued and half-empty. Tobacco smoke filled the air. Farden wandered in and nodded to the innkeeper, who went to pour him a glass of the sweet red wine he was starting to like.

Melting snow from Farden's leather boots dripped onto the floor, making little puddles. He cast a look around the place. A few men leaned against the end of the bar, swapping words in low murmurs. Farden watched them for a moment, trying to listen in, but soon gave up. Another man, a soldier by the look of him, sipped ale by the hearth. His eyes were glazed in deep thought and he absently swirled his ale in his glass.

The warm wine came in a wooden cup. The smell of spices and nutmeg tickled Farden's nose. He sipped the hot liquid carefully, savouring the hot steam on his face. Seeing as he had left most of his supplies at the Arkabbey, he decided he would order some food later. The only things in his pockets were the Weight, the fjortla, and the daemonstone. He found himself pulling a grim face as he thought how pointless the present was now.

The mage looked to another figure, sat in the corner at the back of the inn. A pair of beady eyes stared back at him; familiar rodent-like eyes.

The old beggar tugged on his hair and nodded slowly. Farden hesitated by the bar, staring back at him. He wore the same patchwork getup as before: his wet, dirty cloak pulled tightly around him like a filthy blanket. Bits of snow clung to his straggly, greasy hair. He looked even more haggard than Farden remembered. A yellow smile curled at the corner of the beggar's lip.

Farden looked away and sipped his warm wine. He lingered by the bar, letting the desire swirl about in his chest. Farden hadn't even thought of nevermar since that night in the forest with Elessi. Now it was all he could think of.

With a grunt, he made his way past the men at the bar and meandered through a copse of stools and tables. He sat down beside the old man without a word.

A moment passed. 'It's a cold night,' said the beggar with a cough.

Farden nodded, keeping his eyes on the fireplace. 'Mmm, it is. Storm's coming.'

'A storm 'e says.' The beggar clacked the mouthpiece of the pipe against his teeth thoughtfully and chuckled. 'It'll be comin' sooner than ye think, mage, sooner than ye think.' His laugh was a strange hissing sound. The grimy man flashed blackened gums. Smoke streamed from his nostrils. It made him look like a dragon.

Farden nodded once more and sat in silence, sipping his wine again. His hands fidgeted with his cup. The beggar stared at him with a glint in his eye.

'What brings yew t' my table tonight, then?'

Farden shrugged. 'Nothing in particular, familiar face and all that.' The excuse sounded stupid.

He tapped his nose with a mucky finger. 'Strange that, 'aven't seen yew in a couple o' weeks, mage.'

'I've asked you not to call me that,' warned Farden in a dangerous tone. 'Been busy.'

'Hmm, so I 'ear,' the man chuckled. 'Trouble in Manesmark, was it?' The beggar's words made Farden feel uncomfortable, and he bared his teeth. He could feel his anger rising. *All the more reason.*

'What's the matter?' the beggar grinned, 'Dragon got yer tongue?' He laughed his snake-like laugh and shuffled out of his seat shakily. 'I've seen your room already. I'll be in number nine, if ye fancy tryin' some more. Looks like yew need it, if'n you ask me.'

And, with that, he tottered his way to the stairs and disappeared into the shadows.

Farden sighed. His thoughts spoke all at once, clamouring for space between his ears. The mage went back to his wine, feigning calm, staring into the crackling fire.

Half an hour later, when the warmth of the wine had worked its way to his head, Farden found himself striding up *The Goat*'s well-trodden stairs, eyeing the ascending numbers of the doors.

In the dim candlelight, he found the room and knocked quietly, looking back down the hallway for unwanted eyes. The corridor was silent and empty.

There came a sound from behind the door followed by the click of a cheap lock. An ugly face peered out from behind the door and grinned. Farden nodded silently and followed the beggar into the room. *Strange, that a beggar could afford to stay at the inn*, he thought. Maybe he got lucky with a drunk noble. Farden shrugged. He tried not to think of the last night he had spent in a room like this.

The room smelled stale, like old shoes mixed with damp, or the earthy smell of dirt. Farden watched the snowflakes slip-sliding down the windowpane to join their friends in the street. The city was slowly being covered in a white blanket. *Maybe it was a new beginning*, he thought. A blank canvas for tomorrow to bleed all over.

The man toyed idly with a bag on the bed, coughing and murmuring to himself as he rummaged. *Gods the man was ugly*. In the orange glow from the streets outside, he looked like a scrawny, half-drowned rat, bereft of whiskers or tail but just as twitchy.

After a short while, the beggar cackled softly and produced a long pipe from the folds of his bag. Farden fidgeted all the more.

‘ ’Ere it is. Knew I ’ad it somewhere. Light the fire would yew, mage?’ asked the beggar, flashing a cheeky grin.

Farden bit his tongue and went to the fireplace. He crouched low, hunched over so the man wouldn’t get the gratification of watching the spell. Flame trickled from his fingers and licked at the pile of dry wood. The orange flames hopped from one log to another like a disease and the fireplace began to crackle.

The old beggar stooped beside him and held the end of a long leaf in the flames until it started to smoke.

‘Take a seat,’ he said.

Farden wrinkled his lip at the smell of the man’s rotten breath. He stood up and pulled a threadbare armchair closer to the fire as the man took to a short stool. He grinned his rodent smile as his seat wobbled unsteadily beneath him. Using his leaf as a taper, he puffed on the pipe and the sickly-sweet smell reached Farden’s nostrils, making his insides squirm.

‘I ’ear yew were in Nelska with them dragon-riders,’ muttered the beggar around his pipe. Farden shuffled around uncomfortably in his chair. This man knew entirely too much about his business.

‘You hear a lot,’ he replied.

‘That I do, when my ears still work, heh. Not dead yet then, I see?’

The mage gave the man a stony look. ‘No, apparently not.’ He was beginning to worry him. He asked too many questions. Farden didn’t trust him one bit, but still he eyed the pipe in the man’s claw-like hand.

The beggar shuffled on his little stool, pulling his patchwork cloak around his shoulders. Jabbing the air with the bowl of the pipe, he pointed to Farden’s side, where something strange was happening in his pocket. ‘What’s that?’ he asked.

Farden looked down, confused, and saw a dim glow coming from the inside pocket of his cloak. ‘I don’t know,’ he replied, reaching to fish out whatever it was. It was the daemonstone he had bought for Cheska, and even though it was wrapped in thin paper, it shone with a whitish-yellow glow. Farden pulled it out of his pocket and held it in the palm of his hand. He blinked slowly. It felt cold against his skin. 'That's odd.'

The old beggar shook his head and sniffed loudly. 'Don't look safe t' me. Put it away,' he hissed, with narrowed eyes.

Farden pretended not to hear him and unwrapped the corner of the paper. The golden rock glowed all the brighter. He leaned forwards and it got brighter still, each of its metallic facets sparkling with pinpricks of white light. Farden wrapped it back up again and held it tightly in his hand. The light shone from between his fingers like one of his light spells.

The beggar sucked his teeth and rocked back on his stool. 'Put it away, mage. Ain't natural I say. Glowin' rocks.'

'It's fine,' Farden replied. He could not help but think how much Cheska would have liked her present. He sighed and stuffed the daemonstone back in his pocket, though he kept his hand on it.

Smoke curled up from the pipe as the beggar puffed on it once again. The fire crackled quietly next to them and Farden found himself staring at the smouldering nevermar. The beggar had noticed his eyes and smiled knowingly. He held out the pipe.

'Try some o' this. Different to the last lot,' he said.

Farden took the pipe in his hand and watched it burn for a moment. Grim thoughts shouted inside his head. 'You know what happens if you tell anyone about this don't you?' he warned.

The old beggar shook his head and waved his gnarled hands dismissively. 'I know, I know, for gods' sake. Won't tell a soul.'

Farden watched the pipe dangling between his fingers. Trying to justify it was like trying to wrestle a troll. Even though his dark mood cried out for it, he had promised Elessi. Farden sighed again, knuckling his eyes.

'Are yew goin' t' smoke it or kiss it, mage?' croaked the beggar, impatiently.

Farden glared at him. 'I told you not to call me that.'

'Well, we ain't got all night, boy! Yew goin' to smoke it or not?'

'Fine,' replied Farden. He handed him back the pipe and eyed him with a defiant look. With a grunt, the mage stood up and pulled his hood over his head. 'I think it's time I left.'

The beggar scowled. 'Smoke it,' he demanded. His eyes flashed with anger.

'Forget it, old man. Another night maybe,' muttered Farden, shoving the armchair out of his way and marching for the door. A shout stopped him dead. A shout of a voice he knew very well indeed.

'You've picked the wrong time to grow a conscience, Farden!'

He whirled around. The beggar rose slowly from his stool, shaking and groaning as he did so, as if he were fighting to keep his limbs from running away. The old man stretched upwards before Farden's eyes. His back clicked audibly. His skin warped. Years and lines fell from his face like leaves from a tree. His eyes glowed with a sudden dangerous fire. The man threw off his dirty cloak and flexed his arms and fingers, smiling. His yellow and black teeth shifted to a whiter shade, flashing with a snake's grin. The daemonstone glowed even more brightly in Farden's pocket.

Vice threw the pipe into the fire with a contemptuous snort and watched Farden back up against the door. The mage gawped in disbelief, staring wide-eyed at his friend of many years, the man he had known since his first day at the School, when he had been just twelve years old. He wanted to laugh, as if it were some sort of sick joke, but the humour was lost behind the lump in his throat.

'You?!' was all Farden could manage. His world shattered in front of him.

The Undermage picked at something under his nails and laughed. 'That's exactly what Helyard said. You should think yourself lucky I didn't come while you were sleeping.'

Rage began to boil in Farden's heart. He could feel the white heat running along his spine and shoulders. 'After all this time, you were right here, under my nose?' Farden clenched his fists until his hands went pale. His stomach churned sickeningly as realisation became a thick knot in his heart.

Vice clicked his fingers. 'I'm not here to talk, Farden. But as usual, you take a while to grasp the obvious.' The smile disappeared from Vice's face, replaced by thin lips. 'I suppose your stupidity knows no bounds.'

Farden blinked, fighting the hot tears that had begun to gather in his eyes. 'And neither does your treachery!' he bellowed. He slammed his wrists together with a clang. Fire swirled around his fists, hissing with a dragon's roar.

He cried out, all words forgotten, pure anger pouring from his hoarse throat. He lunged, opening his hands and sending a fireball leaping across the room.

Vice was ready for it. He threw his hands up in front of him, blade-like, and the fireball slammed into a shield moments before it threatened to consume him. The yellow fire billowed around him, yet still Vice wore his sneering grin.

Farden shook with rage. He stormed across the room with his hands held high. Lightning crackled between his fingers.

Vice spun and dropped to his knees, jabbing the air. Farden collapsed in pain that came from nowhere, doubling him over. He had never felt a spell like it. He stumbled against the bed and threw out a hand to steady himself, trying to find breath. The arrow wound between his ribs screamed in agony and he looked up to find the Undermage towering over him. Green light shimmered over Vice's knuckles.

Farden saw what was about to happen and dove to the side just as the fist came down like a hammer. Vice struck empty floor. The shockwave cracked the floorboards and split the fireplace clean in half.

Farden was already on his feet, standing behind the Undermage. He seized his slim opportunity and brought his knee straight up into Vice's ribs, then grabbed him roughly by the neck. Sparks coursed along the Undermage's body and he went rigid, crying out as lightning shivered over his skin.

'Taste of your own medicine, Vice? Like the scholars at Arfell?!' shouted Farden.

Vice threw an elbow into his face, forcing the mage to break his hold. He laughed again, and a curved knife appeared in his hands, glinting menacingly in the firelight.

Farden wiped blood from his lip and backed off. He watched his opponent's hands warily as they moved through the air. The dirty silver blade danced back and forth dangerously. That familiar grin curled at the corner of Vice's mouth again, the one Farden had known for over half his life.

Vice spat. 'You think you're any different? Any better than the old men who died at my hand? Better than those Siren soldiers, or that old fool Åddren? I can dispatch you all as easily as I could an insect.'

The two men circled one another, each trying to force the other into a corner.

'I have watched you systematically ruin your life ever since your uncle died. And let me tell you one thing, Farden, you are no different from him whatsoever. The temper, the nevermar, the voices in your head, you're both as bad and as useless as each other. A waste of my time. And what about that pretty girl in the Spire? That Skölgard girl. What was she called again?' said Vice.

'Don't you fucking *dare* speak her name!' Farden bellowed.

'That one you loved so much. Did you think nobody would notice?' The knife flashed as the blade weaved through the air like a snake. 'She was so easy to get rid of, after all the confusion of the Ritual. The fire did most of the work for me.'

Farden snapped. With a growl of animalistic fury, he punched the air above his head, arms tensed, fingers bent like claws. He shook with the strain, as if he were pulling on the very roots of the sky, feeling power he had not felt since the *Sarunn*.

A rumbling started below the room, slow at first, then building quickly, until the floorboards began to rattle violently beneath their boots. Farden's eyes burnt with vengeful fire, fixed on the Undermage. Magick tore through his veins. Vice began to back away cautiously, wearing a different expression now.

Time stopped, just for a shadow of an instant, as though that one moment could last an hour. The snow froze in mid-air outside the window. The dust hovered in the room. It was almost serene. For the briefest moment.

Then came the roar. An ear-splitting scream that drowned out the world. The floor between them burst into a thousand pieces, as if a volcano had erupted from beneath the bar. With a brilliant flash and an explosion of splinters, a white-hot pillar of fire tore upwards through the room. It blasted the chairs to pieces and turned the floor to ash. It ripped into the roof as if it were no more than a pile of sticks. The bed was catapulted against the wall and the broken fireplace was reduced to charred bricks. Both men flew backwards, trying desperately to escape the flames.

The windows exploded under the pressure, sending shards of glass spinning around the room. Farden shielded his face with his vambraces and scrambled up against the wall behind him to get away from the heat. The column of fire now spun like a tornado, tearing at the ceiling with teeth made from flames and claws of heat and smoke.

But the spell was waning, Farden could feel it in his hands: the shivering power slowly beginning to subside. Between the gaps in his fingers he spied Vice crawling over bits of bed and broken glass towards the cold air outside. The Undermage jumped onto the windowsill and disappeared into the snow-streaked sky.

Farden roared as he scrambled to his feet. Tiredness was trying to creep into his arms and legs again, but rage drove him onwards. He dashed to the window, skirting the dwindling flames. The cold air slapped him hard in the face as he leaned over the window-ledge and peered into the blizzard.

A crowd of people had gathered outside the inn to gape at the fire that billowed from the roof and punctured the snow-laden sky. The street had been washed of all other colours, now a bright array of oranges and yellows. Flames danced on the snow. Pieces of charred wood and cracked tiles were falling from the air, littering the street like a strange new type of precipitation.

The mage scanned the gawking faces below him as he tried to steady his pounding heart. He spotted a figure hurrying through the crowd, hood up, escaping. Farden grabbed the window-frame, ignoring the razor-sharp glass tearing at his palms, hoisted himself up, and leapt from the room to the dark street below.

He landed hard on the snow, rolling to avoid breaking his ankles. He was on his feet in a flash. Farden barged through the crowd amidst angry shouts. Vice had already broken free of the throng and was making his way further up the street and into the city. Farden yelled to the bewildered people in his way.

'Get out of the way! Move!'

Up ahead, half a dozen soldiers rounded the corner, barring the way. Dumbstruck, they stared at the fire pouring from the roof of the inn. Farden shouted to them, pointing wildly at Vice.

'Traitor! Stop him!'

The armoured men broke into a run, heading towards the crowd and the hooded Vice. The Undermage scowled. He wasn't about to waste any time dealing with soldiers. Vice skidded to a halt and stamped his foot hard in the snow. A wave rippled through the cobbles, as if they were marbles floating on a sea. What seemed like a bubble expanded outwards from him, throbbing with magick. The snow scattered and the soldiers collided with an invisible brick wall. Their feet flew out from under them as they crashed to the ground, crying out in shock.

Panic filled the street. The crowd dispersed in all directions, every one of them yelling at the top of their lungs.

A single shout rose above the rest. 'Vice!'

The Undermage turned and chuckled mockingly. 'See you at Carn Breagh,' he yelled, pausing for a moment to let the words sink in.

Vice grabbed something from inside his cloak. Farden sprinted but before he could reach him, there was a flash of light. Vice was gone, leaving the air shivering behind him as he folded into nothing.

'No, no, no!' Farden fell to the snow and stared in horror at the empty air. The wind had died. An unnatural hush had descended upon the streets.

Farden had been cheated of his revenge once more. He put his forehead to the snow, fists clenched in frustration, then rolled back onto his knees and stayed there. All he could do was stare dazedly at the spot where Vice had vanished. Feet crunched in the snow as a few people ran past him, back to their homes, away from the mayhem and the fire. Up ahead, the soldiers slowly picked themselves up and shook the dizziness from their heads. One still lay unconscious.

Farden stared blankly into space and took deep breaths to calm himself. Pain gradually crept back into his body, replacing the adrenaline and burning magick. Deep cuts from the broken glass in his hands oozed. Farden watched rivulets of blood drip down his fingers and land on the white snow, making little red flowers as they seeped in and froze. He could feel people watching him; hear them deciding it was better to leave him be. Farden didn't blame them. He wouldn't have approached him either.

Fury still burnt within him: he could feel it. His clothes were smoking and charred. His face and arms were a patchwork of old scars and fresh bruises.

A trumpeting sound broke his reverie, but still he couldn't move, finding himself numb with shock. The sound of wings beating the air grew louder, and Farden lifted his face to the orange-smeared sky, letting the snowflakes land gently on his hot skin.

Loud thuds from behind him shook the cobblestones under his knees, then came a scraping of scales and claws on stone. Farden watched the soldiers back away, dragging their unconscious friend with them. They stared at something behind Farden, eyes wide and nervous. A familiar, booming voice called to him, echoing through the street.

'Farden!'

He rose, feeling his ribs complain at him, grumbling that he should stay where he was in the snow. Behind him, Farfallen stood with the red dragon Towerdawn. Svarta was the only rider with them. She stood with arms folded, shaking her head as usual. Farfallen's golden face was concerned.

Farden slowly rose to meet them. 'I didn't think it would be long before you spotted the fire,' he said, vacantly regarding the destruction he had caused at the inn.

It seemed like everyone had escaped the fire unharmed, but sadly *The Bearded Goat* was no more. His favourite inn had been replaced by a smoking shell, no more than a mess of rubble, tiles, doors, and glass lying broken in the street. A handful of patrons and the innkeeper stood shivering in the snow. Every eye was now fixed on the two huge dragons that had squeezed themselves into the narrow street. Their wings knocked against drainpipes and gutters.

'It seems that wherever we find destruction and chaos, we find you.' Svarta cast a disdainful glance at the smouldering ruin behind him.

'It's not like I plan these things,' Farden replied. He wiped his bloody hands on his cloak and shunned the pain.

'What happened here?' asked Farfallen. The dragon's scales glittered in the light of the flames. The mage took a deep breath and looked Farfallen squarely in his big golden eyes.

'It was Vice,' he said. His words rang like cold steel.

The Old Dragon's spines rippled and his back arched like a cat's. 'Vice?' The name was a dark growl in his throat.

'I've been so blind!' Farden cursed, clenching his cold fists. 'It's been him all along, this whole time! Helyard, the scholars from Arfell, your Sirens…' *And the most painful of all.* 'The Spire, all him!'

'All this time? You never even suspected him?' Svarta's face was the perfect picture of blame.

'You were the one who was so eager to condemn Helyard! Don't you dare lecture me. Vice has been my friend for years!' Farden eyed Svarta dangerously, daring her to carry on talking. The Siren queen scowled straight back at him.

The mage's fingers crept to where the gold disk hid in his cloak pocket. 'I have the Weight, I can get to him before any of you and stop him,' he said.

'Don't be a fool, you wouldn't even get close,' scoffed Svarta.

'Are you doubting me?'

'That's enough!' snarled Farfallen. It was the first time Farden had seen the dragon truly angry. 'What's done is done, and what matters now is putting an end to this evil. One such as him does not deserve to live in this world. Where is this traitor?'

'He just escaped using Helyard's Weight,' Farden kicked at snow, letting the frustration froth inside him again.

'He's gone?' asked Towerdawn.

Svarta was incredulous. 'You let him escape?!' she spat.

Farden squared up to her, inches from her scaly face. She was unnaturally tall up close. Her yellow eyes drilled into his. 'I swear to the gods, Svarta, one more—'

'I said that's ENOUGH! Both of you, back down! How does this help us?' Farfallen's voice echoed loudly, and the two slowly separated. 'I'll ask you again, where is this foul worm?'

Farden sighed. 'Carn Breagh in Albion, north of Beinnh. He told me before he disappeared. It seems the bastard has deceived us again.'

'What are you talking about?' Svarta glowered.

'Don't you realise? There is no dark elf well near Kiltyrin and Fidlarig, there never was! Vice has been planning to release his monster at Carn Breagh all along, not anywhere near to where we thought he would be. By sending the army south, he's left the Arka powerless to fight back. It would take four or five days' hard marching before the other Written could reach him.'

'And by then it would be too late,' said Towerdawn. His red eyes glinted in the gloom. The dragon sniffed the cold air. 'Something doesn't feel right.'

'We have to stop him,' Farden reminded them. 'He has taken everything from us. I will not let him get away!'

The two dragons swapped glances and Svarta nodded silently, deep in thought but still scowling as she stared down at the snow. 'It doesn't feel right. Why would he tell you where he was going?' asked Towerdawn.

Farfallen simply hung his head and closed his eyes, searching for the answer. They all knew what it meant. The word *trap* hung unsaid in the air around them, tainting the atmosphere with dread.

'We have no other choice,' muttered Farden.

'It's organised suicide, even with all our dragons. He wants to draw us out,' Svarta asserted quickly.

Towerdawn's crimson face was etched with concern. 'We are not seriously considering this…' His question drifted off.

Farfallen opened his eyes and shook the snow from his spines. 'The mage is right. We have no choice. Vice must be stopped at all costs. We have to end this as quickly as possible, even if it takes our lives.' The Old Dragon let the words sink in before carrying on. 'Towerdawn, assemble all of our forces immediately. We have no time to warn the Arka and I doubt they would believe us anyway, not after what happened with Arkmage Helyard. Dispatch two of our fastest, Havenhigh and another, one to Nelska and one to the rest of the dragons in Kiltyrin. We will need all the help we can get. If you want to see this through, Farden, then you can ride with Brightshow, as her rider is in Albion with the others.'

Farden simply nodded, but Farfallen could see the zeal burning behind his eyes, clamping his jaw tight.

The mage was exhausted. Blood oozed from his hands and trickled along his knuckles. Bruises decorated his face and neck. He must have looked like he had when they first met, after the shipwreck. Farden saw Farfallen's eyes slip to the dragonscale amulet peeking out from under the collar of his tunic, and he wondered how much luck he had left.

'May the gods fly alongside us tonight,' said the Old Dragon.

Within the hour, the dragons were tearing through the snowy skies. Their wings pounded the turbulent air and their tails whistled across the cloud tops. Once they had cleared the snowstorm they soared through the crisp air between the clouds and stars. The bright moon shimmered across their scales, turning everything a different shade of silver, monochrome scales glistening under the night sky.

Farfallen was out in front. Both his and Svarta's eyes were fixed on the horizon, resolute determination frozen on their windswept faces. The Old Dragon felt something stirring in him that he hadn't felt in a long time. Svarta sensed it too, as she let her mind entwine with his, each of them mentally preparing themselves for what lay ahead.

Behind them, thirty dragons wore the same expression, their riders bristling with weapons, ready to face anything that reared its ugly head. Every single one of them knew the stakes, the costs, and what might await them at Carn Breagh.

Farden pulled himself as close to Brightshow as he could. With only his spells to keep him warm, he desperately tried to breathe through the rushing air. The sickening feeling when he looked down refused to abate, so he resigned himself to not looking at all, concentrating on conserving his strength. His eyes were sealed tight. Farden felt every single move of the dragon's body underneath him; every sinuous dip of her wings as she snaked through the skies at breakneck speed. Farden dug his feet deeper into the saddle, trying to remove the ache at the bottom of his spine.

Doubt clouded the mage's mind, coupled with dread at the prospect of facing Vice again. Almost everything he had ever learnt had come from Vice. That made him twice as dangerous as any other foe.

It also appeared that the Undermage was adept at the dark art of shapeshifting. Farden wondered who or what he really was. There was something alien about this Vice, as if he were a different person altogether. It was as if the magick he used was older, more ancient, more like Farfallen's. Farden had never known spells like the ones he had felt at the inn. Who knew what else he had hidden up his robe. Not to mention that the whole thing—Vice's entire plan—seemed too precise, too clockwork. Towerdawn had spoken the truth: nothing felt right about this. But they were bereft of choices: funnelled into a lack of options with the odds stacked against them. They were being drawn out to fight. and fight they would.

Farden struggled to force confidence into his thoughts and warmth into his fingers. After all, he was the finest Written there was. If anyone could take Vice down, it had to be him. Farden repeated that like a mantra.

A heavy sword rattled between his shoulders, a loan from one of the other riders. To replace the vial of ice water he had lost, the Sirens had given him a tiny bottle of a dark red liquid that they called *syngur*. The strange stuff was constantly warm and tasted of sickly spices, with a strange underlying flavour of fish. Farden could still feel the stuff burning his stomach; it was helping the spells keep him warm. He counted the hours until they would arrive above Carn Breagh.

He would do this or die trying.

chapter 19

Let it not be said that Farden is just simply skilled; the man is far and above any mage I have yet to encounter. Despite their downfalls, he is of a powerful family, a pure breed. Whatever the Scribe wrote into his Book awoke a magick beast inside him. I've never seen a Written withstand such draining as he does, nor wield such huge spells with ease. It's a shame he ruins all of it with his anger, his battle-rage if you will: the red mist that has gotten him into trouble and danger many times before. Just look at what happened in Huskar after he killed the chieftain's son in a fist fight, all for some ridiculous wager. If Farden learnt to turn his anger into concentration, he could be greater than any of the Arkmages, and if that's treason you can hang me for it.

Taken from the diary of Durnus Glassren

Dawn was slowly breaking over Albion. Pale shades of red, orange, and yellow smudged the skies in the east as the first hints of the Long Winter sun dared to creep over the horizon. A translucent fog hung in the morning air. Thick snow covered everything. It had moulded the landscape into a white sculpture of itself, a mess of rolling mounds and bumps hidden under a crisp blanket. The trees, heavy with snow, sparkled in the weak morning light, as though they blossomed with clusters of diamonds.

Ancient Carn Breagh squatted silently on its grey-white hill, unassuming and peaceful. The ruined walls glistened with the icicles that hung from the ancient ramparts. Its calm exterior belied the malicious evil deep within the castle.

Far beneath the dripping stone, under the solid rock floors, where not even the rats would go, where the torches struggled to burn through the darkness, Vice pored over a small, dragonscale book.

He gripped the stone wall tightly, letting the magick speak to him, allowing it to echo through the dark corners of his mind. Figures scurried about behind him, preparing for the summoning. Dark soldiers in fire-blackened armour stood in the shadows, only the glint of their spears giving their presence away. Somebody drummed their nails on the stone, chipping away at the Undermage's concentration.

'How long, Vice?' asked a voice.

Vice sighed, closing his eyes in quiet frustration. 'If I was left to my own devices, instead of being bothered incessantly, I might get it done quicker.'

'You're taking too l—'

'Quiet! Keep yourself hidden like I said,' shouted Vice. The person behind him huffed in annoyance, then the sound of their footsteps receded into the shadows. Vice shook his head and assessed the buzz of activity around him with narrowed eyes. *All was going to plan.*

He found himself gazing back into the darkness of the vast well that took up the entire centre of the room. The shadows lurking in the stone-lined pit were impossibly dark, a blackness that sucked at the light. The well seemed bottomless, unfathomably deep. Vice could hear the magick from the summoning manual calling to him again and gently he ran his fingers across the spidery script.

There was a bang, followed by a dull thud somewhere deep beneath them. A shout sounded. 'Lord Vice, we're ready!'

'Good,' he muttered.

He swept from the shadows, holding the book with his thumb lodged in a specific page. With his cloak billowing behind him, Vice strode around the walkway overlooking the great well. His jaw was set proudly as he made his way past the others standing in their positions. Vice looked at each of his men and women with a piercing hazel gaze, watching their pale faces melt into expressions of fear and uncertainty. *Weaklings*, Vice thought scornfully. *All they had to do was stay alive.*

The Undermage made his way to the pulpit that perched on the far edge of the dark pit. From there he could lean over the dark depths and concentrate all the magick into one spot. He could already feel it tingling in the air, leaking from the well.

Vice placed the manual on the stone lectern and let his fingers play over the script again. He tried to empty his mind. With his eyes closed, he could feel the magick shivering and pulsing, the others shuffling and waiting, the heightened sense of everything around him. Everything rested on this moment. He had spent too long in hiding, too long pandering to these mortals to fail now. Vice took a deep breath.

There was a loud creak of a thick oak door and a yell sounded from the back of the hall, breaking the anxious silence.

'Undermage!'

All eyes turned to the soldier standing in the torchlight of the doorway.

'They're here!'

The tiniest of smiles might have curled at the corner of Vice's lips then, but it was too dark to see. He simply nodded and looked around the circular room. 'Then let's give them a welcome they'll never forget,' replied the Undermage, and his soldiers and mages sprang to do his bidding.

Vice spread his hands across the manual and put an index finger to the two keys at the corner of the page, the ones that the old Arfell scholars had pointed out to him. A shudder of excitement ran through him. Looking into the impenetrable darkness of the well beneath him, he whispered the pivotal words.

‘Hear me,’ he hissed, and there was a faint rumble in the depths.

High in the atmosphere, where the air grew thin, a swarm of dragons circled above a snowy countryside that was spread below them like a map. The sun crouched on the horizon, a pale-yellow disk that peered into the morning mists. The snow sparkled even from that height.

Farden rubbed his cold hands together furiously as he battled the twists and turns of Brightshow’s body with his tired legs. He looked down through the hazy fog and scattered clouds at the tiny ruin below him and cursed to himself, suddenly regretting their decision to come. A dark feeling unfurled inside him.

He could hear Farfallen yelling to his captains: Towerdawn, Glassthorn, and a huge dragon named Clearhallow who had two riders, one of which looked like Eyrum, armoured up and wielding a gigantic hammer-headed axe in one hand.

Farfallen looked around at his dragons, and Farden swore he could see him smiling. The golden dragon shone in the dawn light, battling the air with powerful strokes of his wings so that he could hover in one place. He drew a deep breath and spoke.

‘I will not waste our precious time with heavy-handed words and long speeches! I do not have to remind any of you how dangerous this will be, nor of how high the cost might be. All I can ask of you is that you remember that we are the first and the last line of defence against this beast. Not since the time of the elves and the gods have we faced such a monstrous foe, such “mouths of darkness.” I see plenty of mouths here today: hungry mouths filled with teeth and fire, strong claws and wings, brave hearts and arms holding sharp weapons. Let us show this ancient beast that things have changed in Emaneska. That we are in charge now!’

A mighty roar followed the Old Dragon's words. There was a metallic screech as scores of weapons were unsheathed and waved in the air.

Farden grabbed his own sword and yanked it free. The razor-sharp blade flashed in the sun's rays as he yelled along with the others. Every dragon unhinged their jaws and snarled. Fountains of flame billowed from their mouths. It was exhilarating.

With another roar, Farfallen folded his wings back and pointed his spiny head to the ground. His body hovered in mid-air for a split second before he dropped, plummeting towards the earth at a frightening speed.

'Hold on, Farden!' Brightshow yelled, and in one dreadful moment, every single dragon tucked their wings to their sides and plunged into the mists like diving falcons.

Farden held onto the saddle for dear life. The air screamed past his ears like a banshee. His heart pounded frantically in his throat. His insides felt like they were trying to escape from his body. The mage pressed himself against Brightshow's back and tried desperately to close his eyes, but something inside him couldn't tear itself away from the terrifying ride, and the sight of the snow rushing up to greet them.

The whole room pulsated and shook with energy. The well was making a deep thrumming sound, as if hammers were striking drums in the depths, getting faster and louder, gathering momentum for their final horrifying crescendo. Vice shook with the strain of the spell, but kept his eyes fixed on the darkness below, feeling the magick swell up from his fingers to his lips as they moved, speaking silent, unfamiliar words.

Something was waking up at the roots of the world.

The Undermage was reaching the end of the page, the final hurdle and most dangerous part of the spell. The booming sounds were getting louder. His head throbbed.

The whole of Carn Breagh vibrated under the pressure. The walls groaned, bending awkwardly as if they were being squeezed by giant hands. Vice's breath came in laboured gasps. The well pulled at him, the darkness trying to drag him over the edge of the pulpit, down into the shadows. He braced himself against the stone with his spare hand. He could hear the final few words of the spell shouting inside his skull, straining to be heard over the deep pounding noise from the well.

A wind gusted around the room, blowing out the torches and plunging everything into darkness. Vice's heart beat so fast that it became a whirring drone in his chest, buzzing like the wings of a hummingbird.

There was a surge in power, followed by a yell as a soldier across the room fell to the floor clutching his throat. A flash of unearthly light came from inside the well as he tumbled into the depths.

Vice watched the body spinning down into the darkness. The Undermage struggled to keep the spell intact while his knees buckled underneath him. Pain wracked his whole body. There was another flash of light, and Vice reached the last word on the page.

A crack of thunder rang out from underground as the tremendous noise reached its peak. Every single person in the hall convulsed under the final wave of magick.

There came a dread-filled moment of silence. Nothing moved. Nobody made a sound. All held their breath, and for an eternity they seemed to wait. Soldiers and mages swapped looks, some concerned, others relieved. Only Vice could feel what was stirring beneath their boots.

Still holding onto the tails of the spell, he slowly backed away from the pulpit. Something was awake now. One last word fell from his burning lips. Then the sky fell in.

Rock erupted from the ceiling as the roof caved inwards with an ear-splitting crash, raining stone and mortar into the room. One man was flattened as he dove for cover, another was knocked senseless and tripped over the edge of the well.

Stone flew in all directions. A vicious wind whipped up a swirling storm of stone-chips and shards. Carn Breagh was being ripped in two. Daylight pierced the shadows as room after room and floor after floor was ripped apart above them and dragged down to feed the hungry well. Snow fell from the hole in great clumps, swallowing the room in a blizzard.

'HOLD!' Vice screamed at the others through the maelstrom. Those that were left grabbed at anything that would stop them from being torn away. Cries of terror were lost in the cacophony of cracking stone. It felt like the entire world was being dragged, piece by piece, into the well. Another boom came from the well, followed by a blood-curdling screech.

Another noise sounded, angrier this time, a gurgling scream. Three gigantic claws reached over the edge of the pit. They ripped the stone apart like rotten wood. Another clawing foot rose up from the well and smashed against the far wall, turning two soldiers to bloody smears on the floor. A stench filled the room that made Vice gag, a smell of sulphur and death, of decomposing flesh. The wind died as abruptly as it had risen.

Out of the darkness below, a head rose; a massive, ugly head, too horrifying to comprehend. Embedded in its dragon-like face were scores of red eyes that glowed like burning coals. They blinked as one. The beast rattled its horns as a clump of snow fell on its head. It turned to Vice. Hot breath billowed from its nostrils, filling the room with steam. The Undermage stood, shaking, to return its gaze, wondering which eye to look at.

Dark whispers hissed in his head—voices he hadn't heard for thousands of years. After a moment of holding that terrible gaze, Vice looked up through the hole in the castle to the wintry skies, to the dark shapes circling above, then back to the monster.

The creature made its whining cry again as it lifted itself further out of the steaming well. Another head rose, and another, and another, and yet another, one by one, until almost twenty heads had reared up from the shadows, fighting for space with snarls and screeches.

Vice couldn't tear his eyes away. He pressed himself flatter against the wall to avoid being crushed by the beast, watching, awestruck, as the monstrous thing rose even higher.

Seconds before Farden thought they would crash into the ruins, Brightshow flared her wings and darted back into the sky. The lurching change in direction made bile jump into the mage's throat, but he forced himself to swallow hard and concentrated on holding on.

He opened his mouth to speak but a crash from behind stopped him. They whirled around just in time to see the castle ripped in two, erupting in a fountain of broken stone. The other dragons roared, dodging the flying chunks with rolls and dives. One unlucky rider was caught by a shard of rock and thrown like a rag doll from his saddle. His dragon, a spiny yellowy-orange beast, let out a terrible cry and went limp in the air. She crashed to the ground in a shower of snow.

'We're too late!' Farfallen yelled, cursing. They barely had time to think before another huge bang rang out. Something was moving around in the gaping hole where the castle used to be. Something older than all of the dragons combined.

'Look!' Brightshow shouted and everyone turned to watch as the monster ripped its way out of the castle.

'IT'S A HYDRA!' roared Farfallen, and with fearful cries and trumpets, every dragon frantically backed away from Carn Breagh. Farden stared in shock.

The sheer size of the thing was terrifying enough. With a thunderous rumble, it pulled the last of its heads from the ruin and stood tall on all four monstrous feet, each one thicker than a tower, and rippling with muscle.

The hydra dwarfed the swarm of dragons as it stretched upwards to eclipse the castle. It was easily hundreds of feet tall. A score of heads sprouted from the monster's wide shoulders, their entangled necks squirming like a nest of colossal snakes. Each fearsome head was larger than even the biggest dragon. Blinking red eyes and teeth fought for space amongst bony ridges and bristling crown-like crests of dark blue spines.

In the weak morning sun, the hydra's grey flesh seemed to pulsate. Its breath steamed in great clouds like an angry volcano. Farden could smell the thing already, a nauseating stench of rotting meat that permeated the air and soiled the snow.

An ear-splitting roar erupted from every one of its mouths, creating an eerie, discordant minor harmony that chilled everybody to the bone.

Brightshow turned her head towards Farden, and they swapped fearful glances. A cold sweat had formed on his brow. He had never seen anything like it: not in his dreams, not in his darkest nightmares, not on the wall paintings in Hjaussfen, not even in the wildest parts of his imagination. The thing screeched again, and Farden found himself staring into its fang-lined mouths. All thoughts of Vice and revenge had disappeared, replaced by numbing dread.

Another part of the old fort caved in under the weight of the hydra. Stones were crushed to sand under its four gigantic feet. Its thick forked tail swished back and forth restlessly. Its myriad red eyes blinked as one.

Farfallen swooped close and barrel-rolled overhead. Farden heard a deep voice in his head, as clearly as if it whispered in his ear.

Go after Vice. We can handle the hydra for now.

Farden looked at the Old Dragon and met his gold-flecked eyes.

Cut the head from the snake and the body dies, said the voice. Grimly, Farden nodded, and the dragon snarled, flashing a dangerous toothy grin back at him.

Farfallen climbed high into the sky, high above the hydra, and let loose a long, trumpeting noise like a battle-horn. The others took up the cry, following him into the air. Below them, the hydra snarled and gnashed its countless teeth together, making a sound like snapping trees.

Farden thwacked his dragon's back to get her attention above the noise. 'Brightshow! Take me down to the castle, I have to stop Vice!' he shouted above the roar.

'Are you sure?' she yelled.

A surge of energy, maybe fuelled by confidence, maybe fear, he didn't know, coursed through him. Perhaps it was imagining what terrors this creature could unleash upon Emaneska, mixed with an overwhelming desire to see Vice's head on a spike that drove it.
'More than ever. Now let's go!'

Brightshow lurched and flapped her wings. 'Then hold on!' she cried.

Farden was growing tired of hearing those words. He tensed his body for the inevitable stomach-churning drop. She plummeted and rolled, making the snow the sky, then back again. Farden fought a wave of nausea, trying to keep his eyes on the gargantuan hydra that was getting uncomfortably close. There were six dragons behind them, wings tucked in and snouts pointed, following him and Brightshow down to the castle. She swerved again and Farden experienced a blinding moment of fear as one leg slipped from a stirrup. His fingers were frozen to the saddle and he found himself praying, to anyone who might be listening, that he be allowed to reach the ground in one piece.

Above them, dark shapes were gathering, roaring, snarling; a riot of colours with claws outstretched and jaws wide. The hydra made its minor-chord wail again as it rose up to meet its attackers.

The dragons and the monster clashed, and chaos filled the cold air. One yellow dragon got too close and was torn in two in a shower of blood and ochre viscera. Another's wing was ripped clean from its side. Farfallen dipped and swooped through the nest of snake-like heads, blasting fire in every direction while Svarta leaned far out of her saddle, thrashing with her vicious longsword.

Towerdawn came up from underneath, flying upside down, and ripped chunks of grey flesh from the hydra's underbelly with his front claws. One head snapped at him, missing his tail by inches. Fire filled the morning sky.

Go! a voice said again.

Farden shouted to Brightshow. 'We don't have much time!'

'I know, I know!' she snarled, rolling left to dodge another snapping head. A blue dragon behind them screeched as the hydra clamped onto its back and yanked it from the air. Sapphire blood splashed the snow as the beast disappeared behind rows of sharp teeth.

With a desperate flap of Brightshow's wings, they found themselves in the clear: behind the monster with only its tail to fear. Brightshow crashed to the snowy ground and gulped air. Farden could feel her huge heart thrumming inside her chest, impossibly fast, pounding with fear. Her yellow eyes were wide with panic. 'Go, while you still can!' she gasped.

'Just keep clear of that thing!' Farden leapt from her side and drew his sword before he hit the ground. The snow crunched under his boots as he landed and he remembered the first time he had seen Carn Breagh, all those weeks ago.

Beside him, dragons skidded into the snow while others hovered to let their riders jump to the ground. A huge hand grabbed the mage's shoulder and he whirled around to find Eyrum standing behind him. His one good eye stared at Farden intently. Even in the excitement of battle, his tone was low and measured.

'Have you still got the scale I gave you?' asked the big Siren. He held his ridiculously large axe in one hand, hefting it as easily as a toy. The sharp blade glinted in the pale light. Farden nodded, patting his chest, and the feeling of the small trinket against his skin comforted him for a moment. A smile hovered on Eyrum's scarred lips.

'Then let us finish this, you and I.'

Farden opened his mouth to speak but was silenced as a vast black shadow passed over them. Somebody nearby shouted a warning, which came out more like a blood-curdling scream, and they all ran for cover. Unfortunately, one soldier was too slow, and a tail as thick and long as a row of buildings flattened him under a cloud of snow.

'Everyone inside! Now!' ordered Farden, and the rest of them sprinted into the shadows of the castle wall, where a small metal door was sunk into the ice-covered stone. The dragons leapt into the sky, retreating. The Sirens took cover, crouching behind blocks of stone, weapons shaking and wide eyes fixed on the monster towering above them. Farden didn't blame them. His own fear chilled him. He would have been mad to have been fearless.

Doggedly, the mage focused his mind and pressed his hand against the cold door. Closing his eyes, he concentrated, blocking out the screams around him. He could hear the swish of wings and the rumbling cacophony of the hydra; blasts of fire and the sounds of things dying. Farden felt the door creak and redoubled his efforts. He strained as he pulled at the door.

'We don't have time for this,' Eyrum grunted impatiently in his ear.

'Just give me a moment.'

'You and your magick,' muttered the Siren.

'I said—' there was a clang, and Farden stepped back to watch the rusty hinges melt away. 'Give me a moment.'

Eyrum raised one eyebrow. 'Hmm, we should stop wasting time. Sirens! With me!' He shouldered his axe and strode into the darkness with the others at his back. There were no torches to light their way. Eyrum turned to the mage. 'A little illumination?'

'Me and my magick,' Farden mumbled, making a fist. White light shivered around his fingers, bathing the corridor in a moon-like light. There was a burning smell in the air, mixed with rot and ancient damp, a smell that clung stubbornly to the backs of the men's throats and made them cough.

'Quietly,' Farden hissed, as they crept into the ruined castle.

They took every stair they could find, anything that would lead them deeper into the ruins. The sounds of battle raged above them: deafening bangs and tremors that shook the walls whenever the hydra moved.

In his head, Farden cursed himself over and over, berating his ignorance. He should have realised the first time he came to this dank castle. Realised that there was something hiding in the darkness. *How had he been so blind*? He tensed his jaw, consoling his guilt with the fact that Vice was somewhere below them and hopefully weakened by the summoning. Farden would make him pay dearly for what he had taken from him.

After what seemed like an age, they came to where the corridors split and the mage looked left and right, wracking his brains to remember the way he had gone before. A tense moment later, he decided to go left, and soon found the room he was looking for.

The mouldy tapestry was still on the dusty floor, seemingly where he had left it, and the narrow spiral staircase led a path into the darkness below.

'This way,' Farden whispered. The others followed silently. He wiped sweat from his forehead and dried his palms on his tunic. The air was becoming hot and clammy. He could feel something different in the magick that thrummed through the castle, though what it was he couldn't decide.

They trudged onwards. Farden momentarily doused his light spell and tried to regain some strength. The others strode past him and further down into the darkness. He felt a hand on his shoulder again.

'What is it?' asked Eyrum. Farden reignited his spell, throwing strange shadows across the Siren's face.

Farden shook his head. He ran his fingertips across the old walls. 'Something is here,' he murmured.

'We know that already.'

'No, something else. Something with magick like… I don't know,' Farden was confused. 'Let's just keep going.'

'Mage!' Someone hissed at them, and they looked up. A Siren with orange scales toting a huge broadsword pointed with her thumb. There was a wide door set deep in the stone.

'That's the one,' Farden nodded, and they all spread out, readying their weapons. He stood in front of the door and let his magick explore the wood. Then he noticed that the massive bolt he had encountered before had been broken open. It was nowhere to be seen. 'It's not locked,' he said.

Eyrum raised an eyebrow in a questioning look. 'Should it be?'

Farden didn't answer. Instead he stood back and held his sword in one hand, letting a blue spark dance on his other.

'Open it,' he said. The Sirens moved towards the door and seized the thick iron handles that had half-rusted away with age.

Farden let his breath slow, feeling his heart stop its incessant nervous drumming and start to steady itself in readiness. His grey-green eyes closed slowly as the magick pulsed along his shoulders. The spark in his palm started to grow. The Sirens watched him, waiting for his word.

All it took was a single nod.

With a squeal of hinges and ancient oak, the door swung open with a puff of steam and the glare of bright, snowy daylight. A sulphurous stench filled their noses. Farden did not care. He charged inside, not even waiting for the others. All he wanted was Vice.

There was no sign of him. Nor anyone for that matter. Nobody alive, at least.

Farden held his sword high and looked around. Mouldy pillars held up a roof that was now rent in two, crumbling with snow and dust. Light poured down on a huge pit in the centre of the room that steamed like a geyser. Dead men littered the floor. Some were twisted in grotesque shapes with their eyes staring blankly into the shadows, while others lay smashed under rubble, lying in pools of blood with their limbs crushed, unrecognisable. Crimson smears painted the flagstones. The room vibrated with the fighting above.

Farden looked around. Trying to ignore the horrible shapes covering the floor, he kept his eyes on the shadows. *Nothing*. He clenched his fist, extinguishing the spell. Farden prayed Vice had not left.

Behind him, the Sirens cautiously spread out and waited. Eyrum leaned close to Farden to whisper. 'Where is he?'

As soon as the words escaped his lips, twenty soldiers in fire-blackened armour sprang from their hiding places in the shadows. They rushed at the small group, their feet stomping through the carnage left by the hydra. For a moment it looked like the odds were stacked high against them, but the attackers hadn't banked on Eyrum being there.

Without a single word or battle cry, the huge Siren calmly twirled his axe in a figure-of-eight, cleaving the first man in half without breaking momentum. The next received a blow to the head and tumbled backwards into his comrades, flailing his arms and screaming through what was left of his face. Blood filled the air.

Farden was quickly by Eyrum's side, trying to stay clear of the windmilling axe and slashing at anything that escaped it. He grabbed one man by the throat and threw him to the floor, digging his sword deep into the soft space beneath his chin. Blade hit bone with a metallic scrape. Lightning flickered in Farden's hand and another soldier flew backwards in a flash of blue and white. The other Sirens stabbed and hacked furiously, trying to even the numbers before it was too late.

The soldiers kept coming, pouring out of hidden doors and shadows like rodents on a sinking ship. Two of the Sirens were already gone, trampled underneath the chaos. Farden slipped on something wet. Farfallen's voice whispered inside his head.

We're running out of time.

The mage knocked his vambraces together and the ground rippled with a shockwave, pushing everyone nearby to the floor. Farden jumped forwards and swung his longsword in wild arcs, trying to clear a path. Then, out of the corner of his eye, he spied a tall figure standing back from the fighting, arms crossed and defiant, a smirk plastered on his smug face, hazel eyes staring implacably at the carnage. Farden snarled, and that familiar rage started to burn in his chest once again.

High above the ruins of Carn Breagh, Farfallen was watching his dragons fall left and right and by the dozen. The snow was an ugly mess of multicoloured blood, trampled and muddy under the clawing feet of the hydra. Bodies covered the ruins, both dragons and riders:

crushed, torn and barely identifiable. Some of the riders still moved, desperately hauling their broken bodies through rock and snow to get away from the monstrous thing.

As he watched, another dragon swooped down and rained bright orange fire on the hydra. Flames engulfed one of the heads and the monster wailed in pain. Before the dragon could escape, another head snatched it from the air, slicing the beast in two. The remaining dragons, no more than half their original number, retreated for a moment and hovered around the Old Dragon.

'We can't go on like this, Farfallen!' shouted Svarta. 'We aren't even hurting it!'

The Old Dragon's golden eyes narrowed. She was right. Most of the heads had been scorched or wounded but they hadn't even slowed it down. The red glowing eyes still watched its attackers with a cold, hungry gaze. Massive claws scratched at the rubble. The hydra swayed in a hypnotising way, waiting for more blood.

Farfallen knew that Farden was close, he could feel it. They had to buy him more time. He turned to face his dragons. Every one of them looked exhausted, beaten, and scared. Half of them were wounded, the other half were covered in grey-blue blood, gasping the thin air. They all had the same look in their eyes, one of fear and terror, and Farfallen was sure he looked no different. The Old Dragon sighed. There was no other choice.

'We will attack one head at a time! We will not rest until they all lie smoking in the ruins, now follow me!' Without missing a beat, he dipped a wing and spiralled downwards.

Farfallen took a deep breath as the air rushed past him. He chose his target. Jaws snapped at him but he was too fast, ducking between the necks with a speed and grace that belied his size and age.

Searing flame erupted from his jaws, bathing one of the larger heads in a river of fire. Farfallen flapped with all his strength and with two wingstrokes he was clear of the monster.

The dragons behind him roared together as they followed their leader in a line. Mouths full of flame, they enveloped the head in a white-hot firestorm that made the air crackle. A few of them tore at the neck with their teeth, claws and barbed tails as they passed, hacking away chunks of flesh.

With a bubbling wail, the head buckled and began to collapse. The eyes blinked frantically. Bluish blood poured from between its fangs. Like a falling tree, the head swayed and finally toppled with agonising slowness. Skin tore apart in a fountain of blood, and the dead head hung at a strange angle, dangling against the hydra's spiny shoulders.

Farfallen grinned and led the others in a victorious roar. He let the air cool him as he circled his remaining dragons. Towerdawn joined him. His rider jabbed the air with a sword and laughed.

'It worked!' he shouted. The Old Dragon nodded and shook his horns. He smiled with grim satisfaction. *Only nineteen more to go*, he thought. But the smile quickly died when he saw was happening below them.

The dangling head had begun to quiver violently. Something moved beneath the ripped skin. The dead eyes glowed, dimly at first, then brighter. They pulsated with a red light as they were stoked into life once more. The jaws twitched. There was a sickening crunching sound as spines started to appear at the base of the broken neck. Another head had started to peel from the skin and grow upwards. As the wounded head began to heal and stitch itself back together, more eyes emerged and blinked, popping up between thick wet spines. Dark liquid dripped from grinning jaws and teeth pushed through black gums.

The smile faded from Farfallen's golden face, replaced by bleak anxiety. The two heads rose up until they stood as tall as the others, as good as new and just as dangerous. The hydra's face seemed to grin mockingly.

This is madness. Svarta spoke in his head. The Old Dragon scanned the horizon for any sign of reinforcements.

'I know,' he simply said, thinking of Farden. *We're running out of time.*

❦

Vice smiled contemptuously. Farden took another step and emerged into the shaft of sunlight that poured down from above. If he had taken his eyes off the Undermage, he would have seen the hydra towering above them, but he kept his glowering gaze fixed on Vice, as if he could burn a hole in his forehead. Farden held his dirty blade out in front of him.

'You never learn do you? You never stop to think,' said Vice. His tone was almost cordial.

Farden scowled deeper. 'I don't need to think about killing you, it's the obvious choice.'

Vice laughed. 'Hah! As if you've ever had a choice. You've been so wonderfully blind to everything since the start. How else do you think I've come so far and achieved so much?'

He unfolded his arms and stalked sideways, away from the well. Farden moved only his sword, keeping it at arm's length, aimed directly at his opponent's neck. The fighting still raged behind them.

'It all ends with you, Vice,' said Farden.

'Does it?' His eyes flashed, and the castle shook as the hydra moved.

Something dark and disturbing stirred in Farden's mind, something he had not dared to conceive until now. Dread loomed from the shadows.

'We're not about to stop now—' Vice's lip curled with scorn.

'Enough talk!' Farden stabbed at him, but the Undermage was fast. A flash of light hit the sword and the blade bounced away with a loud ping. Farden slashed again, downwards, and again Vice parried the blow with his spell.

Farden kept at it, swinging his blade in all directions in a steel blur. He lunged and caught the sleeve of Vice's robe. The sword-tip snagged the cloth, and the Undermage seized his chance. He slammed a fist against Farden's wrist and sent the sword spinning out of his grasp, clattering on the stones. A hand pressed against the mage's forearm and there came a burst of green light. Farden flew sideways as if he had been hit by a hammer, crashing against the wall that guarded the edge of the dark well.

'Who are you, Farden? Who do you think you are?' Vice laughed, a harsh cackle. The mage breathed hard. The sword was no more than an arm's length away, but as he went to move, Vice shocked him with a bolt of lightning and Farden curled up into a ball, squeezing his eyes shut. Ribbons of blue light danced across his body. He felt like his insides were burning, like his bones were about to snap under the pressure of the spell. He could smell his skin cooking.

'I asked you who you were, *mage*? We always thought you would end up like your uncle and run naked through the city gates, but I doubt if we'll ever find out. It seems, Farden, that you've come to the end of your usefulness. And now it's up to me to finish the job the others couldn't.'

Vice's words were a low rumble amidst the crackling that blocked Farden's ears, but he still heard every one of them. Blood thudded noisily against the inside of his skull.

'Are you listening to me?' More sparks fluttered around the Undermage's fingers. He reached for the mage, hauled him upright and pressed him roughly against the stone. His eyes burnt with savage anger. 'Who do you think you are, to stand in my way?'

Farden feebly lifted a hand to push him away, but his skin felt like it was being stabbed with needles.

Go.

Vice cocked his head to one side, like a vulture, and shook Farden. He brought his mocking face close and shouted. Spit flew from his lips. 'Hmm? Answer me!'

'I…' Farden began, but he didn't finish his sentence. With all the speed and strength he could muster, he rammed his forehead into the bridge of the Undermage's nose with a grunt. At the same time, his fingers curled into a fist which he brought up under Vice's chin.

With a pained grimace, Vice stumbled backwards and threw a hand out to steady himself. Farden kicked out hard and caught him in the chest. The Undermage sprawled on the flagstones and spat a drop of blood into the dust with a murderous glare.

A shout rang out from behind them. 'Farden! The hydra!' Farden spun around to see Eyrum surrounded, with only one Siren still standing by his side. He swung his blood-soaked axe at anything that came within reach. Soldiers hemmed them in on all sides, circling cautiously. At least a dozen of their dead friends lay strewn on the floor, many of them missing portions of their bodies. The others were not so keen to get in the way of the big Siren's axe.

Something moved in Farden's peripheral vision and he turned to meet Vice's fist colliding with his face. Sparks exploded behind the mage's eyes. He pushed the traitor backwards with a flailing arm and swung another punch of his own. It landed hard on Vice's chest, winding him.

Farden wiped crimson from his lip and shook his head. His vision was still blurred. He blinked and tried to move slowly to the left, to where he had noticed the summoning manual sitting on a pedestal.

Vice laughed again, sadistically. His narrow eyes mocked Farden's every move. 'You still have no idea. It's dangling right in front of you and you can't even see it. Typical Farden.'

'You don't know me as well as you think you do, Vice.'

'Hah! Who taught you? Who arranged for you to go the Schools, to the Ritual? I did. All of it. *I* was the one who sent you to live the life of a Written. It's just a pity you didn't turn out as I'd hoped,' he scowled, his eyes boring a hole into Farden's.

Farden scoffed, sidling ever so slightly towards the back of the room. 'As one of your loyal servants, like Ridda?'

'Still defending your precious Arka, I see.'

'They're your people as much as they are mine, Vice, you traitor!'

Vice shook his head, sneering 'I watched the Arka crawl from their filthy beginnings! I was there when the first stone of Krauslung was carved from the mountains and I will be there when it falls. I have watched you people grow for a thousand years and I've seen what you've become. Bureaucratic fools, pissing their gold away with the whores and the drunks in the street, meddling in magick they'll never understand. Fools, Farden. Fools that need removing from these lands. And I shall be the one to do it.'

Farden shook his head. 'And the Sirens?' he muttered.

Vice shrugged. 'Two dragons with one stone.'

Farden glared, conveying as much hate as possible in one look. He thought of all the evenings he had spent with the Undermage, sipping wine, swapping stories, discussing the world and its matters. He thought of every lesson Vice had ever taught him, how many things they had confided in the other. *All this time*, he said to himself. The anger and sorrow felt like lead in his chest.

'It must have been exhausting to play dumb all these years, faking all those smiles and kind words,' said the mage. 'I think you've enjoyed every moment of this. Relished every bit of your despicable plan.'

Vice flashed white teeth as he rubbed his hands together, sending a yellow spark floating upwards towards the broken ceiling. 'Immensely.'

Farden kept inching sideways, making sure to hold Vice's gaze for as long as possible. He didn't trust his eyes to look at the manual and betray him.

Orange fire started to curl between the Undermage's fingers. Farden raised his hands, slowly, ready to fend off the spell. He took a deep gulp of air and held it. He could feel magick pulsating along his arms, but he pushed it to his legs and feet and tried to remember everything he had seen in Hjaussfen, everything he had learnt that night, sitting beside the fireplace in the Old Dragon's room, listening long into the morning to the quiet one-eyed Siren called Eyrum.

Go!

Vice flicked his hands outwards and the blistering fireball flew straight at the mage. Farden exhaled, and with one step to the side he made the room blur like a ruined oil painting, pastel shades of grey and white mixing together.

He watched the crackling orb of flame roll through the air, lazily making its way towards him. The crystalline flames blossomed and whirled, and for a fleeting moment he considered reaching out to touch them, to see if they would snap in his hands. But he was moving too fast. Farden slid to the side as though the earth had tripped beneath his boots.

The fireball burst against the wall in an angry flash. Farden was already several yards away. Without wasting a moment, he dove for the pedestal and the manual.

'NO!' Vice yelled, leaping to catch him. Farden skidded to a halt and grabbed the book, letting the magick flow back into his hands and erupt in white-hot flame from his fingers. There was a distant thud from somewhere deep in the well and the room started to shake around them.

The yellow pages curled and crumbled as the fire ate into them. The room shook even more. Farden lifted the manual up and let the flames consume his entire forearm until the manual was a smouldering mess.

It took Vice the same amount of time to reach him and land a blow to his ribs, right where the arrow had hit him. Uncurbed pain knocked Farden to the floor. Something or someone was standing behind him, but as he turned, a heavy object collided with his skull. The world went black.

Farfallen took another deep breath and blinked the smoke from his amber-flecked eyes. A pitiful number of dragons were left now. The sounds of their screaming below made his beating heart sink heavily in his chest. He felt Svarta putting her cold hand on his scales, sending her thoughts into his head.

'We have to fall back. The mage has failed,' she said aloud.

The Old Dragon shook his head stubbornly. 'I can still feel him, somewhere in there.'

'Farfallen,' she said, and he could no longer ignore that she was right. He looked down at the hydra below them, still snarling and biting at his dragons. They fought on bravely. Riders still swung their swords as their mounts ducked and wheeled under and over the squirming heads to breathe fire on the monster's back and legs.

Farfallen could feel their exhaustion. He watched with sad eyes as yet another of his dragons was ripped to pieces by two ravenous heads. One held the screaming beast by its tail while the other tore at its head. Sulphurous breath steamed in clouds through spear-like teeth. Emerald blood ran in rivers down the hydra's shoulder. Farfallen let a wave of pain pass over him and nodded slowly.

'Then let us get away from this thing. We have done our best. Emaneska will have to fight it another day,' he said. He let out a mighty roar, tinged with disappointment.

Screeching in reply, the dragons retreated, flapping away from the hydra's jaws. Every single eye, both rider's and beast's, was wide with relief. The hydra chased them, hissing, drenched in blood and gore yet still not satiated.

'Keep clear of it!' Towerdawn yelled, as the diminished ranks flapped higher into the clear blue sky. One unlucky dragon lost the tip of its tail as a head snapped its grey fangs, but it managed to escape and join the others.

The dragons could barely summon the strength to beat their wings. They watched Farfallen, waiting for their next orders. As the Old Dragon opened his mouth to speak, a moaning from below interrupted him. They all looked down.

Dust was starting to rise up around the hydra's claws. Its eyes had begun to flicker, pulsating amidst writhing, sweating skin.

'Something's happening!' shouted a nearby rider. Farfallen inwardly prayed that it was not another one of its tricks and that it was not about to sprout wings. The dragons flew higher as smoke began to pour from one of the hydra's mouths. The dust turned to ash and cinders and billowed in great clouds around its legs. A huge boom resonated from somewhere inside Carn Breagh.

Farfallen squinted at the monster. Its skin was starting to darken. Great black blotches erupted all over the creature. The marks seethed and smoked until all of the hydra's flesh smouldered like burning paper. The smell was horrible.

The remaining dragons soared on the rising air to get clear of the beast and save their strength, and from high above they watched the hydra burn, wondering what would happen next.

Another deep boom sounded from within the castle. One of the hydra's legs dissolved into ash, then its tail started to deliquesce into swirling clouds of smoke.

Just before its heads started to topple like fire-gutted towers, crashing and burning against each other, it wailed one last time. With a loud sucking noise of rushing air, the hydra folded in on itself with a rumble. It was like watching a mountain burn up and die from within.

As the thunder reached its crescendo, the hydra exploded in a gigantic cloud of ash. The shockwave turned the snow black and filled the air with dust. Trees were flattened. The rest of Carn Breagh crumbled to the ground.

The dragons rode the blast, and in a moment it was over. They flew in its wake, gliding down towards the ruined castle, swapping exhausted smiles and disbelieving grins.

Farfallen had only one thing on his mind. *Farden.* The little spark had disappeared in his mind shortly before the hydra had collapsed.

'To Krauslung!' he roared.

chapter 20

A long time ago, when elves and daemons still haunted the lands, the oldest of the gods held a secret meeting deep in the deepest woods. Fearful of being heard, they whispered no louder than the softest leaf.
'The daemons are growing bolder by the day,' said one, a tall, glowing goddess.
'They have called on Orion, the oldest of the daemons,' replied a second, one of the earth-gods. 'He roams the shores as we speak, hunting for us.'
In reply, the ageless one nodded, and listened to the cawing of the ravens in the firs. He sighed with a rustling of ropes. 'He will spell our downfall if the elves have their way. We grow weaker,' he said. 'Above and below us, the lands of fire cool and the lands of ice melt with every passing year. We must take action now or be lost forever.' The others hummed and murmured in agreement, but the god of the earth, a great beast of stone and moss, wagged his mistletoe finger. 'We have forgotten the others.' And with that he pointed, through copse and bramble, to a scrawny group of figures huddling around a campfire in the distance. Another god, a scaled man with wings that fell like hammers, shook his head.
'They are the slaves of the elves; they will never amount to anything.'
The tall pale goddess held up a hand. 'They shall have my gifts, and none will stand in their way when we are finished,' she said.
The ageless one knocked his stick against an oak tree. 'It is decided. We will go forth.'

And so the gods decided. They burst forth from their hiding place and fell upon the elves. Orion himself was almost overwhelmed as he lay with his slave mistress, but they fought and fought, for a whole year, until finally the gods pulled the elves and the daemons into the sky to remain there for ever more. Only three escaped that fate: the dark spawn of the daemon Orion, and taking their shapes, they hid amongst the campfires with the slaves, pale kings in drab clothes.
And as the stars began to sparkle and the wolves howled at the ghostly moon they decided to split the barren land in three, to go their separate ways as each saw fit. The red sun rose above the cold and empty land and they left, to the three corners of the world, to carve their own destinies and rule over these new people.

Old fairytale

Something smelled like burning. The smell of scorched flesh under the rags that were the mage's clothes.

Something bound his wrists, rasping at the skin underneath, turning it rough and bloody. His vambraces were cold.

Something in his head ached like a firework had gone off inside his skull, as if his brain was trying to smash its way out.

Something made his skin tingle and burn, itch like ants biting, or cats scratching. It made him think of a cat from a ship he had been on once, perhaps.

Something was deeply wrong.

Fragments of a fight, or maybe a great battle, floated in his memories. Flashes of a great beast towering above a snowy land, orange blood splashing on rocks. *Screams*. It was like waking from a dream he could have sworn was real, a strange familiarity amidst the scattered images. Farden attempted to open his eyes, but the pain was too much. He would rest.

No. It was all too real. Farden saw himself being punched and kicked, watched the world blur all over again, wanted to reach out and grab the tendrils of a crystalline flame that floated inches from his face. His skin burnt under yellow light. A smile sneered from the shadows. Something collided with his head.

He had been there, in that place from his dream, with a daemon towering over him and reptile shapes in the pale blue sky high above. He had fought a man. A tall man with piercing eyes. He had done something, or was in the process of doing… *something*. Farden remembered fire and a book.

Then it came to him. The realisation of being tied to a chair in a cold, empty room struck him like a wet rag around the face. Farden jolted upright, forcing his eyelids to open and his eyes to focus.

Pain wracked him, but blurry shapes and dark objects slowly took shape. There was blood on the floor, smeared as if something had been dragged across it. Farden rubbed his fingers and felt something sticky between them. His head ached.

He looked around, slowly recognising the pillars that lined the walls of the hall. Light was coming from somewhere behind him but it was too painful to turn his head. His arms were tied fast with tight ropes, and so were his legs. They felt dead and heavy as if no blood could get to them.

Farden strained, the rope and chair creaked, but the agony of pulling against the bonds was too much. He slumped back into his seat, feeling utterly exhausted and quite alone. A quiet but annoying noise whined in his ear. At least it let him know he was alive.

Farden waited, though for what he had no clue. It was all he had to do. He closed his eyes and let the rhythm of his breathing take over.

❦

Outside the room, behind the locked door, down the long hallway and up several flights of curling stairs, in the highest part of the fortress,

Vice strode back and forth between the pillars and tall windows. His boots scuffed against the smooth marble.

Anticipation churned inside him as he felt the final pieces of his plan sliding into place. His victory was close at hand now. There was only one problem left to deal with, and he was tied to a chair downstairs in one of the empty dining halls. Vice would take care of him shortly.

Then came the sound of clattering armour and the thump of boots on marble. The Undermage turned. A soldier ran up to him and saluted abruptly. The man seemed agitated. Vice gestured for him to speak.

'Your Mage, they're here, in the city,' he blurted.

Vice allowed himself a shiver of excitement. 'King Bane?'

The soldier nodded eagerly. 'Yes, my Lord. His soldiers are rounding up our men and going about the streets telling everyone to stay inside.'

'Good. Tell them not to resist and to follow their orders. Bane comes in peace; do you understand me? None of the Skölgard are to be harmed in any way. You can escort the king to the great hall at his leisure, and tell him I shall await him there,' ordered the Undermage.

The soldier clicked his heels together with a metallic clunk and hurried back down the hallway.

Vice smiled. It was time to pay someone a brief visit.

Farden was concentrating on staying conscious. He hadn't felt so close to slipping away since the shipwreck, when he lay on the cold table with the healer standing over him. He focused all his energy on breathing, on encouraging the magick to creep back into his body.

The warm glow soon started to comfort his cold, aching bones. There must have been something wrong with his eyes though, because the floor and the walls in front of him were painted with harlequin patterns of different coloured light. Red, green, yellow, and blue; Farden blinked, but the colours didn't go away.

There appeared to be a wide door at the end of the room, atop a small flight of steps. A long hardwood table lay against the wall on the left, surrounded by wooden chairs, some lying awkwardly on the floor, others stacked between the pillars. He squinted at the crest hanging on the wall to his right, a golden pair of scales, equally balanced, emblazoned on a white shield topped with tiny mountain flowers shaped from polished steel.

Farden was in the Arkathedral. He was somehow back in Krauslung, not Albion. He pondered how long he could have been there, tied to a chair in an empty room. His tongue was dry enough and his stomach ached enough for it to have been days. Farden had no way of knowing.

He was startled by a bang and the sound of jangling keys twisting in locks. There was another bang, followed by a slow creak. Two blurry figures strode briskly into the hall, a tall one and another. Farden couldn't make them out. The tall one walked straight towards him, rubbing his hands. He appeared to be smiling. The other disappeared into the shadows.

Farden blinked slowly, like an owl, lifting his head to look at the stranger. The multicoloured light swirled over him and turned his robe into its canvas. It dyed his face strange hues of red and yellow.

Vice came close to Farden and laughed. He seemed to be in a good mood.

'I'll take these,' he said, reaching into Farden's pockets to retrieve the Weight and the daemonstone. It glowed fiercely in his hand and Vice narrowed his eyes at it. 'Aptly named,' he muttered, and slipped it and the Weight into a pocket of his own.

Farden tried to spit at him, but there was nothing in his mouth. He panted instead, feeling his furry tongue rasp against his dry teeth.

'Manners, Farden, we have company,' said the Undermage.

'Wh—' the mage croaked.

'Why? When? What? You still have no idea what's going on, do you? Poor, blind Farden.'

Vice stepped back to admire his prize, helpless, weak, bound tightly to a chair. Farden turned his neck, looking at the huge stained glass window that dominated the wall behind him. It depicted a huge arching portrait of the sun shining over the Port of Rós with a man standing in the centre of it: a proud-looking old mage accepting a ball of light from the white goddess above him. Vice followed his eyes, scowled, and began to pace back and forth.

Farden coughed and spluttered. He eventually managed some hoarse words. 'I killed your hydra, it's over.'

'Hah, you may have killed my hydra, but it is far from over. No. I find that highly unlikely. I might as well tell you that at this very moment, the good King Bane is perusing the newest addition to his realms. After all of the trouble with his lovely daughter, he is most anxious to see order restored to the Arka, especially after all the mess they have made.' Vice sneered. His teeth glowed red in the odd light. 'And Farden, the so-called saviour of the proud Arka, will be charged with treason and sent to the gallows to hang for all to see. It seems that you have gone mad, my good mage, just like your uncle did. It was you who committed the murders at Arfell, it was you who stole the tearbook from the Sirens, and it was you who tried to summon the hydra for yourself. Thank the gods that I was there to stop you in time. You see, Farden, Bane is here to announce the new and only Arkmage, his very loyal subject, the Undermage Vice. I wouldn't be too surprised if Åddren did not survive the next few weeks.' Vice grinned, his complete masterpiece divulged. There was a moment of silence as the pieces finally slotted into position, and Farden was left to stare into space.

It was all for power. Utter, ruthless, and absolute power. 'You're nothing but a common thief,' spat Farden.

'Oh, I am much more than that, dear boy, I am a merchant of chaos. There will be all-out war again, if the King of Skölgard and I have anything to do with it. The fall of the Siren kingdom will take a year or two at most, but we will break them in the end.'

Farden narrowed his eyes, thinking of all the things Vice had taken from him. 'You disgust me, Vice. It should be you hanging from the gallows, not me,' he said.

'Then tell me why it's you that's tied to a chair, bound and beaten, and clueless as usual? It has taken us years to get this far. And if you hadn't been such a disappointment then you wouldn't be in this current situation,' replied Vice, jabbing a finger at the mage.

Farden grinned a weary but insolent smile. 'Then why is it so hard to kill me?'

The Undermage shot him a dark look. 'Because you're a stubborn bastard, and I needed your stupidity. Of course, it's not that things went without any complications. The sorcerer I placed on the *Sarunn* with you was one of my oldest, but he was a moronic fool. He was supposed to wait until you got back from Nelska, once you had delivered the precious tearbook to that Siren Queen, Svarta. He obviously got greedy. And after all this time, to think that Farfallen, that ugly beast, had survived his wounds? That I did not expect. But it was a bonus, as his memories confirmed my suspicions of Carn Breagh. It was all about looking in the right place. Unlike the old golden fool, I can hold onto my memories, long as they are. That's why I had you sent there in the first place. But despite you finding nothing, it all fell into my lap, and my plan unfolded accordingly.'

'What about Helyard?'

'That dreary old fool was doomed from the start. His hatred for the Sirens made him an easy target, and with the power he had it made sense that he was behind it all. You saw for yourself how quick the dragon-riders were to condemn him, and the amount of dignity he displayed on leaving the hall. The old bastard deserved everything he got.'

'You love hearing the sound of your own voice, don't you, Vice?'

The Undermage backhanded him hard and he spat blood on the floor. The blow made his head throb even more. He rolled his eyes and tried to focus again. Vice was still talking.

'What did I say about manners in front of guests? You're about to miss the best part, Farden, patience please. Do you want to know what you are? Why you were so perfect to manipulate?'

Farden shook his head, very aware that a pair of eyes were watching him from the shadows. Vice crossed his arms triumphantly.

'You were an experiment, Farden,' he said. 'A test to see if a Written could withstand the deeper magicks and attain a new state of perfection. I was the one who originally brought the Scribe to the Arka all those years ago, and I had him write a few special things into a few Books here and there, things an ordinary Written couldn't survive. Things that in the end, turned your own uncle mad.' Vice paused to sneer again as Farden glared. 'That's right, you heard me. You were to be another weapon, just like your uncle Tyrfing. But one that didn't fail.

'But you weren't perfect either, oh no, by all definitions you were yet another disaster. A reclusive, self-involved individual, impeccably dupable, with a strong sense of duty, hanging onto every word that dreary vampyre of yours had to say and too stupid to see past your own anger. So you became a tool, Farden: a pawn for me to manoeuvre and exploit as I wished while I waited for another exceptional individual such as yourself to come along. Someone of better upbringing, with ideals and power like mine, somebody who would follow and serve the true power in Emaneska.'

'I guess that true power would be you, then?' Farden scowled, straining uncomfortably against the ropes.

Vice's eyes flashed with a deep, murderous fire that Farden had never seen before. 'You Arka are just lambs for slaughter to me. Meat to be sold and bartered with. I have watched you since the first sun rose above these mountains, when you were over-confident and weak, and I have watched you grow into a spineless nation of magicians and prostitutes. I've spent too long simply watching, and now what is there left to do with the Arka but destroy them? I just happened to save two of the better ones for myself,' he snarled. Vice slowly lowered his head until his eyes were level with his captive's, inches from his face.

Farden stared straight back at him, eyes fiery. 'What are you?' he asked, and the Undermage tapped him on the cheek.

'That's a story for another day, my dear mage, one that you won't be hearing.' He tapped him again, harder. 'You're not curious, Farden? Not at all? Who else I have under my wing besides Ridda, and that idiot, Karga? Could it be Åddren? No, of course not, he's catatonic after the loss of his precious Helyard, too busy soiling his robe with fear and weak indecision.'

Slap.

Farden's cheek stung. He didn't care anymore. Vice had taken everything from him that there was to take. But the Undermage continued.

'Not any of the Sirens, no. Who could get closer to you than anyone? Let me see, maybe the man you buy nevermar from, that good friend of mine? No, closer still, even more than your precious Durnus.' Vice chuckled and stepped back to swing an arm wide. He beckoned to the shadows. 'Come say hello to Farden,' he said.

Footsteps echoed on the stone, and a familiar figure walked from the darkness. A figure his hands had explored every inch of, wearing a smile he had kissed countless times, gazing down at him with eyes he had stared into for hours on end. Eyes that he had emptied himself into, that he had told all his darkest secrets to except one: that he loved her more than anyone or anything he had ever encountered.

Cheska threw him a little wave and smiled at him mockingly. She stood in front of him with her hands on her hips, smiling with her mountain-lake eyes, purple and green in the strange light. Farden was breathless. His heart felt like it was grinding to a halt.

'You died. In the fire,' he managed.

Cheska stalked closer. 'The fire was Vice's idea, but it was necessary to make you believe I was gone.' She shook her head. 'You always were a strange one, Farden, so emotionally complex for a Written. You're so concerned with this heroic facade, so afraid of becoming your uncle, you don't give any thought to who you actually are.' She leaned in to whisper in his ear. 'You're like fire, you only come alive in the dark.'

Farden could smell her, that same scent that she had left on his pillow. He choked back something, not daring himself to speak. She smiled. 'It was fun, for a while,' she said. 'And we got what we needed.'

'If you're curious, Farden, the only thing I needed from you was *you*,' said Vice, in a low, mischievous tone.

Farden looked up, feeling the same darkness he had felt in the bowels of Carn Breagh. Something was deeply wrong. He stared straight into Cheska's face and saw the sick truth hidden there. She stepped slowly back, devoid of all emotion. There was no fondness in her eyes.

Vice walked up behind her and let a pale hand rest on one of her shoulders. He watched Farden with glowing eyes, victorious and arrogant. His other hand curled around her waist and pressed against her stomach.

'A spark of life grows inside Cheska's womb: a child of pure power, born from two Written. There is a reason the offspring of such a union is outlawed, Farden, and that reason is very simple. Your child will be the finest mage Emaneska has ever seen, and my finest weapon yet, bred for one purpose.'

Farden bucked against his restraints, seething with anger, grinding his teeth at the two of them. His face went red with exertion, and his breath came in ragged gasps. The ropes held fast.

'At least you were useful in the end, hmm?' Vice chuckled, then he turned to Cheska. 'We must go upstairs and leave the good mage in peace for a while, to mull over what he's learnt. Your father will be eager to see you,' he said, and she nodded.

Vice examined Farden with his ever-present mocking smile as he rocked back and forth, pulling feebly at the chair. The Undermage put his foot on Farden's thigh and pressed hard against his ribs. He gasped in pain. Vice pressed once more, then relented, stamping his foot back on the floor. His smile didn't falter once.

'I will be back for you. First, I have a princess to return, and a throne to claim,' he said, then turned to leave.

The door slammed behind them. Farden started to convulse with rage, yanking and straining the ropes in all directions. The chair and the knots protested with squeaks and groans but still didn't budge. He was too weak to try magick. All he could do was tug and pull and hope something would give way. His skin was rubbed raw.

Minutes passed and still Farden fought. With each twist and pull he growled and coughed, fighting against the grief and anger and sorrow growing in his chest. He sucked in air, exhausted, sagging in the chair with his head down and spit dangling from his mouth. A tear crawled from his eye and down his dirty cheek. Farden watched it drip onto his shredded tunic and soak into the fabric.

He gave in then, and cried, with uncontrollable sobs and anguished breaths, letting hot tears of frustration burn channels through the dust on his skin.

Farden relentlessly repeated every word, every tortuous moment of the conversation in his head. Every heart-wrenching wave and whisper drenched him with renewed sorrow. He stared into the coloured patterns on the floor and tried to banish his thoughts. Nothing happened. Farden closed his eyes and let the painful darkness envelop him.

❦

'I don't understand why you had to tell him about the child. He's already going to hang, why rub it in?'

'Are you turning soft on me, Cheska? The man has caused us endless trouble, he deserves to suffer. And if I recall, you were the one who wanted to come and show your face, not me, so don't you dare lecture me on rubbing it in.' Vice glowered at her, and she looked away.

Cheska remained quiet as they made their way through the Arkathedral. She watched her feet tread the marble steps and took several long, deep breaths.

They walked up another flight of stairs and emerged into the long hallway leading to the great hall. The council and the king would be there waiting.

Vice rubbed Farden's blood from the back of his hand and straightened his black and green robe. There was no need for haste, he reminded himself, he had all the time in the world. He turned to Cheska as they reached the huge gilded doors.

'Just remember what I told you,' he hissed. The two soldiers standing guard raised their spears and pushed hard on the heavy handles. The doors swung inwards with a low moan.

Vice pasted an affable smile on his face as he walked into the bright sunlight inside the hall. He looked around at the council, noting the mass of Skölgard soldiers that surrounded them all, holding tall halberds and wearing thick armour that was a rusty copper colour.

Arkmage Åddren sat on his throne looking small and agitated. His dark sapphire eyes were hollow. His hair looked thin and unwashed. There was an awkward hush in the room. Vice inwardly laughed.

The King of Skölgard turned around to face the newcomers. He stood in front of the statue of Evernia with his hands on his hips.

Bane was a huge man, maybe seven feet tall and almost as wide. He looked half-man, half-bear, with a hungry smile and dark green eyes that shone in the daylight. His hair was short, slicked down with wax, and his beard was braided into two forks. A scar carved its way down one side of his jaw. A silver necklace of miniature skulls hung around his thick, bristly neck, dangling over an enormous silver and pale green breastplate depicting two wolves fighting. Wrapped around his shoulders was a long fur cloak, the tails of which had dragged muddy streaks across the pure white marble.

When he saw Cheska, King Bane opened his massive arms wide. His numerous bracelets rattled noisily. With two gigantic steps, he closed the gap between them and swept her up into her arms, looking directly at Vice as he did. Vice nodded almost imperceptibly.

'Cheska, my daughter! It is good to have you back in my arms once again!' announced Bane in a booming voice. 'Where is the bastard who dared to endanger the first princess of Skölgard?' he glared, examining each and every one of the council. Nobody moved.

'Have you caught the traitor, Vice?' called Åddren, looking confused. The Arkmage's voice cracked as he raised it to shout. 'Who is it?'

Vice sighed and looked to Åddren with a grave look. 'Your Mage, esteemed council members. The traitor behind all of this was none other than one of our own Written. A mage this council put a lot of faith in. A man we have honoured more than once. He has been in league with the dragons this entire time, and together they sought to destroy this council from within.'

'What of the beast?' came a shout from the council.

Vice held up a hand and nodded. 'That, at least, is good news. I have just returned from Albion where this traitor attempted to summon a hydra. The beast was stopped, luckily by myself.' Vice paused for effect. He heard more than a few sighs of relief. Satisfied, he continued. 'I caught the traitor and brought him back here.'

Åddren sat up, feebly, in his throne. 'Well, tell us, Vice. Who is it?'

The Undermage pointed a long finger at the Arkmage. 'You should know, Åddren, he's the mage you put so much trust in, the mage that you gave your own Weight to, allowing him his escape to Albion before I had a chance to stop him. The traitor is none other than Farden, Captain of the Written.'

A wave of shocked murmurs rustled through the crowd. Bane took a few giant steps towards Åddren. 'You allowed him to escape, Arkmage, after what he did in Nelska? After he almost killed my daughter?' The king was incredulous. *And playing his part well*, Vice thought to himself.

Bane signalled to his men. 'Drag him from the throne!' he shouted, and his soldiers sprang to his bidding.

Panic erupted. The council and the Arka guards were torn, but any that moved immediately found blades in their faces. The Skölgard soldiers had the great hall surrounded.

Åddren leapt up from his throne and tried to call for order, but before he could utter a word he was grabbed and escorted roughly across the hall to stand in front of Bane. Shouts echoed around the hall. Vice felt the Arkmage's magick flare, but then suppress itself.

'Leave him alone!'

'Arrest the traitor!' they cried.

'Quiet!' yelled the king. He looked the frail-looking old man up and down, curling his lip in scorn. 'You are not fit to rule these people.' Bane waved a hand dismissively. 'Take him to the cells,' he ordered, and his soldiers dragged Åddren away towards the doors.

Unlike Helyard, the Arkmage didn't protest. He allowed himself to be silently removed from the hall, simply gazing back at Vice with sorrow in his eyes.

The Undermage smiled and glanced to the King of Skölgard. Bane nodded back and turned to the council members and the Arka soldiers standing in small groups behind his men. His voice boomed again.

'You are all witnesses to this! From henceforth, the lands belonging to the Arka will be held as a vassal of the Skölgard Empire! My soldiers will remain here to keep order as your new Arkmage sees fit. Since he has saved this council from betrayal and chaos more than once, I am appointing Lord Vice as the head of this council, to rule alone. Too long have the Arka worked unchecked. It is time to add true balance to your scales. My word is final! Do we all understand?'

There was a resounding chorus of agreement from everyone there, including the Skölgard soldiers. Vice walked towards his new throne, victorious.

As he passed the statue of Evernia, he reached inside his robe and dropped both Weights into each of the scale pans with two loud clangs. Fire trickled from his fingertips, lighting each candle in turn, just as tradition stated. He flashed the goddess a mocking glance and continued walking.

The council began to clap as Vice put his foot on the marble steps. One by one, he marched up them, then turned to take his place on the left throne. He looked over the gathered members of the council and then to Bane, who stared confidently back at him with what might have been a smile.

The crowd was on the verge of cheering when a huge, rending crash sounded from somewhere below the hall. The room vibrated with the impact and the goddess' statue trembled. Dust fell from the marble beams. Vice barked orders at the nearest group of soldiers. 'Go find out what that was, immediately!'

'Yes, your Mage!' they shouted, bowing briefly before running off. After the doors had slammed with a bang, an eerie silence fell upon the great hall, broken only by the tolling of the twin bells below. Vice drummed his fingers on the marble throne, staring at Bane.

❦

Sunlight burnt his skin, making it prickle and sweat in the dry heat. The hot wind made it worse. There was sand between his toes.

Farden sighed; this was not what he needed now. He tried to keep his eyes shut but the fine grains of sand wormed their way beneath his eyelids and scratched at his eyes.

Something pawed at his leg. Farden opened his eyes to find a black cat staring at him. He blinked, partially blinded by the sun, and looked around. Only sand greeted him. There were no mountains, no cliffs, no birds, just endless sand from horizon to horizon, east to west, north to south. The sky was bigger and bluer than it had ever been, and Farden wished he could melt into it and never wake up.

The cat yowled at him and he looked down. He could feel tears drying on his cheek. The wind whipped his naked body. His red and gold vambraces glinted in the sun. He stared into the cat's obsidian eyes, trying to match its impassive gaze. He knew it was waiting for him to speak. Farden shook his head.

'I told you to leave me alone.'

You're not finished yet, said the familiar voice in his head.

'I'm done. I give up. All I have to look forward to is the rope around my neck. I don't care who you are, but I would appreciate it if you left me to enjoy my last few hours.'

So this is it? All the help I've given you and you just give up?

Farden hung his head and the cat hissed at him through its needle-like teeth. 'I don't even know who you are.'

For the third time, I'm just like you. We never ask for this, nor do we ever complain, we just do what we're told. It's what people like you and I do: we fight, and we never ask for anything in return.

'I want to be left alone,' replied Farden.

No, you don't. You want to fight. You want to march upstairs and take a sword to his head and watch the blood drip on the floor, for both of us. The voice was impatient now.

Farden shook his head. The cat crept a little closer. 'It's useless. He's won. I'm a failure just like my uncle.' He slumped down into the hot yellow sand. The blue sky looked so empty.

The voice hesitated for a moment. The cat crept closer and raked its claws down Farden's leg to get his attention. He didn't even flinch. The sand shifted around his shoulders and he closed his eyes, letting the warmth surround him.

They found me naked and screaming. They found me painted in someone else's blood. They found me biting the tips from my fingers. They found me scraping words into my legs with shards of window glass. They found me swearing and cursing and yelling his name until they filled my mouth with rags. They found me clawing at the city walls and wanting to run. Then they gave me a blanket and a gold coin to do with as I saw fit. They sent me out into the wilderness. They didn't kill me, they let me go. I didn't fight, I left. I was lucky. I was not becoming someone different, I was getting to know the person I already was. He had changed me, he had tried to use me, but he failed. He had failed, not I.

The sand crept over Farden's neck and swallowed one of his arms. The cat bit his thigh, drawing blood this time. Why him? Why had all this happened to him? Was it his destiny to be tortured and chased, just because he was some failed idea Vice once had? The hot sand moved up to his ears, blocking out the noise of the wind. But the voice still spoke deep inside his head.

All the help I've given you, and you're just going to give up.

'What help?' Farden felt the sand tugging at his legs. It wanted to eat him alive and he wanted to let it. He didn't care anymore. Vice had taken everything.

Who are you, Farden? Are you his tool?

His foot was enveloped by the warm gritty earth.

Are you his tool, Farden? His weapon? I asked you a question, mage!

The sand sucked him further into the ground. The cat now scratched furiously at the sand, digging for his limbs. He was engulfed up to his chest.

Are you going to let him win?

The sand moved over his skin like a yellow river, like time falling through the waist of an hourglass. It had completely swallowed his chest and arms and begun to creep up his neck. The dragonscale amulet pulled at his throat and he opened his eyes to find the cat's black eyes staring straight at him like two scrying mirrors reflecting his bruised and battered face.

What was he? Farden felt the sand on his chin. There was a reason he had been so useless to Vice, and that reason now burst alight like a candle in the mage's dark and stormy mind.

You are not becoming someone different, echoed the voice in his head.

Instead of doing what Vice wanted, instead of falling into treachery, he had gone out and sought his own life, tried to make a difference in the wild world. Farden thought of all the creatures he had slain, the towns he had saved, even the bandits back in Beinnh he had slaughtered, and decided, yes, he had made a difference, at least somewhere in Emaneska. Vice had failed, not him.

Farden sat up a fraction, and felt the claws of the cat on his chest. The sand fell back slightly. Whatever had been woven into his book made him angry and vengeful, yes, but it also made him powerful. If he could learn to tame it he could make everything right.

With Vice's cards now spread openly on the table, it was his turn to make a decision. It was his turn to play his hand. Farden began to push against the hot sand. He heaved and strained as he yanked his limbs from the ground.

'I am simply getting to know the person I already am,' whispered Farden, the hot wind catching in his throat. The cat danced on its hind legs as he pulled his body free and stood up. He raised his hands to the blue sky and felt something he had never known before.

You're no coward. Keep an eye on the weather, Farden, said the voice, as a single wisp of cloud appeared above him in the endless blue, and the desert began to fade.

❦

Farden snapped back to consciousness. A wave of dizziness hit him, the colours on the floor swirled and shifted, and he took a deep breath to steady his pounding heart and suppress the nausea. A large shadow scudded across the patchwork of colours. A repetitive whooshing sound grew loud in the dark room.

Farden blinked owlishly, wondering why his blood was pounding so loudly in his ears. Before he could make sense of what was happening, an almighty crash came from behind him, followed by a huge gust of air that knocked his chair over. Gold wings towered over him, glittering in the sunlight. Shattered pieces of stained glass crunched under heavy claws.

The dragon raked a razor-sharp talon over the back of the chair and Farden's bonds sprang open with a twang. Ignoring the skin-shredding glass underneath him, he wriggled free.

As soon as the ropes were no more than a tangled, frayed mess on the floor, Farden stood drowsily and started picking bits of glass from his torn clothes. The whistling noise in his head was back. He wiggled a finger in his ear to no avail. Shielding his eyes with a hand, he stared out of the smashed window. It was a clear, crisp day over Krauslung, and the bright sun made the mountains sparkle.

Farden looked up at the Old Dragon, who grinned at him, then he made a hurried movement with his wings, but Farden moved to the door.

'The King of Skölgard has taken over the city, you don't have much time to stop Vice! Come with me!' said Farfallen.

'I have to try. Just keep them off my back,' he replied, hobbling towards the door. Farfallen nodded and crouched to move further into the hall. Behind him, other dragons swooped, circling the fortress. The twin bells were singing over their roars and screeches. Archers were filling the ramparts.

Farden reached the door at the very moment that it flew open under the boots of a dozen men. They stormed into the room waving their swords but Farden dodged to one side, still holding his ribs.

'Farfallen!' he shouted. The Old Dragon closed one golden eye and blew a stream of orange fire at the doorway, sending the men diving for cover. Farden was already up and running.

Ignoring the flames at his heels and the pain in his side, he darted down the corridor and sprinted up several flights of stairs, towards the highest part of the Arkathedral, the great hall.

Farden heard shouts and the banging of weapons behind him but he kept running, skidding on bloody feet down the marble hallway. The Arka soldiers at the door saw him coming and lowered their spears. Farden did not break his pace.

'Out of my way!' he yelled.

'Halt!' they shouted, starting forwards with their spears in front of them. Farden still didn't stop. One of them held up his hand in an authoritative gesture.

'Stop, I say!' he bellowed.

Farden flicked his bedraggled hair out of his face and pushed against the air with both hands as he continued running. The soldiers flew backwards against the wall with a crash of armour. He didn't waste a moment. He ran straight at the gilded doors and kicked them open. Gritting his teeth, Farden strode into the hall and let the doors slam shut behind him. He was breathing heavily. Pain seared him.

The great hall was deathly quiet. Every eye was on Farden, standing there: dishevelled and dusty blood pooling around his bare feet. There were no whispers, no shouts, no clamouring of any kind from the gathered men and women, only silence. Farden looked around, trying to calm himself.

A huge man, who Farden correctly assumed was Bane, the King of Skölgard, stood in front of him. One hand held Cheska and the other was at his belt, resting threateningly on the hilt of his sword. Vice was standing in front of the Twin Thrones, glaring at Farden.

The mage looked at the statue Evernia, at her calm expression, then at the unbalanced scales swinging gently from side to side, two gold disks sitting in each pan. The sunlight was touching the edges of the skylight above her marble head. The sky was as blue as it was in his dreams.

A booming shout broke his reverie.

'Seize him!' yelled Vice.

A group of nearby soldiers ran to the mage and grabbed him roughly by the arms. Weak though he was, Farden still struggled against them. Vice stormed across the hall towards him. Shadows fluttered across the floor and the new Arkmage peered up into the clear sky to see a swarm of dragons circling above like vultures.

'Have you told them what you told me, Vice? Have you told them about who started the fire? About Cheska?' Farden barked. A soldier elbowed him in the ribs, knocking the breath out of him.

Vice marched straight up to Farden and struck him in the face. Indescribably hard. It was a punch without grace or mercy, and it sent the mage sprawling into the hands of the soldiers. Vice hauled him to his feet and shook him, eyes blazing with murderous fire. The council was talking now. Bane moved Cheska behind him and his soldiers inched forwards.

'I've had enough of you,' snarled Vice.

'Tell the council what you really are, old friend' Farden gasped.

Vice shook with rage. His hazel eyes bored into Farden's, but the mage kept staring straight back at him. 'You're a stubborn bastard, Farden, just like your uncle. I will have you hanged immediately!'

'You'll have to catch me first,' Farden whispered. He grinned through bloody teeth, breaking his gaze for a moment to see a small white cloud drift across the crystal blue sky above Evernia's head. A voice whispered in his head, and suddenly Farden understood. *Keep an eye on the weather.*

With every ounce of magick he had left in his exhausted body, Farden pushed against the floor.

Amidst surprised shouts and yells, Farden flew out of the grasp of the soldiers and soared into the air. He swung his fist as he broke free, focusing all his energy into one crucial blow.

He struck Vice squarely in the jaw like a bolt of lightning. Sparks exploded from the mage's fist as his knuckles met skin and bone. There was a blinding flare of light, and Vice fell to his knees, stunned. Chaos erupted in the great hall as screams filled the air.

Farden landed awkwardly, stumbling on his injured feet, and bolted for the centre of the room. With a metallic scrape, Bane unsheathed his gigantic broadsword and swung it at Farden's neck with a loud grunt. Farden dove into a roll as the blade whined over his head, missing all but a strand of his dark hair.

The king roared and darted after him with a speed unnatural for a man of his stature. Farden could hear the huge man bearing down on him, but he kept running, eyeing the others closing in on him. All he had to do was get to the statue and it could all be over: Vice, Cheska, the Arka, they could all disappear. His chest was about to implode with exhaustion but still his legs pounded the floor, propelling him onwards.

Just as Bane reached out to snatch at Farden's clothes, he flung himself in a mad jump for Åddren's Weight. The king grabbed at nothing but empty air as the mage crashed into the scales with cry of pain.

Farden rolled to the floor in a shower of hot wax and spitting candles. He snatched at the gold disk as it almost tumbled out of his hands. As soon as his fingers curled around it, Farden bent his whole concentration on it, pouring everything he had left into its golden surface. Like a pouncing wyrm, the magick bit, and began to drag him in. Farden gritted his teeth and roared.

He watched as the world ground to a halt, ignoring the men hanging over him with swords and halberds; ignoring Vice staggering to his feet; ignoring Bane frozen mere inches away, hands outstretched and his face a boiling mass of anger.

Farden looked only at Cheska, staring into her pale blue, expressionless eyes. He wondered what his child would look like, whether it would have his hair, or her eyes, and whether she would miss him in any way whatsoever. He looked into those eyes and found she was not the same person any longer, just a hollow shell of what she had pretended to be for all those years.

There was a rush of air as the world folded in on itself, and Farden was dragged into a white light.

FOR ALL THE THINGS TO COME

As the orange sun peered over the craggy, ice-locked mountains in the east, a pair of grey-green eyes watched the light spill over the rocks and ignite the drifts of snow with a warm yellow glow.

The man stood atop the highest mountain for miles and miles around, braving the icy winds that tugged at him. He closed his eyes and let the cold bite his cheeks. The air was so clear.

Below him, in the places the sun hadn't yet touched, shadows fell amongst the black rocks, turning the snow a deep blue. The man squinted as he peered at the jagged skyline in the distance, where wispy clouds huddled together. He could see smoke rising from the city in the south. Beyond that, the sea sparkled like a blanket full of jewels.

He crouched and pulled his cloak around him, careful not to drop the gold disk that he clutched in his hand. His clothes were torn and his pale face was a mess of bruises and scratches, but he didn't look as though he cared. For the first time in his life he felt true release. Serenity.

Farden stayed there for a while, letting the sun warm him, letting his thoughts wander, then he stood. With a flash of light and a flurry of powdery snow, he was gone.

❦

Later that morning, the mages found that the old vampyre and his servant had disappeared sometime in the night. Their tent was empty but for a few items of clothing.

At midday, hawks arrived carrying messages saying that the Written were to return home. The dragons flapped away northwards, silent and brooding.

Modren watched them as they left, as he stood on the shore on the outskirts of Dunyra harbour. The waves licked his boots. He watched the dark shapes disappear into the sky, one by one. With a sigh, he crumpled the parchment in his fist and threw it into the sea. He left without a sound, heading for the bubbling quickdoor and Krauslung.

❦

A week later, a small boat approached the snowy shores of Nelska with three passengers sitting on its wet benches. The man in the middle of them was working the oars. The gentle grey waves lapped at the soggy boat, splashing against its sides. It creaked and moaned with every move. The wind was cold, but calm. It ruffled their hair and played with their clothes. It looked as though it was about to rain.

Farden paused his rowing and looked behind him. He noticed a welcome party standing on the shingle. The people looked cold and miserable, but the dragons glistened as brightly as always.

Durnus looked uncomfortable, shuffling around in his seat. He was a touch paler than usual.

'What's wrong?' asked Elessi. 'You've been fidgetin' around this whole time.'

'Nothing is wrong, maid. I am merely tired and not fond of the sea,' he said.

'You told me you loved the sea,' Farden said.

'Not in small boats, now leave me alone, woman,' replied the vampyre. Farden nodded.

Elessi wrung her hands and tapped Farden on the back. 'Are the dragons dangerous? I've never seen a dragon.'

'Well, you're about to meet one. They're as docile as big cats. It's their queen you have to watch out for,' he said. He pulled hard on the oars and the little boat skipped across the waves. His ribs twitched with a faint stab of pain, but then it was gone.

After some arduous rowing, they reached the shore. A pair of Siren soldiers dragged the boat up above tideline to where the others were waiting for them. Farden hopped out of the boat and offered his hand to Elessi. She smiled and jumped to the sand with ease. Durnus scrabbled out of the other side and immediately got as far away from the water as he could.

Farden walked to the dragons and smiled at Farfallen. Svarta and Eyrum were on his left, Towerdawn, Havenhigh, and Brightshow stood on his right with their riders. The Old Dragon smiled his toothy smile. When he spoke, Farden felt Elessi jump behind him.

'Well met and good wishes, friends.'

Farden bowed. 'And to you, Farfallen. Thank you for your offer of hospitality, but I'm afraid we won't be staying long. As soon as the weather improves I'm heading to the south.'

'You may stay as long as you want, Farden,' replied the golden dragon. He wore a sombre expression for a moment and lowered his voice. 'Any news from Krauslung?'

Farden shook his head. 'None. That last we heard she was out of the city and in the north, with her father. Vice remains in the Arkathedral for now.'

Towerdawn crunched pebbles as he shifted his weight from foot to foot. 'Dark times are ahead; he has no love for us dragons.'

'You should have killed him when you had the chance,' said Svarta quietly, more like a regret than an accusation. Farden nodded.

'Who have you brought with you?' asked Brightshow, excitement flashing in her yellow-flecked eyes. Farden smiled and moved Elessi out from behind him.

'This is my friend Elessi, from Albion. She's never met a dragon before,' he said.

Farfallen bowed his head in a formal gesture. The others followed suit. 'Well met and good wishes, Elessi of Albion.'

Elessi smiled and looked as if she would start giggling. Farden rolled his eyes.

'And this is my superior, Durnus.'

Durnus stared at Farfallen with his pale blue eyes and bowed low to the ground.

'I've heard a lot about you. Let me tell you what an honour it is to meet you,' said the vampyre, with a polite smile. Svarta looked rather taken aback at the sight of his fangs, but Farfallen lowered his head once again.

'Well met, Durnus. It is a pleasure to have you all in Nelska,' replied the Old Dragon.

Brightshow piped up again. 'In case you forgot, Farden, you left something behind the last time you were here,' she said, looking behind her at her rider, Lakkin. The tall Siren moved forwards, holding a box. Farden looked confused.

Slowly, Lakkin crouched down, tipping the box gently on one side. Out crawled a small black cat and Farden's weathered face creased into a smile.

It was Lazy, the ship's cat. The little creature stretched and looked around for a moment, but when it saw Durnus standing there it made a curious sound and came straight for him, daintily stepping over the wet pebbles. The cat came to a stop a few feet from him and curled her tail around her body.

Then, to everyone's absolute amazement, the cat opened her mouth, and spoke aloud.

'I have a message for the vampyre,' she said calmly. Every eye turned to Durnus, whose mouth hung agape.

Elessi leaned close to Farden and whispered in his ear.

'Is this normal in Nelska?' she asked.

'No.' Farden couldn't take his eyes away from the cat. 'Not in the slightest,' he replied.

to be continued

Farden's story continues in the rest of

The Emaneska Series

BOOK TWO
Pale Kings

BOOK THREE
Dead Stars - Part One

BOOK FOUR
Dead Stars - Part Two

SHORT STORY
No Fairytale

acknowledgements

4th of October, 2010

This was my first book, and mark my words it shall not be the last. It's also been a long time in the writing, and thanks to the following people, I actually finished it. So without any much ado at all, let's begin:

First I would like to thank my parents, Paul and Carol Galley, and this is for two very basic reasons. The first is quite simply that they produced me. The second is that as a child they insisted, nay *demanded*, that I read everything in sight. Without those two reasons I would not be where I am right now, scribbling this on the back of an envelope. (I'd like to thank the post office for the envelope).

I'd like to thank the incredibly tolerant people who, for the last sixteen months, have had to put up with my constant badgering. Nancy Clark read and edited the first ever manuscript, as did Roger Clark, and their feedback and suggestions were invaluable to me. Nancy made sure it was suitable for all you Americans out there. Charlie Elwess was there to keep the Yorkshire tea brewing and point out any irregularities. To Sarah West, my eternal thanks, for the final edits, and for a room in her house, for which I am utterly grateful. Spotify, for your musical archivery, and my thanks to the music of the innumerable artists that have provided the emotions. Thomas Bulfinch, for the stories and myths, Mikael Westman for the cover, and Oliver Latham, for giving me a book that changed my whole perception of writing. I don't think he even realises what he's done. I'm expecting a phone call any day now…

And thank *you*, for reading my debut book, I promise I won't take this long to write the next one.

Ben Galley

DID YOU ENJOY THE WRITTEN?

If you liked **The Written**, then feel free tell a friend, spread the word on social media, or leave a review on Amazon or Goodreads. Every little helps an indie author like me.

Follow me to stay up to date with new books, competitions, fantasy content, and news. Follow on Facebook and Instagram:
@BENGALLEYAUTHOR

Or on Twitter and YouTube:
@BENGALLEY

Visit my website for all the details on my fantasy books:
WWW.BENGALLEY.COM

Join The Guild for a monthly newsletter of behind-the-scenes stuff and the exclusive prequel short story **The Iron Keys**:
WWW.BENGALLEY.COM/GET-INVOLVED

THANKS FOR READING!